THE HIDDEN HISTORY

OF

ESSEX LAW SCHOOL

EDWARD J. BANDER
Law Librarian Emeritus

Order this book online at www.trafford.com
or email orders@trafford.com

Most Trafford titles are also available at major online book retailers.

Printed in United States of America.

ISBN: 978-1-4269-3077-5 (sc)
ISBN: 978-1-4269-3078-2 (e-book)

Library of Congress Control Number: 2010925811

*Our mission is to efficiently provide the world's finest, most comprehensive book publishing
service, enabling every author to experience success. To find out how to publish your book, your
way, and have it available worldwide, visit us online at www.trafford.com*

Trafford rev. 4/13/2010

 www.trafford.com

North America & international
toll-free: 1 888 232 4444 (USA & Canada)
phone: 250 383 6864 ♦ fax: 812 355 4082

TABLE OF CONTENTS

CHAPTER 1

MARY McCARTHY

MEMORANDUM November 7, 1940, 3:52 pm

I have just returned to my office from a weird experience at this law school. I want to make it clear that I was not willingly a participant in the event I am about to narrate.

On this date, about 3pm, I received an abrupt phone call from Mary McCarthy, Dean Adam's secretary of long standing, and I do use that term deliberately.

"Is this the new librarian," Miss McCarthy shouted into the phone.

"Yes, it is, Miss McCarthy," I responded.

"Well get your ass to the Dean's office this minute – and bring your keys."

For the record, I informed my assistant, Adele Gray, of my destination, also made sure I had the master keys for the building in my pocket and proceeded to the Curley Building, where (I am being very meticulous) I ascended one flight of stairs to the ridiculous two person elevator, which I took to what I call the loft floor that housed the Dean's office. I knocked (timidly as I was aware that that was the required procedure), and was met with, "If that's Bender, come right in." I tried the door. Sure enough it was locked. I inserted the key, opened the door, and there was Miss McCarthy flat on her back – actually flat on the back of one of those old desk chairs with four legs that operated on rollers. On top of her was the Dean obviously in a state of semi-consciousness.

I rushed to the phone announcing, "I'll call an ambulance."

1

"You'll do nothing of the sort. Call Dr. Kelly in the Health Services – make sure that you speak only to him, - and tell him to get his – to get right up here." I did as I was told but could not help observing the scene. The Dean's pants were down. He had obviously had an orgasm. God help me! As the Dean had rolled over by this time, her bloomers were still on but I could not help noticing they were conveniently open at the crotch. Dr. Kelly came, as if on cue, and ordered me twice to leave as I was in such shock I did not hear him the first time. I reversed my steps and got back to my office at 3:31.

As this is my first day on the job, I am in a quandary as to what to do. I have a family to support, and I am writing this memo to protect my interests.

Edward O. Bender

And that was what Tom Jones was thinking about when he visited Mary McCarthy on Bass Harbor in Mt. Desert Island, ME. Tom had taken the shore route to get to his destination, Route 95, to get out of Massachusetts and then a lobster lunch at Ogunquit, a crab roll in Camden, a nap in the parking lot at Walmart's in Ellsworth, and finally the concourse into Mt. Desert. He stayed at an inn in Southwest Harbor for the night, and the next morning took a short ride to Bass Harbor and had breakfast at the Sea Ketch before walking across the street to the old sardine factory that had been turned into condos. Tom's first thought as he noticed the neat brickwork, and the sailboats tied up at the slips, was, "How do you do this on a secretary's salary?"

Tom proceeded to the docking area where Mary said she would be seated probably with a coffee cup in her hand.

Mary McCarthy was short, stout, and ordinary. Her gray hair was prim and neat and she was wearing a white shirt, buttoned down the front, a brown skirt that buttoned around her waist. Sandals and no stockings. At most she was five feet tall, and her stocky build seemed to have been with her for a long time. For a woman at least in her eighties, Tom surmised from his background information, she rose with difficulty and reached out to shake Tom's hand in a firm grip.

Tom was first to speak. "You picked a beautiful place to retire, Mary.

"I was born on this island, Tom. So was the Dean for that matter."

"You know why I'm here."

"I know, but tell me again," asked Mary.

"Let me create the scene for you. Dean Oberal is making big plans to celebrate the 100th year of the law school. In his own inimitable – or should I say irritable way, he dropped into my office to let me know that he has given great thought as to who is most capable of writing a history of the law school. Now he knows that I know that he has been turned down by every member of the faculty that he asked to do the job, but he can't resist polluting the atmosphere with undeserved flattery. The irony is that I'm happy to do it – and if I was the Dean, I would add, I would have picked me – for no other reason than to come to this beautiful island – and to see you."

"I wont buy all of that Tom, but two things – why interview me and, for a librarian, you certainly come on strong."

"Mary, you are a legend at the law school, and I don't think I'm flattering you to say that you were there practically, shall I say, at the creation and probably know more of the beginnings of this law school than maybe even dear departed Dean Adams."

"I do, but I don't think your history will reflect half of what I know," and Mary shot Tom a knowing wink.

Tom laughed. But he certainly knew that Mary was pretty close to the creation. His research, he recited to Mary, showed that when Seth Adams started the law school in Massachusetts, there were only three law schools that counted. There was THE law school – Havad. There was the Protestant law school – Commonwealth Law School, and the Catholic law school, St Francis. Tom discounted that there was a Portia Law School that at first only admitted women, an anomaly that could only happen in a city that had "Boston marriages," a dormitory for working women, and a Watch and Ward Society to protect its inhabitants from books and magazines that threatened the purity of its inhabitants. There was also a Huntington Law School, and even a New England Law School. Law schools sprouted in Boston like mushrooms in the Arnold Arboretum.

So, in retrospect, Seth Adams, a graduate of Commonwealth, full of Yankee ingenuity, found the soil of Boston fertile enough for a new brand of fungus.

Mary interrupted his thoughts, "He resented those Boston Brahmins. He never stopped talking to me about how he went to every damn Yankee

Boston law firm and was turned down. Why? Because his Yankee family never made it. They farmed, they did odd jobs, they stayed out of the cities – one or two of them became lawyers by clerking in law firms. His father was a hard-scrabble doctor, and Seth made it to Commonwealth Law School after two years of college because he was also hired to coach the swimming team."

"He did practice law for a couple of law firms if my information is correct."

"Yes, he did. And he noticed that they were all family affairs. He was never going to make partner. The system was that outsiders like himself didn't have a chance. They would pick him dry, and not keep him long enough to steal any of the clients. The legal hierarchy in Boston was like a guild that kept the riffraff out.

"That's when he came up with the brilliant idea of starting a law school for the kids who couldn't get into Havad, or didn't have the cash, or were limited by quotas, or were black.. Don't get me wrong. He was no civil libertarian. I could tell you a few things he said about some of these students."

"He was selling a new brand of soap."

"It was more than that, but not much more."

Tom was having second thoughts about his quarry.. But Tom tried to look back sixty years and he saw a woman, with all her plainness, that could have surprises for him. Does this woman fit the Memorandum he read by Bender as well as some of his other memos that showed a woman who had more to do than only taking dictation? Well, let's see what she has to tell me.

And Mary gave him time to think. And it gave her time to size up this librarian. She, who had run roughshod over quite a few librarians in her time was thinking this young man might have a little more backbone.

She eyed Tom carefully. Medium height. In his thirties. No belly bulge. Quick smile. Dressed carefully. Full head of hair and a hat. Not a baseball cap, but a brown hat with a nice weave, and a visor that ran a shadow over his brow. He wasn't a best-foot forward guy, and he might be fun. There were a few things she would like to get off her chest and she wouldn't mind talking him into driving her into Southwest Harbor for lunch. She could prolong this thing and get an errand boy in the bargain.

The eye contact continued until Mary broke it, "Let's have lunch. I want you to drive me over to the Claremont Hotel – I have a reservation in a quiet nook on the pier where we can talk and you can tell me what is going on at that den of inquiry."

"Iniquity?"

"Inquiry. Isn't that what this is all about."

The Claremont Hotel, like all select inns on the island, was situated facing a harbor, in this case Southwest Harbor. It was an old wood shingled hotel with a circular gravel path, tennis courts, and a pier that accommodated a lunchroom and looked out on a bevy of sailboats, lobsters boats, and miscellaneous craft. Mary and Tom were ushered to a seat with a view and it was obvious by the nods as they passed some of the tables that Mary was not a stranger here.

"I like it here. Quiet. People mind their own business. The tourists are well behaved and take up most of the seats."

"Must be expensive."

"No – I think if you compared it with Boston prices you would find it moderate."

After drinks, Tom ordered a lobster. Mary had flounder and explained, "When I was a kid, lobster was what you ate when you had nothing else to eat. The state saved money by feeding them to the prisoners. I had friends who would dive for lobsters. I like a plain piece of fish – broiled. At my age, I have to be careful of what I eat."

Tom, at this point, removed a pad from his jacket pocket. "Let's get to work."

Mary laughed. "All right, you asked for it."

"Let's start from the beginning. When did you start working for Dean Adams?"

By this time Mary had finished her first drink – apparently the spirits loosened her tongue and she seemed to like being with this young guy. "Tom, the beginning was long before I started working for Seth. I told you we both came from Mt. Desert. His father was a doctor – a country doctor. My father was a drunk and my mother was a mouse. Ma did housework for Dr. Adams, and for all I know a few other things. To keep me away from my old man, she would take me with her when school was out. I wasn't a bad looking girl then – I was good at sports, Pitched, played the outfield, hit home runs. I did my homework. But Seth ruined all that. Why that funny look on your face?"

"I'm sorry. I'm giving myself away. When I met you, I wondered about all those rumors."

"Rumors? About moi? Hold it, Tom, you aint heard nothing yet. My mother was cleaning house. I was taking the trash out to the barn, when Seth showed up – probably was following me. I'm guessing, Tom, but he decided to do to me what his father was doing to my mother."

"And you let him?"

"You are a sweet kid, Tom. I was thirteen; he was thirteen. Lots of hay in the barn."

"Were you in love?"

"Are you crazy? Next thing I know, I am pregnant."

Tom was indignant. "Did he offer to marry you?" Tom was taken back by all this. He was compiling a history of a law school. He planned on writing two histories; one like the ones he had read about Havad and Columbia, and one that would have all the dirt and stench that go into the making of institutions. But the last thing he anticipated was what looked like something out of a Hawthorne novel. Looking at Mary's picture he found it hard to believe the memorandum he had found in the archives; looking at Mary, a woman in her eighties – plump and still rosy faced – short, even dumpy looking – and telling me she was pregnant at thirteen by the future dean of Essex Law School. And why is she telling me all this?

Mary waited patiently as she could see Tom was having trouble digesting what she was saying but Tom spoke up again..

"Did he offer to marry you?"

"Where were you brought up?"

"Me, Roxbury, a part of Boston."

She laughed. "Maine is no longer a part of Boston or Massachusetts or anywhere else. Having a baby out of wedlock, as you misfits in Boston would say, is no big deal. You just have a baby."

"How about your parents – your mother?"

"They really didn't care. The interesting thing is that Doc Adams did care. When my baby was little – and he looked a hell of a lot like Seth – those big ears, long face, thick lips – anyhow, Doc came to me and told me I was too young to bring the lad up and he knew a nice young couple who could not have any children and would like to bring my son up. I think he wanted to get that facsimile as far away from Mt. Desert as possible."

Tom couldn't think of anything to say so he asked, "What was his name?"

"I called him Seth the third which I knew didn't go well with either of them. Not that Seth didn't chase me into the barn after that. That's why I went to work at Mott's BarBQ in Bar Harbor. Old Doc hired another, and younger, cleaning woman and I had to support myself. Tom, once the word gets around that you had a baby, you get a reputation. I lived about five miles from Mott's but I never wanted for a ride home. Came closing time, one of the boys at the bar would offer me a ride home in his pick-up truck. That's why they call them pick-up trucks."

Tom had a squeamish look on his face. Unlike Mary, he was taught that if you got a girl in trouble, you would marry her. Tom dreaded the thought that when they write the 150th year of the law school some innocent will come visit me and I'll tell my story.

Mary continued as the waiter, without apparently being asked, brought over another round. She had picked up his look. "Tom, we're talking about Maine, Down East and Northern Maine. I'm told New Hampshire and Vermont aren't much different. And it's worse in Newfoundland. People use to call it New Foundling. The winters here are cold and dark, not many people, and not much to do. Today it may be different – the tourist trade has changed things. The Rockefellers changed things. The rich are buying up camps and turning them into cottages. Working people now live off the island. Try leaving this island at four pm."

"Mary," and Tom looked at his notes, "you are now working at the BarBQ. How did you get back to Essex Law School?"

Mary laughed. "The things I can laugh at now. Well, Seth started the law school." Before she could begin another sentence, the waiter approached her and dropped a note on the table. "Heh, we have to get back to my condo." She got up and headed down the ramp leading to the hotel, while Tom was frantically looking for a waiter. "Just sign the slip, Tom – c'mon I have to get back to take some pills and I have to meet somebody."

CHAPTER 2

THE CONCORD CONNECTION

Tom rushed Mary back to the sardine factory. "Tom, I have to take my pills – I am an old lady – atenolol, plavix, God knows what and that note advised me that an acquaintance – a business acquaintance – wanted to talk to me. I'm going to call the Dean and tell him to send you back up here. I have lots to tell you."

"Can't we continue tonight?"

"No!" They had pulled up at the sardine factory and Tom helped her out of the car but she refused any further assistance and slowly made her way into the lobby of the condo.

Tom shook his head. What a crazy dame. There was something masculine about her. Something feminine. Was she flirting with me? More than once she brushed her hand on his lap to make a point and he could see she was evaluating his response. Tom said to himself, "I'm going to get this story, but I'm certainly going to stay away from office chairs with rollers."

His mission over he started driving out of the driveway when he noticed a Jaguar parked in the lot. It obviously had just arrived as it was still breathing from the heat of the engine and the cold November air. It was a convertible, a couple of years old, red, and had Massachusetts plates. And in the rear mirror was the unmistakable logo of Essex Law School. He thought: could that be Dean Joseph F. X. Dooley's car? He stepped out of the car and checked the license plate – "Essex2" It was Dooley. What next? Next was to head home. It was none of his business. There may be a connection. Maybe not. Whatever, his concern was to write the history not to inquire into the affairs of other people.

Tom had nothing left to do but start home and he took the fast route. Stop at the Lucerne Inn for a coffee and a view that was pure Maine with a little bit of Switzerland thrown in.

He took out his cellphone and called home.

"Janet, Tom, I'm on my way home."

"What!"

"She called off the meeting – something came up."

Hesitation. "Tom, take a few days off. You love Maine."

"If you were with me – I invited you to come – if you were with me I would but I don't feel like hanging around here alone. Why don't you drive up with the kids …"

Hesitation. "Tom, the kids have school. It's too sudden. But please don't come home."

At this point Tom became a little belligerent. "Mary, I'm on my way home. I'll be home by seven or eight. I want to come home, okay?"

The phone slammed shut.

Tom got back in the car and bypassed Bangor, bypassed Augusta, 95 to 295 using the Portland bypass, 95 again into Massachusetts and then 495 to Route 2 to and home in West Concord, MA. Six hours and only 7pm.

Tom's home in Concord was not his.. It had been three generations in the family name of Wright. The Wrights were old Yankee and Janet's father Frederick actually kept a family tree that traced his lineage back to the Mayflower. Janet would tease the old man that all he could come up with was Cabots and Lodges. Where were the horse thieves? When Tom suggested that the downfall of Tess of the d'Urbervilles was due to the father's obsession with his royal lineage that was the last straw as far as any paternal relationship would exist between father-in-law and son-in-law. It was bad enough Janet married a non-Yankee but one who did not listen attentively to his latest discoveries of kinship with the founders of the Republic.

Fred's descendents were not very prosperous. They were trades people and Fred was the only graduate. He had gone to Amherst and emerged into a modest career as a manager of estates for the Merchants National Bank of Boston. The house they lived in was built by a Wright in the 1850s – three layers with a mansard roof and the wooden shutters to keep the cold out in the wintertime. The shutters had the Wright emblem, a cutout that resembled the appearance of an open book. In the cellar were bared beams that could have held up a ten story house. The gigantic coal stove took up a substantial space but now included within its bulk an oil burner. Buried in the lawn was a 500 gallon oil tank.

Grandfather Wright was a staunch Republican. Hoover, Landon, Willkie were his heroes and F.D.R. a turncoat villain. In one election, he refused to drive his wife to the polls for fear she would vote for a Democrat. He wrote letters to politicians telling them how to conquer the New Deal. Fred, now in his 80s, invited his daughter and son in law to live with him when his wife died. In some ways he would have preferred to live alone in his eleven room, coal heated, drafty house, but the thought of his daughter living in Roxbury, as she was, with her mixed breed husband, was more than he could stand.

Tom was not in favor of the move either. But Janet was pregnant and their one bedroom flat in Egleston Square called for more room than Tom could afford on a librarian's salary. Both Tom and Fred knew that neither was particularly in favor of the final solution, which was what made it palatable. So Tom put up with listening to the old man's non stop talking at dinner time and also his non stop smoking and leaving ashes everywhere but in the ash tray, Fred put up with a son in law not of his choice. Janet was pleased with the new arrangement. It made her father happy to have her around and she would do the errands to provide him with seed and soil so that he could spend his retirement growing things – flowers, tomatoes, cucumbers so that the one third acre looked like a farmer's market in midsummer.

Fred was out in the yard on his knees and may have grunted as Tom drove into the driveway. Jack was riding his bicycle in the middle of the street and Tom's search for Janet was unsuccessful. He picked Jack and the bicycle up and put him on the earthen sidewalk. "Jack ride on the sidewalk. See that automobile going by – the street is for automobiles." "Street is better," said Jack. Tom looked sternly at Jack. "Jack, you will not ride on street, understand?" Jack looked meekly at his Dad, "Yes, Dad," and rode down the bumpy street and into the driveway, where a shiny red convertible, hood down despite the cold November day, was parked awkwardly which had prevented Tom from putting the car in the garage.

Tom was greeted with an uproarious laugh as he entered the house. "Tom, how are you." When Tom did not answer, Brick Bronson took another tack. ""Would you believe I drove in from Michigan, got to 495, and had to drop in to say hello."

Tom eyed three empty quart bottles of beer. "Must have been about five minutes ago."

More boisterous laughter. Tom looked at Janet, "I just put Jack and his bike on the sidewalk. It's seven o'clock. Couldn't you at least drink your beer on the porch and watch the kids, and how come he isn't in his pajamas? And where is Janice?"

"Janice is in a sleepover. I goofed. Aren't you glad to see Brick."
"No!"

Bronson got up a bit unsteady. He was a big man and although overweight had been a good athlete until his propensity for quart bottles of beer got him kicked off the football squad at Commonwealth. "Well, my mission has been accomplished. I got to see Janet" and with slight hesitation, "and you Tom, two of my best friends at college during those glorious years." Brick put on his suit coat, and then did an about turn as he started to leave. "Must use the bathroom."

Janet was bristling with rage. "Did you have to do that? Throw him out."

"I didn't throw him out. I gave you an honest answer. He's your guest not mine."

As Bronson left the bathroom, he muttered, "Am I forgetting something?"

Janet started to run upstairs. "Yes, you almost forgot your suitcase – I'll get it."

The two men stood facing each other. Brick, a good six feet; Tom a shade under five foot six. Janet returned and put the suitcase down; Brick picked it up, shrugged his shoulders and left.

Now it was a face off with Janet and Tom. "I couldn't let him go home drunk."

"Call him back. He's still looking for his keys."

Janet ran out the door and reached the car as it was pulling out the driveway. You could see Brick shaking his head, then reaching out and kissing Janet full in the face before driving away.

Janet brushed by Tom as she walked in the house. She briskly went upstairs. Tom whisked Jack off to bed and returned downstairs to clean up. He added the three quart beer bottles to two others in the pantry.

He mopped up the table strewn with bottle caps, cigarette ashes, and the remains of what looked like roast beef sandwiches.

It all took Tom back to that fateful day when Janet suggested a walk around Walden Pond. It was a beautiful fall afternoon with the sun shining on the placid water. They walked pass the mound of rocks that heralded the spot where Thoreau built his cabin and defied the world by listening to his own drum beat. Janet was extraordinary quiet because their walks around Walden Pond were glorious affairs. They would find a bare patch of land and read from Louisa May Alcott, Ralph Waldo Emerson, Thoreau, and Hawthorne. And that was where they made love. It was all laughter and shouts, running and jumping, quoting and pantomiming. To Tom, Concord was hallowed ground and to find the girl of his dreams showing him all the sights and sounds of this historic spot was heaven itself.

But Janet was walking slowly and kicking the leaves as they made the turn. Tom respected her mood. He knew something was coming. In the three years they had been seeing one another, they had, you might call it, broken up. She had returned his Commonwealth liberal arts ring more than once only to accept it back on her finger when things quieted down.

Finally she sat down. Tom followed. "I'm pregnant." Tom looked querulous than pleased. "It's not yours." She slipped the ring off her finger and put it in Tom's lap. "Is there something I can do?" was all Tom could offer. "I guess you could get me an abortion." "Well I do have some savings. Janet, what can I say? I'm shocked, yes. I love you. This is crazy, but I'll help you in any way I can." Tom walked off about fifty feet and returned. "Janet," he cried helplessly and went to the ground putting his head in her lap.

"Tom, things happen. I've never pretended to be anything but what I am. I've enjoyed your company – friendship – love – whatever, but I've never given much thought to things. I was out drinking one night, had a little too much, and ended up getting laid. He wasn't as careful as you."

"Bronson?"

"How did you guess."

"Does he know?"

"Yuh."

"Are you going to marry him?"

"The subject never came up."

"Abortion?"

"Subject never came up. Tom, Brick is in love with Rebecca. Rebecca will not marry him because he is not Jewish and it will kill her mother if she marries him. I am not in the picture and Brick is just that big cuddly bear who grows on you ..."

"Like a hangnail."

Tom stood up. "Janet, I don't want you to have an abortion. Now here is my solution. I don't want you to shame your dad. We will get married. Please, don't interrupt. This is a business proposition. We get married. You have the baby. You don't like the arrangement. I don't like the arrangement. We break up. Worst that can happen is that you go back to your parents with a legitimate child." Tom slapped his hands. "I think this is the last time I want to see Walden Pond, and I think Thoreau was the only guy who spent a night on Walden Pond who didn't get laid."

What was on Tom's mind when he came up with this solution has passed into inconsequence. To Janet it was more of the same. But it was a Concord solution. The people of Concord were no different than others. They had the same problems but had different solutions based on the novels of Louisa May Alcott, Nathanial Hawthorne, the self-reliance of Emerson, and the individuality of Thoreau. In the minds of Tom and Janet, they had met their forebears, and it was them. No letter would be found on Janet's breast for they were people of the letter.

CHAPTER 3

THE FACULTY MEETING

It was a more boring than usual faculty meeting. Tom was seated next to Josh Wittberg. Wittberg was one of the few in the faculty of whom Toole was cautious. But it was generally agreed that he was a competent teacher. He did all that was required of him. He had written a primer on contract law that was popular with law students and fulfilled a requirement that faculty should write. He not only met his classes but had schedules to meet them after class. He attended faculty meetings, although he was known to leave early. But outside of these activities, he was nowhere to be seen. He did not attend functions, speeches, dinners and rarely went to the faculty library to connect with his colleagues. When classes met in September, Wittberg, a big man of some two hundred pounds, would appear clean-shaven, suited, and well-appearing. Imperceptibly, a change would take over him and by January, as the second semester began, he would balloon to some three hundred pounds, a beard, and dungarees. In Tom's first year, he wondered who this bearded giant was until, upon introducing himself to what he thought was a new faculty member, was told, "For Christ's sake, Tom, I'm your buddy who keeps bugging you to keep only one of my books on reserve so that the students will have to buy it."

At faculty meetings, Wittberg would find fault with every speaker who took more than three minutes to discuss an issue. At this meeting he became particularly exasperated with Joseph F.X. Dooley.

Professor Dooley: "This debate has gone on long enough. We have spent ten minutes, at least, debating whether commercial law should be a two semester course with two credits for each semester or a one semester course with three credits. The world will not come to an end either way. I suggest we put this to a vote and stop these *megillah*s from carrying this meeting into midnight."

Professor Wittberg [aside but loud enough for everyone to hear] "One thing I can't stand is an Irishman speaking Yiddish."

Professor Dooley: "I heard you, Wittberg, what, do you have to be circumcised to use Jewish words?"

Professor Wittberg: "No, except you don't know what you are talking about. *Megillah* is what you talk."

Professor Dooley; "Well, you know what I mean."

Wittberg – "Try *macha*"

Professor Dooley: "So I was wrong. So I'm a schmuck. How is that?"

Wittberg: "Now you're talking."

Dean Oberal: "What is this a Yeshiva? Back to business."

The meeting broke after thirty more minutes on the point total for Commercial Law and ending with sending it back to committee for further discussion.

As they left the meeting, Peter Toole patted Wittberg on the back. "Josh, I complement you on your behavior. We are brothers under the skin."

"We are not," replied Wittberg.

"Maybe not, but you and I see through a gloss darkly."

"There's a difference, Toole. You're a cynic, I'm a skeptic."

Toole thought for a moment but just walked on.

The Dean motioned to Tom. "Can I see you in my office, Tom?"

Tom nodded. The Dean's office adjoined the faculty meeting room through a side door so Tom followed the Dean.

"Let's get down to business." The Dean looked at his watch. "I have to catch a plane to San Francisco to address an alumni group there tomorrow. Then to Chicago to meet with a group of alumni who want to give us some money. Why I gave up a nice cushy job teaching Constitutional Law for this, I will never know. Any suggestions?"

"Maybe to get away from the wife. Money. Prestige. How about getting an offer from a top tier law school."

"None of the above. Let's get down to business." The Dean looked at his watch. "Tom, I asked you to interview our oldest alumnus, Caleb Cushing. I got a phone call before the faculty meeting from him saying you disappeared in the middle of the interview – and he was really pissed. This guy contributes every year to the school – he's our oldest alumnus. It seems like he'd be a natural for your legal history."

"He'll be in our history Dean. I drove to a little town north of Albany to see him last week. He lives alone in a small house. Bungalow type. Widowed. Met him on the porch. Introduced myself."

"'Come on in young man,' he says. 'Sit right there and let's talk.' The room was the same size as the porch."

The Dean looked at Tom and then looked at his watch again.

"At that point he let off a fart that I thought would be followed by lightning. He said, 'Excuse me young man – when you get to be my age you don't stand on ceremony – you sit on it – I would never have done that when I was practicing law in Albany, but once.' And then, Dean, he told me this story. Maybe you have heard it.

"He was arguing a jury case in Albany. Everything was going fine until it was his turn to address the jury. He had a spicy meal that afternoon and it was getting to him as he began his closing argument. Not two minutes into it, he felt his stomach expanding and that the gas that was accumulating was either going to rise up in his esophagus or head down in the other direction. At that point he thought if he put his hand on the railing that separated him from the jury and bent over just a bit, he might get silent relief as well as impress the jury with his Clarence Darrow down-home approach. As he bent, he could hear a noise like a kettle reaching its boiling point. According to your oldest alumnus that went on for at least twenty seconds. The only sound in that courtroom was gas escaping from the rectum of Caleb Cushing. Mr. Cushing, by his own account, looked every juror straight in the face – his expression stoical and non committal. He then looked at the judge who he could see was about to go into hysterics. Suddenly the judge reached for the gavel, called a recess and disappeared from the court with his robe hiding his face."

"What happened after the recess?" asked the Dean.

Tom ignored the question. "The air in the room was clearing and I asked Mr. Cushing, 'When did you graduate Essex?'" Tom always carried a notebook to take notes for his history of the school. He stopped to find the page he was looking for. "He graduated in 1910 or 1911. And I quote from my notes, 'I had intended to be a vet. Liked animals. But Dr. Hennepin said I talked too much - particularly to the animals – dogs, cats, sometimes sheep. I could tell you some stories. Said I'd make a better lawyer. I think he was afraid I'd take all his business away. I'd heard of Essex. Worked my way through. One semester, my tort teacher paid my tuition because I took care of his three dogs. I did well enough. Passed the bar. I took every kind of case – personal injury, malpractice, wills, even criminal cases. For thirty years I represented people. Their case was my case. I was on call. I dressed like a lawyer. Even wore tasseled shoes that raised me an inch to make a better impression. To be honest with you, though, made most of my money in real estate.

'I have to tell you my first case. I was working for a couple of lawyers on Washington Street. 294, if I remember correctly. I promised myself that if I was going to be as bad a lawyer as these guys – by the way, Commonwealth grads – I would go back to my first love. Anyway, Gavin – I wont tell you his last name – had a gas station as well as a practice. One of his employees was in trouble and he tells me to meet him at the office and take care of his problem. I meet this guy who obviously was told to dress for a court appearance and – you know – shabby elegant. Soup stained tie, ill fitting suit coat, and denims. Hands me a piece of paper. *Capias.* Court appearance for 9:00am in the morning. It was 8:45 am. I grab my coat and brief case and hustle him off to the courthouse, instructing him to tell the court that, if given another chance, he would pay his custody on time in the future. He tells me he was sick and wasn't working. We no sooner get in the courtroom when they are calling out his case. I drop my brief case and coat on the bench and approach the judge. By the way, my client's name was O'Sullivan. He was black. The judge's name was Sullivan. He was Irish and he had the appearance of someone who had overcooked his three minute eggs that morning. Have you ever seen a bull released into the arena and is looking for a fight? His rear legs are clawing at the turf – his head is lowered and ready to charge. That is Sullivan not listening to my plea for mercy for this poor guy. His wife is standing with her lawyer. She is dressed as if she is going to a ball. Her lawyer presents to the judge the work sheets of my client showing that at the time he told me he was ill he was working. The judge would hear no more. Sixty days. No kidding, I felt relief when the bailiff came to take my client away. I thought it was for me. I go to retrieve my belongings. No coat. My beat up brief case sat lonely on the bench.'"

"At this point, I said to him. 'You not only lost your suit but your coat.' He didn't laugh.

"'Never got thanked. If I won a case they thought I charged too much. If I successfully defended a criminal, he thought he could have done better representing himself. It took me a while to learn to get my fees up front from these bastards. After my third wife left me – the thanks I got from getting her a fantastic settlement from her husband, I had enough. Turned the business over to my one and only son. I got a lot of thanks for that. The ungrateful bastard – I think he thought he was doing me a favor. Put me into assisted living. Had me sitting looking out of a window. I'd lean to the left, someone would straighten me out. I'd lean to the right, someone else would straighten me out. Couldn't even fart in that place. Walked out, found me this place and that no good son of mine won't pay me a visit. Calls me every day. Big deal.'

"At this point, Dean, our oldest alumnus veered to one side of his rattan chair and farted four or five times. After each fart, he would rate it in baseball terms. The last one being a triple. A silent one was a steal home. Dean, you cannot believe the stench in that room. By this time I was getting sick to my stomach but, Dean, I am on a mission in completing the task that you have assigned to me."

"I'd still like to know what happened in that jury case."

"You have to hear this last bit, Dean. He then insisted on telling me a case he had involving some bull's semen that didn't work. He told the jury of a farmer that had hired a bull to service his herd. The bull was not cooperating so they sent for a vet. The vet had the farmer's assistant bring him his medicine bag and he concocted a cream that he put on the bull's teeth and don't you know it but that bull got up, shook himself thoroughly, and proceeded to service the entire herd. The farmer said to his assistant, 'Did you see what that concoction was?' And the boy answered, 'No, I didn't but it tasted like vanilla'. I told the jury you never can predict what semen can do for you and the jury bought it'."

The Dean by this time had edged his way out of the room and was heading out of the building and reaching for the door of the waiting cab.

Tom followed him. "That's the end of the story Dean. Caleb Cushing laughed so loud as he finished that story, that he told me he thought he had shit himself and headed to the bathroom, the door being just off where we were talking. He said to me, 'Keep talking son, we're just beginning.'"

"At that point, I took off." At this point the Dean was getting into the cab and the last words he heard Tom say were, "Oh, and as to the jury case, the verdict was…."

CHAPTER 4

TOM ARNOLD, L.L.B.

Tom decided that his next interview was going to have to be with someone of a more cerebral character. He was pouring over an article written by Mike Bailey whose law review production was phenomenal. Commercial law, Patents, Sociology and Law, and an article in the alumni publication extolling the purpose and aims of Essex in turning carthorses intro trotters. It also dwelled on Ivy League quotas and lauded Essex for opening its doors to the poor, the huddled, and those discriminated against by quotas at the leading institutions.

"That man has no shame," said a voice over Tom's shoulder. It was Professor Peter Toole, unquestionably the most able teacher at the law school despite not a chip on his shoulder, but an entire forest. "He wants a chair so bad he can't sit still. Can you show me one law review article that he has written that is anything more than a rehash of cases – and that article on the law school. Rubbish!" Toole was Havad, Havad Law, and a frequent guest at the Havad Club on Commonwealth Avenue.

"Dean Toole," Tom always referred to Peter Toole as Dean knowing that he was Dean of a law school for three years and left when the faculty gave him a vote of no confidence. The vote was because two members of the faculty had nervous breakdowns because of his legitimate, if cold-blooded, criticisms; three had left for less paying jobs, and he had a habit of sitting in on classes, and at times, questioning the teacher. People in the legal profession who did not know him admired him for the two law review articles he had written some years ago– one on the tort of emotional disturbances and the other on military law. He was also a brilliant teacher, who gave credence to the Socratic method. He was irascible with unprepared students, but gentle and prodding with those who were trying and had promise. He was a hard grader and merciless with those he did not believe should have considered law as their profession. Unwanted impulses – "The Imp of the Perverse" – seemed to shoot up like lava from a volcano. A famous example of that was when Tom Arnold, a powerful member of the Massachusetts Senate, decided he should get a law degree to further his political ambitions.

You have to set the stage for the monumental battle when the immoveable force of ambition is pitted against thrusting force of implacable integrity. Tom Arnold was a product of Boston Irish politics. The politics of James Curley and Honey Fitzgerald. He was tough, beleaguered, stubborn. He rose from a ward heeler to state representative to state senator to President of the Senate. On the one hand people knew better than to get in his way; on the other he took care of his constituents even if it had to be at the expense of everybody else's constituents. He was the unemployment bureau, the Medicare, the Medicaid of his constituency. A snap of his fingers would send an army on its way with turkeys on Thanksgiving for the "deserving" poor.

How a short, big jowled, wide-eyed, big bellied Irishman with long arms, short legs, small feet (no one called him "footsy" to his face) made it to the top of the ladder was a mystery to those not in his district. He may have looked like something put together by a committee, but he was no fool, except in his idiotic idea to become a lawyer.

Tom's high school yearbook predicted that he would be the grandmaster of the St. Patrick's Day parade. He belonged to only one organization outside of politics. He was a scrappy hockey player known as "the hyena," as he worked the corners, often leaving behind a trail of split lips, bloody noses, and black eyes as he fought for the puck as if he were scavenging for a carcass. Tom, now in his sixties, still plays in a league and is no less ferocious.

He served three years in the United States Navy after graduation from high school and spent the entire time as a striker in the radio shack aboard the battleship Massachusetts. According to one of his secretaries who served on the same ship (Tom called his bodyguards secretaries), he was very famous for another aspect of his anatomy. He was known to have the biggest penis in the fleet. This all started when the ship passed the equator and all on board passing it for the first time were initiated into what was variously called the Royal Order of the Ancient Deep or the Imperial Domain of the Golden Dragon. Pollywogs became Shellbacks and after recovering from the ordeal were rewarded with a certificate of proof of their initiation which contained the usual "whereases" and "wherefors." Initiations or punishments were handed out by the honored shellbacks. There was a king and queen (the youngest and prettiest of the ship's company) dressed in the royal regalia of white robes and crowns of torpedo steel made by the black gang. The ingenious crew that prepared this initiation built a pool and all initiates were required to dive naked into the pool, instructed to kneel before the queen with their their heads between "her" knees and drink a concoction that stirred the recipient's imagination of its contents. After being shorn of their locks, the pollywogs then exited by way of a chute constructed of bed sheets and low enough so that posteriors were visible enough to the vassals of the royal entourage so that they could be soundly lambasted with bats made of sturdy canvas.

An officer, who always wore his Yale tie in defiance of regulations, was an observer mainly to see that things did not get out of hand and see to it that the ship log properly recorded the event, had noticed the size of Arnold's appendage and jocularly requested a measurement of all initiates as they left the tunnel. This eventually came to be called the royal yardstick. Arnold won hands down and thus a legend was born. Ships would challenge the Massachusetts and send over their contestant. There is documentation that Arnold met the challenge of the best of over one hundred ships. Arnold's certificate making him an honorable shellback included the designation as holder of the award of "numbskull and boners." Arnold, who was known to get in line more than once at Honolulu whorehouses, was very proud of this attribute, and there were many who thought it served him in better stead than his brains.

He had barely passing grades entering his final year of law school and his political responsibilities clashed with his efforts to take courses with members of the faculty who were afraid to flunk him. There he was, a former sailor in the Navy, taking a course with an Irish professor, who tried to maintain the same bearing as when he was brigadier general in the army. This almost turned out to be the biggest mistake in Arnold's career. He rarely attended class. Even sent Toole a bottle of wine and a box of his favorite cigars, with, of course, no note as to identifying the sender. Toole's flunking grade meant he would not graduate. The situation was brought to the attention of Acting Dean John (Duke) O'Brien, who was aware of the power of Tom Arnold to hire Essex students, to provide legislative comfort to the school, and the well-known vindictiveness of the Honorable Tom Arnold to his actual and supposed enemies. O'Brien approached Toole with the chicken scratchings of Arnold's exam on the Code of Military Justice. Toole was adamant; O'Brien was threatening. The grade never appeared on Arnold's record and he was awarded points for his legislative service by the Board of Trustees. The rumor was that Arnold passed the bar the same way. He was subsequently defeated in his run for the United States Senate and spent his remaining years as clerk of the Massachusetts Supreme Judicial Court, where his office had emblazoned on its door: "Tom Arnold, L.L.B, Esq., Clerk of the Massachusetts Supreme Judicial Court."

The Dean of Essex grabbed Toole when he learned of his "expulsion," and hired him with the idea that a new atmosphere might make him less obstreperous much as general managers in sports hire cantankerous stars in the hopes they will help his team as well as take on a new attitude in life. Toole had been humbled but had not lost his zest for being himself.

Toole recognized that Essex was a school of no pretensions. Unlike top tier schools, the Essex faculty was not composed of prima donnas waiting for the call to Havad Law School. There was no pecking order where assistant professors looked up to associate professors and associate professors looked up to professors. This faculty was not as sensitive and when Toole showed up at one class and questioned the professor, he was shut up by "Professor Toole, I only answer questions like that after class – will you please see me later in my office."

"Dean Toole, Can you show me one law review article in the past five years that was not a rehash of cases.?"

"Are you Jewish, Tom. You answer a question with a question."

"It so happens I am half Jewish, Professor"

"My God, if I had known that I would have voted against you – you came into this faculty on false pretenses." As he could see Tom was getting his dander up, Toole caught himself.

"No, Tom, you belong here. But I'll tell you what. And this has nothing to do with your being half anything and sometime you can explain to me what it means to be half Jewish. Of course, no one I have ever known claimed to be half Christian. If it was up to me I would not have given you tenure – I don't think librarians should be faculty, let alone have tenure. They didn't when I was Dean"

"Dean Toole, I'm going to let you in on a secret. The reason faculties give tenure to librarians is that most of them are women. Law schools like to boast they have women on their faculty so they give librarians faculty status and it makes them look good as to diversity when they come up for accreditation before the ABA and the Association of American Law Schools."

"But you are not a woman or are you holding out on me."

Tom started to unzip his fly. The two of them were at the main desk of the library and students were cued up to get books or ask questions. Toole raised his hands, "No, no – We believe in crucifixion not circumcision. I never thought of that angle. You may be right. But let's get back to Bailey He wrote an article on Dean Pound and sociological jurisprudence last year that on one page had two lines of text and the rest of the page in footnotes. He writes articles to impress rather than to be read"

Tom could sympathize with Toole's view of Bailey. He was the most ambitious personality he had ever come across. A Havad alumnus, whose career was in advising undergraduates at Huntington on career development, he had gone to Essex evening law school and graduated with top honors. His law note for the *Essex Law Review* was on discriminatory practices of Boston's top law firms. One of them was already under investigation and Bailey was hired by the firm that had experts in every area of law but discrimination. Bailey's efforts got the firm out of a jam, but now they no longer had need of him. Anticipating this possibility, Bailey ingratiated himself with the Essex dean by the fact that he was one of the few graduates to achieve law firm status and was put on Essex's payroll. He began as an adjunct faculty, made friends with other faculty members, helped with the moot court team, and then successfully interviewed for full faculty status. And then began what turned out to be his writing career. He taught commercial law but managed to turn out books on copyright law, civil procedure, bankruptcy and other topics that legal publishers gobbled up. At one point he was called Seth Adams the Second.

No one was more gregarious than Bailey. He accepted speaking engagements, talked to the press, anticipated the next wave of concern about lawyer practices. He noticed that a media personality who was critical of personal injury lawyers made a profession out of it. He had a TV program that was a joy to corporate America. His books claimed that tort lawyers were destroying corporate America with fake science such as frivolous actions against companies using silicone in breast enhancement, grandmothers burning themselves on hot coffee turned out by franchises, class actions that were the bane of free enterprise. Bailey, who was now teaching and writing about torts, began a campaign against this person. He was invited to speak at many law schools; he debated him at conservative think tank forums, and then he decided to write a book about it. In a feverish three weeks, with the help of Tom and his staff, and two student assistants, Bailey finished the book. Then came the problem. He tried to get the trade publisher who had put out a book on tort reform to take it. Not interested.

"It's a conspiracy," Bailey told Tom. "Trade publishers are corporations. I am attacking corporations. They hate class actions. Class actions are the public's defense against malfunctioning automobiles, medicines that kill or maim, toys that poison children."

As a last resort, Bailey went to the Huntington University Press. The book was published, reviewed in the *Essex Law Review*, and left to die.

"Tom," said Bailey, "I'm going to run an expose on university presses. Did you ever hear of a university press paying royalties? On the other hand, if they're against me, I'll never get published again. Tom, can you get me a list of awards given to books. Nobel Prize for Literature, Booker Prize, all of them." Tom gave him a list of some fifty awards handed out for books, and all of them received a copy of "The Case Against Tort Reform." Not only was no award forthcoming, but when Patrick Donavan saw the bill for sending out these books, he refused to pay it. Samuel Cohen's terse comment to Tom was "University presses are to universities what earmarks are to the federal government."

This was occupying Tom's mind and because he did not want to agree with Toole on the subject, he went on another tack. "Dean Toole, Let us get on another topic. I just had a horrid experience interviewing an alumnus of this school. You'll read about it in my history of the law school."

"No, I wont."

"I am looking to interview someone who can tell me about the law school without revolting me. Someone that can give life to my project besides information. I was looking over this list of prior Deans of the law school. As a former Dean, and therefore an authority on how one should be a Dean, can you suggest one of our former Deans to provide me insight, experience, knowledge, that will turn my history from a pedestrian piece of work into a memorable monograph."

Whether Toole smirked at this to indicate that either a touché was called for or that Tom could write a memorable monograph will remain a moot issue.

Toole looked at the page Tom had opened which listed the prior deans:

> Seth Adams, 1906-1942
> Fred Sampson, 1942-1952
> Acting Dean John O'Brian, 1952-1957
> Fred A. McGuire, 1956-1964
> Ronald Sampson, 1964-1972
> Joseph A. Coalfield, 1972
> Francis Aloysius Seargent, 1972-1973
> Edward V. Petty, 1972-1988

"Let's stop at Petty and go through the list."

"Please, I don't think my stomach could take going through the list. Please, give me one name that will make my day. One name that won't be a waste of the school's money. Can you do that?"

"Ronald Sampson. Good man. His father was Dean here. Wrote this idiotic book about the law in Massachusetts. Black letter law. His son kept it up as it was a good money maker."

"A lot of people passed the bar exam with it."

"I'm not so sure. But Ronald was a good teacher. I sat in his classes. The school made a big mistake in getting rid of him. Do you know why?"

"I am sure you are going to tell me."

"The Chairman of the Board of Trustees, Patrick J. Donavan, and the President of the University John M. Sullivan both wanted their sons to be Dean and neither had the power. And guess how these sons got to be Associate Deans! When Sampson reached 65, as a courtesy, he notified the President of his age and asked President Sullivan if he had any suggestions as to his future. I think he was looking for a raise, or even a birthday card..

And you know Sullivan was in charge of disbursement and he actually kept a record of the use of toilet paper in the building. If a toilet exceeded its quota for the month – that was it. And you could get splinters from the toilet paper he authorized. I know Samuel Cohen had his own supply." Toole took out a handkerchief and wiped his brow. He was not a tall man. He had a permanently red face and a rather large pock-marked nose. Big jowls. Always wore a tweed suit, a Havad tie, and in the faculty lounge he would smoke a pipe. He took a deep breath and continued, "Sullivan saw this as an opportunity to get his son, Esau, into the Deanship of the law school, and replied to Sampson: "Happy birthday. We at Essex wish you a most satisfying retirement." Somehow word of this got to Donavan and he let it be known that he had a better choice for the job, and his name was Frank Donavan. I am ashamed to say, my half-Jewish friend, that the two of them were a disgrace to the legal profession if not to their heritage."

"What happened?"

"Well, John M. Sullivan was twice the size of Donavan but Donavan was fast on his feet. When the Board met to decide the fate of the school after Sampson notified the school he was accepting the Deanship of that new New Hampshire law school, only the two of them showed up. The rest of the Board absconded to the 18th Amendment, the bar across the street from the State House. After a lengthy debate, punctuated with a substantial intake of alcoholic beverages, they voted to approve whatever the victor proposed."

"And what was that."

"A draw. Both bided their time and I advise you to get Sampson's view of the matter."

CHAPTER 5

BENNINGTON LAW SCHOOL

Bennington Law School was a short ride from Tom's home in Concord, Massachusetts. Tom had arranged for an interview with Dean Sampson and decided to make it a family affair, by camping out at the Calvin Coolidge National Notch for the night and then proceed to the Bennington campus the following day. It was a gorgeous morning and the four of them packed a good lunch and loaded their eight year old car for the two day trip. After paying the entry fee to the park and being assigned a camp sight, they drove to their spot and were exhilarated by the view. They were at an elevation where they had a clear view of what New Hampshire was all about. Nothing in sight but nature.

On the way they had stopped at a general store and purchased a cut of cheddar cheese from a big wheel of displayed cheese that looked enticing on the counter. It was enclosed in a plastic cover and the proprietor lifted the cover by a pulley secured to the ceiling. He gave each of them a taste and Tom was forced to get a pound, which he did not regret. They added the cheese to their ham sandwiches, drank chocolate milk, and had Twinkies for dessert.

"Mom," said Jack, "I could stay here forever." Janet had stayed behind to clean up and Tom, Jack and Janice trekked up the side of the mountain that had been marked by the rangers with the warning, ""FOLLOW THE BLUE." Janice piped in when they returned, "Mom, you have to come with us to see the river, and you can see the town from up there." It was Tom's turn. "Yes, you can see the campus from the water tower. It's an hour's climb and there is a cliff side trail they want to hike. I think you should go up there with the kids. One trip is enough for me. I could use a nap and I have a few law review articles that Sampson wrote that I want to read before the interview tomorrow."

"Let's go kids," Janet announced and jumped up, snapped on her water bottle and knapsack and headed for the trail with Jack and Janice right behind her.

Tom napped for an hour and then started reading Dean Sampson's articles. It was the most refreshing time that he had ever had in reading law review articles. One article proposed that contracts should be the only course taught for the entire three years. It suggested that the accepted notion that there should be consideration in contractual relations was belied by the practice in civil code jurisdictions. Williston and Corbin, giants of American jurisprudence should be pitted against French and German theorists. An entire semester could occupy the minds of the geniuses that occupy seats in American law schools. He suggested that after the first year, everything was a rehash of first year studies and that a thorough absorption in that one topic would better prepare the young lawyer for any problem he may come up with in his practice. It was a *tour de force* and Tom thought they could do the same thing with the good Samaritan law and other topics that he knew teachers at Essex covered only by giving the majority rule, the minority rule, and the rule in Massachusetts. This could be some interview, he surmised.

Tom looked at his watch and it was 5pm. It was taking the three of them longer than he thought and he started up the trail only to find Jack and Janice rushing down into his arms. "The cliff route is even better Dad. We saw a train rounding the mountain," yelled Janice and Jack piped, "The diorama on the side of the mountain showed us where Massachusetts is." Tom was holding both children in his arms. "You guys are getting too heavy for me," and he looked up the trail and asked, "What happened to Mom." Jack piped in "We had to ask for directions to get here and when Mom realized how close we were she told us to run down and meet you."

"OK, kids. What do you say we put up the pup tent and make a fire and cook some hamburgers and put some of that great Vermont cheddar cheese on it?" The country air infused the three with hunger, and they were soon on their second hamburgers, chocolate milk, and more Twinkies, while Tom, every fifteen minutes or so looked up the trail for Janet. It was getting dark and Tom was not about to leave the children and get lost on the trail and he contemplated what to do about it. Janice was reassuring, "Mom never gets lost, Dad. She always gets delayed." Tom knew this was so and busied the children in setting up the pup tent. This was a first for all three beginning with camping. Tom was brought up in Roxbury, a part of Boston, and had been to camp once – a Jewish run camp in upstate New York, run by the Workmen's Circle. His only memory of that experience was when he got home the first thing he did was rush into the toilet and flush it. The camp had only outdoor facilities. It was now nine o'clock and what had been an occasional mosquito bite turned into a frenzy. The kids, who at first insisted on sleeping in the tent, begged to go into the car. Ten o'clock no Janet. Ten-thirty. Eleven and then a rustling in the direction of the trail. Janet came in distraught. "Where the hell have you been?"

Janet sat on the ground. She was sweaty and ignoring the mosquitoes swarming about her. "Just leave me alone and let me die here."

Tom could sense one problem. "You have been drinking!"

"If you must know – and you must, yes. I asked this guy for directions. He very kindly gave me directions and invited me to have a drink. Any problem with that." She looked at Tom and decided there was. "I was tired so it seemed like a good idea so I knew the kids could find there way back so I decided on another. And, if you must know, another."

"Are you aware that your blouse is practically ripped off your shoulders?"

"Probably got tangled in a branch – look are you accusing me of anything?"

Tom just looked at her.

"If you must know, I was drinking with three homosexuals. Yes, homosexuals."

Tom threw up his hands. "Janet, it is late. You are going to wake up the children. I have an interview tomorrow morning and then you can tell me how you determined you were drinking with three homosexuals."

At this point it started to rain. Not rain. Pour. Janet started to crawl into the pup tent, eager to avoid any more questioning, and knocked over the pole holding the tent up. Tom repositioned the pole and then started to make a ditch around the tent using the tire iron. Janet crawled out of the tent backward, crying "The God damned tent is soaking wet" and sat in the passenger side of the front of the car. Tom, partly to dignify his efforts, and partly to ignore his wife, crawled into the tent. He had no sooner got into his sleeping bag when he heard someone say, "So there you are, sweetie-pie." Tom started crawling out of the tent and knocked the pole down, and saw this fellow, this big fellow in shorts and a sweat shirt looking in the window at Janet. He had a bottle of liquor in his hand and was waving it at Janet. Tom got to his feet and had the tire iron in his hand. When the fellow saw Tom, he bowed, "Ooh, excuse me, wrong car," and wandered away back up the trail. During the night the rain eased, but the thunder and lightening had the children huddling together. There were trips to the outhouse with Tom and Janet taking turns and the mosquitoes found new territory to conquer.

The next morning few words were exchanged as the four took advantage of the campsite washroom to clean up and get into fresh clothes. The radio promised a fair day and the original plan was that Tom would leave them, do his interview, and they would spend another night at the camp. But Tom was packing the car. There were no protests. As Tom started the car, Janet said, "Where are we going?" "I want to be in time for my interview. When I get there, I will give you the keys and leave it to you where to spend your time until I am through with my interview." He looked at his watch, "Let us say, 3pm" Janet noticed that there was a Bennington Bed and Board across the street. "We may be at the B and B, or I may go back up the mountain. They still owe us a night." There was a note of defiance in her voice. "I think I can find my way home," Tom replied and headed for his interview. Janet wavered, "Please, Tom, try the B and B."

Bennington Law School had only a few buildings. It had only been in operation for a year, the invention of a man who had had a successful career representing inventors. He believed technology would solve all the problems of the world and long before Bill Gates took Microsoft to the heights, he had addressed the American Bar Association that communication would bring the world together. Despite being long on talk and short of money, he managed to buy an old farm of a few acres. The farmer had built a house to contain his wife and twelve children, to which Kniles had added an extension large enough to contain a classroom of seventy five students. To one side there were two low leveled structures that you would have mistaken for cow stalls except for the fact that students were milling around them and there was no smell of cattle.

Tom walked over to the cow barn and noticed that each stall was marked "BULL PEN" followed by a number. He asked a student where he could find Dean Sampson. "He's in that classroom teaching Contracts," the student said pointing to the extension. "It's over at eleven sharp and if you watch that door, you'll see him come out followed by about twenty students. That's going to take another twenty minutes,"

Tom watched Dean Sampson patiently converse with the students and approached him as he made for the front door of the law school, Above the door was hand-chiseled lettering proclaiming: "BENNINGTON LAW SCHOOL – Reaching out to the Legal World."

"Dean Sampson, Tom Jones. I wrote you about an interview for the Essex Law School's 100th anniversary history project."

"Follow me, Tom." They walked into the foyer. There were classes going on in what was once a kitchen, a dining room, and a parlor. There were students filing into the room that the Dean had vacated from the rear. They walked up one flight to Sampson's office and he motioned for Tom to take a seat.

"First. For our interview. What do you know about me?"

Tom looked at his notes. "Commonwealth Law Degree, also liberal arts there. Your father was Dean of Essex for many years and published an annual survey of Massachusetts law which you continued until you came to Bennington. You were Dean at Essex until Bennington snatched you …"

Dean Sampson broke in and laughed. "You should know that I was not the first choice to be Dean of Essex. I was sixty when they hired me and I think they figured that if they made an old codger like me Dean, Donavan or Sullivan could sneak their son to take over when I died – I'm sure you know the story."

"Dean Toole told me all about it."

"Dean Toole, that's rich. Hasn't anyone killed him yet. Donavan hired him despite my objections. And let me tell you about Donavan, the most irascible judge that ever set his ass on the Superior Court. I remember him sentencing a defendant to five years on a one to five. Counsel, which happened to be me, approached the bench and said to the Judge, 'Judge, my client is seventy-five years old. He has a heart condition and diabetes. He has a sick wife and three children. He'll never make it through five years.' The old bastard interrupted me, 'Tell him to do the best he can.'

"Tell me about John M. Sullivan."

"Another graduate of Essex. Became a big shot executive. Made a lot of money and devoted himself to the school. He became the man in charge of the money. No committee. You came to him on bended knee. He assumed all teachers practice law so that he paid them poorly unless they were his favorites. You have to remember when this school started there was no Association of American Law Schools to inspect and report on a school. Not that I am a fan of the AALS. Absolutely ruined legal education. I think they tried to bankrupt new schools by creating standards that only the elite could afford. Small classes. Library requirements."

"You don't believe in small classes."

"No, I don't. What you get is four teachers teaching torts when only one of them has any competence. And just because Havad Law has a million books that none of those giant intellects use, doesn't mean you have to impose a similar standard on a school in East Squahosh. What it does is raise the cost of tuition which brings up another problem – the established schools want you to think that if tuition is that high, go to the established schools."

Tom was taking all this down. "Dean, everything you say fascinates me, and I am sure that you realize that I am writing a company report and may leave out a few things."

The Dean laughed. Sampson was quite tall. What was left of his hair still retained a sort of orange tint with wisps of it reaching over his ears and down his neck. He wore moccasins, argyle socks, chino pants, and a sport jacket with elbow patches. Despite his years, he gave the appearance of vibrancy. He had a habit of blinking his hazel eyes, but his face was kind, even wizened. While sitting, his left leg tapped continuously.

"I assumed that, Tom, which brings me to the next point. Essex always had devoted and competent second rung people. It would have gone down without them. Luck also plays a part. World War II was the best thing that ever happened to the school. For one thing, they were forced to have an accounting system to collect all that GI tuition and loans. Before that it was chaos and mayhem."

"From my perspective the school taught pretty much black letter law."

"Correct. We left social policy to Yale. Corporate competence to Havad. Excellent teachers to Hastings which hired retirees from the best institutions. There were no hypothetical arguments about what lofty goals the school should attain to. Essex law students wanted to pass the bar exam and my job was to prepare them for it. Every student, in every course, had to buy the Dean's handbooks. You know what they were?"

"No," replied Tom thinking that would be the appropriate answer to keep Sampson reminiscing.

"His Commonwealth notes. He was a copious note taker in law school. - converted those notes into hard bound handbooks. And we were required to use them. Contracts, Torts, Personal Property, Equity, Bills and Notes – you name it. The old black letter rule – three rules, in fact. The majority rule, the minority rule, and what I liked to quaintly call the Massachusetts rule, because we were basically a Massachusetts law school. They were no better than the annual survey that my dad wrote and I continued but my book was not sold on campus – had to get it at the Pemberton Law Book store – another racket. But," and the Dean continued before Tom could interject, "the boys were better off with Seth Adams's books than the casebooks of Langdell."

"Why?"

"Why? They learned the adversarial method. Two people disagree. They go to court. The sharper guy wins. Not necessarily the one who should win. Asa Allen, my teacher at Commonwealth, would point out that on the same basic facts, he represented a defendant in one case and won, and a plaintiff in another and won." You know the old saw about the law clerk who notified his senior partner that their case had been decided and justice won out. He immediately said, "Appeal at once."

"Is that why lawyers make good politicians?"

"That's why lawyers make lousy politicians. Now you sit right there – this isn't going into your history – if any of it does – but I tell my students to practice law and stay out of any other field of endeavor.

What a student learns in law school is not to have an opinion. He spends three years reading other people's opinions. That is why I have moot court in Bennington in the third year. Two years of other people's opinions is enough. The entire third year is moot court. Every student is obliged to argue in moot court and he has to defend whatever side he gets. If his side has to argue that it is free speech to burn the flag, he is taught to argue that with brain and brawn.

Now don't get me wrong, Tom. The men and women who come to

law school may have high ideals. But they take the best offer they can get and for most it is the only offer."

"I remember," interjected Tom," asking my labor law professor why he only represented corporations and not labor unions. He answered the corporations offered him the job, first. So you're saying that lawyers are just hired guns?"

"I think Veblan said that many years ago but it's too simple an answer. It's the training you get in law school. Lawyers are not general practitioners. They gravitate to personal injury or class actions or malpractice. Others represent insurance companies. Once you fit into a slot, you become its slave not its master.

"And when they get into politics?"

"That's the problem with our country, son. Why do lawyers go into politics? Lawyering is the only profession that has the time for politics. Most lawyers are lucky to see two or three clients a day. They join the Elks. They make their presence felt at their law school and at charitable functions. But what is crucial is that most lawyers didn't know what they wanted to do with their life. Doctors, architects, biologists usually have an idea of what they want to be when they grow up. People who become lawyers don't have a clue – and this goes for those whose parents are lawyers..."

"And so ..."

"They are the very worst people to do anything but practice law and the electorate should avoid lawyers like the plague. All they are good at is taking sides – not justice, not the good of the commonweal – if they happen to do good it is a mistake. I have never voted for a lawyer in my life, which means I don't vote in lots of elections."

The Dean looked at his watch. "I have a class in fifteen minutes. Let me just leave you with this and you can write your history any way you want. Why am I at Bennington and not at Essex? I had not heard from Sullivan since my appointment. I had served honorably for five years. I was not yet 65. I had signed no papers. I received a salary check each month. No thank you for services rendered. So I facetiously sent him a note thanking him for his card on my birthday and five years as Dean. He replied by accepting my resignation. I guess it was time for his son to take over the reins."

Professor Sampson got up and smiled graciously. "All I miss is Durgin Park. I went there every lunchtime with Samuel Cohen – loved their poor man's special and split the strawberry shortcake with Samuel. I have to tell you about Samuel and Patrick Donavan. Sam grew a beard while he was here. Not a rabbinical beard – just a healthy growth. So I decided to grow one. Donavan calls me and questions my judgment. I mention Sam and he tells me, confidentially that Sam being Jewish is obligated to grow one but that it is not the Christian thing for me to do. I shaved it."

Tom reluctantly got up from his seat. Sampson gathered his notes and a couple of books and left the room. Tom made the following note for his history of the law school. "Professor Sampson was Dean of the law school from 1973 to 1978. He taught many courses and never left a class without a retinue of students following him. During his tenure, he added elective courses, increased the size of the faculty, and was responsible for the law school being accepted into the Association of American Law Schools, a step that brought the school respectability and a student body that reached out beyond Massachusetts to the New England states and even beyond."

It was noontime when Tom left the law school. He had wandered through the law school, sat for a few minutes in a class on Patents, spoke to the editorial advisor to the law school publication dedicated to intellectual property, bummed a cup of coffee as he visited the law librarian's office, and then stepped out into the cold, refreshing New Hampshire air. He walked over to the Inn across the street. He asked at the desk for his room and went upstairs to find his two children having a picnic of sandwiches and soda.

"Where's mom?"

"She went to get cigarettes."

Tom went downstairs and there she was, sitting at the bar, smoking a cigarette, and talking to the bartender.

"Hi, dear."

"Hi, sweetheart." It was obvious that the empty martini class was hers.

`"I guess we better go upstairs and pack and get back to Boston. I had an interesting interview."

Janet looked at the bartender. "Frank, it's been nice knowing you. I was hoping we could stay longer and learn more about your wife and children. Put your face over here." He did. She kissed him on the lips, edged off the stool and said to Tom, "I love bartenders – they are the only ones who understand me."

Janet looked tenderly at him as they made their way to the second floor. "Darling, let us go upstairs and pack." Tom then said in a low voice, "I think that bartender was a homosexual."

The ride to Boston was sullen. No conversation. Then Janet edged closer to Tom. "Darling, I hope the meeting went well. The weather was miserable. The tent," and then she laughed, "you obviously were never a boy scout. But I'll make it up to you tonight." And she patted his thigh and could sense agreement. He returned the pat, That night Tom dreamed of that tent and that every time he tried to get the pole in the right position, it would shrivel up and turn into a rope.

CHAPTER 6

MOOT COURT

Moot court is the most lavish function run by a law school, and Essex was no exception to the rule. It did not exist during Seth Adams's reign, but upon his hastened departure the new administration followed lock step the ivy tradition. The competition in most schools would begin in the first year of law school. At Essex, the four hundred first year students would be broken up into four sections A, B, C. D. Each section of one hundred students would be broken up into classes of twenty. Each class, after preliminary lectures, would then be entered into the moot court competition. A memorandum, consisting of two legal issues, would be contested by the entire class in groups of two.

The instructor, usually a recent graduate, would pair off the students, and, sometimes, with the help of faculty, alumni, local judges, create a judicial atmosphere where one student would argue against the other on the issue – appellant versus respondent. Winners would be announced and the judicial panel would offer a critique of the student's performances. Within each section the contest would narrow down to the winner of each class of twenty. These winners would compete until there was a victor in each section. The semi-finals would consist of the winners of A, B. C, and D. The finals would be held in the moot court room. The school would attempt to get leading judges and lawyers from the community to preside over this event.

As the same issue was argued throughout the contests, the winning students sounded quite professional at this point. The winning argument went to the person with the best prepared brief, most skilled argument, and keenest response to questions from the bench. Most judges were sympathetic to the contestants, and also had the advantage of a memorandum specifying what the moot court considered to be the most significant cases and ruling on matters pertinent to the issues. Of course there was always the overbearing judge like Professor Ribet, a leading constitutional authority, who presided one year as part of a three judge court. His colleagues were unstinting in their praise of the contestants' performances and brief. Professor Ribet was faint in his praise and also suggested the case should have been decided on other grounds and was critical of the moot court memorandum. He was not invited back.

But this was not all. The second year was also moot court time. This time it was voluntary. Second year students would pair up and vie for the biggest event of the school year. The students entering this contest would also find themselves wooed to enter intercollegiate contests – The National Moot Court Contest – The Patent Moot Court Contest – The Trial Practice Contest, and many others. A Federal Judge was usually courted to preside over the contest. The Dean and faculty had front seats reserved for their presence. A reception was held and the winning team's picture was taken, usually with their family members looking on proudly.

To make the occasion even more significant, one of the large classrooms was converted into a courtroom. The room was paneled, there was a jury area, the seats were padded, a dais was provided each contestant as they faced the court. The room actually looked better than most court rooms in the Commonwealth. The one thing it lacked was a name. The Board of Trustees created a commission headed by Dean Dooley to find an appropriate name for the room. The committee decided it had to be named after a United States Supreme Court Justice. This proved to be a hard task as quite a few of the names had been taken, and quite a few of the names did not appeal to the committee. Implicit in the thinking of this group was that it was not going to be a Havad person. Finally the committee put it in the hands of the chairman, and the room, now and forever, is "The Justice McReynolds Court Room."

Tom Jones was a frequent judge at these contests and he was asked to work with the moot court team to come up with a hot bench for the finals. The court also honored Tom by asking him to be one of the judges, and to search out colleagues. Tom then got an immediate affirmative response from Judge Kaplinsky. As this year's issue involved a criminal issue Tom decided to go after Gerhard O. Deutsch. Tom knew Deutsch from his librarian days at Cahn Law School. He was six feet tall, slim, his hair blond. He had a large forehead, a slender nose, thin lips, high cheekbones. Not only did he look German, but at fourteen, he served on a Uboat in the German Navy during the waning days of World War II. His clipped English disguised a faint German accent. His early education was English; his legal education American. His manners were continental. The only thing missing to make Gerhard complete would be a few scars inflicted during a duel. No woman was ever seated in his presence without his slowly edging the chair in place for her. Although some suspected he felt his charm was irresistible, Tom felt it came very natural. And most important, he was a scholar. His text books were used abroad as well as in the United States. He had worked on the formation of the International Criminal Court of Justice. He crisscrossed continents on speaking engagements. And Tom was honored when he accepted the assignment.

He sought out Tom when he arrived at the school. "Tom good to see you. Thank you for inviting me. I have heard great things about you." And he whispered close to Tom's ears, "We need you back at Cahn." He winked. "Now you know why I am here."

"Professor Deutsch. We are honored to have you." And Tom added, "I am quite happy here."

"Confidentially, Tom. You are paying my expenses here. My daughter is at MIT. By the way, I am having a party at the Commonwealth Club tonight. Please bring your charming wife. 9pm"

"I'll try Gerhard." When Tom was at Cahn, it seemed he was always invited to Deutsch's parties. And there were many held at his spacious apartment on the East Side overlooking the F.D.R. drive. They were extravagant affairs. And not just faculty. There were diplomats, United Nations officials, prominent attorneys. English was not always the dominant language. And there was Tom, sometimes with Janet, spending most of his time lifting delicate items out of trays passed around by attendants better dressed than he was. Tom decided ungraciously that his being Jewish must have something to do with it. Even half-Jewish seemed to qualify him.

The finals went well. Deutsch and Kaplinsky fell all over themselves in complementing each other on their questions to the contestants. Both claimed to be overwhelmed by the oral arguments and expressed their sorrow at having to decide on a winning team. Tom wisely did not intrude on the time of the other judges or the contestants and also agreed with them as to the caliber of the contest.

Refreshments were served and the tall Deutsch and the short Kaplinsky were surrounded by students and both exulted in the attention. The Dean then gave plaques to the winning and losing teams, and a gift to the three judges.

Tom suddenly felt spent. His role in gathering together a judicial team, reading the briefs of the contestants, reading the memorandum and checking cases had taken their toll. He was tired. As he was leaving the room, his exit was barred. There was Janet in all her finery.

"Hi dear."

"Janet!"

"Let's go to the party."

"What party?"

"Isn't Gerhard giving a party?"

"I don't know anything about it."

Janet stood aghast. "He's giving a party and he hasn't invited you? He always invites you."

"Janet. I am very tired. I have had a hard day. If you want, I'll be happy to stop and get a bite to eat with you. But my goal now is to get home early and get a good night's sleep."

Janet stood with her hands on her hips. She shook her head. "I can't believe it. We should have sunk that dumb German's Uboat."

Tom and Janet went straight home.

CHAPTER 7

FACULTY LIBRARY

The faculty library was on the fourth floor of the law school – the same floor as the law library. Tom Jones could enter by key from the library but the faculty would enter by taking the elevator to the floor or using the stairway. There was a basic collection of Massachusetts Reports and statutes as well as sets recommended by faculty. There were two work rooms where faculty could secrete themselves. Along one wall were some forty lockers of an odd shape. They were purposely not big enough to hold anything more than one's working papers. By tradition, they turned into a secure place for a bottle of wine or something stronger. Each locker was locked and numbered and faculty could request one for their personal use. The library provided coffee and tea. There were carrels along the wall and the center contained a large circular table much scarred by spilled coffee, wine stains and other signs of much use and much careless drinking.

By tradition, only senior faculty members sat around the table. Instructors, assistant professors, and newly minted full professors used the carrels and talked softly to one another. By some process of osmosis, as chair holders died, a carrel user would ascend to the round table.

Seated around the table on a Friday afternoon were the Associate Dean Joseph Francis Xavier Dooley, Josh Wittberg, Mike Bailey, Peter Toole, Samuel Cohen and Earl (Rhino) Warren. Warren's chair was a rocking chair given to him for thirty years of service to Essex. The other chairs were simple library chairs with arm rests. No one but Warren sat on the rocking chair. He would enter the faculty library. Go to his locker. Open it. Pour himself a drink. Return the bottle to the locker. Close it, and sit in his rocker, and slowly sip his drink. You had to know what you were talking about or the rebuke from Warren could silence you for a week. Peter Toole, when he first came on the faculty, found this out when he opened a conversation one day with, "I read in the *New York Times* today.." He got no further then that when Warren thundered, "Do you think I can't afford the *New York Times*? Who cares what you read in the *New York Times*?" Warren abruptly rose from his seat, downed his drink, slammed the glass on the table and left the room.

Warren prided himself on his broad-mindedness. He was of Scandinavian stock, but considered Mexicans, Jews, homosexuals, transsexuals, transvestites – any and all creeds, races, sizes, and colors to be his equal. However he had no patience with stupidity and women in his classes.

Women, like his wife, best serve society barefoot and pregnant. When the gates barring women from a legal education came crashing down, Warren had no answer except to refuse to call on them. When complaints to the Dean about this practice proved futile, a women's group protested to the state's civil rights commission. Warren avoided being hauled before the commission by compromising. He instituted "Ladies' Day." On a designated day each semester he would only call on what he described as "the fair sex." It was a circus. Male students, encouraged by Warren, would hoot down sub par answers to his Socratic forays. Women students would often leave the class in tears. Not unexpectedly, the practice caught on and there was usually one law professor in many a law school that adopted the "Warren method." As one of Bender's memoranda put it, "The practice stopped when women outnumbered the men in class and the women started hooting the men."

Some people think that Professor Warren got his nickname, Rhino, from the way he thundered in the classroom. He was not above calling a student "stupid," and he would cite a case and ask someone to compare it with another case. Then he would cite another case and ask another student to compare it with another case. Then he would want someone to compare the first group with the second group. It is folklore that after going through this procedure, he called on a student who said that he had not read any of the cases. Warren dressed down this student for five minutes and was so worked up that the large mole on his forehead just above the base of his nose had turned a livid red that he took to staring at the student. The student calmly said, "Professor Warren, thank you for your knowledge of my pedigree, but even without reading the cases it is obvious that this is a *Rylands v. Fletcher* situation that can only be resolved by some application of absolute liability." Warren looked at the young man quizzically, and the young man answered, "my colleague sitting next to me has that underlined in his notes." Warren shook his head, "Young man, I take back everything I said. You have the makings of a great lawyer."

So there was Warren seated on his rocking chair daring someone to say something. Josh Wittberg, who once said that having tenure made him fearless, started things by moaning, "How did this school get the name Essex. For God's sake we are in Suffolk County. We should be called Suffolk Law School." "Bad idea," said Samuel Cohen, "hundreds of businesses are called Suffolk and I think there is a Suffolk County in New York." At this point Kelly Kindregan, a recently appointed clinical instructor not familiar with the rules of the round table came into the law library, poured himself a cup of coffee and sat in the one empty chair. Mike Bailey decided to offer something. "The answer is simple. Norfolk means North folke. Suffolk means South folke. It is ridiculous that we call ourselves Essex. How about Folke Law School. Professor Warren shook his head wisely and everyone turned to hear his view on the matter. "I think it is too late to make the change, but it is something we could play with." At this point, Kelly Kindregan piped in. "Isn't this a university?" Everyone turned to the newcomer, and he added, "Folke U.?"

Silence. Warren rose from his seat, finished his drink, and sauntered out of the room with nary a repartee.

That pretty much broke up the party and everyone but Dooley left the table.

While this conversation was going on Tom Jones was sipping a cup of coffee in a carrel, looking out the window that faced the Old Granary Burying Ground. Buried there were the parents of Ben Franklin, James Otis, Samuel Adams, John Hancock. On the far side of the cemetery was the rear of the Boston Athenaeum, that sacred library that housed a painting of John Marshall, the famed Chief Justice of the United States. The Park Street Church was off to the left where Henry Lloyd Garrison lit the fires that turned into the Civil War. Essex had much to live up to.

"Tom Jones, you look to be deep in thought. Do you mind coming over here. I want to talk to you. Sit in Warren's chair, the warmth might inspire you to great thoughts." This was not said in a tone of friendliness.

Tom declined but took a seat at random. "My great thought is which of the men buried across the street would want to sit at this round table."

"You are a smart ass, Tom. I just spoke to Mary McCarthy. She tells me she has invited you up there. She wants you to do something for her?"

"I can't say no to one of the most knowledgeable people about the start and success of this law school. As a matter of fact, I didn't get to finish my interview with her for my history. And I might add, I intend to bring my bike and see if I can make it around the island."

"Want some advice?"

"No!"

"You shall get it nevertheless. Mary is a very nice lady. She is way up in the eighties and a bit dotty. I would make sure you get substantiation for anything she says. But that is neither here nor there. What does she want you to do for her?"

"I have no idea. And I don't intend to report to you what she does want."

Dooley rose from his seat. "Is the school paying for this?"

"It was, but if ..."

"No, no, no. Go up for the interview. Do what she asks you. She is a legend – what kind I have no idea. But do me a favor – forget we had this conversation."

"It's a deal."

Tom made the trip alone this time. He purposely notified his wife to make reservations for him at the Kimball Terrace in Northeast Harbor for two days. He flew to Bangor, then rented a car and drove Rte .95 to 1A passing the Lucerne Inn, stopping at Ellsworth for lunch, and then on to Northeast Harbor where he pulled into Kimball Terrace. After lugging his bag to his room, taking a shower, he walked down to the pier to check out the sailboats in the harbor. The first thought that came to his mind was that if he ever bought a sailboat, he would never park it at Northeast Harbor for, as far as the eye could see, there was an armada of sailboats and yachts that would make anything he could afford look like a scow. He watched people scurrying around the fleet like ants at an anthill. They were pushing carts loaded with food, water, and gear. One woman had scaled half way up a forty foot mast and was either patching something or scraping paint. One not atypical gentleman with a walrus mustache, a captain's hat with a scrambled eggs visor, short pants, navy blue suit coat with two yellow bands at the wrist area and sneakers. He was helping his rather obese wife into a row boat. After seating her, he got the outboard motor running and Tom watched him putt putt to his sailboat in the middle of the harbor. It was a struggle for the two of them to get into the sailboat, but that they did, and Tom watched them motor out of the harbor until they got to a point where they could unfurl the sails. It was work and Tom was reminded of Mr. Dooley saying that it was work if you were paid to do it, and it was pleasure if you paid to do it. Maybe he would forget about a sail boat.

It was late afternoon, and Tom returned to his room and gave Ms McCarthy a ring.

This time they met in the recreation room of Mary's condo. She called it the Sardine Factory because at one time that was exactly what it was.

"The sardines are gone. This place was empty for many years. The sardine business gave way to crabs and lobsters."

"And tourists," Tom added.

"And tourists. They've bought up all the property. We've also got a few labs here. The Jackson Lab is world famous for its mice. There is a novelist who lives next door to me who is writing a novel about all the mice escaping from the lab because of a crazy scientist there. Mice with cancer, Mice with heart disease. And one breed that grows larger each generation and unless he is captured the planet will be overrun and god knows what. I think it is possible. How about you?"

"Mary, I can't get interested in of mice and men. I want you to tell me about your early experiences at Suffolk. "

"Well, I don't remember where we left off. Seth Adams came up to visit his Dad. He was now married and had two kids. His wife was a rather prim young lady, and Dr. Adams was quite proud that Seth had married a nice Yankee gal – a Cabot – who had some pedigree and some money. Seth had started the law school – some say in his bedroom, which wouldn't surprise me.

"I don't know whether he knew I was working at Mott's Bar-B-Q, but he showed up alone one morning and I could see by his quivering lips that he hadn't had a good lay for a while. He actually took me to a hotel that afternoon." Mary could see that Tom wanted to convey his abhorrence at her giving in to this man, but she raised her hand to silence him. "Tom, I was pretty easy. It was sort of for old time's sake, but this time I could take care of myself. But then he made me an offer."

"An offer?"

"He asked me to come to Boston and work for him. Tom, he made a lady out of me. I was his secretary. I went to the Gibbs Secretarial School and learned to type. They also taught me what they called decorum which I practice religiously except when my master wanted me. To my complete amazement I found that I was pretty smart. That I had a curt tongue. That I could keep his papers in order. Handle the telephone."

"And tell off students and faculty when it was called for."

"And, I could be trusted to keep a confidence and – this is very important – and handle the money."

"He trusted you to run the school?"

"Not exactly. But do you know how we collected tuition in those days?"

"No."

"Waste paper basket. As students filed into class they had to buy a ticket for each class. I would take the money – give them a ticket and the lecture would begin."

"How did he get the students?"

"He advertised in the *Boston Post*. The turnout was more than he anticipated, and he soon talked the proprietor of a secretarial school to sublet him a room. The Essex School on Essex Street. Harold Schwartz was the proprietor and he specialized in legal secretaries. Seth like to tell me how he outsmarted Schwartz. Made a deal with him. He would take over the teaching and give Schwartz half the net from both Seth's law students and the secretarial school."

"I don't see Schwartz's name anywhere?"

"He died the following year and Seth convinced most of the secretarial students to become lawyers. He just put "Law" between "Essex" and "School," as if it was like that since the school began. Seth was not one for paying rent and he bought an old building – a former print shop facing the State House.

He had a neon sign erected on the top – facing the State House – 'Essex Law School'. He made speeches. He wrote articles. He even became a radio personality. You can't believe how hungry the immigrants in Boston were for a legal education. We had Irish cops, Italian street peddlers, all the Havad, Commonwealth, and St. Francis rejects."

"No qualifications."

"In those days, you could get into law school without an undergraduate degree. You could become a lawyer by clerking for a lawyer. Seth, in no time at all, hired three lawyers to help with the lecturing. All using his notes."

"How did you pay them."

"Out of the waste basket. I would carry that basket around from class to class. Lunch time, Seth would look into the basket and say, 'Hmm, I think we can afford Durgin Park today.'. It became a standard with him. 'Gentlemen,' he would say to the other teachers, 'I think it's Locke-Obers today.'"

"And then what?"

"Then I would count the money and find time to put the rest in the bank. After my first three years we owned the building we had rented."

"And you were the only one that counted the money.?"

Mary looked sternly at Tom. "That's right. When I asked what my salary was, he said, 'Twenty five a week,' and that was what I took out for myself. I never removed a dime from that waste basket that didn't belong to me."

"I suppose at some point a more formal arrangement was made."

"Yes, and I hired the registrar – Nancy Sergent."

"Isn't there a painting of her in the lobby?"

"That's right. She was our first female law student. Seth protested at first but, at my insistence, relented. She was the best student we had and business was so brisk that I asked her to take over the tuition thing. She created an office in the building. She supervised applications for law school, made decisions on scholarships, worked out arrangements for tuition, students called her Mother Teresa and practically every year she was voted most valuable faculty member – that was after she also taught equity and contracts – she never missed a faculty meeting, and was the Dean's best point man at faculty meetings. She also put an end to people dipping into the waste basket for money"

"I thought only the Dean did that."

"No. We had four I guess you would say faculty members. Dooley, Dougherty, Hancock, and Gargarian. Four practitioners that were hired by Adams for two reasons. They made a good enough living practicing law that he didn't have to pay them much and they actually enjoyed doing it. I called them the lunch brigade."

"Adams put up with it?"

Mary looked scoffingly at Tom :"What's the big deal." Mary noticed that Tom still had his doubts. "All right I was uneasy about it. Particularly when Dooley decided that he would act for the four of them – sometimes even for Seth and scoop up the cash and say, 'Follow me gentlemen and we shall partake of the victuals.' And off they would go to Durgin-Park, or Dino's, or the Union Oyster House."

"And Nancy ended it?"

"Abruptly. She was great. We were now a thriving corporation, and Nancy, after she passed the bar, passed the mantle on to an accountant and began teaching equity. Probably the most dedicated person Essex will ever have. I have to tell you about Tony Canzonari. Had a barber shop across from the State House. A lot of his customers were Essex faculty and students. So he decides to go to law school and sees Nancy. In those days you did not need a law degree. She enrolls him. His last semester he runs into financial problems. Reluctantly she agreed to let him provide the faculty with haircuts – it saved his law degree and his business. Ed Bender used to have us in stitches about Tony."

But Tom's thoughts at this moment was more with Professor Charles Gargarian. Ed Bender left a raft of memoranda behind. He was the most persnickety librarian Tom had ever come across. He was also very thrifty, no doubt due to John M. Sullivan's need for signing off on even the purchase of catalog cards. He wrote his memos on the backs of unused printed forms. Librarian Bender had installed a wire cage in the stacks in which he secured the library's valuables, books awaiting cataloging, supplies, equipment in need of repairs, and his personal file cabinet. In these memos he vented his anger, praised himself, made a record of things that might be necessary to protect his reputation, integrity, and sensitivity.

From what Tom had been told of Ed, and from his memos, he could picture this fellow. He was boyish, short, but in very good shape. He made a point of noting that he was always on duty between five and six pm when the day crew left and the night crew came on. There were three sure ways to get fired. One was leaving early before the night crew came on, two was being late to relieve the day crew, and three was using the telephone for personal business. "These are traits not only leading to criticism of library efficiency but of insensitivity to others and I feel I am not only doing my job as librarian but creating good habits in my regular staff and the part-time law students," he wrote in a long essay on personal habits. He had an inquisitive mind – inquisitive enough to publish not very scholarly books about Shakespeare, Justice Holmes, and Charles Dickens. He was a voracious reader and his memos were arranged by topic – Shakespeare, Dickens, Dunne, anecdotes, faculty members, and a voluminous one on "short people." His memos constantly quoted a Mr. Dooley but this Dooley, on inquiry, turned out to be no relation to the associate Dean.

About Gargarian, Bender was very suspicious. According to Bender, his lawyer job was being counsel for a local hotel owner who was starting to expand into Maine and Florida. According to Bender, Gargarian was a little below average height, a mite on the hefty side, and his voice was never lower than a shout. He bragged of fixing traffic tickets but he confided to Bender that most of the time he would pay the fine and charge the fixee twenty dollars over the price of the fine. Bender was particularly merciless about his classroom work. Twenty percent of his class had to do with case material and eighty percent were war stories from his practice of law, or as he put it, "being in the pit." No conversation of Gargarian was without the word "indubitably," always said with gusto and not always pertinent. Gargarian always talked of his influence with the Massachusetts legislature. He, in fact, did what is now called lobbying for his hotel. Ed related how on one occasion he was walking down Tremont Street with Samuel Cohen when Gargarian accosted them and insisted they accompany him to a hotel for dinner. When the dinner was finished, the manager came over and said there would be no charge, and then invited them to the lounge where Al Hirt was playing the clarinet. Gargarian herded them about – actually bullied them – and both Bender and Cohen went along with less than vigorous protest. Bender vowed in his memo to avoid Gargarian. He was particularly disdainful of Gargarian's efforts to get him to invest in property. Bender tells of an argument between Dooley and Gargarian as to which was responsible for the real estate transaction that resulted in Mary McCarthy getting her house in Mt. Desert Island when she retired. Bender concluded, "Mary obviously let it be known she wanted to retire in Mt. Desert. Gargarian probably contacted his hotel friend to locate a real estate agent in Maine and helped get Mary the spot she wanted. But as far as handling the real estate closing and all the paper work, as between the two, I would give Dooley the credit. He had handled the work when I bought in Dorchester."

"Tom, a lobster claw for your thoughts," Mary broke into the long pause while Tom was deliberating on how much of this belonged in the school's history and how much in his hidden history.

"What's on your mind?"

"How long did this dipping in to the waste basket take place. How do I get this into the history of the law school?"

Mary thought about it for a second. "I'll leave that up to you – maybe you should check as to how other law schools got started."

"A good thought. Let's see. Brown University used slave trade money. Duke is great today because of tobacco money that probably has accounted for more deaths than World War II. Stanford is railroad money which means buying Congressmen. Vanderbilt, and Tom paused, "maybe was the first tycoon but at least you have to credit him with establishing interstate commerce. And Essex's founding proved that there is such a thing as a free lunch.

CHAPTER 8

FEDERAL JUDGE STRONG

"Where are you Mr. Jones." Elizabeth Hughes queried as she faced a mound of books on his desk.

Tom laughed. "I'm right here Elizabeth. I asked a student worker to bring me everything Judge Strong has written so that I can prepare an exhibit on him for his talk here tomorrow night."

"The Dean is very proud that we got him," said Elizabeth. Elizabeth had been at the school for some thirty years and she was not shy about reminding Tom that she was not without influence at Essex Law School. She had come to the school as a student in the post World War II period when it became Essex University to accommodate the GI Bill of Rights that gave every returning veteran an opportunity to go to college at the government's expense. It also gave Essex an opportunity to cash in on a windfall of returning GIs who opted for an education. While matriculating she worked in the law library and then decided to get a law degree. At this point the law library was expanding from a meager two thousand volumes of the Massachusetts reports and statutes into a library that was attempting to get accreditation from the American Bar Association. Elizabeth became the assistant law librarian through a succession of male heads of the library. When Tom's predecessor, Francis Burke, a military man, decided to retire, the faculty decided it would need a librarian with credentials. It probably also decided that managerial jobs are best left to men because, when the appointment committee finished its work, no women were interviewed for the job. Elizabeth herself would not have worked for a woman.

"Well," said Elizabeth, " I deserve a little credit for that. I gave the Donavan Honorarium Committee six names of distinguished legal people who had a background in writing for law reviews." And that was the key. The *Essex Law Review* was desperate for established writers. Trying to compete with ivy league schools for top articles was getting nowhere. Tom tried to argue that although the ivies got top scholars, no one read the articles, particularly law students; and it made better sense to go after some unknown assistant law professor who had something to say. That was turned down because as Dean Dooley pontificated, "People cite the Tribes, the Ackermans, the Sunsteins; they don't cite assistant professors. We need to up the number of times our law review gets cited." That won the day and the Donavan Honorarium Committee set up a sum to invite distinguished legal scholars to speak at the law school. The understanding would be that the speech would appear in the *Essex Law Review.*

And Judge Strong, a Federal Judge, had all the credentials. For one, he knew the law school prided itself that it had admitted black students before Havad Law School. For another he had written for many of the top law schools and he had agreed to all the stipulations presented to him. That is, except for expenses. He was notified that a room had been reserved for him at the Parker House. He notified the school that he only stayed at the Ritz and had reserved a suite. He also rented a BMW for his two day stay. And he never ate alone at the Ritz, but managed to find colleagues to join him for sumptuous feasts. When John M. Sullivan saw the bill for his stay, he threatened to end the program. Only when it was agreed that a member of the faculty would be the next speaker did his rage subside.

If he knew the rest of it he really would have ended the program. As Tom went through the Judge's three books on slavery, and thirty-seven articles on slavery, he noticed that there was not a lot of difference in them. Nevertheless, he filled three exhibit cases with the work of the judge. Found pictures of him in the *American Bar Association Journal,* as well as material sent along by the Judge's secretary. As he was admiring his work, a young man nudged him. "Nice work. The Judge will like it. Hi, I'm Judge Strong's law clerk. I told him I would drop by and look over the premises so that he will know where to go tonight."

"Are you part of the Judge's retinue?" Tom asked wondering if this was going to be another expense to be accounted for. The young man laughed, "No, I went to Havad but I used to study here unless your predecessor – he was an animal – would kick me out. I love the girls at Essex – unpretentious and not competition – and I have a date with one in about ten minutes. I told the judge I would be around for whatever need be. I'm Abner McCoy."

"I'm Tom Jones, nice to meet you. I didn't overstep anything about retinue, did I?"

Abner laughed. "You would have a hard time doing it. The Judge does what he does and that's the end of it."

"Do you help him with these articles?" Tom asked delicately.

More laughter. "Judge Strong wrote that article twenty years ago. He gives the same speech whenever asked, and then he sends a written copy to the law review with the following instructions: 'You may alter, amend, delete or do anything to this article that you like except send it back to me for my approval.' Law review editors love that. That speech of the judge has a different look every time it appears in a law review. Most of the times for the better."

Tom looked incredulous.

"Every time, he is asked to give a talk. He says to me, 'Sonny, it's pay back time.' Nobody reads law reviews anyways," and Abner strode off with a lively gait.

And Judge Strong's talk or sermon or lecture was a great crowd pleaser. "It is a pleasure to be here and I look forward to talking to some of you students at the reception they are having afterwards. Let me tell you who I am. My grandfather was a slave brought to this country in chains from Africa." He then pointed to the audience. "Some of you may have descendants who were in that business." The audience tittered. "He was a big tall man – probably bigger than me, and I am sure he brought a good price in the commodity market of those days." More titters. "He was so impressive, my father tells me, that he was adorned in a livery costume and greeted the colonel's plantation guests with the utmost courtesy. He also charmed the colonel's oldest unmarried daughter, who gave birth to my father and introduced father and son to the underground railroad that brought them up north. My grandfather passed away before I really knew him. I have no idea who my grandmother was, but every time I watch a Senator from Alabama or Georgia or Mississippi on television, I look for a resemblance. Dad became a cog in the industrial revolution and worked the coal mines and oil rigs of the great Commonwealth of Pennsylvania where he met my mom and I was soon conceived as well as eleven other brothers and sisters. My friends, I was a good student – not a great one – and a good enough basketball player to earn my way through the University of Pennsylvania. My coach called me "Ass," and he would say to me, 'Ass, you think too much to be a basketball player.' I played defense. I could have been a scorer, but that meant getting your feet stepped on, hands clutching your shorts, and elbows in your face. When you play defense, the opposition wants no part of you. I was drafted, folks, but I opted for three piece suits and tassels on my loafers. No brogans for me. Law school followed and I'm going to tell you the secret of success in law school. Find a study group. I noticed that there were a group of five young men who sat together, lunched together and always engaged the professors in lengthy discussions. They all wore skull caps. I intruded on these gentlemen, and little did I realize that I started affirmative action at that institution. They judiciously included me in their group - I am invited to their Passover seders - and when I organized a basketball intramural competition at the law school, I was their star center. We didn't win a game, but I graduated with pretty good grades, passed the bar exam and was hired by one of the better Philadelphia law firms. Affirmative action. Is that what you're thinking? No sir. I told the hiring partner that if they hired me it would improve the firm's standing in the community. How did I get to be a judge? Well, after a suitable period of time – and this is something every one of you should realize when you yearn for a position at a top law firm – you are either a partner in that time or you are on your own. I guess they decided I was not good enough for partner – and folks, I left the office at five pm – and too valuable a token to let me loose, so they made me a Federal District Court Judge. During the last election the President wanted some black votes, so he made me a Court of Appeals Judge. What I have just given you is the black version of Gilbert and Sullivan. And now let's get on with my talk which will be published, I am told, in your inestimable law review.."

The audience applauded, except for the distinguished lawyer, a senior partner in the firm that hired Strong, who had introduced him and who happened to have spent five minutes telling a different story of Judge Strong's career.

Judge Strong's speech was duly published in the *Essex Law Review* with extensive footnotes provided by the *Review* staffers, and some original insight on underground railroads that managed to trace the path the

Judge's grandfather took in his escape from slavery. This information was supplied by the Judge's law clerk to his girlfriend, who was a member of the law review, and so impressed the Judge that she was hired to be his clerk on graduation. Needless to say, these two married, and have a successful lobbying firm in Washington, D.C. to this day.

CHAPTER 9

THE CAMP

Tom could not get Tony Canzoneri out of his mind. In the back of his mind he wanted to put up a display of early graduates of the school. He wanted diversity. Italian, Irish, Black, women, policeman, fireman, whatever. So he trekked down to the Cage, as he called the archives, and checked to see if Billy Connolly had anything on him. Sure enough, there was the Bender memo:

"Tony Canzoneri. I usually avoid his barber shop or he whistles me in. The guy is now a lawyer but he really doesn't practice law. He helps out his friends but that is about it. A real character. He talks to me just like he came off the boat. I have heard him in class and in court, and he not only speaks without an accent but sounds better than I do. So I asked him 'Tony, why don't you give this up. I'll bet you could be a good lawyer.' So he answers me in his fake Italian, which I wont imitate: 'Heh, here I'm the boss. I practice law, client is boss. I have people waiting for me in my barber shop. If I practice, I have to wait for them.'

"Last week, I'm deep in thought and I accidentally pass his shop. He whistles me in. He decides I need a shave and a haircut, and in the middle of the shave, he tells me

'Mr. Bender, would you please get up from the chair and sit over there a minute?' I do as I am told, and I look out the window and see someone opening the back door of a Chrysler, and the Governor getting out. Tony says, 'Mr. Governor, so good to see you,' and in a sweeping motion invites the Governor to take my seat. He gives him a trim. Afterwards, I am invited back to my seat and Tony finishes with me. Now this is long after he had graduated from the law school and I wanted to pay him, but Tony says to me, 'No, Mr. Bender, the Governor always pays for his and the person he replaces.'"

Tom was always proud of his displays in the law library. His display on "The Path of the Law" that listed all the significant legal events in Boston's history from John Adams' defense of the English soldiers of Boston Massacre fame to the infamous Sacco-Vanzetti case. James Otis, Daniel Webster, Oliver Wendell Holmes all were commemorated and located on the streets of Boston. It was a permanent display as you entered the law library, and Associate Dean J.F.X. Dooley was admiring it as Tom was leaving the library during the lunch hour.

"Can I invite you to lunch, my friend?" asked Dooley.

This sudden invitation and tone of friendship put Tom on the defensive, but although he was looking forward to a quick lunch at a pizza place in Quincy Market, a canoli at Mary's, and a cappuccino at Mike's in the North End, he had no qualms about giving it up to see what Dooley had in mind. Tom was aware that Dooley's usual luncheon companions were four Irish contemporaries of his that met in a cafeteria in the McCormick building. He had obviously grown up with these South Boston locals. Tom would occasionally lunch with Samuel Cohen at the cafeteria and there would be Dooley and his buddies carrying their trays to a secluded corner and Samuel would notice that they would all talk with a brogue as if they had just come over on the boat. Sam would comment, "Professional Irishmen. They're not proud to be Irish; they are arrogant about it. A lot of my *lentsman* think those bozos are anti-semitic. They are just mad that we thought of the idea of a chosen people before they did."

"I am honored," answered Tom, "honored that you are choosing me over those guys I see you with at the cafeteria."

"Something I want to talk over with you. Mary McCarthy called me today and told me she has invited you up to Maine again. Is that right?"

"Am I obligated to answer that question?" Tom answered as they proceeded along Tremont Street and passed the Parker House.

"No. I recognize that Miss McCarthy has legendary status here and I was only offering my help. Mary and I have been friends these many years, and I am proud to say that I was the one that made it possible for her to enjoy her retirement in Maine."

At this point they had reached Dinos on Tremont Street across from the Boston Common. Dinos was a popular restaurant for the legal crowd as Dino himself directed traffic as people entered the restaurant. Lawyers, judges, elected officials would enter and be greeted with, "Ah, Mr. Jones, I have your table – please follow the waitress." And lawyer Jones would be escorted to the left and seated. If you were not recognized, you would wait for an opening on the other side of the restaurant.

"I am sure she will express her appreciation if the subject comes up. Mary is well into her eighties, and she has asked me to come up for a few days and straighten some things out for her. She has invited me and my wife to stay at her camp. Have you stayed there, Dean Dooley?"

"Stayed there. I handled the purchase and sale. I negotiated the deal with the builder. Do you know what that place is worth today?"

Tom nodded that he did not, and Dooley continued, "I just want to express a few things when you go up there. As you say, Mary is well up in years. Her memory is very bad, and she can be very testy. My advice to you is to stick to fundamentals. She has also been a very generous person, and it was all I could do to prevent her from giving her money away. That rehab place that just went up – it was on her property and I had to rush up there to make sure the town didn't" and Dooley caught himself, "er, knock the price down."

Tom listened carefully as Dooley continued to express doubts about Mary's memory and that if any financial matters came up he would be happy to offer his advise. "From what you tell me, you would be a better choice …" but Dooley interrupted, "I would be but we haven't got along for years now. Something came between us – I'm sure you are not interested, These things happen. I would be the one but," and Dooley looked wistful and penitent, "things just didn't work out." Dooley got up, looked at his watch, signified to the waiter that the tab would be on him, "Take your time, Tom. I have an appointment with, believe it or not, the Governor," and Tom saw him cross the street, and make for the side entrance of the State House. Tom smiled as Dooley crossed the street. "Don't fool with me, Tom," Dooley was warning, "I have friends in high places."

It was early Friday afternoon, and Janet had agreed to pick Tom up at the school. She gathered the children and drove into town where Tom was waiting at the corner of Bromfield and Beacon Streets and off they drove to Mt. Desert Island. Everyone was excited about the trip. They were to stay at Aunt Mary's, as they decided to dub Miss McCarthy. Mary had arranged for a Kayak tour on Saturday morning on Seal Cove . It would end at Bosc's Landing where Mary's caretaker would pick them up and bring them to Mary's camp at 72 Mill Marsh Road. That night they were to meet at Thurston's for lobster dinner in Bernard. Tom had promised to rent bikes and circle Eagle Lake and then to Jordan Pond for lunch with their famous popovers. Tom would have to fit in time to talk to Aunt Mary, but the children were more interested in the activity than whether Tom would be in attendance.

Tom and Janet shared the driving on the three hundred mile trip from Boston. Their route was 95 to 295 to 95 to 1A and then follow the signs to Somesville, pass the post office, pass the theater on the left, take a right turn at the fire station, and follow that road to a sign "Marshfield." Take a right until you come to a sign that says mischievously "Downtown to Bosc's Landing." At this point slow down and watch carefully for a sign that says, "Mill Marsh Road." Turn right up the path for about a mile and turn left when you see the numeral "72" posted on a tree. As they drove up the path, two deer bolted about thirty yards in front of them. Janet shouted with excitement which woke up the children and they were disappointed at missing the sight. Mary had arranged for the caretaker to leave the lights on. The keys were left under the door mat.

It was evening when they arrived, but the children were now awake and they rushed down the terraced steps to the house. They ran from the kitchen to the study, from the study to the bedroom, from the bedroom to the bunkroom – their room where they immediately argued as to who was to get the top bunk. Then down to the cellar. The entire house was lit up. As the children emerged from the cellar they looked for their parents. Room by room. Toilet by toilet. Finally they noticed that one entire wall was of panels of glass. One panel was slid open and they rushed out to the deck and there was mom and dad reclining on a lounge chair, huddled together, and looking at a full moon. The deck was the width of the house, and on the side was a stair well, and some hundred feet beyond the deck you could watch the tide coming in. It was full tide and full moon and the tidings were good for a glorious weekend.

The morning was just as exhilarating. The house, or camp, as the natives called it, was dead center on the cove. Off in the distance was the Blue Hills. A sailboat tacked into the cove and then returned to sea. On the left, a short distance from the cove was the far end of Bosc's Island, an island owned by the Pebblepals. There was nothing else to be seen except nature. They just had time to walk the rocky beach and climb over rocks to the far edge where they could see another camp, and then a log cabin perched at the entrance to the cove. A dog barked and they all went back to the camp to prepare for their day.

Mary McCarthy's camp was usually rented from July to September, except for two weeks that Mary reserved for her own use. A real estate agent in Southwest Harbor took care of the rentals, and her caretaker took care to open the house in June which meant activating the well, turning on the electricity, notifying the telephone company, having the grounds sprayed for termites, and a cleaning woman come in to tidy up.

Tom went along for the kayak trip. The caretaker drove them to Seal Cove on the quiet side of the island. A truck came along with the kayaks and the driver turned out to also be the instructor and the Jones' were soon fitted with equipment and assisted in putting the kayaks in the water.

The instructor led the group from Seal Cove, circled Bosc's Island and paddled to the shore at Bosc's Landing. They pulled the kayaks onto the rocky beach, shed the awkward garments they were required to wear, and the caretaker gave them the option of walking the mile back to 72 Mill Marsh Road or riding in the back of his truck. Hungry as they all were, they decided to walk back. As they made their way up the path and crossed a concourse that separated the marsh from a body of water that led out to the cove through a reverse waterfall, two young deer bolted fifty yards in front of them. The first reaction of Jack and Janice was to huddle near their parents, but as they disappeared in the brush, they shouted with glee. Hand in hand, the four made it to the house and dug into the ham and cheese, cookies, and milk that had been stocked for them by the keeper.

Tom then left for his meeting with Mary and promised to be back in time for the promised lobster meal that evening.

CHAPTER 10

THE WASTE BASKET

The message that Tom had received from Mary McCarthy was not to meet him at the Sardine Factory. Mary had notified Tom that she had fallen and broken her hip and was recuperating at the Bar Harbor Residence for Seniors.

Tom had made inquiries and learned that it overlooked Frenchman's Bay and was a combination retirement community with a rehabilitation component. The first floor of the facility was for people capable of taking care of themselves. The second floor was for rehabilitation, and the third was hospice. Mary was on the second floor and Tom found her literally in the hands of a person holding on to her from behind as she maneuvered on a walker.

Mary's eyes sparkled when she saw Tom. "Can you believe it. I fell off a ladder."

"I'm a little younger than you, Mary, and I don't get on ladders."

Mary turned to her helper. "Jim, I think I've had enough. Get me to a chair, I want to talk to this guy." Jim did as he was told, and Mary was maneuvered back to her room and carefully positioned on a chair.

"The doctors tell me that I am going to be fine. I played baseball – I mean hard ball in junior school. This was during the war when Ted Williams and Phil Rizzuto and all the good ball players went into the service. I was a star pitcher and outfielder for my middle school team. I think this break came from those days. When I pitched, I pushed off on my left leg and it would hurt for three days. When I get out of here, I'll show you my clippings."

"Mary, I'm the one to be showing you my clippings, if I had any." Tom stopped suddenly. Knowing Mary's background, he realized he might be treading on dangerous ground, but Mary shot back, "I think I have it right. But, I want to get down to business, Tom. I feel good. I think I will live forever. But there are some things I have to take care of and my instincts tell me you are the one that can do it." Tom was about to say something, but Mary would have none of it. "Tom, I let you in on a few things the last time you came here. I was checking on you. I know in my heart that any confidences I share with you will stay with you. I have to believe that. And I also believe that some things have to be taken care of and you will help me take care of them."

"Mary, don't you think you are taking a chance with someone writing a history of the law school?"

"The history is the perfect set up for us. It is my excuse to talk to you about our glamorous beginning, and I am sure that I can tell you a lot of good things about the law school. But it will also permit me to get you to help me – I don't know – correct wrongs – do the right thing – at least let me put my situation in the right hands."

Tom had not seen Mary in such a serious mood. A few seconds followed in complete silence. "Mary, what is it you want me to do?"

And Mary tells her story. Mary tells how she wanted to go back to MDI – She wanted the respect she had innocently lost. She goes to Maine on her summer vacations and begins to look for a place she can call her own. She buys her own kayak and keeps it where she has set up her mother on the quiet side – a small cabin – her mother is overweight, diabetic, but Mary has made an arrangement with two waitresses at Southwest Harbor – they live in the cabin and do the shopping, etc. and more or less care for her – take her to the doctor, etc. Mary kayaks to a cove she had sighted on one of her trips to the island. She kayaks into the cove, pulls the kayak up high enough so that the tide wont take it out to sea and begins exploring the area. A big dog barks and Mary talks with the owner who lives in a log cabin that juts out on the south side of the cove. Turns out she has just been divorced and given a large share of the acreage. She is willing to sell – she actually knows of Mary – part of it so that she can share expenses for the path that she has built that leads to the road to Bosc's Landing. Mary returns gleefully to Essex and turns to Dooley, who teaches real estate. He agrees to go to Maine and look it over. He thinks she is crazy to want to build in a wilderness but arranges with a local lawyer to pass on 10 acres and three hundred yards of ocean frontage that Mary has picked out. She gets a local builder, Raymond LaGrange, that she knew had built on Long Pond He convinces her to build the house with a cellar, big porch – nothing New York or Hampton. Mary had saved up money by this time and paid for the land but needed a loan for the down payment for the house. Dooley arranged for the financing. By this time, Dooley became interested in Maine. He took a few tourist rides around the island. The Pebblepal estate, the sailboats at Northeast Harbor. He was at that time building on the Cape, and inveigled Mary to buy some property in her name for him.

"It's a great story Mary, and Janet and my kids are at this very moment enjoying the fruits of your foresight."

"I wish that were all. Did I tell you how in the early days students paid per class?"

"And they put the money in the wastebasket between your legs. And the Dean dipped in for lunch money."

"I never paid much attention to it. The Dean took. Dooley took. When I spoke to Dooley about wanting to buy that property, I knew what I was doing. I didn't have the guts to take a dime, but I must have known Dooley would see this as a great opportunity."

"He had an accomplice."

"He arranged for a safe deposit box in Portland. In both our names. To make a long story short, that safety deposit box paid for the house."

"And …"

"And, I signed documents Dooley brought to me. I have no idea what they were and I need you to help me out of this dilemma. I want to do right, but I don't want to besmirch the school, and I have given money to some local charities, and," and Mary stopped and tears, a drop at a time, ran from her eyes.

"And you are worried about Dooley."

"At my age going to jail doesn't bother me. But, I've got my reputation back. It's going to come out and I am a loss to know what to do. Maybe all I am doing is getting this off my conscience. I had to tell someone and you are it. I'm a crook, and God damn it, you are my priest."

Tom went over to Mary, and hugged her. "Mary, Your first job right now is to get your strength back, You concentrate on walking again, and I'll concentrate on our problem. Right now, let's be practical. Nobody is accusing you of anything and nobody may ever accuse you of anything. But what I want you to think about, before I come back here for another interview about the history of the law school, is: Do you have a will?"

"Yes and no."

"Think about it. And I promised I would get back to that wonderful camp of yours and take my family to the Thurstons for steamed clams, corn on the cob, a pound and-a-half lobster, and some blueberry beer."

Mary laughed and as they waved good bye, she shouted, ""Make that blueberry pie."

CHAPTER 11

SIMON KRUPNICK

The ride home from Mt. Desert Island was about as pleasant as Tom could want. Memories, memories. Pancakes at the Jordan House in Bar Harbor, lobster at Thurston's, the swimming on the fire road, picnic at the Marshfield picnic ground all made for an exciting, healthy fun packed three days. Although Janet enjoyed herself, she was perplexed at how little attention she drew. "My God, I wore my two piece bathing suit to Thurston's, with my bra practically falling off and, would you believe it, one guy actually warned me it was falling off as if it was affecting his appetite." "It probably was, Mom," shot out Jack. And Janice shot out, "And the kayak leader told you to put your bra back on. I heard him." Janet sniffed, "I just wanted to get an even tan, the prude." Janet looked at Tom, to see if this elicited any reaction. Tom looked straight ahead, traveling at his usual sixty miles an hour, as cars sped by him. "Next trip I am going to have one of you go with your father and report to me on his peccadilloes. Darling, do you want me to take over the driving?" "Yes, dear," answered Tom with his mouth puckered up, "I will pull in at the Kennebunkport stop and we can get something to eat and you can take over." That was done, and Janet took over, upped the speed to eighty and they were home in less than two hours.

When Tom arrived at work the next morning, Elizabeth Hughes was at her desk. The circulation desk was busy. Student workers were shelving books. People were at their desks in the catalog department. Tom went to his office. He sat at his desk and could think of nothing to do. Tom could just wonder at his good fortune in his job at Essex. He had spent twenty years at Cahn Law School. He had tenure. He was an Associate Professor of Law. But there were some gnawing details in his past.

A new dean had been installed at Cahn. The new Dean, Norman Needleman, got on Tom's nerves. He had either a nervous tic, or was laughing at his own jokes. This would not have been a problem except that Tom found that, when in the company of the Dean and others, and the Dean laughed, he was the only one not joining in. Then there was the alumni magazine that Tom was asked to edit by the previous Dean. On the issue that the old Dean had approved, but came out as the new Dean was installed, there was a picture of a streaker running through Professor Wallace's last class. Dean Needleman, without informing Tom, had a new editor in place, which Tom only found out when a new issue appeared. Needleman also had a wife who liked to suggest improvements. Tom was sure she was behind a lavish stairway that was cut into the center of the reading room. The stair way led to the first stack level where an enclosed area was created with mahogany book cases with fixed shelves.

The final blow came when Isaac Small, the law librarian retired. Isaac was an icon in the law library field. A past president of the American Association of Law Librarians, at one point he was made Dean of libraries at Cahn to correct some inefficiencies, and he was an author of seminal books in library science, legal biography, and legal bibliography. Tom realized that he did not have the reputation of Isaac, and that he had no right to expect to be offered the throne, but the complete silence by both Isaac and the Dean, left Tom with the impression that they would be happy to see him go.

And go Tom did. By a stroke of good fortune, Essex was losing its law librarian, who was retiring at sixty five. Francis Burke, a former lieutenant colonel in the Judge Advocate Division of the Army, had been hired by the school to be its librarian. In effect librarian Burke was a figurehead. Elizabeth Hughes ran the library. Burke considered his job to keep order in the library. He would sneak up behind a student who had his bare feet on a library table, and shout, "Get your God damned feet off this school's property." If a student had more than six library books in his vicinity. Burke would stand over him with a piercing eye to let him know that that person was responsible to reshelf those books. But the crowning anecdote of his career, was reported by Walter Herlihy. Burke was on one of his raids and was silently stalking through the library, when Walter approached him to ask a question. Burke turned on him and shouted, "Never interrupt me when I am talking to myself." Although Burke dressed in mufti, he saw himself in an officer's uniform at all times. This fact was duly noted by the committee set up to find a replacement. Esther Goodman, who taught admiralty law, and whose husband was Provost of the university, was chair of the committee to find a new librarian. She sent out letters to librarians all over the country asking if they had a second in command they could recommend to take over Essex. Tom's departure from the school was rather abrupt. Tom learned from his successor at Cahn, that the library staff implored the Dean to be present at a short ceremony in the library's recreation room. The Dean presented Tom with a brief case, said a few words that had him cackling for two minutes, with the staff joining in, and Tom, as usual, not getting the joke.

Tom shook these thoughts out of his head. "If I have nothing to do," Tom said to himself as he sat at his desk and watched students being taken care of at the circulation area, "who should I interview next.?

Tom had a subscription to a clipping service that provided him with newspaper items that identified people in the news that had graduated from Essex. What caught his eye was Simon Krupnick, an Essex graduate of 1965 who had just returned from Europe as a member of a committee on the Law of the Sea. Krupnick had been a member of a leading Washington, D.C. law firm, a Federal Judge for a number of years, was "of counsel" for a leading New York City firm that had offices in the major cities of Europe. Tom knew he had been editor of the law review and had never received a mark lower than an A. Professor Toole had told a story about Krupnick that stuck in Tom's mind. Toole was in his office while final exams were being given, and Krupnick knocked on his door and asked to speak to him about the final exam he had just taken in Toole's course. Toole was quite put out that anyone would ask questions about an exam. It was sacrosanct that you take a final exam and you wait until the professor corrects them all. But Krupnick persisted and said that if three of his buddies were right about the answer to one of the questions, then he was going to flunk his course. So Toole listened. And sure enough, Krupnick's analysis not only differed from his buddies, but also from Toole's, and Krupnick was correct. A tacit agreement was reached with Krupnick to keep the matter to themselves. Krupnick got his A, and Toole admitted to Tom, "Krupnick was the smartest student – and I have taught at Havad, Yale, Villanova – that I have ever met. And a whiz with the Bluebook."

Professor Cohen attested to his Bluebook skills. "I was the faculty advisor the year he was editor in chief of the law review. There was no citation he wasn't the master of. "op cit.," "ibid," you name it. He knew the position of every comma, semi-colon, indentation. He could have written the *Kama Sutra*..

He was a little guy. I don't think he was five feet tall. I think he was in love with that Sheila girl."

"Sheila?" But Cohen had walked away, leaving Tom wondering who Sheila was. He decided to check Bender's memoranda so down he went to the cage where among the rare books, discarded carrels, books needing repairs, were the file cabinets that contained Bender's acid thoughts. In all the musings Tom had read, not one good word was said about anyone. It was as if all his frustrations were taken out in print and stored in these cabinets. They were intermingled with his annual reports, expense accounts, copies of exams that he had given, and even a certificate awarding him a Methew Bander Publishing House scholarship. Tom was indebted to his archivist for the work he was doing for his legal history, both hidden and public.

And there it was – labeled "The sorrows of Werther." : "I have to tell the Krupnick story. He was such a pain in the butt. Didn't like the cataloging system. Insisted on a key to the faculty toilet. Walk into my office with impunity, and always called me 'Bander.' A New Yorker. Manhattan no less. I heard his father was a judge. Passed away which is why he is at Essex. I was told this story and I believe it. He buys a beat up old Cadillac. Parks the car illegally and goes to the movies. The movie no sooner begins when an announcement comes over the loud speaker, 'Will the owner of a Cadillac 8788M1 please move your car. It is blocking the parking area.' And out strides this little fat guy as if he had the most expensive car in the city.

But everyone has their comeuppance. Sheila Cohen makes law review. Krupnick is the big cheese. He falls in love with her. I mean head under heel because she was a head taller than him. He knew she was at the theater when he parked his Cadillac illegally. Every excuse, he would be in her company. Teaching her. Explaining her class notes. They would lunch together, I'm sure at his insistence.

Now for the tragedy. I knew it would come. I didn't know how, but it did. Of course, like all semi-geniuses, Krupnick outsmarts himself. Professor Robert Posner, our most distinguished professor. The man who brings Supreme Court Justices to the law school. *Havad Law Review*. Classes are always over subscribed. He is writing a seminal paper to be given at a conference at Geneva. The genius who single handedly invented the litmus test for Supreme Court nominees – that if they did not pay obeisance to *Roe v. Wade* the Senate would reject them. In lock step, practically the entire legal academic community backed him up and denied approval to a candidate whose qualifications far exceeded his replacements. That opinion was the worst reasoned opinion ever handed down by the Supreme Court and Louis Brandeis would consider it not a self-inflicted wound but an infection on the Constitution. I believe in a woman's right to an abortion, but I also believe that states, not nine Justices, should be the experimental chambers to work out this problem. Posner asks Krupnick for help. So what does Krupnick do. Ordinarily he would welcome the opportunity to work with Posner, but Cupid takes an arrow out of his quiver, and shoots it up his you know what. He offers Sheila to Posner. I won't go into details. Sheila and Posner spend a lot of time going over footnotes or playing footsie, and Sheila not only graduates magna cum laude but as Mrs. Posner.

That was the original memo, But Bender would update it: 'Posners have a baby boy,' 'Posners have a girl,' 'Krupnick spoke to the law review last night. Posners were there, but Krupnick didn't seem to notice."

CHAPTER 12

THE VISIT TO LESLIE FORSYTH

Tom Jones had decided to visit Leslie Forsyth. He had dropped in on the Development Office with the idea of compiling a list of alumni who would be fodder for his interviews. He particularly wanted someone who would be more representative of what Essex was all about. Someone who made a good living and would be an advertisement for the law school.

Salvatore Lombroso, the Placement Officer, had the ideal person to interview for the law school history. "She is a natural," he said. "Was a paralegal. Took over her boss's practice. Very successful real estate practice. Hires Suffolk students all the time. Affable – you'll like her."

Lombroso was a tall, gangling fellow who was made for what he was doing. No matter how desperate the job market was he had words of encouragement for the 400 or so graduates of Essex Law School. He arranged for law firms to visit and plied them with lunches. In turn, the firms sent their hiring partners, particularly those outside of Boston, who longed for a day out of towns like Waltham, Worcester and points west and north. Other New England states sent representatives as well as state and federal agencies. The military came seeking Judge Advocate candidates. Salvatore always invited a few faculties to these luncheons. Quite often, the interviewer was an Essex graduate and it was good socially and ideal from a public relations standpoint. The only problem was getting faculty to attend the luncheons. Some faculty had good excuses. They were either at class, preparing for class or had interview hours for law students themselves. Some like Professor Dooley found them boring, a waste of money, and that law schools were to get students by the bar exams and should not be expending time, money, and energy in finding them jobs. "In my day," he would say, "you either found a job yourself, started a law firm, or went into the real estate business." Of course, he did not mention that after law school he went into his dad's business. Tom on the other hand was happy to attend the luncheons and he had a standard invitation from Salvatore which he kept assiduously. Students were not invited to these luncheons but could usually be found sitting nervously outside the room waiting for their interview.

And so Tom gave Ms Forsyth a ring and off he went to 294 Washington Street, ninth floor, where he was met immediately by a sign that pointed to "Leslie Forsyth, Attorney-at-Law." The door to the office listed Ms Forsyth and also contained, in less prominent letters, the names of additional attorneys. Tom presented his card to the receptionist, she spoke into a receiver, and out of the door sprung Ms Forsyth.

She was a woman in her forties. She was what those with a smattering of Jewish would call zaftig. She was a bit on the short side but walked with a stride that belonged to a six foot woman. She was not pretty nor was she ugly. But she did radiate friendliness. She did not dress like many of the successful female lawyers that Tom knew. She wore a frilled white blouse, and a Navy blue skirt that seemed a bit too short for someone her age and her position. Her greeting to Tom was full of *bon homme*.

"Hi, Tom – I know you – the librarian. You have a great library and I'll have you know that my most proud accomplishment was writing a law review article in one of your cubicles."

"Thank you – I think that all happened before I was hired but I hope I am keeping up a great tradition."

"Come on in." Tom accepted the invitation and found himself in a large room with a large leather couch, heavy furniture including her desk and chairs. The walls attested to her profession and one included the fact that she had the best grades of her class in the subjects of Jurisprudence and Property. There were also pictures of her with her law review classmates, and one where she was the only women among a group of tuxedoed men.

"That was taken two years ago at the law school banquet where I was honored with the title of – I think – "Distinguished Alumnus of the Year." It should have been "Alumna" but the galoof that did it either didn't know his Latin or didn't know I was a female."

Polite laughs follows and then Leslie went on non-stop.

"One thing I think that a history of the law school should make known is that Essex is, and I hope always will be for, the poor, the people who want to get ahead, like me. I was a legal secretary to Ted Liscomb. He had a great practice. Real estate title searching. He would do them for the banks. He would do the same one for the mortgagor. He had practically the entire town of Concord title searched. When a search came up it was just a question of bringing them up to date. Each year he would hire a recent graduate – always from Havad, occasionally Yale – they would work for one year and he would let them go because he didn't want them learning too much, knowing too much or networking with his clients.

I picked up title-searching very easily. It wasn't long before I was teaching these muck a mucks how to check to see if there were any liens on a piece of property or if the state were planning a highway and were going to take a slice of property by eminent domain.. Strangely enough, I found it fascinating. We had a summer clerk one year who was doing a paper on Justice Holmes – I'm sure you know who he was."

"Havad graduate, I think."

"Yes he was – but you know he quit a teaching job at Havad that led him to become a Justice of the United States Supreme Court. Anyways, I was able to locate where Justice Holmes – his father had the same name – lived in Boston which was very helpful to this guy. So the idea came to me – why am I a paralegal? I want to be a lawyer. On my lunch hour, I headed down to Essex and spoke to the Registrar, Ellen Dougal."

"She's still there," Tom chimed in. Ellen Dougal was a tall, spindly woman in her late sixties. "She came in after Nancy Sergeant passed away. Registars are the bulwark of this law school. Rumor has it that Ellen was married some forty hears ago when things came apart. No one will speak of it but it is said that her husband is a drunk and sits on a corner of Tremont and Boylston panhandling. And when he is half-way sober he walks into the law school and sits in on classes. He's been doing it for years, and no one thought much about it, until he once embarrassed Dean Dooley on his interpretation of the Rule in Shelly's Case. Dooley found out he was a local bum and ordered the guards to keep him out of the building. I understand he still sits in on classes, and uses our men's' rooms for his toilet."

"I don't know about that but Ellen granted me an interview. When I told her I worked for Ted Liscomb, she called him up and - I will be damned- she listened to that man for about five minutes. When she hung up she said to me, 'He doesn't think you should go to law school. Says you are a woman and a great paralegal and you would be very unhappy to get involved in the messy business of law.' I started to sputter and she stopped me. 'Ms Forsyth, you couldn't have got a better recommendation. That bastard has never hired an Essex lawyer. When we petitioned for accreditation he was one of the Havad guys that opposed us. Now where did you go to undergraduate school.' I told her I went to a secretarial school. 'I guess that will have to do – see you in the fall.' End of story."

I was taking notes and thought the interview was over.

"Not so easy, young man. I want you to get the entire story. "Call your wife – you are married aren't you – and tell her you'll be home a little late." Tom did as he was told. This was the kind of story that he envisioned for the history. A success story. A woman. The role of the law school. A hit on Havad. Wow! Tom moved to the couch to get comfortable and indicate that he was ready to give her all the time she wanted to tell her story. Leslie followed him to the couch.

"I thought he was going to fire me. The reason he didn't was because I knew what he didn't want the Havad Law students he hired not to know. I made it clear to him that I needed time to go to law school, to study for exams, and there was plenty of time to take care of his practice.

One year, he kept a Havad guy on longer than the one year which turned out to be a bonanza for me. We wrote an article together on "Title Practice." Leslie reached on her desk and picked up the article and planted it on Tom's lap with her wrist under the article and nudging Tom's penis. He smiled at Leslie to indicate that no harm was done, and Leslie smiled back indicating that she knew that men's laps consisted of more than two thighs.

"Liscomb immediately fired the Havad guy, and here comes the surprise. He tells me that there is no reason for him to hire anyone else to do searching but me. That he is getting on in years, and that the law business is mine if I want it."

"Damn nice of him."

"Not really. The Havad guy wanted me to join a lawyer friend of his that was doing title work. When we both graduated, we would join him as equal partners."

"Did Liscomb know this?"

"I don't think so. But he was no dope. His kids weren't lawyers. He was in his seventies. He gets a piece of the business. And I have all this." She stood up, raised her arms as if encompassing a globe, and then descended on Tom and gave him a big kiss on the mouth.

She looked coolly at Tom and said, "When I think of all this, it makes me sexy as hell." She went to her desk and flicked on the intercom. "I don't want to be disturbed until I call again."

She then, lifted Tom out of his seat. Turned the couch into a sofa bed, lifted her dress, dropped her panties, eased herself on the couch, spread her legs, and said, "C'mon big boy, wet your whistle."

Tom felt he had no alternative but to comply. He dropped his pants and obliged the woman. When he was through, she still wanted more and directed Tom's hands into her pudenda and starts stirring and grunting. It reminds Tom of when he was painting a wall in his house and was stirring some coloring into the paint to get it to the right shade. Soon she grasped his wrist with both her hands and was rotating it with such force that Tom thought his wrist would break or he would never recover his knuckles. He was now a Cusinart. She finally lets out a yelp and releases him.

"Do they think you are beating me up or I am beating you up." "I couldn't care less – get dressed quickly," she added, "I have an appointment in five minutes." She wiped herself off, applied some lotion here and there, straightened herself out, looked into the mirror to add some lipstick, and as Tom headed for the door, she said, "This is a one time deal, my friend." Tom did his best to look disappointed as he disappeared out the door.

Tom made it home about eight o'clock that night. His wife yelled out from the bathroom, "Tom, I just got home with the kids. We went out for pizza. I'll be right out. Open a can of sardines or something."

Tom reached for a can of sardines, but realized his wrists were too sore to turn the can opener. He settled for cheese, crackers, and chocolate milk.

Janet enters the kitchen and says, "Not hungry dear," and then, "you smell funny dear. Like you just came from a whore house."

Tom was riled. "No, I haven't been to a whore house. And how do you know what a whore house smells like? I've been cooped up with this crazy real estate lawyer for two hours. I've been on the go since this morning, and I'm eating cheese and crackers for dinner and being accused of going to a whore house."

Tom stomped out of the kitchen and headed to the bedroom. As he undressed, he realized that he was wearing his shorts during his rendezvous with Miss Forsyth. He put his bathrobe on and went downstairs, located his brief case, and dumped his shorts in under his interview notes. He then showered and when Janet came to bed, she smiled at Tom and sweetly said, "You smell better now dear."

As Tom snuggled up close to Janet, he whispered, "This history business is more than I expected – I wonder if the guys who wrote the histories of Havad and Yale had to go through what I am going through."

Tom arose early the next morning and apologized to the children that he couldn't help with the breakfast as he wanted to get to work early. He made sure that he took his brief case with him.

The morning was hectic. He no sooner arrived than he had a message from Dean Oberal asking him to come to his office to meet Sarah Greenlease, who was being interviewed for possible appointment to the faculty. Essex's procedure in looking for faculty was to advertise the position in the *New York Times*, then check over the responses, and invite two or three to make a presentation to the faculty at a luncheon. Professor Greenlease had arrived early and Tom immediately set in motion the schedule for the day. Coffee and fruit at 10:00am with faculty invited to meet Ms Greenlease and question her. Copies of her resume were made available. She then accompanied Tom to the library where he provided space for her to recover from this ordeal and prepare for her after luncheon address. It was Tom's turn to introduce her to the faculty after the luncheon. And then she would give her talk.

After the talk came the questioning or sometimes inquisition. Sybil Latke could be counted on to spend five minutes digressing on the topic until she could work in a question. Vickie Dodge would add another five minutes without a question. Wittberg could always be counted on to end the torture with a short question that would begin with, "I'd like to ask this question before we break for classes and give a hand to Professor Greenlease for a great presentation." That would follow and then Tom, as the host for the day, would then bring the guest down to the dean for goodbyes and his escorting for the day was done.

The day and afternoon spent, Tom decided he just had time to do something with his interview with Ms. Forsyth. He used the phone in the faculty meeting room adjoining the Dean's office to call Elisabeth

Hughes and ask her if she had a person available to type up his notes on Ms.Forsyth and drop them on his desk. The notes were in his brief case somewhere in his office.

Tom went to the staff room for a much needed cup of coffee and was greeted by the librarians and secretaries who were there with much camaraderie and jollity. More than usual, he thought. He knew his predecessor never had coffee with his staff, and he was sure he did so not as a boss but as a fellow employee.

When he got to his office there was Ellen, a staffer, with his notes and the typed copy for him. She smiled brightly, displaying two glimmering rows of teeth, and then placed the typed notes neatly on his desk. "Oh," she added demurely, "I always wondered why they called them brief cases – now I know," and she left laughing. Tom's brief case lay open on a chair near his desk, and there was the incriminating evidence. Tom picked up the briefs and, without assistance, disposed of them in the disposal bin in the basement of the building.

CHAPTER 13

TOM LEAVES CAHN LAW SCHOOL

To: Dean Oberal
From: Tom Jones, Jr.

Re: History of Essex Law School – Progress Report

The first part will recreate the school's beginnings with Seth Adams starting an evening law school that provides "opportunity's open door" for those who had to work for a living, lacked educational credentials, or who could not afford the higher tuition of the day schools.

I will next report the remarkable rise of the school. Its growth from an evening school to a day and evening school. I will show how elite law schools, elite law deans, and even Presidents of elite universities attempted to eliminate Essex by inveighing against Essex at bar association meetings, law school associations, and even legislation. The hero in all this will be Dean Adams, who fought for the common man. Essex pioneered in making the law available to all religions, creeds, colors, gender, and economic status. Statistically, I will show that Dean Adams' instructional method proved that he could turn "plow horses into show horses."

The report will feature interviews with faculty, present and past, success stories of our graduates who have excelled in the practice of law, in politics, in business, and even in teaching. I will interview donors and supporters of Essex. This will subtly show how we have grown from a Boston institution into a national ornament with a promise of global prominence.

The report will be about 150 pages, but I will preserve all my notes and drafts, so that fifty years or one hundred years from now, when another history is written, this material will provide a basis for that history.

From: Dean Oberal
To: Tom Jones, Jr.
Re: History of the Essex Law School – Progress Report
    The Dean asked me to congratulate you on your progress report of the history and to keep up the good work. Please keep the expenses down.
                            Ellen,
                                    Secretary to the Dean

Tom could see that he was on his own on this history. The Dean was planning an anniversary that would celebrate the school's one hundredth year, but Tom knew his role was going to be perfunctory. The usual speeches, the usual galas, the usual pitches, the usual promises. Essex was secure in its role in attracting students who could not get into the first tier law schools, but could provide all the features of a first tier law school: legal publications, moot court teams to compete nationally, a faculty with some outstanding teachers and scholars, financial aid, student bar activities, legal clinics, and all the rest. Essex, like all fourth tier law schools, was sucked into expensive programs by the ivies that veered them away from their initial purpose – to provide education for those who were not affluent. What Essex did have going for it was subliminal. It had a reputation, not really earned, as being the law school for the misbegotten, the rabble, the oppressed, the anti-Havad. It was also located in an unparalleled intellectual and social center. Within a small radius there was professional and amateur theater, universities that specialized in music, international law, and one of the largest concentration of students in the United States. And you could not spit in downtown Boston without hitting some spot of legal significance. And then there was THE museum, THE golf course, THE college, and that smug Bostonian attitude that it was THE Athens of America. You could always tell a Bostonian, but you could not tell him much, which Tom remembered reading in one of Justice Holmes' many collections of letters. Tom was going to inject some of that in his history and he found it fascinating that he was writing one history for the Dean, and one for posterity.

Best of all, from Tom Jones point of view, was that the history of Essex would show that it was on its way to having a top tier library. This was no thanks to the administration but the work of Esther Goodman, an Associate Professor at the law school, who was asked to head the committee to replace the retiring law librarian, Francis Burke, who had reached sixty-five. She surprised the Dean with the energy with which she tackled the job. She went through the *Directory of Law Schools* and noted that many law schools listed head librarians as being on the faculty. Many of them, like herself were women. As one of only two females on the faculty, Esther did a quick study of this phenomenon and found out that law schools were being pressured to hire more women, more minorities, and more blacks. Librarians, in many cases met this need. So law schools, by making librarians, who were predominately female, faculty could solve one problem of diversity. This was an ideal solution to a large body of male professors who didn't mind diversity so long as they did not have to associate with it. Goodman herself never doubted her standing in the Essex faculty. She was a Havad Law graduate, she had practiced law with a major Boston firm, and it was irrelevant that her husband was the provost of the university.

Professor Goodman sent a letter to the law librarians of major law schools asking if they had a second in command they might recommend to head the Essex Law Library. She received three answers, one of them being from the New York Abraham Cahn Law Center, where Tom Jones was the Associate Law Librarian. Cahn had come from nowhere to become a leading law school. Columbia Law School was the ranking New York City law school with a rich history and ivy league status. However a perfect storm eroded its standing. For one thing it was located in an area of Manhattan troubled by civil strife, crime, and poverty. There was also internal strife between the faculty and the administration. A murder-robbery of a prominent professor started a chain reaction that led many faculty to retire early or accept positions in other parts of the country, particularly California, which was partial to aging ivy league faculty.

Cahn, on the other hand, was one of many schools with day and evening students and local lawyers, many part-time, making up the faculty. Then a confluence of events occurred that propelled Cahn into top-ranking. A new Dean, Newton Rockefeller, a former Chief Judge of New Jersey energized the school. He raised money to erect a new Law School in Greenwich Village. He originated full scholarships, including room and board, that attracted bright students from all over the country. A rabid Yankee fan, he used their techniques to hire away talented professors, young and old, to upgrade his faculty. Although Rockefeller was not from the oil family his name was magic, and he became prominent in bar association and law school association affairs. He created an Institute of Constitutional Administration that brought judges from around the country to its seminars. His biggest coup was interesting a tobacco company in a stock arrangement designed to reduce the company's tax obligations. Eventually the Tax Court disallowed the tax benefit but allowed the stock arrangement which resulted in Cahn benefiting to the extent of fifty million dollars. Fifty million dollars can do wonders for a law school's standing in the legal community.

The second in command at the Cahn law school library was Tom Jones. Tom had been at Cahn for eighteen years. His boss, Isaac Small, was one of the most eminent members of the law library profession. A past president of the American Association of Law Librarians, an author of books on legal history, Justice Oliver Wendell Holmes, and a master politician. You had to be adept, vigilant, and merciless to get ahead at Cahn as it rose in prominence as a legal institution. Rockefeller, an ardent admirer of Franklin D. Roosevelt enjoyed pitting his petty scholars against one another. He created a tax department, an international law department, a copyright department, and reached out far and wide to find heads of these departments. For the graduate tax department it was Fred Wallace, a former assistant to the head of the Bureau of Internal Revenue. Fred had turned the tax department into the leading tax program in the country and the nine hundred graduate students it attracted made it the biggest money maker at Cahn. A gracious man but when imbibing, he could be brutally frank in his assessment of other faculty members. His *bete noir* was Gerhardt O. Deutsch, who taught criminal law, and who lectured extensively throughout the world. Deutsch, a submarine enlisted man in the German Navy at the close of World War II, had an ebullient personality,. an unmistakable Germanic underpinning to his clipped English accent, that just seemed to set the former commander of a PT boat in a rage. Wallace's power was such, he could reign supreme in the makeup of his department. No faculty member would vote against his choices; no Dean would question his judgment. When a junior tax associate decided to change the cataloging system so that books in his courses would be together on the shelf, three members of the catalog department were fired for defending the integrity of the cataloging system in use in law schools throughout the country.

Wallace's classes were oversubscribed. His wry wit such as his calling the Tax Code the "Pension Plan for Tax Lawyers," and his ability to place students in well-paying positions, made him the darling of the Cahn community. His only competition for popularity was Henry Youngerman, who taught evidence, trial practice, and professional ethics. Youngerman, a Havad graduate, turned down acceptance at Havad Law School to attend Cahn on a full scholarship that included room and board. On graduation, he immediately turned to teaching and was an immediate success. In the classroom, he held the students in the palm of his hand. He would play witness and then stand and cross-examine himself. He would analyze not only decisions but the judges who rendered them. His lectures were taped and used in courses throughout the country. Plaintiff lawyers hired him to write briefs, and in one instance, he was hired to handle a multimillion dollar personal injury case. He lost the case but the publicity from the case was worth every penny to the law firm.

Students looked forward to attending the last lecture of both men. Some prank was bound to happen. In Wallace's case, a stripper was slipped into the class and during Wallace's opening comments, she took off her trench coat and sauntered, red hair flaming from top to bottom, down the aisle, past Wallace, and out an entrance behind him. Wallace never missed a syllable. Youngerman outdid this performance. His wife was suing him for divorce and she agreed to come to his class and was seated in the front row. Youngerman, unphased, got down on his hands and knees and pleaded successfully for another chance. Only at Cahn.

Tom's decision to leave Cahn was a combination of factors. He was unhappy with his New York life. It was a time of civil strife in New York and the school system was in chaos. His wife was drinking a little more than he liked, and he was unhappy with the code you had to live by in New York City academia. He and Janet would get invited to a home, where the hosts would have the event catered. Servants, hired by the hour, would rush in and out with canapés and drinks. In one instance, in Riverdale, it was poolside, with a caterer preparing crepes for the guests. On this particular occasion, the host ripped off his clothes and jumped into the pool, followed by a few idiots, including Tom's wife. Tom did not have the facilities, the money, nor the inclination to reciprocate and he had a suspicion that he continued to get invitations not for his conviviality, but for his wife's seductress presence.

There were two more factors and this overshadowed all the rest: The new Dean, Norman Needleman and Isaac Small's retirement at sixty-five. The new Dean was a graduate of Yale, law review, and was given a leave of absence to become Solicitor General of the United States. When a Supreme Court appointment was not offered him after four years of service, he returned to Cahn, and immediately, on sensing that the current Dean, Miguel de Cervantes, was overwhelmed with his responsibilities, began campaigning for the job. Cervantes, a former Olympic fencer, did not bring his talent to the job. He could parry but not thrust, Although an able teacher of corporate law, he had written only one law review article, and it was a faculty joke that it was the only law review article that had never been cited. He retired after three years as Dean, and returned to Mexico and was never heard of again. Meantime internecine warfare broke out at Cahn. It was dubbed "The Norman Conquest" for Needleman had an opponent, Norman Dawson. Jones remembered Dawson paying him a visit. He had never so much as acknowledged his presence before, but Dawson was now gracious and friendly and telling Tom how much he had contributed to the law library's standing. Needleman, heir to a pawn shop fortune, held a party for the faculty at the Havad Club in Manhattan, where in the presence of a stuffed elephant, courtesy of one of Theodore Roosevelt's hunting trips, guests ate, drank, and mingled while Needleman and his wife made the rounds. Tom found himself in one of these rounds, and noticed that Needleman would make a statement and giggle hysterically. All those within hearing would follow with some degree of amusement, except Tom, who did not believe in laughing to impress anyone. And Needleman was not unaware of Tom's presence, nor did it escape him that some admired him for his courage.

So now Needleman was Dean and Small was retiring. Needleman had already removed Tom from editing the school's alumni publication. He also had made Diana Vincent, the foreign law librarian, an associate. When Tom received Professor Goodman's invitation to interview at Essex, he did some hard thinking. He had tenure – they could not fire him. In twelve or fifteen years he could retire. It would mean tense moments with the Dean giggling and Tom searching for the humor. Working for Small was not exactly paradise, as he was frequently away, and Tom found himself running the library, teaching an introductory course, and supervising the cataloging, acquisition, and other departments of the library. And then there was the thought that maybe it was time for him to run a library. Three times in the past, law schools had attempted to pry Tom away from Cahn, and three times Tom had notified Small of the interest. Three times Tom had received raises to stay and was rewarded with better titles. In fact, it was a source of wonder to him that he started as a Reference Librarian and now had the title of Associate Professor of Law, Associate Law Librarian, and Associate Curator. And then came the letter from Professor Goodman. Tom applied but this time he did not notify Small of his intentions. After accepting the job, he dropped into Small's office to notify him and was met with a handshake and, "Congratulations Tom, I have assured Essex that they will not be sorry in hiring you, as I will be in losing you." It was Isaac Small at his best.

CHAPTER 14

TOM AT ESSEX

Actually Tom was ambivalent about applying for the law librarianship at Essex. Tom had been with Cahn for eighteen years. Essex was Cahn eighteen years ago. Today Cahn is a top ten law school. The law school was vibrant with activity. Judges and justices from all over the United States and abroad visited the law school, attended its conferences, lectured to the law students. And the school's gamble to provide a free legal education to students who had graduated with high honors from leading colleges had paid off handsomely. Cahn boasted of its graduates who were partners in the top one hundred law firms, the current attorney general was a graduate, and, the biggest bonus of all, two of its recent graduates were now law clerks to United States Supreme Court Justices. Little was spoken of the United States Senator graduate who resigned his seat when he was accused of multiple instances of sexual harassment.

So when Tom received a letter at his home asking if he would like to be considered for law librarian at Essex, he bragged a bit about it to Janet, and then threw the letter in a waste basket. Janet picked it up.

"Heh, Tom, look what you did for Cahn. Maybe Essex, too, will rise from the ashes under your leadership. You always tell me that the law librarian is far more important than the Dean in a law school. I think you should go for the interview," she suggested.

"Why?"

"You don't have to take the job. They will pay for the trip. We can visit family."

"No way. It would not be right. And I don't think I could pull off faking an interest in a job I wasn't interested in."

"Tom. You hate the new Dean. And, remember the last time you interviewed. at Wayne State, I think. Cahn gave you a big raise to stay."

"And Wayne State didn't make me an offer."

They both laughed. Tom folded his arms on his chest and started shaking his head. "Maybe it's time for me to be a law librarian."

Tom arranged for the interview. They drove to Concord on a Sunday and Janet's father greeted Janet and the children with open arms, and a cigarette hanging from his lips. He never did acknowledge Tom until he tried to carry a piece of luggage into the house and found it a bit heavy for him. "Tom, you're a big strong boy – see if you can carry this into the house." The old man hadn't changed a bit. He accommodated his widening girth by sewing a gusset in his pant waist. He sat his daughter down and talked to her incessantly until Tom interrupted and suggested that they better get the children to bed. Interrupting the old man was a trial. A clause would hang in mid air while he caught his breath. His pauses would be in mid sentence. When Tom learned the trick, he would break in with his own thoughts regardless of where the old man was, and that was when conversation between the two ceased.

On Monday, Tom took the train into North Station and walked to Beacon Hill where Essex was located. An unpretentious building six stories high on a street leading down into Cambridge Street. The street was in the process of being paved, and Tom was beginning to have misgivings about leaving Cahn, which was Taj Mahal compared to Essex.

By prearrangement he met Esther Goodman and she introduced him to the members of the committee. Off they went to Locke-Obers for a delicious lunch. Tom had the lobster bisque and finan haddie. After lunch he was introduced to the acting librarian, Elizabeth Hughes, who showed him around the three floors that made up the library. Ms Hughes was a big woman. At least six feet tall and big boned enough to look like a college line backer. Elizabeth was a little aloof, but he learned later that he was her choice. Elizabeth had been at the school for thirty years. As Professor Toole told him soon after he introduced himself to Tom, he looked like someone she could handle. She had started when the law school expanded into a university which was accomplished to take advantage of the GI Bill of Rights. She worked in the library while an undergraduate. She then decided to go to the law school. Passed the bar but continued to work in the library finally becoming the assistant librarian. That was her career. And the faculty committee was careful to advise Tom that Elizabeth was an institution at the law school, and whatever great things he could bring to the law school, she still had a role to play.

Elizabeth then brought Tom to the room where faculty meetings were held and he was introduced to the entire faculty available at that moment. Compared to Cahn, a group of twenty was not imposing, and the questions put to him not unfriendly, so that Tom was beginning to enjoy the day. He then was ushered in to Dean Oberal's office that adjoined the faculty meeting room.

Oberal was a big man with a round face and the modulated voice of someone who knew how to sway a jury. Oberal was a storied graduate of Essex's evening law school. He was credited to have the highest average ever recorded before or since at the law school. He was a successful tort lawyer with a small law firm. His reputation as a trial lawyer was such that other firms hired him to try their cases. It was not unusual for him to be called into a case the day before trial. He would be briefed by the lawyers on the fundamentals of the case, plaintiff's witnesses, the insurance company's case, and Oberal would storm into the court as if he was a witness to the accident. One of his great assets was a phenomenal memory and an ability to speak extemporaneously in well constructed sentences. You never heard a "you know" or an "um" or a pause in his delivery. When no-fault insurance was proposed in Massachusetts, he was the hired gun to defeat the legislation. Although the legislation passed, it was so watered down as not to make any difference to the income of personal injury lawyers.

Orberal taught at Essex while practicing. He enjoyed the prestige of being a professor and the camaraderie of his colleagues. The one flaw, the Achilles' heel, in his armor was that he did not have an undergraduate degree which was not required to attend law school in the 1950s in Massachusetts. In the classroom or in the courtroom, you could only admire the skill and competence of his delivery. But the only Shakespeare you could get out of him came from *Bartlett's Quotations*.

"Tom Jones, sit down." Tom sat. "I don't know why but I expected a Roy Mersky or a Dan Henke, or a Dusan Djonovich - a law librarian name. Tom Jones sounds to me like a regular guy who works at the Silver Dollar Bar."

"I think my dad wanted me to be like the fictional Tom Jones. I disappointed him. My mother's maiden name was Bloom. He named my sister Molly, and she also disappointed him."

Oberal knew he was missing something, so he got right down to business.

"Tom, you have excellent credentials. I must say they pay well at Cahn because you make as much as our tenured faculty." Oberal noticed a dark shade coming over Tom's face and he added quickly, "Not a problem. We do have some more interviewing to do but I would say we like you very much. We need someone with your experience and coming from Cahn would be very much to our liking. Now your predecessor taught military law, but we do have other slots available and I like to get your thoughts on it."

"Dean Oberal, I have done a bit of research about Essex, and yesterday I took the liberty of going through the library as a visitor. There are big gaps in your primary collection, particularly state statutory material. I notice that you lock up your Westlaw and Lexis material, and ..."

"Whoa, Tom, I'm impressed. We'll talk about those things when you get here. Right now we are awaiting inspection by the Association of American Law Schools and let's forget about teaching for now." Oberal got up. They shook hands vigorously and Tom was to hear shortly that he would be the new law librarian at Essex.

Tom needed a drink after that immersion and he noticed a bar on Bowdoin Street. The New Ritz . The closest thing he had ever seen to a bar like this was McSorley's in the East Village that had a reputation of not serving women. It was the seediest looking affair: The floor could have used some saw dust. It had booths that were not secured and one was so far separated from its table that the woman occupying it was lying prone on the seat with her legs spread. And no underwear. Tom ignored her beckoning glance and sat at the bar and ordered a draft beer.

The underwear unencumbered lady sauntered over to Tom. "The least you can do is buy me a beer." "A beer for the young lady, bartender." "Are you a student or a professor?" Tom looked closely at her. He took her for about twenty. She had a hard look but with soft eyes. Her blond hair needed a good washing as did the flimsy dress she was wearing. Before Tom could answer, she said, "I'm not a prostitute, mister, I'm just easy." Tom replied, "I'm a librarian. Just applied for a job at Essex. Wore me down.

So I thought I'd have a beer to cool off and then go home to my wife and kids." "Right now," she quickly replied, "I'm between guys with wife and kids," and she took the beer and went back to her booth.

Tom finished his beer and remembered the brand, Fagawi, because he would make sure its foam would never touch his lips again.

He made the 6:15 pm train to Concord, walked up the hill to his house. The door was open – he had never known it to be closed. There was no sign of activity until he looked out the kitchen window and there were Jack and Janice helping grandpa Wright with the gardening. Tom walked out the back door and the children were so busy with their activity that they just shouted out, "Hi, Dad" and kept on with their work. "Where's Mom." "She left a note on the kitchen table, Dad." Grandpa Wright had reached that age where he needed help getting up off his knees, and he looked up at Tom and said, "You know when I was your age, and saw an old man on his knees, I'd go over and ask him if he needed any help getting up." Tom walked over and pulled the old man up and said, "But you're not an old man, Grandpa." "I'll give you this, Tom. You are fast with a quip. If you were as fast in some other ways, Janet would have stayed here and helped with the gardening." "Fast in what way, Gramps?" "Forget it," and Mr. Wright limped painfully back in the house.

The note read: Gramps and sis agreed to put the children to bed. Join me at HoJos for a little jazz.

HoJos was a restaurant on Route Two between Concord and Acton and two nights a week featured jazz with Ricky. Ricky's son was part of a state program that brought black students from Roxbury to Concord. Ricky came to Concord when the school had its annual family-student event. The high school band played, the chorus sang, and the teachers and students decorated the school for the occasion, and soft drinks and home made cookies graced each table. Ricky was a local entertainer and he was asked to play a few tunes. The manager of HoJos was impressed and thus began Ricky's career as an entertainer in Concord. What made Ricky endearing was that there were a number of successful people in the area who had once entertained ideas to having a musical career, but gave it up to follow in dad's insurance business, or become a doctor or an engineer. Careers that would make it possible to marry into a good family, send the children to Concord Academy, and make it possible for them to follow in their dad's footsteps. They would come on Ricky's nights with their instrument and Ricky would give them a hearing. A nod from Ricky would mean you could unclasp your instrument and join in the swing of things. Fun was had by all, including an occasional singing of a raucous song. On some occasions, the number of instruments in play equaled the audience. The house gave no free drinks.

Tom found some slices of venison in the refrigerator. Gramps had been out hunting and brought home a deer and hung it in the shed. He had obviously sliced and cooked some for the children and fortunately a few piece were sitting on a greasy plate. Tom made himself a sandwich and a glass of milk, read the *New York Times* he had started reading on the train, and then left for HoJos. He was not in a hurry, as about twenty minutes of jazz was about all he was interested in, and he knew that Janet's main interest in his being there was to get a ride home, if that.

As he opened the side door to HoJos – the main door was for the restaurant – he could hear Cashew Marconi singing, "Wop, Wop, Wop." Everyone was clapping widely and Cashew followed his verses with a bit of harmonica. Janet was sitting on the piano stool next to Ricky. There were two gin and tonics on the piano top and Janet was sipping on another with one hand, and the other hand on Ricky's shoulder.

Tom joined a group at a table and ordered a beer. People would holler out suggestions for the next song, most of which Ricky ignored. A few more numbers, and Ricky announced he would take a rest before he began the next set. As he got up, Janet also got up and kissed Ricky on the lips. At that point, Doc Rickerson, the trumpet player, and the Wright's next door neighbor, got up and whispered into Janet's ear. She turned and saw Tom.

"Tom, darling," she gushed and holding on to Ricky's hand she went over to Tom's table. "You know Ricky, and he tells me that his son will be in the same class as Janet when we move back to Concord." Ricky struggled to get his hand free, and said, "Excuse me, hi Tom, but I've got to get to the boy's room."

Janet was exercised. "Tom, you didn't say hi to Ricky."

"I think we were both embarrassed. I think he was happy to get away from both of us."

"Oh, for God's sake. I kissed him so what."

"So nothing. Look I'm tired. I figured you asked me here to drive you home. I'm ready to go home."

Janet thought for a moment. "Okay, two more songs. Ginny, two gin and tonics."

"Just one."

"You are a party-pooper."

Ricky returned to the piano. Janet nursed her drink nervously. Janet arose and brought her drink over to the piano and sat next to Ricky and said something in his ear. He shook his head and turned nervously to look at Tom, as if to say, "Heh, mister, do something." Tom walked over to the two of them. "Janet, we agreed on two songs and then we would head home. Ricky is finishing his second song."

"You go. I'll walk home."

Tom shrugged his shoulders and started to leave.

Ricky stopped playing. Doc Rickerson started blasting, "When the Saints Come Marching Home." Ricky joined in. Janet pleaded, "Just this song and I will go, please."

They sat, listened, and left.

Janet fell asleep in the bedroom with her clothes on. Tom slept in the sun room. The next morning Janet was cheerfully making pancakes for all and they packed up that morning and drove back to their Riverdale apartment in New York City. All Tom could think of was that he would soon be starting a new life in Boston and he was not off to a good start.

CHAPTER 15

ELIZABETH HUGHES, GEORGE BURTON, PETER TOOLE and LAVINIA

Tom's appointment began in September. He made it a point to consult with Elizabeth Hughes on every move. He was also surprised at the acumen of his two reference librarians, Susan Sanders and Janet Klein. Both were graduates of Simmons College Library School, and Janet was also an evening student at the law school. But his first move was to ask to appear before the Student Bar Association in a question and answer session.

The student bar president excoriated the previous librarian, a former officer in the army. Francis Burke would parade up and down the library looking for students in bare feet and, to the annoyance of other students studying, berate the student in a cadence that sounded like he was leading a regiment to battle, instead of a student out of the library. He left all library matters to Ms Hughes, whose many degrees did not include one in the library field. Tom immediately put Janet in charge of instruction in Westlaw and Lexis and before the fall semester was out, one-third of the class had received instruction by signing up for it. Susan was to make sure that the library had the latest statutory code of every state and territory. Tom took over the collection which had three sets of the National Reporter System but none of the early state reports. That was corrected by Tom's purchase of microfiche. He next arranged with used book dealers to send him their listings as the library was sadly deficient in legal history, jurisprudence, and classic texts in constitutional law and other fields. Tom realized that because the library was seeking approval by the Association of American Law Schools it needed to increase the size of its collection and it had gone about it by scatterbrain purchasing of books in law enforcement, juvenile delinquency and other fields that were strictly, and at best, inter-disciplinary. He made the library a government depository of material. He also discovered that the library still used IBM punch cards and single-handedly convinced the associate dean and the business manager to provide him the funds to set up a computer lab in the library. Ten personal computers were purchased. They were linked to two printers by the university's reference librarian and two evening law students who worked at Digital Computing (who were in fact his unpaid advisors). Tom had given up his office to accommodate the equipment as the administration showed little interest in providing any other support for his venture. Before Tom could even announce the new addition, students had poured into the room as if it had been there forever.

His last move in his first semester was to get into an argument with the faculty advisor to the school newspaper, *The Cert*. The editor was selling advertisements to the paper, and he was using the proceeds to hold meetings with his staff in the North End at Joe Tecce's. The faculty advisor thought the money should go into a general fund for student activities. Tom, who made it a point to be quiet at faculty meetings, brought the matter up and said it was only just that the student staff had to forage to get these ads and deserved some reward for their efforts. The faculty advisor defended his position and concluded that if the faculty were to agree with Tom maybe he should be the faculty advisor. The Dean did not even bring the matter up for a vote and Tom accepted his task with the comment, "I do not remember the last time I spoke at a faculty meeting. I look forward to reverting to my former self." That evening Tom was regaled at Joe Tecce's by the staff, but despite a few more glasses of wine than he intended, his parting remark to the group was that he intended to look closely at the financial statement of the newspaper and make sure that some disbursement was made to the student bar. The Associate Dean Dooley told Tom, "My friend, I must confess to you, I thought you were wasting your time and the school's money with those machines. I was leery of you with that business with the school paper. If it was up to me, I would have fired you the day I saw those kids hooking up those idiot machines. I guess you knew what you were doing." "Dooley," Tom replied, "If I had known being a librarian was so dangerous, I would have joined the army instead."

In all of this, Tom knew that Elizabeth Hughes was watching closely. Elizabeth was a big girl and she towered over Tom. He knew from Professor Samuel Cohen that she had played baseball in a woman's league. According to Cohen, her team actually played a one inning exhibition game against the Boston Bees and she struck out the side. "She was a good pitcher I was told," he told Tom, "but when she reared back to throw her breasts practically burst through her uniform. My guess is that distracted the batters. I have it on good information that the Bees were interested in hiring her. Thought it would bring in some customers for a last place team."

Tom added, "I guess if they could have a one-armed outfielder and a midget playing in the major leagues, a woman makes sense."

"Don't let Elizabeth hear you say that."

Ms Hughes' relations with the reference librarians was very touchy. Elizabeth came off the street to work her way up to running the library for Tom's predecessor, and now finding that her new boss was a hands-on law librarian, posed psychological problems of a large order for Tom. Somehow there had to be a *modus vivendi*.

Elizabeth had ambivalent feelings about her worth in an academic setting that was male dominated. She had the territorial ferocity of an animal about her role now as second in command. She was also overwhelmed by an inferiority complex about her limitations academically and intellectually. Her ability to perceive a slight was only matched by the ferocity of her reaction. Add to this the administration's realization that she was the most dedicated person to the welfare of Essex University then one can understand Tom's delicate position. Her position did not give her faculty status, and she recognized that her role was to do the cataloguing, manage the staff, including the part-time law students, and take care of the budget. But she used every opportunity to let the reference librarians know that she was their boss. For instance, she kept an accurate check of their time, their sick leave, and vacation time. She would complain to Tom that Janet spent too much time teaching Westlaw, and that law students had no one to go to for assistance at the reference desk. And Elizabeth's irritation would show up once a month like clock work. In one instance, she complained to the Dean that Tom did not keep her informed of what was going on and that bills were coming in for computers – and that she had no orders for them. Should she pay them or was something fishy going on. The Dean called Tom in and berated him for not keeping Elizabeth up on things and asked for an accounting for the bills he put in front of Tom. Tom took the bills and knew he did not order them. After putting in calls, it turned out that there was a standing order for OCLC computers to replace the old ones. It was a technical service transaction that Tom advisedly left up to Elizabeth. He left the information on Elizabeth's desk, and then headed down to the Dean's office to acquit himself. The Dean was too busy to see him. As Tom went back to the office he realized what had happened. The Dean was happy to have Tom handle Elizabeth's monthly problem, and by berating Tom, he had made Elizabeth happy. It was all too simple and Tom decided he could handle one problem a month.

Tom finally broke the ice with Elizabeth. He had developed a very bad and lasting cold. After two days of this, Elizabeth approached him. "Mr. Jones, you should do something about that cold." "Any suggestions, Elizabeth." "It's obvious that you are out of alignment, Mr. Jones." Tom looked at her querulously. Elizabeth directed him to turn around. The next thing Tom knew, she had gripped him by the shoulder and vigorously brought the left shoulder forward and the right shoulder backward. The sounds of bones crunching and crackling followed, and Tom was sure he would be in a cast for the rest of his life. He sat down. "Does that feel better? I'm going to give you the name of my chiropractor." Tom was about to say, "Now that you are through how could it not feel better." But then he realized he did feel better. His cold was gone in one day. And also gone was the wall between the two. He also became careful about catching colds.

Tom's activities with the student newspaper brought him in closer contact with the school's past. It also fit in with his writing the history of the law school. This brought him in contact with the school's archives, such as they were.

The archives were in a caged area in the stacks. In fact they were not called archives. The staff referred to it as "The Cage." Tom was aware that when the law school was started in Seth's home there was no library. When word got around that there was a "law school" for the misbegotten, Seth eventually took over the bottom floor of a defunct printing plant on Beacon Hill. The dribble soon became a stream, and Seth gambled and bought the building. Being an old printing plant, the floors were wide open and easily converted into classrooms. The first library consisted of a second hand set of the Massachusetts Reports that were stored in the same room that was set aside for the first faculty members. Seth Adams taught from his notes, and made copies of the notes for his faculty. Seth was a copious note taker during his student days at Commonwealth Law School. With prodigious labor he typed up his notes, converting the many mnemonics he had developed into plain language and produced copies for his colleagues. Eventually these notes became hard bound books which were sold to the students, providing Seth with a good income. The faculty, practicing lawyers, were happy to have a crib to bolster their own knowledge, particularly considering they were required to teach in areas in which they did not practice. One teacher, whom Seth thought to be very good, was not hired back when he attempted to require the students to buy his own production.

In the forties, Seth faced with requirements by the legal profession that law schools accept only graduates of undergraduate schools, he took steps to obtain a charter from the Commonwealth of Massachusetts so that he could create a College of Liberal Arts. He wisely recognized that his quarry was poor students, that he needed a college poor students could go to so that they could continue at the law school. Seth suspected that this requirement was a conspiracy by established law schools to put him out of business. Seth would face many threats to put him out of business, particularly led by the snobbish ivy league schools, but he proved to be more than a worthy adversary. The archives contained a diary by Seth, spiced with vitriol, that listed every attack, and his plans to oppose it. He may have been a dirty old man, Tom concluded, but he was up to those Havad intellectuals.

With his new college and new building, Seth started to have a dream. Originally, he was trying to prove to the world that he could make lawyers out of the common man – make race horses out of plow horses. Now he had an institution on his hands. And the end of World War II turned into a golden opportunity. The mostly young men coming home from the war were no longer armed with weapons of war but the fire power of the GI Bill of Rights. Students that were eligible for this education had their tuition paid, the books paid, and were given a stipend that increased if they were married. Essex soon became the law school with the largest enrollment of any law school in the country. Classes could be as large as two hundred students all required to buy *Adams on Equity, Adams on Constitutional Law,*

Adams on Agency, and so on. Money flowed into the coffers of educational institutions including Essex beyond their fondest dreams of avarice. New faculty had to be hired, facilities enlarged, and for Essex, a library. And Seth now envisioned an institution to rival any in the City of Boston, and, maybe, even Cambridge.

With the outpouring of money from tuition, and his credit established, Seth moved ahead rapidly. He purchased an adjoining lot, hired an architect, and within a year had a six story building erected. The old building became the liberal arts and business college, and the new building had emblazoned on its roof a neon sign with that lettering: ESSEX LAW SCHOOL. Deans of the local law schools made unflattering remarks at this display, and even challenged it as unprofessional advertising before the Overseers of the Massachusetts Bar. The complaint was turned down as "while it would be unprofessional for an attorney to so advertise, we have no standards for law schools."

At this time, there was a movement by a Havad professor, a recluse who believed law to be a science, and that cases were the lodestone to discover law's true meaning. He was Christopher Columbus Langdell, and his movement spread from Plymouth Rock to Alcatrez. But to Seth Adams, case law was nothing but a conspiracy to put his black-letter rule books out of business. No one was more outspoken on using cases rather than experts to interpret the law. What judge's decision could compare with *Collier on Bankruptcy* or *Williston on Contracts* or *Scott on Trusts*, or *Wigmore on Evidence*, or *Story on Constitutional Law*, or *Backstone's Commentaries on the Law* or Adams on anything.? As Tom mused over the case law controversy, he admired Seth Adams, though it was in a losing cause.

Adams recognized that if he was to have standing with the prestigious American Bar Association, he would need to bow to having other than his own books in the law school library. Faced with having a university and needing library books, and, in his mind, having the law school as the jewel of the university, he hit upon the idea of hiring the university's history professor as librarian and entrusting both the university library and the law library to his keep.

George Burton had no trouble teaching history and being the librarian. For one thing he had Elizabeth Hughes to handle the day-to-day activities. For another, students were too busy with their assignments in the medley of Adams' books to wander among the volumes of the National Reporter

System, the basic depository for Langdell's theory. Adams also now looked the other way when the faculty began using case books as supplementary to his texts. George Burton was a librarian because it added to his meager salary as a professor at the university. He also had a love that dared to mention its name, and that was the Welsh language, about which no one questioned his authority, and few lingered to learn from him. His one self-confessed claim to fame was that he had published a book on it, and he could segue any conversation into some mention of it. One reason he was very happy to have the title of librarian was that he would frequently go to interlibrary loan and determine which libraries did not have his book. He would then start a campaign to see that they ordered it (from his publishing company). This resulted in a second edition and you could be sure that when he found a reason to mention his book in conversation, it was always with "As the second edition of my books states." Despite his foibles he was both affable and conscientious, and handled his classes and the library adroitly. He was no academic, but like many academics, was not aware of it.

Burton was a bachelor. He was short, stocky, bald-headed and had the bulldog look of Winston Churchill. People, upon being introduced to him, would sometimes mention this likeness, and they would be friends of his for life. This included Samuel Cohen, the first Jewish member of the Essex faculty and the two of them could be seen having coffee in the basement cafeteria of the law school. Burton would often question Cohen about Jewish words, on the pretext of seeing if there was any relationship between Welsh and Hebrew or Yiddish words. It got so that Burton used more Jewish words than Cohen. Burton's favorite expression when he was questioned about some of his assumptions and had to admit error, would say, "What do you expect from a goyishe kop?" He would then flash his teeth, have a hearty laugh, plop an unlighted cigar in his mouth, and then pronounce a Welsh word of twenty or thirty syllables that he would claim had the same meaning. Cohen was also short, but had a theory about height. He claimed that his upper body had the dimensions of someone about five foot ten, but that his short legs reduced his overall height to five foot six. Samuel had everyone pegged. James Stewart, the actor, was six foot four from the waist down, but only five foot seven from the waist up. He conceded that Tom Jones was five foot six any way you looked at him. Cohen was someone who probably looked old at the age of sixteen. Add to this a full head of salt and pepper hair, a facial growth that was less than a beard, a slight stoop and you had a law professor who taught commercial law and taxation.

When Oberal became Dean, he was obsessed that the law school have a separate identity from the rest of the school. He made sure that only law classes were taught in "his" building. He would send an Associate Dean to university functions. And he demoted Burton to college librarian, and reached out to Francis Burke to be his law librarian. Burke had been in the army in the role of a Judge Advocate. He was a graduate of St. Francis and desperate for a job now that he was out of the army. As Burke was a friend of another former military man, Salvatore Lombroso, a former Captain in the Navy's Judge Advocate program, who had been hired to be Placement Officer at the school, he was welcomed aboard the U.S.S. Essex. Burke was interested only in a faculty appointment. But Lombroso convinced him to take the library job. "Heh, I don't tell people I'm in Placement. I tell them I work at a law school and teach military law. Heh, the guy who shovels behind the elephant in the circus tells people he's in show business." The two alternated teaching Military Law. Burke became the terror of the law library. when he wasn't at lunch with Lombroso, his military buddy. Students were required to wear suits in the law library, The only noise was when Burke was shouting at someone for wearing sneakers, or bringing food in the library. The hiring of Burke and Lombroso was not an anomaly, as Essex probably had more faculty with military ranking than any other law school in New England. The fact that Tom Jones had been an enlisted man in the Navy did not work against him.

The hiring of Tom Jones was the final piece in the completion of the project to legitimize Essex Law School. Seth Adams had since passed away, but Dean Oberal had ambitions that matched his. Essex now had a separate building for their liberal arts program. They then added a science department, and followed that with a graduate program in business administration. Some said that they were what they were in name only, but low tuition and a solid base of eager young, poor New Englanders anxious to get ahead in the world paid the bills and put students in the classrooms.

But the law school was the tail that wagged the dog. Oberal was quick to hire disgruntled faculty from other law schools, of which there was always a fair share. A perfect example was the hiring of Professor Peter Toole, the former Dean of Huntington Law School. Toole was an excellent teacher, an author of prestigious articles on law and technical innovation and unintentional torts. He would have been sought after by many law schools except for an unforgivable personality trait. He was perfectly honest about his colleagues' ability. As Dean at Huntington he enraged tenured faculty that had outlived their usefulness. He went too far when he suggested that the President of the University, Paul S. Pell, was a coward for refusing to present the Pell award to the most outstanding student of the school because he had resigned as editor of the university newspaper when it was forbidden to write an investigatory report casting suspicion on the entire Board of Trustees. Pell ran the school as a fiefdom and his run in with Toole made headlines in the Boston newspapers. Toole would have continued in his Deanship, except, by design or coincidence, the faculty had signed a letter of protest about Dean Toole's "inept and boorish" running of the law school.

Toole resigned and Oberal offered Toole an appointment, wisely suggesting that it would be interim if Toole found a position elsewhere. In one swift move, Oberal had the best tort faculty in the country, for it also had Professor Lambeth and Professor Evans, whose stay at Essex was also of convenience. Toole did not change his colors at Essex, but as the faculty were more practicing lawyers than academic prima donnas, his barbs rarely penetrated their hides.

Tom meanwhile was turning a rag tag collection into a manageable whole. He arrived while Elizabeth Hughes was in the midst of arranging the collection to conform to other law schools by adopting the Library of Congress Classification, which included the designation of much of law under "KF." Unfortunately, probably due to a snag in the computer system, the KF classification was reversed and all catalog cards and markings on volumes were marked with "FK" with the corresponding subject numerals, author identification, and other library markings to individualize each book in the collection. Students would come to the desk and ask "Where in the FK is 128?" and other smirking variations. Tom's first task was to correct this problem. It was easy with the computer catalog, but you can still find books on the shelf with the FK marking.

As the National Reporter System did not include early cases, he arranged to obtain them on microfiche. The statutes of all states were obtained. A book dealer notified him of an excellent collection of treatises that included names like Ames, Arnold, Beveridge, Darrow, Laski,

Wellman and many others. His suggestion to the Dean that all alumni and alumnae who contribute to the law school be given access to the law library was adopted. When the Association of American Law Schools admitted the law school to membership, it commented on the caliber of the collection. Tom turned out to be exactly what the law school needed to improve its standing in the legal community, and, without asking for it, became both a force at the law school, and an object of suspicion by those jealous of their power. An example of this was when Tom went in search of the archives. The archives were in the stack area and shielded from the rest of the collection by a cage. The room contained broken furniture, rusted filing cabinets and other equipment discarded for one reason or another. Sitting at one of the discarded desks was the archivist, Billy Connolly, son of Archie Connolly, the well known Fugawi beer distributor, and member of the Essex Board of Trustees.

Tom Jones learned later that Billy was hired by the Associate Dean Dooley at the request of his father. Billy was fifty years old and had held more positions than a utility infielder. He was not stupid but he would go on a toot for two or three weeks and then appear as if it was the next day of work. Dooley was proud of himself for creating this job for him as his presence or non presence did not interfere with the workings of the law school, and it did not hurt him with the Board of Trustees.

Strangely, the title of archivist impressed Billy. Not only that, but he found the files and boxes of material fascinating. Newspaper clippings, the student newspaper, old exams, announcements of events, photographs of graduating classes, diplomas not presented, tickets from the early days of the law school when a ticket was needed to enter a classroom, a mountain of papers required before seniors graduated (with little evidence of faculty perusal), exams that were so old they were crumbling. Some of the files and boxes had labels. But most stood, some one on top of the other, covered with a layer that looked like a combination of coal dust and soot.

But there was also evidence that someone was assembling the material. It was haphazard but the fact that he could recognize certain categories impressed Tom. In fact, Tom had had one experience with Billy. He had called down looking for material on an alumnus that he thought would be a good prospect for an interview, and Tom was presented with a file that included a photograph, three newspaper clippings, and a silver bowl that indicated the person had judged a competition.

As Tom went into the room, he nodded at Billy, and Billy nodded back. Tom then opened a file, peered in, opened another and his fingers went file by file into what looked like material covering the 1950s. It was a revelation. He knew that these files would be a great source for his history. Tom was no fool. He was aware that his history for the Dean would be embroidered. It would be all light and no heat, all watts and no short circuits. As you read the history, angels would flutter overhead, and virtue would be epitomized in his fifty or sixty pages that would be distributed to Essex alumni, the press, potential students, and political notables. The Dean had made a big mistake in thinking Tom was going to limit himself to angels and virtue. The prospect of writing the true history of a law school intrigued him. His final product may never see the light of day but he was going to produce the true history of a law school. It was not going to be the watered down version he had read of some of the more celebrated law schools like Havad and Columbia. Interviews were silver, these files looked like platinum.

A shadow descended over Tom and he looked around to find Billy. Connolly. Billy was a very substantial person. A good six feet tall and some 250 pounds, he took up a lot of space and he had a look about him that you shouldn't be nosing around without his permission.

"Can I help you, Mr. Jones?"

Tom shrugged his shoulders. "I have no idea what I am searching for but I thought this would be a good place to find some rich material for the history of the law school that I am writing."

"They shuda had me do the history – Cripes, I'm down here all day – I know more about this school than anyone. I'm pissed they didn't ask me. My father said he is going to talk to Dooley about it."

Tom realized that he had to be at his most diplomatic at this point. Billy, at most, had graduated from high school. As zealous as he was about collecting material, it was obvious it was indiscriminate. "Billy, I wish you had. I did not volunteer for the job."

"I'm not blaming you, Mr. Jones. Gee, I go upstairs and see all those computers you put in and I wish I knew how to use them."

"Great idea, Billy. I'll arrange for you to get a computer down here and for someone to teach you. I think you can be a big help to me in showing what a great school Essex is. You know what I mean. All the information about our graduates is right here in this room."

"How about Salvatore Lavinia? I have a whole bunch of newspaper clippings and stuff about him. I think he was one of the greatest lawyers this school has ever made."

Tom had no idea who Lavinia was. He knew Essex graduates who had made a lot of money. An impressive list of state legislators from Maine down to Rhode Island – even one from Connecticut. Graduates who were appointed or elected to the bench. He had a list of Essex law teachers, not a long list since law teachers usually came from the Ivy League or the so-called ten best law schools, but Lavinia was new to him, so he humored Billy.

"Can I see them?" Billy went to a file cabinet and fingered through the manila folders until he came across the file he was looking for. "Here she is Tom – er, I mean Mr. Jones. A lot of this stuff was all over the place – some was alphabetic – some by date – but I put Lavinia all together." He puffed up proudly.

Tom felt an obligation to look at the file. As Tom pored through the folder, his admiration for Billy grew immensely. He had collected a gold mine on the most eccentric character Tom had yet to come across in the annals of Essex history. Here was a fellow with no background for the job – nepotism at its worst – and yet he was doing a better job than people more qualified for the work. Salvatore Lavinia was a treasure and Tom got permission to take the file up to his office on the promise that it would not leave his office for any reason, and that Billy could come and get the file anytime he wanted. "Yuh, Mr. Jones" Billy responded, "I'll find more stuff and I'll make sure it gets into that file."

"Thanks a lot, Billy, and by the way, please call me Tom."

Lavinia was no where to be found in any Essex record. They assured him of this in the Registrar's office. He also went through the school publications for the years that he thought Lavinia might have been a student. On one year the school honored an Italian consul who was visiting Boston, and the invitations to people invited included the names of students and faculty on the reception committee. No Lavinia. The school had started a law review during this period as well as an alumni magazine and Tom combed through both without results.

Tom was undaunted. He remembered researching a Howard Cousell, a noted announcer that claimed a degree from Cahn. He turned out to be a Cohen. Samuel Cohen told him of two boy friends, Bernard Schwartz and Tony Curtis. Bernard wanted to be a movie idol and Tony wanted to be a law professor. So they changed names.

Lavinia, Tom found, turned up as the commencement speaker at Essex in 1965. He was introduced, according to the school's newspaper, *The Cert*, by Professor Charles Gargarian as from that class of lawyers who "worked the pit" and earned their keep by representing the downtrodden and humiliated. Gargarian said he not only could argue round, he could argue flat, and if that didn't work, he could argue cube. Lavinia was now a Doctor of Humanities, a title that he treasured far more than other Essex recipients did. He had been an annual contributor to the law school – not a vast sum but a steady amount every year. The newspaper accounts always identified him as an Essex graduate. Somewhere along the line he received the sobriquet of "The Little Pistil," a title he did not relish and few would use it in his presence. The title came from the observation of some that he emulated Fiorello LaGuardia; others suggested it was an anatomical observation. A survey of elder statesmen reporters at the *Boston Globe* and *Boston American* unearthed a horde of stories. One clipping by a featured writer at the time, Bill Runningham, proclaimed, "Lavinia – the Howe and Hummel of Boston." Kevin Kerr, an irascible reporter of the *Boston American*, who once wanted to award a medal to the cab driver who severely injured the manager of the last place Boston Bees, said he was a fraud. "I don't think that guy graduated high school let alone law school. I once got a court stenographer to give me her recording of one of his closing arguments. I heard that argument. It sounded beautiful. The jury came in with an acquittal. There was not one complete sentence in his argument. Not only that. There is something suspicious about his accent. There's a little bit of Litvak in those oratorical flourishes. It changes with the makeup of the jury. He sounds Irish sometimes, Italian mostly, and no one could identify his accent the day he defended an Englishman and gave his closing address wearing a monocle."

If that was so, somebody must have written his commencement speech. It was better than any Tom had attended. He talked about how early in his practice he had a lot of time and few clients. He told of how Daniel Webster got fifty dollars for a case that took two weeks of research, and later got five thousand dollars for a case with the same facts later in his life that took no research. And he knew someday he would be famous so he wrote speeches on Law Day, Memorial Day, the Dred Scott decision. He wrote on his hero, Abraham Lincoln, and on the freeing of the slaves. He wrote on Sacco-Vanzetti, Justices Holmes and Brandeis, and the founding fathers, particularly Massachusetts' own John Adams.

He wrote on the Constitution. Someday, he orated, he would make a collection of all his undelivered speeches. He concluded by telling the class the one speech he never thought of writing was a Commencement Day speech, and he asked their forgiveness. It was probably a very serious speech, but the papers reported it as being quite humorous, but to Tom there was a note of pathos in it.

The newspaper articles made much of Lavinia's appearance, and Billy probably did not miss one of them. He was very short – about five feet generously. He was stout. He wore a frock coat and his vest – he had many and colorful vests – always had a gold chain from one pocket to the other that suggested a Phi Beta Kappa Key. On occasion, he also had a Masonic ring which he would flash if he thought it might sway a judge or a jury. He was never without spats, impeccably clean, and of a tan suede. And then there was his *coup de tete*. A large felt hat with a broad undulating brim. It was either on his head, nestled at his heart, or resting on the table at his place in the courtroom. When asked if he was emulating La Guardia, he would look at his accuser with the innocence of a virgin, and say,"Who is he? I never heard of anyone in this august Commonwealth with that name." And that would be the end of it.

The newpaper reports made it clear that Lavinia represented mostly down and outers. Petty criminals were his specialty, although he would occasionally be asked to represent someone accused of murder. Most of his business came from the courtroom. The accused would come before the judge and be asked if he had counsel. If the accused said no, the Judge might seek out Lavinia, standing demurely in the background. "Attorney Lavinia, if your case load isn't too full could you provide the defendant with your erudite counsel?" And Lavinia would agree but not before he made a flowery speech extolling the judge for his learning and fairness, the Commonwealth for its provisions to provide a fair trial to the accused, and so forth until the judge would say, "Attorney Lavinia, thank you for your kind words but we must get on with the business of the court." Lavinia would then "bow to the majesty of the law."

One of Lavinia's great assets was his likability. Newspaper items and personal recollections abounded. The press loved him for the copy he provided them, and, much to the chagrin of opposing counsel, the juries loved him as well. He may not know the law as well as most of the attorneys, but he knew how to get a ten year sentence down to two years. Plea bargaining was his specialty. One instance was reported many times. The newspapers covered it. Many lawyers remembered being in the courtroom when it happened, but, if so, the courtroom had to be as large as the Boston Garden. It occurred when Judge Canavan was presiding in Worcester. Lavinia's client was given two months for arranging poker games in his candy shop. Lavinia asked to approach the bench. He looked Judge Canavan in the eye and said, "Judge, if you sentence my client to two months, how am I going to get home? We came here in his car" Probation followed. Attorneys, particularly those who were opposing him in court, thought their lofty language in praise of him was their way of belittling him and showing up his limitations. Lavinia knew his limitations, and knew the limitations of those that thought they had his measure.In a much repeated episode in Lavinia lore, Judge Wyzanski, a Federal Judge with little patience, took over the examination of one of Lavinia's witnesses and chastised the lawyer for his inadequate grasp of the Federal Rules of Evidence. Lavinia began removing a handkerchief from his sleeve. For a while it appeared that he was about to do a magician's trick, but seconds later it was all withdrawn and Lavinia mopped his brow with it, and said plaintively to the Judge, "Judge, I am doing the best I can, and if you are going to take over my case, please don't lose it." He then held himself erect by grabbing the railing behind which the jury sat, and looked balefully at each one. Wyzanski thought twice before interrupting Lavinia in court.

As to knowing the law, Lavinia was known to fudge the issues a bit. His small office was barren of books. Each year, he hired an evening Essex law student to take phone calls, accompany a client to a doctor's office (sometimes they wandered into one of the many bars that lined Washington Street), or serve a subpoena. The office consisted of two chairs, his and his client's. His desk was a roll-top that no one had ever seen opened. In a capital case, the prosecution attempted to get a search warrant to open the desk on suspicion the corpus delicti was in that roll top. Lavinia opposed the petition but did allow the prosecution to smell the outside of the desk. Levinia won an acquittal, and the desk was always referred to as the "Corpus Secundum delicti." On occasion he would appear at the Essex law library and inquire of the librarian, "Where are the books on torts?"

He would then instruct that person to march him to that section. Fifteen minutes later he would be out of the library and probably on his way to interview a tort client. On more than one occasion, when a case was dead against him, he would reach into his vest pocket, pull out a folder of safety matches, open it, look as if he were absorbing his jottings on it, look the judge straight in the eye, and say with authority, "Your Honor, my position is supported in the Massachusetts case of *Jones v. Smith* at 295 Mass. 421." As one of Connolly's clippings had it, the judge would listen patiently and then erupt, "Mr. Lavinia, don't give us any more of your phony citations," to which Lavinia would immediately reply, "Your Honor, the citation may be erroneous, but the principle of law is sound."

From court documents and newspaper accounts that Billy had collected Lavinia must have had hundreds of clients. He was good copy and he had no qualms about bringing his client to the offices of a newspaper editor and proclaiming his innocence. No theory was too outré for Salvatore. One of his clients, a doctor was given two years for performing an abortion, illegal at the time. His defense was that the prosecutor's case was a miscarriage of justice, which so infuriated the prosecutor that he brought a disbarment proceeding. Lavinia, always ready for a debate, said the prosecutor was not a miscarriage of justice but a miscarriage, and the Boston tabloids ate that story up for a week. Lavinia may not have had a classical education but he could quote Shakespeare and Dickens with the best of them and there were few on the bench and bar who could or cared to dispute their authenticity.

The most bizarre case that Tom came across was when a charitable organization petitioned the warden to permit them to hold a Thanksgiving Dinner at the Charlestown prison. It was granted and the press was there covering the event with pictures and copy. During the festivities, it was discovered that a female cook, brought in to supervise the cooking, was having sexual intercourse with a convict who was serving a life sentence for murder. She was indicted under a law that called this kind of activity rape regardless as to whether it was consensual or not. Lavinia was at his best and the press quoted him extensively. "Ladies and gentlemen of the jury. Can you imagine the state bringing a prosecution against this poor woman? Can you imagine a law of this nature being on the books? When the British imposed a tea tax on the colonists do you know what the colonists did? They threw the tea in the ocean" He then walked over to the prosecutor, who was seated, and looked him right in the eye. "Ladies and gentlemen, we still have an ocean," and he strode away. "This is the state that had Shay's Rebellion. Peter Zenger was tried for sedition and the jury voted to affirm the principle of nullification. Alexander Hamilton, the patron saint of this country, defended that man. I am no Alexander Hamilton, ladies and gentlemen, but I ask you to free this woman not from the embraces of that criminal, but from the embraces of the law." It is a truism that nothing is more perishable than courtroom oratory, unless in a compendium of anecdotes. Tom had to conclude that Lavinia was one of the most colorful, if not intellectual characters in Boston, and he deserved a place in Essex history. After all, if they could put up a statue to a mayor who spent time in a Federal penitentiary, Essex should be able to provide a few paragraphs for this man who had no humility but a lot of chutzpah. How he would manage it was a problem for the future but he had plenty of material.

Only the *Boston Globe* carried an obituary for Lavinia. A short item that had more misinformation than facts. Essex had no symposium in his honor. The local and state bar associations had no messages of condolences. There was no indication of family. It was as if Lavinia did not exist. After all, no doctrine of law was established by him, he was not involved in a *cause celebre*. He was a solo practitioner who eked out a living and brought a bit of levity to a profession that takes itself too seriously. He must be remembered.

Tom went back to the Registrar's office and checked through the years that Lavinia may have graduated. This was not the age of computers, and many stretches contained only records in handwriting. When he came across a Schmu-el Levine he did remember the Hearst's reporter's comments. He paid no attention to it then considering the tripe that paper published, but now he decided to he had to track it down. He went through some *Polk Directories* that listed people by name and street. He found going back to the early 1900s a Benjamin and Rebecca Levine that lived on Fernboro Street in Roxbury. They had a son Schmu-el on a subsequent listing in the North End on Salem Street Schnu-el Levine did graduate Essex Law School, but there was no indication of his practicing law. This was the period of much anti-Semitism in Boston. Father Coughlin preachings of hatred were condoned by many Catholics. Father Feeny preached hatred on the Boston Common. Gerald L.K. Smith filled Protestant places of worship with his Protocols of Zion falsehood. Gangs were known to roam through Jewish districts beating up Jewish boys, and when Jewish organizations complained of the violence, the Irish police and priests passed it off as the playful exuberance of the young. Maybe this Levine decided the only way to get ahead in Boston was to change his identity. He was living in an Italian neighborhood. There were some who believed that there was an affinity between Jewish and Italian people. How much would it take for Levine to become Lavinia? The area that Levine grew up no longer existed – the victim of a horrendous redevelopment project that replaced a historic section of old Boston with impersonal high rises and ugly overhead train lines. Somewhere in the debris of that period, the true history of Salvatore Lavinia is buried.

CHAPTER 16

JANET DOES TIME

Tom Jones was concluding the Law Library Committee Meeting. "Thank you all for coming here. This was a very productive meeting of the staff. I appreciate the Student Bar Association sending someone to attend our meeting. I regret the faculty liaison did not come but ..."

Associate Dean Dooley burst into the room. "I think I am supposed to be here. Sorry to be late. What can I do?"

"You can make the closing remarks, Dean."

Dooley did not look troubled at all. He seemed pleased the meeting was over. "I am sure all went well, and you can also be assured that if there is anything I can do for the library, I have the ear of the Dean, and it will be done."

All left the Conference Room, except Dooley and Jones.

"You do look natty today, Dean. Corduroy jacket. Matching chino pants. The usual cuff links, but no bow tie. I don't ever think I have seen you without a bow tie?"

"Tom, bow ties do not go with corduroy jackets."

"Particularly with elbow patches. Did you wear out the elbow?"

"Wise guy. You are probably the worst dresser on the faculty. Look at the crease on your pants!"

"Sorry, Dean."

"Never mind. I think we hired you to set an example for the students in this school. A bunch of slobs. Place looked a lot better when Burke was here."

Tom smiled and headed for the door but was cut of by Dooley.

"Hold it. I want to compliment you. "

"Moi?"

"Tom, are you striking for Dean here? First I catch you up in MDI fooling around with Mary McCarthy, then you take over the school newspaper, you've got the library humming, the Dean goes around saying we have the best law library in Cambridge, and now you are making out with the Board of Trustees."

"I must have a doppelganger."

Dooley made a face then continued. "Had lunch with Archie Connolly the other day and he told me that you and Billy Connolly are on a first name basis."

"That's right, Dean."

"Dumbest Irish kid in the world. Even got thrown out of that school in Worcester."

"Seems to have a knack for what he is doing."

"I put him there to get him out of the way. His father is a big donor. The kid's been on drugs, alcohol, you name it. I hope you will be easy with him – the old man can be a terror."

"We're working together."

"I admire you, Tom. I really do. We should do lunch sometime – heh, let's go have a beer now."

Tom looked at his watch. "I'd like to Dean, but it's been a busy day and I'd like to get home at a reasonable time for dinner.

Tom walked out the door leaving the Dean to eye him suspiciously.

Tom made the 5:20 train to West Concord. He lived five minutes from the train station, and went up the hill to his mansard roofed home. Grandpa Wright was more than happy to have his daughter and grandchildren live with him after Tom accepted the job at Essex. Tom, he put up with, as necessary baggage. With all the good Protestant young men in Concord, how his daughter settled on a part Jewish, part Catholic librarian was anathema to him. At least he should have been rich.

There was a car in front of the house which was unusual. Across from the house was a Catholic church, and Janet's father had protested to their parishioners parking in front of the house on church days, and blocking his driveway. The town agreed and put a no parking sign in front of the house.

As Tom entered, there was Janet sitting with her arms folded. Something was brewing, and Tom, acting nonchalant, went into the kitchen saying, "What is for supper?"

No answer. He put his brief case down, took off his suit coat, untied his tie. "I see nothing in the larder. Maybe I'll run down to John's and get some cheese – maybe a can of soup?"

Still no answer."I've done something wrong. What is it?"

"I'm going to New York."

"OK"

"I've got a job."

"Is this sudden? Have we talked about this? Do the children know?"

"Do you remember when I helped you edit the *Law Library Journal*?"

"Yes, and I gave you the money I got for it. I also gave up the editorship because you drove me nuts taking your time editing the damn thing."

"Well, I applied for a job at *Item Magazine*, and used my editing of the *Journal* as an example of my work. Surprise – they hired me as a copy editor. I start Thursday. Beverly Brooks is outside. Isn't it wonderful? She drove here to take me back – and she is putting me up until I can get an apartment. Do you want to know my salary?"

"Beverly Brooks. That's the gal whose husband the psychiatrist divorced her to marry his receptionist. The gal you have coffee with at McDonald's. If I remember correctly, you told me how she threatened to expose his cheating the IRS."

"That's right. She got his apartment in Riverdale, custody, and is having a ball."

"It should be fun, Janet. May I ask if you have given any thought to your children?"

Janet's face flushed. "Is that another of your digs that I am a lousy mother? Yes, I have given it thought. My sister has agreed to work nights at Emerson Hospital. Dad will take care of the kids in the morning as he does now. Rebecca loves the kids and will be there after school. I'm sure you love your children and will do your part. And – let me finish – I only work from Thursday to Sunday so I will be home the rest of the time. When you think about your absences to conventions and meetings – about which I never complain – it will amount to the same thing."

Tom shook his head. "You and Beverly Brooks. I fear for Riverdale."

"She happens to be a fine person and a real friend."

"Yes, I can still picture her telling a bartender the right way to make an Irish coffee, for the fourth time."

Grandfather Wright came in from the rear of the house with an armful of tomatoes. He was shaking his head as if he had postponed coming into the room. "Janet, why don't you invite those people to come in and have a bite before you go. I caught some trout at the lake this afternoon. Look at these beautiful tomatoes."

"No dad. We have to go. I'll be back Sunday. Well, are you going to kiss me goodbye and wish me luck?"

"One more thing. Didn't you have an appointment with your shrink this afternoon?"

"It so happens, I did."

"How did that go. I'm curious."

Janet had picked up her suitcase. But dropped it. "It went very well. You want to know if I asked him about this move. I did. Did he approve. Shrinks don't approve, but one thing is clear from my going to him. I resent being owned. I am my own person. I'd like to be loved, but I wont be owned."

"That is very heavy. And I guess I am guilty. If owning means family, and family means responsibility, I guess owning is part of it. You know Janet, we had an agreement many years ago. It still holds."

Mary stamped her foot. "You want a divorce."

"I'm not leaving, Janet. You are leaving."

"I'm not leaving. I'm taking a job. And I'm going."

Mary picked up her suitcase and rushed to the car. A man got out of the back seat and jumped in front, and Janet got in the backseat. A man was in the back seat and the car turned around and was about to make a left turn to head into Route 2 when Rebecca and the children had just made it to the corner of Dixwell Street and Highland Avenue. The girls rushed to the car and kissed their mother and happy words were exchanged.

As Tom was viewing the scene, Grandpa Wright ambled out. He awkwardly put his hand on Tom's shoulder and said, "Strong willed, that girl. Just like her mother. Mark my words, she wont last a week and things will be just as before."

Tom laughed. ."Gramps, I hope she lasts more than a week. I think she is more like her father, and my guess is our relationship is like a tire.

You wear out the tread, and its time to retire." Tom turned to go into the house.

Rebecca at this time was perched on the porch. "Wait Tom, we brought you a hamburger, some fries, and a coke from the Station Café. I thought it best for the kids to stay clear while you two fight it out."

"Thanks Rebecca. No fight." Tom couldn't help noticing how Rebecca, one hand at her hip, the other leaning against a door jamb, a cigarette dangling from her lips, resembled her father in voice, posture, and habits.

Tom then went into the house and ate his make-do supper. He slipped into the bedroom and began changing into something comfortable. He then opened a top bureau drawer and noticed a little box where he kept the ribbons that he had earned when he was in the Navy, a set of cuff links his father in law had passed down to him, a gold necklace with a pendant that bore the Star of David with a cross in the background given to him by his wife on some occasion, and the gold "rubber duck" his father had passed on to him. He looked down on his left hand. He slowly twisted the gold band off his index finger and put it with these memories. He put on a pair of chinos and laid down on the queen bed and fell asleep.

Tom was awakened by the cries of his children. "Dad read us a story."

Tom went up to the third floor with its slanted walls and his two children met him. "You were asleep Dad. We washed, brushed our teeth, and put on our pajamas and now we want a story." Tom went over to the book shelf. "How about 'Cat in the Hat;' we haven't read that in a long time." Jack said, "No, no I want Tom Sawyer." "Yes," Janice the elder cut in with authority, "we left off when Tom was trying to rescue Mr. Jim – you told us not to use that word, Dad." Tom smiled and he then read his two little ones how Mr. Jim made his escape from slavery.

CHAPTER 17

PROFESSOR TED REDELL

One way to unburden your mind of personal problems is to get interested in something that will grasp you like a vice. Tom's fascination with the history of Essex Law School was just that thing, and Professor Ted Redell was just what Tom needed to forget his personal problems.

Essex could not afford, nor did it seek the outstanding law professors in the country. Unlike Cahn, it did not go after the elite the way major league baseball teams went after ball players who were free to negotiate. However it was wise enough to offer a home to those eccentrics who had become unwelcome at other institutions, and others who were looking for a change of location. In the case of Toole, they were able to put up with his barbaric criticisms of mediocre faculty. At other times, they would offer a visiting professorship to some celebrated faculty who wanted to spend a year in New England, and a summer at the Cape.

Professor Ted Redell was a separate case. His escape from Havad Law had something to do with both a sexual harassment scandal and a run-in with a faculty member over his fiancée. He was also an embarrassment to the law school for his writings on emotional disturbance. He loved to quote Calvert Magruder's article that, when it came to sexual matters, there is no harm in the asking. He also wrote bawdy limericks for humor magazines, and at Association of American Law School conventions, he provided substitute words for popular songs that did not make him popular with his targets.

One would think that with his reputation as a womanizer that Redell was tall, dark, and handsome. He was tall, dark, but not handsome. He liked to think that he was Lincolnesque in appearance but only those that sought his approval could come to that conclusion. His face was too long for his body. His cheeks appeared as if he was sucking them in. His eyebrows were thick enough for shearing. In his early days, he sported a beard but he found it made him look too old for the conquest of young female law students.

He accepted Essex's offer, after an intermediary told the school he was available, and the daily papers made much of it. One article quoted an unofficial Havad source as saying that Redell was a great scholar but a bad influence on both faculty, students, and the profession. It continued, if ever there was a reason for an ivory tower, a very high one, Redell belonged in it. Redell's response was a threat to sue, but he actually enjoyed the publicity.

Tom Jones's interest in Redell had been piqued by one of his predecessor's memoranda. He also had some clippings from Billy Connolly on the same topic, and some interviews with some librarians who were around at the time. Redell had been invited to speak at a Convention of the Law Librarians of New England. The invitation had been extended by Associate Law Librarian Roy Myerson of Yale who was President of the Association. A week before the event, Myerson called Bender, who was Vice President, to notify him that he had just accepted the librarianship at the University of Texas and that the program was in his hands. Bender, for the first time, found that the meeting was not just for law librarians, but that Myerson had included all library associations in New England and that the function was to be held in Swampscott at a shore side facility. At this point, as Bender reported it, panic set in. Redell decided not to come, and Bender, frantic to avoid not having a main speaker, prevailed on Professor Redell by sending him a poem, "Ode to Redell," with the recurring rhyme, "What the hell, Redell." Redell agreed and asked to be picked up at the Commander Hotel in Cambridge. Bender found Redell at the bar, and with some persuasion, managed to get Redell and a double martini into his Volkswagon and off to Swampscott. It was getting late in the afternoon, and Bender, normally a moderate driver, was pushing things a bit, when Redell suddenly said, "Stop the car!" Bender stopped the car, and out bounded Redell and off he sped into a bar. "Just one, my friend," said Redell and he ordered two martinis. Bender said indignantly,

"Professor, I don't drink martinis." Redell answered, "I am glad to hear that young man." At the bar were two not so young ladies, known in the vernacular as B girls, whose combined age was still less than Redell's. As Bender tugged, Redell became more amorous and the ladies more willing to negotiate. Bender, in a rage, though half the size of Redell, dragged him off the bar stool and stuffed him into the Volkswagon.

Once again, they sped to Swampscott. Bender parked illegally at the entrance to the banquet room, and pulled and pushed Redell into the ballroom, where Elaine Ferguson, the secretary of the NELL, was filling in for Bender, and fumbling with her notes to keep the evening going when she spotted the two and waved frantically for them to come to the dais. Bender made the mistake of waving back, for Redell had spotted the bar and was swishing a martini when Bender caught up with him. He finally wrestled Redell up to the dais, and then noticed that there was no seat for him at the head table. Bender meekly found a seat at one of the tables and was both cursing Myerson for getting him into this fix and praying that Redell would not pass out.

He should have prayed for the passing out, for Redell somehow captured his youth and ranted and raved for three quarters of an hour about Thayer, Holmes and Frankfurter and how they had disgraced constitutional law, legal education, and diluted freedom of speech. Bender left in the middle of the speech, and fortunately reached his car before it was towed away. He sped for home and learned later that Redell was not discommoded as he spent the night with the matronly secretary of the New England Law Librarians.

Redell's career at Essex had many misgivings for many. He not only antagonized every member of the faculty by beginning each of his contributions to faculty meetings with, "At Havad, we handled the situation at follows" but spoke up whenever the occasion moved him and expected everyone to listen, including the speaker who had been interrupted. He thought himself the Oracle at Essex.

Redell's activity with women became no less notorious at Essex. If he found a young female law student attractive, and his judgment came from the neck down, he would manage to get into a conversation with the young lady and eventually he would get around to "That's an interesting concept you bring up, why don't you drop into my office this afternoon at three and we'll have a go at it."

The young lady would be thrilled to talk constitutional law with the man who had written a seven volume history of the United States Supreme Court, monographs, law review articles, and a number of articles that appeared in *The Nation, Fortune Magazine,* and the *New York Times Magazine.* At 3:04 pm, he would say to her, "I'm extremely attracted to you, young lady, and would like to fuck you." Most left in a huff, but the few that stayed were enough to satisfy his lust. He looked at sex the same way he looked at baseball averages: "Three out of ten can get you in the Hall of Fame."

It took an Essex law student to provide his comeuppance. Evelyn Bryan was a savvy twenty-seven year old when she started at Essex. She was a single girl who was single minded in her pursuit of a mate. That was why she decided on law school, and why she decided that a lecher like Redell could be her man. Knowing his crude technique, she set out to be a decoy and sure enough she found herself being propositioned.

"Fuck, did you say you want to fuck me, Professor Redell. Here!"

"Young lady, that is exactly what I said."

"Professor Redell, I find your offer attractive, but I don't fuck in offices. I've worked for lawyers, you may not know."

"But I'm not a lawyer, I'm a professor. My dear girl, I'm very much in need of a fuck. It concentrates my mind. Can we just make an exception this time?"

"No."

"What do you suggest?"

"A hotel."

Off the two went and Evelyn insisted on the Ritz Carlton where the two trooped in and Professor Redell, who only stayed there when speaking invitations paid for the room, signed in and the two of them soon found themselves disrobing and enjoying themselves immensely.

As they unraveled, Evelyn insisted they talk about the topic that got her in Professor Redell's office in the first place. And soon, naked as the day they were born, the two thrashed out the parameters of the First Amendment with emphasis that Justice Holmes had it wrong when he said that you cannot yell fire in a crowded theater. Afternoon turned into evening, evening into morning, conversation into sex, sex into conversation, and before they parted they had had breakfast at the Ritz that included the best poached eggs over corned beef hash, blueberry muffins, and coffee that were ever eaten after a night of revelry.

EDWARD J. BANDER

Redell wanted more, but Evelyn insisted it was a one night stand for her and she was not going to deny the other women in the class their opportunity. The two were eventually married in Nassau, New Hampshire in a quiet ceremony. Evelyn published her paper in the *Essex Law Review*, resigned from the *Law Review*, dropped out of law school, led the uninteresting life of a faculty wife, adopted a young Chinese orphan, and spent her time in Cambridge going to adult extension courses. She also was aware that marriage was not going to change her husband's colors, but only insisted that he use a condom as she was not taking a chance of his contracting a venereal disease.

Redell was not a young man when all this transpired. Drinking and carousing had not been kind to his features. He became thin to the point of anemia, his prominent nose had an unhealthy red pock-marked hue, and his receding hair made his forehead look large enough for him to pose as Frankenstein, None of this affected his drinking, debauchery, or excellent appetite.

"Tom," he announced when Tom visited him at his retirement village in St. Petersburg, Florida, "I was biggest pain in the ass Essex ever had. I was a drunk," and he pointed to Evelyn, "and she really saved my life. I still like my martini but she holds me to one a day. I hated going to Essex. A shit law school. The reason I left was that Debby Baker, that smart ass lawyer, was going to sue me and claim I raped her. That was bull shit. She consented and I fucked her in my office. Her word against mine and all those other broads ready to testify against me. The Dean got her to drop the suit, if I left the school."

"Professor Redell," Tom asked, "don't you feel guilty about taking advantage of those girls."

"What! We're not talking about some priest ripping off an altar boy. They needed it and I needed it. Society doesn't realize that guys like to get laid all the time, and guys like you, are too stupid to ask for it.

Tom was not happy being included in what sounded like a false syllogism. For one thing, in his experience, it was the fair sex that was more forward as far as his life was concerned. But he decided to steer the conversation to an anecdote that Samuel Cohen told him about Redell.

"Oh, that, it's true. When Essex went about renovating to make the place habitable for the handicapped, disabled, diseased, and disinherited, the Dean went all out to accommodate. In a faculty meeting, Alan, I forget

118

his last name, who by the way, considered himself, falsely I think, a ladies man – he once said to me how easy the Asian ladies were. I told him, the President of the ACLU shouldn't be talking that way. Any how, he insisted that the urinals should be of different heights. It would discriminate against dwarf students if the urinals were too high. Turned out to be a good idea. I happen to be well-equipped. I have a big schlong. Want to see it? No, I didn't think so. I always used the dwarf urinals as I was afraid my pinky might stir up the cigarette butts idiots, including myself, leave there.

Well, it so happened that the faculty toilet was being cleaned so I went to the student facility. There I am taking a pee, and three students are lined up similarly occupied and smirking at me. I figured they were admiring my package and turned my head to them and shrugged my shoulder as if to say what you are seeing is at ease. At that point my eye caught the hand dryer, and there was a sign on it that said, 'PRESS THIS TO HEAR PROFESSOR REDELL ON CONSTITUTIONAL LAW.' Well, my head not only turned but so did my body and there I was pissing on all three students."

Although Tom had heard the story before, he laughed so loud and he started coughing and Evelyn came over and patted him on the back. "That's not the end of the story. Can I finish it for you. Fred?" He nodded

"Professor Redell was unmoved by all this. He apologized brusquely to the students and then proceeded to his class on Constitutional Law followed by the three students who had taken the lavatory smell with them. In the excitement, the esteemed Professor Redell had neglected to zip his fly. That is number one. Professor Redell did not wear boxer shorts or underwear of any kind. When he unzipped his fly he was ready to pee or screw without any fumbling around. Number two. Professor Redell was a drinker and students tended to leave the first row unoccupied as his breath could inebriate a crocodile. And he usually put one foot up on a chair as he discussed the issue of political thickets, and there he was exposed to even the back of the room with one hundred students staring incredulously, and for once not copiously taking notes."

Both Redell and Tom Jones were laughing.

"Until one student," broke in Redell, "shouted 'Professor, your fly is open.'"

Tom looked at Evelyn. "Was that you?"

"That was me and that was how I got his foot in my door."

But in retrospect, Tom knew that Redell's final act dwarfed these antics. Before retirement, he decided to really get even with the institution that sent him to the minor leagues. His book, *Woe Unto You, Law Professors* crucified institutions such as Havad, Yale, Michigan and all those institutions that made the top tier of the *U.S. News and World Report* of the best law schools. The book made the case that three year law schools were obsolete. At most, law schools should be one year where contracts, torts, criminal law, and civil procedure were taught. All other courses were but offshoots of these courses and were simply a way of extorting money from many who could least afford it, and not only putting students and their parents into poverty or bankruptcy, but making it impossible for less well endowed law schools to survive, let alone prosper. After the first year, Redell proposed, a passing student would be obliged to sign up with an attorney, a legal aid organization, a corporate law department or any politically oriented group that used the legal system to advance its program. When that organization put the stamp of approval on the student, he or she would become a member of the bar. No bar review ("a bar-baric institution"), no bar exam, no legal structure: that was simply intellectual masturbation. Redell argued that this was not a novel theory of his but that American legal history began with young men clerking for lawyers. Check the careers of John Adams, Abraham Lincoln and many others that founded and sustained this republic. Read the biographies of some of our great lawyers like Clarence Darrow and see how little formal legal education played in their careers.

His particular scorn was for law reviews. A waste of bright student's time. No one reads the damn things. To call what goes into law reviews scholarship is to debase the term. He cited Louis Brandeis and Charles Reich as the only two authors who had written law reviews of any enduring value. As to footnotes, he wrote, they were nothing but an attempt to increase the obscurity of the articles. His particular scorn was for those who rated law schools by the number of citations their faculties could generate. The only salvation for law reviews, in his opinion, was that an old tradition should be revived that no author of a book or an article should be cited unless he had been dead fifty years. There were no footnotes in Professor Redell's book.

Law libraries, Redell claimed, were an anomaly. Only the incompetent lawyer needed law books. Requiring them was a conspiracy between law professors and the law publishers. The truly competent lawyer found intelligence, rhetoric, and a broad education in the humanities as responsible for their winning cases, creating legislation, and running the Republic. Law schools housing a million volumes, a dean, four vice deans, an assistant dean were a drain on the country's resources. They should be turned out into the real world and earn a living.

And Redell proposed a four point retrenchment plan that would have law professors practicing law (and he suggested many of them would fail badly at it, and end up in real estate, accounting and state agencies), deans becoming financial advisors, librarians operating as separate entities, and the host of hangers on searching for their place in a platonic hierarchy.

He also suggested that the legal profession was vastly overpaid, and a committee of philosophers should determine the comparative advantage of each field so that people could enjoy the good things in life instead of the life of good things.

The publication of the book brought swarms of reporters to Essex only to be told that he could be found in the Havad Yard. And there he was seated on the lap of Johann Havad, holding a copy of his book that had just placed first in the *New York Times Book Review* listing.

The reviews were mixed. Chief Judge Poseiden of the Seventh Circuit, not just a rival of Redell in the output of books, but one who had published more books than the entire Federal Judiciary for the last thirty years, was his severest critic. "This is the worst book published by a person who has been a member of an elite law school faculty," he wrote.

Professor Redell, reaping the financial benefits of a best seller and a Warner Bros. option to make a movie of the book, retired to his home in Florida, published no more and his agreement to talk to Tom Jones was his only concession to the legal world.

The book, of course, accomplished no reforms. A copy resides in most law school libraries where it is occasionally discovered by a student who thinks it makes a lot of sense but keeps it to himself. The only real consequence of the book is that it brought Essex fame and reputation. A permanent exhibit of Redell's accomplishments resides outside the Dean's office. The Redell Chair in Legal Writing for Popular Consumption was endowed by the Cato Association, and is over-subscribed each year.

A Redell plaque is given each year for the best brief written by a student in the moot court competition, and a photograph of his being given a Pulitzer Prize for non fiction hangs in the law library. The American Bar Association had a committee look into the reforms suggested by the book, and although kind to Redell decided they were not appropriate for this time and place and tabled it for future consideration. Each year doctoral dissertations are written on Redell and his books, mostly by sociologists.

Tom Jones looked over all he had uncovered about Professor Redell. He felt that all of it belonged in Essex's legal history, but that only his last paragraph would be judicious.

CHAPTER 18

THE FERRY RIDE

"Hello everybody," shouted Janet as she briskly walked into the house. Grandpa Wright looked up from the stove. He was cooking some trout he had caught that morning. He had taken Jack with him, and Jack shouted to Janet, "Mom, I caught a trout and Gramps is cooking it for lunch." Tom walked into the kitchen on hearing the commotion and had a sullen look on his face. There was a Red Sox game on television in the room that Tom had left.

"Darling, I'm so sorry. I fell asleep on the train and didn't wake up until I got to South Station." Janet was holding, actually pulling on the hand of the person she had come into the house with. "And this feller saved my life. Jim, this is my husband, Tom."

Tom nodded and sat down at the kitchen table. Jack and Janice were devouring the trout, but Tom just took a small piece from the mound that sat in the middle of the table. He was not crazy about his father in law's cooking. Everything doused in lard.

His silence activated Janet. "I didn't wake up until this gentleman nudged me that we were in South Station, the last stop. It's a long story but he insisted on driving me home." Janet started giggling. "Oh, God, you poor thing. And you came all the way to 128 to pick me up."

Tom nodded. "I ran through the train cars looking for you, Janet …"

"You didn't," Janet shrieked. "You ran through the cars?"

"No, I did not." Janet tried to hide a look of relief. "I didn't want to take a chance the train would start with me in it and my car parked at 128, so I drove home knowing you are a big girl and would work something out."

In the meantime, Jim was working his way out of Janet's hand, and finally headed toward the door. He whispered a quick good bye and was on his way.

"I am dead tired. I am going upstairs and get some rest. Maybe you can come up later, Tom and I can tell you what a wonderful job I have."

Tom was now picking at the trout. Fresh trout is delicious even doused in fat.

Janet had one hand on her hip. "Anyways, It's a standing invitation, if you know what I mean," and Janet slowly ascended the stairs.

Janet did not awake until ten that evening. Tom had put the children to bed, and was at Janet's side reading "The Dud Avocado." Janet rolled over. "Tom, put that book down, turn out the light. I haven't seen you for three weeks, and I am desperate to get laid." And Tom did as he was told.

As Tom learned more from Janet about her job, he had the feeling that it may have been the best thing for her. Being a copy editor at *Item Magazine* required her utmost effort. It meant reading every word that went into each issue of *Item Magazine*. It meant looking for errors in spelling, meaning, and content. She proved she could be intellectually competitive with the other copy editors. She would take a train to New York City on Thursday morning and some thirty five working hours later until the early hours of Sunday morning be at the job. When she edited the *Law Library Journal* for Tom, he would be constantly prodding her to work, so much so, he gave up the editorship after two years.

She couldn't wait to tell Tom her latest coup.

"Sydney Rosen is the back page editor. This week end, the entire editorial staff has been invited to get on a ferry and circle Manhattan Island. There is going to be food, dancing, and you will get to meet all the big macha machas. Well, maybe not meet them. I'll point them out to you."

"I gather you are inviting me?"

"Darling, of course. Now, This Rosen guy. He thinks he is perfect. He is about five feet ten. Good looking in a sort of Jewish way. Don't look at me like that. That is the only way I can think of to describe him . If you go into his office, there is a picture of his wife and two children next to his BMW in what looks like the Hamptons. I'm sure she is the President of Hadassah, and his children will also go to Havad.

"Now, the word is that no one – but no one – ever corrects his copy. So last Friday, I was reading his copy to my copy mate – that is what we do – when I notice something. I think about it for an hour. Then I decide. I ride down to his floor, barge into his office and say to him, 'Mr. Rosen, in your back page editorial you have used the word "regrettably" and I think it should be "regretfully." I barge right out, sashaying in a new skirt I bought at Macy's. Saturday night, Mr. Rosen, seeks me out at my cubicle and invites me to the executive dining room for coffee to thank me for my suggestion. What do you think of that!'"

"I was thinking about his height. Do you know when they built the Panama Canal they scouted the county for men five foot ten. That was the perfect height for loading mules."

Tom accepted his wife's invitation and decided it would give him an opportunity to drop in on his old place of employment in Greenwich Village. He would call up John Teehan, see a play, go to his wife's *Item* shindig. He would have lunch at Monte's – who knows maybe Joe Gould would be there – stroll through Washington Square Park, watch the chess players, and buy some pastry at Sutter's. Maybe head up to the Tickets booth at Duffy Square and get half price for a Broadway show.

These thoughts raced through Tom's mind as he and Janet sped through the Mass. Turnpike into Connecticut, into New York, Cross County, Henry Hudson, 246th Street exit, Fieldston, pass the Horace Mann School, Ethical Culture, Manhattan College, to Janet's drab two bedroom apartment on Drexel Street. It took two turns around the block to find a parking space. "Don't expect much," Janet had told him. I'm only there Thursday to Sunday. *Item* pays for my cab rides home. I eat out, and then I am back with you and the kids." No mention of the fact that her homecomings were in three week intervals.

Janet had the bare minimum. One bureau, a full size mirror fixed to the inside of a closet door, a stuffed chair that probably came from Goodwill, one bed, a minimum of kitchen utensils. Tom dropped their bags into the apartment while Janet waited in the car, using the rear view mirror to arrange her lips. Tom hadn't maneuvered New York streets for some time and getting on Major Deegan, F.D.R. Drive, and then Sixth Avenue to the Item Building took some effort. Getting a New Yorker, even a cab driver, to help a tourist was not only frustrating but dangerous. At one point Tom inadvertently found himself cutting off a transit bus, but jamming his breaks just in time to avert a collision, heard the bus driver yell at him, "Where were you, I was waiting for you."

Arriving at the building, Janet jumped out of the car and raced into the building. "My God," Tom thought to himself, "I never thought I would see her racing to work."

Tom drove back to the apartment. Found a parking space and opted to try and see a play in the Village. The apartment was two blocks away from the IRT, and Tom made good connections that brought him to the Public Theaters on Lafayette Street. He lined up at the ticket office and decided on a play called "Colored Girls." As he neared the booth, he heard the ticket person indicate that that show was sold out. He was going to get out of the line when he was approached by an older man.

"You look disappointed, sir."

"Yes, I was going to see ..."

"Let me be your fairy godmother. I have a complimentary ticket, two if need be, for "Knife," I think you will enjoy it."

Tom deliberated. He had nothing better to do. Free ticket. "Just one, thank you so much."

It was an opera. It was about a guy who was married and had three children and decided he wanted to be a woman. He goes to Amsterdam for a sex change. His wife gets a divorce and marries his boss, and refuses to have anything to do with him. The lead was pretty good. At one point, on a raised platform, he sang an aria that presaged the change and only when he finished did Tom realize he was wearing high heels. Mandy something, but what intrigued Tom more than anything was the intermissions. He found himself next to the man who had given him the ticket. At each intermission, the man would yell out, "Frank, meet Tom, Bruce meet Tom, Alan meet Tom."

When he left the theater, he ambled up Sixth Avenue, stopped at the Strand Book Store. Not one of the half-price best sellers that the store featured interested him. He looked for Klein's on Fourteenth Street. It was gone. The street had turned to shlock. He stopped at a diner for a coffee, and watched a guy bolt from his seat and out the door. "I knew that bastard wouldn't pay. He wont live through the night with that fish stew I served him," He looked at Tom sipping his coffee. "Don't worry about your coffee mister." Tom was a little worried because it was the worst cup of coffee he had ever tasted.

Tom still had time to kill before meeting up with Janet for the ferry ride around Manhattan. He stopped in at the Public Library at 42nd Street, went up the escalators at the Trump Palace, and then, not sure how to get to the pier, managed to get a cab. As he arrived at the pier, he noticed a crowd surrounding the slip that would house the ferry. It amazed Tom how much it must cost *Item* people to dress informally. Designer jeans, cashmere sweaters, men with berets, and one person dressed in a tuxedo and smoking with a cigarette holder. People greeted each other with hugs and kisses. Tom conceded it was a good looking crowd. Everyone seemed to feel superior. Except Tom. He felt like a sore thumb in a paraplegic ward. Even his wife ignored him, until he felt her grabbing him by the hand and hustling him over to a group that sounded like canaries in an aviary. As he was being introduced to Mr. Rosen, he never got to shake the man's hand as the crowd was now edging into the ferry, and he was the last to board.

There were food stations all over the boat. Roast beef, shrimp, Chinese food, a full bar. There was chamber music aft, and dancing music fore. Conversation was vibrant. Tom wandered around and bumped into Janet. "Hi, darling. Enjoying yourself. Have you met Sydney Rosen?" They shook hands this time. "Oh, look, darling, there is Mr. Swerling. Our retiring editor-in-chief. And with him is the new editor, Michael Strate." Tom took this as good bye and decided to sidle up to these very important people and recognized that they were talking to the chairman of the Federal Reserve. Their conversation was most enlightening. For four minutes, he listened to these three men, one with a heavy German accent, disparage the Democratic Party, savage the wife of one of the editors, and grumble about the choice of a ferry ride by a certain Larry. "And here he is heading straight toward us. Shall we ignore him?" "No," said another, "let us humor our gay eminence." Tom decided that he had enough and continued his circle of the boat circling Manhattan.

As they circled Manhattan, a loud speaker pointed out various sights. The Empire State Building, the Statue of Liberty. It also pointed out where suicides occurred, and even threw in a bawdy story. Tom guessed he was the only one listening. The ferry entered the slip, the gate opened and the crowd dispersed. No Janet. A number of cabs had been lined up to take the crowd home, and when Tom noticed only two were left, he decided he did not want to be left alone at the dock and was about to get into the last cab when he heard a shriek. "Tom, wait for me." Janet rushed up to the cab holding in tow a stocky young man. "This is Bruce. He is a neighbor of ours and we can drop him off at 256th Street and Riverdale Avenue." Bruce was a very amiable guy and he could not wait to tell Tom about his latest activity. He put his hands together in joy, and announced "We are doing 'The Odd Couple.'" When Tom indicated he knew the story line, Bruce added, "I know you've seen it with two guys. Did you know it has been done with a female cast?" Tom shrugged. Bruce then gushed, "We are doing it in drag!" At this point they had arrived at Bruce's address. As he left the cab, he kissed Janet warmly, and then shook Tom's hand, adding, "Heh, how come she wears a ring and you don't?" "Maybe it's because it makes us both look attractive to a certain species." As Bruce was closing the door he shouted out to Tom, "Maybe when you come to the play, you better put that ring on."

As Janet nestled into the cab, she chortled with a look of smug satisfaction, "Did you enjoy yourself? Tom. Isn't it wonderful? Aren't you proud of me?"

"Whoa! Whoa! Whoa! Those are three tough questions. I'll only answer the first. No."

They arrived home around two am. Tom had bought some Danish at Balducci's earlier and made some instant decaf, and they both sat around talking about their day. Janet was upset when he told her his experience at the theater. "You should have at least bought the guy a cup of coffee." Tom answered, "If I bought him a cup of coffee, I would have had to buy all those other guys a cup of coffee."

By this time, both were dead tired and went to bed.

The next day, Tom dialed the number of John Teehan, and gave him a call.

"Tom Jones, Junior."

"Tom," shouted John. "How is it being in the ninth circle of law schools?"

Tom got right to the point. "I am driving my wife to her job at *Item Magazine* this afternoon. Do you have a few minutes today, tomorrow, anytime?"

There was a slight pause. "Yes, I heard something about that. There are people here that haven't forgotten you. Tell you what, let's have dinner tonight at the Worsthaus on Fourteenth Street. They have venison on the menu. How about six pm?

"Perfect John. See you then."

Tom dropped Janet off at *Item*. Drove to Janet's *pied a terre* and had plenty of time to kill before meeting John. .

John Teehan taught American legal history at Cahn. You can always tell a top tier law school by the number of courses it offers that are irrelevant to the bar exam, and, in many instances, to law. Legal history to John was Indians. One semester it might be the Hopis, or the Sioux, or the Navahos. His research would take him to the Huntington or a cattle ranch in Wyoming. He would then prove his versatility, by writing an article in the *New York Law Journal* comparing Chief Justice Doe to Oliver Wendell Holmes.

Another semester he would concentrate on the tribes that met the Pilgrims. Ironically, his forays into New England tribes contributed to the many law suits brought by Indian tribes reclaiming their territory. In one brief in Connecticut he was referred to as "The Great White Father of the Casinos."

John was full of ironies. He was Irish, and dressed and acted English. He was Groton, Havad, Havad Law, and turned down teaching at Havad to accept an appointment at Cahn. The reason he would give for his choice was that New York City had better Irish pubs than Boston. His parents would return to Ireland each year which John would characterize as "their annual pilgrimage to show off their wealth." His clothes were Saville Row, his umbrella of sturdy English stock. John was a bachelor and lived in a Cahn dormitory across from the law school that was once a twenty story hotel . Despite a shortage of dormitory rooms for law students, John had two connected rooms. It looked like an English lodge. An replica of an elephant's foot, in leather, contained his walking sticks and umbrellas. He collected English coats of arms and they hung in each room. There was also a rubbing from sarcophagi of a medieval English king and queen that went from floor to ceiling. You felt as if you were back in the Middle Ages in the apartment.

Other than his sartorial selections and suspiciously clipped English, he was an affable sort. Physically he had only one demerit, a roving left eye. When he looked you in the eye, it appeared his other eye was looking for someone else. John's father was a celebrated doctor, and you had the feeling that much money was spent to correct this deficiency, only to make it worse. It did not trouble John at all.

Tom spent the afternoon reacquainting himself with Riverdale. He walked by the palatial homes in Fieldston, visited the Community House on 256th Street where Janet had starred in a few productions of the Riverdale Community Theater, had a hot dog with sauerkraut at the deli, and was tempted, but did not go into The Steakhouse, where he and Janet would go on weekends. He remembered Gary Abrezio, who sang at the Steakhouse on week nights. Gary had a heavy Bronx accent but when he sang it was pure Sinatra. Tom remembered once praising Gary after a session, and saying to him, "You really had the adrenalin going tonight, Gary." Gary, his Bronxese returning, replied, "I never take drugs." Tom then skipped the bus and walked the couple of miles to the subway station. He took the A train to 59th Street, then transferred to the AA train so that he could get off at 14th street. He then walked to the Wursthaus.

The Wursthaus was, as the name implies, a German restaurant. For the neophyte looking at the menu of a German restaurant does not inspire confidence. Sauerbraten, something with blood in it, sausages of various colors and size, food things the size of shillelaghs, hanging from the ceiling. But venison was something Tom could handle and he liked the beer.

John Teehan was already sitting at a booth. Tom slid in opposite him. A waiter immediately approached and soon Tom and John were drinking to each other's health. "I presume that you and Janet are in the process of getting a divorce or does absence make the heart go pitter patter?"

"John, I came here to find out what is happening at the law school. Has it gone to pieces since I left? Are you still splitting your sides at Dean Needleman's inimitable repartee?

"To the first, no; to the second, you have me wrong. I never laughed with the Dean, I laughed at you and the Dean."

"Me?"

"I made it a point never to be in the Dean's presence at a gathering unless you were part of it. I would watch the Dean attempt a bon mot, then observe his laughter followed by everybody but you. Then I started laughing. Back to the first point, your successor is not going to last long. When the Dean isn't driving her crazy, his wife is. I hold her responsible for the new construction going on. The reading room is being destroyed by a staircase smack in its middle that Busby Berkeley could use for one of his dance sequences. The usual sniping is going on, but nothing that compares with that run in with you and Walter Duesenberg. "

CHAPTER 19

WALTER DUESENBERG

Walter Duesenberg was a refugee from Nazi Germany. He and his family wisely left when Hitler came into power. Walter was a young lawyer in Bonn at the time. He was married, had a very successful practice, was not particularly religious, and thought Germany to be the most cultural and civilized nation on earth. But when Hitler came to power, and his non-Jewish legal colleagues not only supported Hitler, but some rushed to write legislation that specified Jewishness. Their disingenuousness was only exceeded by their cravenness. The writing was not only on the wall but in the legislative, judicial, and executive chambers.

Duesenberg had an easy transit to America. He had been to New York City on business. He knew the language, and had spoken at conferences in Los Angeles and Chicago. He also had family. His problem, as well as the problem of most professional immigrants, was that they were not transferable to America. Doctors became nurses, lawyers became librarians. The reason was the difficulty of learning a new language. That was not a problem for Duesenberg. He decided to become a New York lawyer and enrolled at Cahn. He became a member of its law review, passed the bar exam, and immediately became a leader of the copyright bar, a discipline he had some experience in while practicing in Germany.

He became a founding member of the Copyright Association of America and its first and last president, as no one dared volunteer to succeed him. When he became a professor at Cahn, he arranged for the offices of the association to be at Cahn. He made every effort to shed all vestiges of his German ancestry except for his speech. His guttural accent gave him away immediately. He became a valuable member of every international conference on copyright. Every year he arranged a cocktail party at Cahn over which he presided with stealth. When Jim Gabrelle, a recent addition to the faculty, requested to teach a copyright course without first approaching him, Duesenberg showed his displeasure by striking his name from the list of invitees. He also did not hesitate to berate him when not in his company. No one who had incurred his displeasure was ever known to be pardoned. He made an exception for chess players. Once a week, he would sit down at one of the chess tables at Washington Square Park and challenge the savants that sat there looking for easy marks at the chess table. Walter would occasionally come away a victor, but even then, he would pay his cohort for the privilege of the opportunity.

And that brings up Tom. When Tom was at Cahn, he had written a piece for the school newspaper about the administration being top heavy with tall people. It was a gentle satire that suggested that blacks, woman and others were protesting discrimination, and that a new category should emerge. The article found fault with clichés such as "being tall in the saddle" and Tom suggested that being short might be more advantageous as the rider was less of a target. It wasn't all whimsy, and Tom received a host of letters from readers attributing failure to lack of height. And now comes the estrangement with Duesenberg.

A member of the Cahn faculty familiar with Tom's humor, was teaching at Bennington for a semester. Bennington was having a copyright symposium, and he suggested that Tom be the banquet speaker. Tom accepted and was having the devil of a time trying to come up with a "banquet" speech, until he attended a Cahn faculty meeting. Duesenberg had received notice of the symposium. Not only was he not invited, but there in alphabetical order was the list of speakers including the name of Tom Jones. At the faculty meeting, Jim Gabrelle, still smarting from his disgrace, suggested that the faculty authorize two people to attend the conference. The Dean looked to Duesenberg, absolutely unaware of what was going on. Duesenberg stood up, he looked up and down the long table for Tom Jones. "Vy are you asking me for comment. He," and he couldn't think of Tom's name, "is the copyright authority." And Duesenberg threw down the symposium announcement and sat silently through the meeting.

And that was how Tom Jones gave a talk on "How to Be an Expert."

CHAPTER 20

BETTY LU

After the dinner, John Teehan suggested they go to a party at the law school.

"What party?"

"Tom, don't you know that we are the best catered law school in the country. This party is for faculty who have written books in the past five years. All by University Presses, by the way, which guarantees that more will be given away then bought. It will give you an opportunity to meet your old buddies. Norman Dawson is being featured for his latest epic. His wife is teaching at the law school now. I hope the same fate does not befall him that befell Michael Stinger, another of the honorees tonight."

Tom was well aware of Michael Stinger. A well-known civil liberties lawyer, he came east with the understanding that his wife would teach an introductory course. She had been his student, was law review, and, in Tom's opinion, was a very capable teacher. Michael was a star. His lectures were well attended, he wrote articles that were accepted by *Michigan Law Review, California Law Review*, and he was usually recruited to chair a session at the annual meetings of the Association of American Law Schools. He had a slight flaw, you might say an academic disease associated with young legal scholars. He was easily seduced by the ever larger number of women that began to attend law school after World War II. What was once occasional at Michigan, or proliferating at William Mitchell where he visited, became an epidemic at Cahn.

The tolerance of women for a philandering husband varies with the economic and social circumstances. In academia, a wife hesitates to give up the wonderful gatherings of academics, the summers off, the trips to conventions in San Antonio and other select vacation spots, and the short notes to alumnae not as well positioned in life.

But blatant indiscretions, telephone calls from what she called his "call" girls, and denials that suggested her imagination was running wild took its toll. She ordered him out of the apartment.

All this was related to Tom, by John who was happy to pass on any scuttlebutt that occurred at the law school.

"It seems to me that you were following this closely, John," suggested Tom.

"Only because the young lady came to me. Being a bachelor, Tom, has its advantages. More than you can ever realize. She came to me for advise. Should she resign from the law school. Would her presence at faculty meetings be an embarrassment to the school?"

Tom was about to offer an opinion, but John's hand shot up.

"I told her 'My dear lady. You have not done anything wrong. You have no need to be embarrassed. You made a terrible mistake in marrying a law professor. For that I cannot forgive you. You have two children to bring up. You are a good teacher. You have an appointment. If you enjoy your work, continue at it, and let him suffer at the faculty meetings.'"

"Did she take your advise?"

"She did indeed."

"And how about Michael."

"He will be a visiting professor at Essex Law School next semester."

It just dawned on Tom, he had heard that Stinger was coming to Essex. He wondered why a professor compared to Ronald Dworkin, would come to Essex. He now knew why visiting professorships were so popular in legal academia.

And off they went to the party at Cahn. The reception area was on the main floor of the law school. The room was large enough to comfortably hold about five hundred people. There were three or four tables dispensing a wide selection of beverages, including hard liquor. The food table was bulging with food. A turkey roasted to perfection sat in the center, with Adele, a long time employee, doing the carving. Tom remembered in the sixties at the height of student uprisings, the protest that these gatherings were plantation affairs, as black servants were serving the whites. The school promptly arranged for whites to be part of the carvers and dispensers necessitating the firing of some of the blacks. There was roast beef, a pate shaped like a large cod, a large bowl of shrimp, and other delectables.

Tom had had enough to eat and opted for a gin and tonic, a drink he had given up since leaving Cahn. He stood in the middle of the floor watching the pecking circles. Full professors spoke to full professors, associate professor to associate professors, assistant professors to assistant professors, clinical teachers to clinical teachers. The same with alumni. The big shots with the big shots. On one occasion, an assistant professor approached a full professor. Tapped him on the shoulder. A few words were exchanged and the full professor did an about face that had the effect of turning the assistant professor's face redder than a delicious apple. Tom was having a wonderful time observing the legal comedy when he was tapped on the shoulder. It was Thomas Collins. Tom taught labor law and arbitration, and was influential in Cahn politics. He was a big supporter of Diana Vincent, the foreign law librarian, to succeed Small in the job. Maybe it was that, or maybe it was the bravado with which he approached Tom Jones.

"Tom Jones, what are you doing here?"

"Me! Oh, The Dean asked me to stand in the middle of the floor and if any of the faculty had no one to talk to, I could be available."

Tom Collins took off like a shot.

That was not the only incident in Tom's night. He stayed away from the Dean. He held himself to one drink. He did partake of a slice of turkey and two shrimps with cocktail sauce. And then he felt it was time to leave. As he was leaving, Betty Lu Lisbon, the head cataloger, was on her way out.

"Tom, what are you doing here?"

"I had dinner with John Teehan and he suggested I drop in. I've had enough. Time to go home."

"Tom," and Betty Lu hesitated, "can I speak to you for a minute." Tom followed her to her office in the library.

"I have a terrible problem."

"Betty Lu, you look as if you dropped a catalog tray. Run in your stocking. What is it."

Betty Lu was not only young, maybe twenty five, but younger looking. She was about 5'2", slim, and about as average as a girl can be. But she did look frantic.

"My problem is that I agreed to have a drink with Professor Kohan."

"What's the matter with that. He's written the most significant treatise on Federal practice. Columbia grad. You should be honored."

"His hand."

"His hand? The guy was born with no fingers on his left hand. Heh, You won't have to worry about being pawed by both hands."

"We are not amused," she glowered, and then softened.

"Tom, you have to do me a favor. If it was up to me you would be the librarian here. You know that."

Tom didn't know that, but he went along.

"You'll come with me and the three of us will go for a drink."

"No way. I'd feel like an idiot." The look of desperation of Betty Lu softened Tom. He could see she was struggling – close to panic. She was telling him that librarians must stick together against the onslaught of tenured professors.

"I'll tell you what. Where are you meeting him."

"In the lobby"

"All right. You go in the lobby and meet him. I will leave here in five minutes and go into the lobby. Call me over to chat, and I will leave it to you to insist I accompany the two of you for a drink."

Betty Lu thought it over. It was that or despair.

Kohan had no idea who Tom was when he passed the two of them in the lobby. But Betty Lu gushed over him as if he were carrying myrrh. She had to have Tom tell Professor Kohan about the KF mixup, and dragged the two of them across McDougall Street to the Canteen.. Kohan knew a brush-off was in the making. He let himself be seated, ordered drinks for the three of them. Excused himself politely when they arrived and dropped a sizeable bill on the table as he left. Betty Lu put her head to one side as if to say I hope we didn't hurt his feelings. Tom said nothing but sipped his drink, and they shared the third.

It was now after ten o'clock, and Tom suggested a cab, but Betty Lu knowing Tom was feeling bad about the situation, suggested that she only lived a few blocks down in the East Village and she coyly asked Tom to walk her home. She lived near Tompkins Park It was more than a few blocks, particularly since Tom had more to drink than usual. When they got to her building, Tom opened the door and she reached in for her key to open the security door to her walk up. Betty Lu then turned to Tom.

"Tom, you were wonderful. Thank you. Thank you." She put her arms around Tom and kissed him full on the lips. Not bad. And Tom responded. The kisses turned to necking, and Tom found himself reaching under her blouse and fondling her large nipples that represented all of her breast. Betty Lu then slipped through Tom's arms and went to her knees and bit his penis. They then looked eye to eye. Tom said, "Let's go to your room." Betty Lu's bag was open. She found her key. Opened the door. Let herself in and closed it without admitting Tom.

They stood looking at each other through the glass panes for a full minute. And then Betty Lu proceeded up the stairs. It was no time to be yelling. And as Tom thought about it, he decided it was a fitting end to his evening. His problem was that he still had an erection, and his testicles were beginning to feel that they were either swollen or slowly turning to brass. As he left the apartment house, he realized that he had to get from Tompkins Park to Seventh Avenue to catch the IRT. It was approaching eleven pm, and this area was no place to be walking at night, particularly if you were not fleet of foot. Tom did make it safely, although the IRT proved to be somewhat of a nightmare. Somewhere around the Harlem area, three strapping black young men entered his compartment. To Tom, they looked to be up to no good. He made it through East Village and now he was going to be beat up on the IRT. He was wrong. The three men proceeded to leap frog one another. They did gymnastics on the straps, and whirligigs on the poles of the car. After five minutes of a remarkable display, one of them went through the car with a hat looking for donations. Tom reached for his wallet, drew out a five and dropped it in the hat and was greeted by a big grin and a "You're the dude."

It was a short walk to the apartment and Tom just walked into the bedroom and sunk into a chair and fell asleep. At three am, Janet came home. She turned the lights on and shrieked, "Tom what are you doing in that chair." "You don't want to know." She shrugged. "I sure do want to know. You have lipstick all over your face and" She stopped. She waited.

Tom took pains to explain his evening and how a grateful Betty Lu wanted to show her appreciation. He got an unsympathetic nod from Janet. He then made it clear that nothing happened. As his mind cleared, he heard himself saying out loud, "How did I let myself get into this. I knew that girl at Cahn for three years and she had about as much appeal to me as a scarecrow, which she resembles. How in the hell do I get into these situations?"

Janet, eyeing the suspicious blotch on his fly, shook her head, "Who is it that said something about protesting too much. Tom, please, no more, or I'll think you are lying like a rogue." Janet did not bring the subject up again, but did notice that Tom' pants were being sent to the cleaners.

CHAPTER 21

WALTER HERLIHY

New York City was proving a little too much for Tom. He was drinking too much, and all he could think of was the many times he had tangled with Janet about her flirtatious adventures. Maybe he was no better. But he also had told the administration that he was going to New York City to interview one of Essex's very successful alumni. Not just a successful alumni, but one that made it out of New England. This was important to the school which now had ambitions to attract students nationwide.

Walter Herlihy agreed to an interview and the only time he had was a Saturday afternoon which was fine with Tom, It was time to get a little business in to justify his listing it as a school expense.

Tom met Walter at a booth in Hallohan's on 51st Street and Tenth Avenue.

The waiter approached the booth in which Tom and Walter Herlihy were sitting and put down a shot of scotch and a glass of water in front of Herlihy.

"What'll you have, Tom?

"If you'll forgive me Mr. Herlihy, I've had my share of liquor since my arrival in town."

"OK – you want to know about me and Essex. Let's see. I graduated in the 60s – law review – worked for a plaintiff law firm – Cohen and Rattigan – for five years. Went over to the other side. Was offered a job by the New York Insurance and Indemnity Company. Took the New York bar. No trouble.

"Let me tell you the case that made me partner. We were sued by a longshoreman who claimed he got a spinal injury while unloading a ship. They claimed the ballast on the ship had tipped the ship to one side making the lifting precarious and causing the injury. At trial, I suddenly had an inspiration. I whispered to the young lawyer sitting in on the case with me and in twenty minutes he came back with what I wanted. A cross section of the hull of a ship with a ruler hanging from the top that could be rotated. Stillman, the plaintiff lawyer – a very good lawyer by the way – had a bunch of stevedores lined up ready to testify as to the listing of the ship. Stillman would put them on the stand and they would testify as they were told, if I might add. I would cross-examine with my – as you know – demonstrative evidence. I would go to the easel and ask each one of them, "Show me on this ruler (and I would move the ruler back and forth} how much the ship listed." Some had 30%, some 20% and so on. Jury for the defendant."

"Do you ever feel sorry for the plaintiffs?"

"Always. I've been faced with cripples, people on wheel chairs and once the court had to make arrangements for a guy to testify on a stretcher. His lawyer, Max Gannett, was the most flamboyant – that's a charitable word for him – I have ever run into. I still remember my closing to the jury – 'Ladies and gentleman, this is a court of law. Counsel for the plaintiff has stressed the terrible suffering that his client has undergone. What he hasn't stressed is that plaintiff went through a red light, lost control of his car, swerved in the opposite lane and hit the defendant's car as it was coming out of a driveway. That is not an instance of what he calls last clear chance. Your job, ladies and gentleman, is to serve the law. That requires a verdict for the defendant. Now if you feel for the plaintiff after doing your duty, I suggest you all dig into your pockets and offer a donation. I will contribute $100.00.' The jury agreed with me as to the verdict."

Tom smiled both at Walter and within himself. That last bit was an anecdote he had heard many lawyers tell as if it was original. "Did you get a good legal education at Essex?"

"Yuh. No fancy courses like they have today. Contracts, Torts, Procedure, Equity – Domestic Relations with Flaherty which was a farce. Can you imagine a guy who doesn't believe in divorce, abortion, and anything against the strict teaching of the Catholic Church teaching that course? It would be alright if he didn't go into a tirade about these matters, but he had to stick in his religion which antagonized the hell out of me."

"You know he doesn't teach Domestic Relations - and they don't call it that any more – Teaches Trial Practice now – which I believe you also teach as an adjunct professor. You're not anti-Catholic are you," said Tom a bit facetiously.

"I'm a Catholic, Tom. My grandparents were Catholic. They came from Ireland and settled in South Boston. My parents and brothers and sisters are Catholic. I have five brothers and sisters and all are Catholic and have families. One of my kids converted to Judaism and lives with her husband in Israel and I pray for her, not to convert, but I'm scared as hell as to what is going on over there.

But I am not a professional Catholic like Flaherty whose views, politics, and daily life is obsessed with his religion. Some years ago, he asked me to help in a brief denying a gay Irish group the right to participate in a St. Patrick's Day parade. I refused. Flaherty is one of those Catholics who hates the Jews because they claim to be the chosen people, a designation he believes belongs to the Irish. He's angry and I think he's angry because he wants to play golf on Sunday. He's angry because he can't practice birth control. At least, that's my reaction to his tirades about Jews and blacks and anyone that doesn't conform to his specifications. My religion is a personal thing and I have no wish to impose it on anyone else. One of my partners is gay and thank God he brings in a lot of gay business. A great gay guy."

At this point, Herlihy, motioned to the bartender and another shot and a glass of water was brought to the table.

"Can you make me a wine spritzer," Tom asked the bartender and when given a querulous look, added, "a half glass of red wine and add some soda water."

"Does that come with a straw."

"No."

Walter laughed. "This is an Irish bar, my friend. If it wasn't for me he would probably have thrown you out of here."

"So you are a good Catholic."

"Heh, wait a minute. What's that mean? Look. On any given Sunday you can find me on the golf course as well as in church. Why am I a Catholic? I was born a Catholic. My friends are Catholic. Above that I love the ritual – the pageantry. I like the platonic idea of a Pope. Now I know you are thinking: what about the Inquisition, the Crusades, the pogroms. I remember having a professor of European history. He gave a lecture on the Reformation and it was all about bad Popes, indulgences and the worst infirmities of the church. A student got up and protested and accused Novak – that was his name – of defiling the Church. Novak smiled beatifically at the young man, 'Sir, what you have just heard from me is history. You can look it up. Now if you want religion, I suggest you come to the church teachings I give at St. Mary's Catholic Church in the Back Bay.'"

The bartender resupplied Herlihy and Jones, without a nod from either.

Herlihy continued. "Last week I was at a boondoggle – excuse me – convention in San Antonio. I turned down a golf scramble and went to church. I guess it was in the Mexican part of town because I certainly looked out of place. A six foot two guy, a complexion so white five minutes in the sun would have turned me into looking like a cooked lobster, 240 pounds and speaking English. Beautiful church and after church you never saw such a gay, colorful crowd. They swarmed around that church showing off their children, their clothes and their Spanish was like music. I don't ever remember feeling so spiritual and I didn't understand a word that was spoken. Mr. Dooley once mentioned the Apostle's Creed never sounded so good as when it was spoken in Latin. Something to that. What about you, Jones."

"Probably an atheist, but I'm half Jewish, whatever that means. Maybe I'm a deist. I love to walk, climb mountains. I have a friend who takes me sailing, weather permitting. I read Voltaire and Emerson and Clarence Darrow and Ralph Ingersoll and they kind of mess up my feelings about organized religion. I don't buy immaculate conception, the trinity, and I don't think the whale business makes much sense. But I'd feel a lot better about it if most Catholics had your perspective. If I ever have to choose, I'd probably be a Reform Jew or an Ethical Culturist."

"Fair enough. I'll tell you my gripe about the Jewish religion. You read the Old Testament and what do you find – a God endorsing, encouraging and even abetting murder. You people have a *mezzuzah* on your door front so the God will know whom to save from his wrath. Jesus is all love. He doesn't talk about any mayhem except maybe tossing the money lenders out of the temple. I take my religion directly from him and all I ask of my priest and my cardinal is to conduct religious services with pomp and circumstance.

"Wow, Walter. Just think if Shakespeare's Henry V thought that way, we would not have those wonderful speeches of the value of Catholic Englishmen killing Catholic Frenchmen."

"Alright, touché," broke in Herlihy, "let's conclude our religious discussion with this thought. I believe there is one camp all people can live under and that is the camp of justice. Catholics, Jews, Mohammedans, atheists, anarchists, cannibals, you name it. That is the canopy where we can find agreement. Enough!

Let's talk more about this legal history. Why did I go to Essex? The price was right. No other reason. Obviously I made the right choice as I am completely content where I am. I probably could have gotten a scholarship to Havad and where would I be? I'd never have made law review. I would be in with a bunch of snobs. And nothing makes me happier when I win a case from a Havad guy with a Havad guy sitting on the bench. The big point I want to make about Essex is this. The faculty doesn't think it's special, the students are not the crème de la crème, no one is going to steal your notes to get a step up on you, you meet guys who drink beer. My senior year I roomed with three guys. Bunk beds. Week ends we would end up at the New Ritz on Scollay Square – they call it the Government Center now. I gotta tell you this. Charley McGovern was my bunk buddy – he had the upper. As nice a guy you would ever want to meet. We go to the New Ritz and spent a good part of the night there. There is this babe sitting alone in a booth. These booths by the way – the whole bar was a disaster area. The booths were not rigid and they moved so that one booth could look into a part of the other. This babe catches Charley's name and suggests Charley pay her a visit. Charley was feeling no pain and I guess he felt honored to be singled out and wriggles out of the booth and into hers and yells to the bartender for two beers. This babe makes no bones about wanting to sleep with Charley – and for all I know Charley was a virgin. Next thing you know they are heading out of the bar and it is obvious she has a wooden leg. Well, we watched the two leave the bar and we stayed at that bar until it closed. We were all drunk as we climbed up the three flights to our little nest. The young lady was strapping on her leg and extolling the virtues – or maybe – the vices of Charley. She extolled them all the way down. Every time this lady got drunk she would trudge over to our building, profess her love for Charley and thump her way up three flights of stairs. If you knew Charley, you would realize that he never could hurt the lady's feelings. We never mentioned the goings on to Charley. As she climbed the stairs, we would all trudge out of the room until midnight. He practices law in Providence, married, three kids, makes a living. I see him in court once in a while, had a beer with him about three weeks ago. I should tell you about Milt Wexler, the Passer, but another time."

Herlihy put on his broad brimmed hat, gave a "See ya, Martin" to the bartender and motioned to Tom to follow him out.

"Mr. Herlihy – I can't tell you how much I appreciated this interview, and believe me, it has been very helpful. I'm going to stay away from religion and Charley in the history but the rest of it makes some valuable points about Essex.

"Good to meet you Tom. If I think of anything else I'll give you a ring. The Dean picked the right man for the history. You are a good listener. Even if I don't think of anything else, maybe I'll catch you at the school if I ever go to an alumni get-together and you can tell me about your progress."

"Sure thing" They both rose and were heading out the bar when Tom realized they had not paid. He turned to correct the situation, and Walter's hand kept him towards the door. "Tom, this is an Irish bar – they let me keep a tab."

Walter's car was parked in front of a hydrant at the bar. Tom noticed there was no ticket on the windshield. He dropped Tom off at the IRT subway stop and his last words, "Tom, stay away from those Ethical Culturists."

Tom made it home without any incident. That night he slept with his clothes on since Janet and he had decided to drive back to Concord as soon as she got home. She awoke Tom around 5am and off they went. Both were very quiet until Janet suggested they stop as she had to go to the bathroom. They pulled off the road in the Hartford area to "Jake's New York Deli" where the rest rooms were labeled "Queens" and "Menhattan." They ate in silence, and returned to the car.

"Cat got your tongue?" asked Janet.

"No, I'm awake now, Janet. How was your day in the big city? You used to ask me that when you waited for me to come home from work." And he added, sarcastically, "Wearing a pretty apron, and the smell of baked potatoes and roast chicken wafting through the air."

"You'd love that wouldn't you? It so happens Tom, that I can see now that I was meant to be a working girl. I love it."

"Yes, you can't get away from it. I guess you spent every day of that three weeks away from Concord parsing every sentence of *Item Magazine*."

Janet smiled. "Wouldn't you like to know, Mr. Jones." She then thought better. "In fact, I have become quite a lover of jazz. Beverly Brooks and I have found a great jazz band."

"Just you and Pat."

"No, I have experiences like you had with that cataloger tease, you told me something about."

They drove in silence until they came to the Massachusetts border and Tom pulled in at a large road side chain.

As they sat sipping coffee, Tom said, "I'm not complaining, you have been a much healthier person since you are working. You don't seem bored any more."

"Funny, Tom. I felt the same way about you."

Tom laughed. "Let's be serious. We're like a divorced couple. You have visiting rights to see your children. You come when you feel like it. We don't question each other's conduct."

"And?"

"Well, I've been looking into it. I spoke to Cohen about it the other day. The Dominican Republic has made it easy to get a quick divorce. You fly there and are met by an attorney. The package includes a vacation hotel. You spend a half an hour in court. Voila. A valid divorce."

Janet shrugged her shoulder. "Why don't you get one?"

"Simple. I have the papers in Concord. All filled out. All it needs is your signature."

"Tom," and Janet broke the stirring stick to her coffee as she answered, "If you want a divorce you will have to get it without my signature. I will not agree to a divorce."

Tom was non-plussed. "Janet, I have no intention of - it is either amicable – it is something we do together without lawyers or mediators – or" and Tom stopped talking.

It was Janet's turn. "Tom I like the idea of being married. As a matter of fact it was your idea in the first place," and she spread the fingers of her left hand to feature the gold band on her index finger.

"Well, I was just thinking back to when we agreed to get married."

"Yes, and you told me that if I wanted to change my mind, I could. I haven't."

From the Massachusetts border to Concord was approximately two hours. Two hours of additional silence. When they arrived home, Grampa was on his knees tending to the flowers that lined the path to the doorway. The children ran to greet Janet. Jack then said, "Dad, are we going to ride the bike path like you said?" Janice jumped in, "I'd like to go to the Magic Forest." Janet got out of the car and after kissing the children, and patting her kneeling father on the head. "You kids work it out with Dad. I didn't get through work until around 5 am. Your father has been giving me a headache, and I am going right upstairs to get some sleep."

Tom took the children to the Bedford bike path. He promised the Magic Forest next week. Around seven pm Janet got up, and, at her suggestion, the four of them went to HoJos for dinner. Rebecca, her sister, figuring Janet would not be home again, arrived to put the children to bed, and Janet insisted she accompany them to dinner. After dinner, she mockingly pleaded and cajoled that Tom drive the others back, and that Tom come back for her so that they could listen to a little jazz. A morose Tom said nothing but did as Janet suggested. After a half hour, Janet thanked Tom for letting her blow off a little steam, and picked her bag off the bar and headed towards the car. Tom followed and they drove home silently.

They both got into bed. Tom in his pajamas. Janet in a red night gown. She moved close to him. "Tom, I don't know what they put in that drink, but if you don't screw me tonight, I may get that Nicaraguan divorce."

CHAPTER 22

ASSISTANT TO THE DEAN

Tom liked to get to Essex early enough to get a cup of coffee at the school coffee shop before he headed up to his office on the fourth floor. The Dean was usually there. The business manager was usually there talking to the Dean. And occasionally they would invite Tom over which gave him an opportunity to subtly suggest matters to both so that when they came up at faculty meetings, at least, the Dean had some inkling of what Tom wanted. This was the procedure that Tom used when he wanted to set up a computer lab. The Dean, and he was better informed than most faculty, had no idea what computers could do. The lab proved to be a success, and now Tom wanted to take it another step.

"Tom," the Dean began, "I've heard that Commonwealth sent some people over to look over our computer lab."

"That's right, Dean. Our next step is to go online."

The Dean threw up his hands. "Tom, I'm a little busy with Dan here. Take it up with Dooley or better still, with Bill Solide."

Bill Solide was one of four assistant Deans. One for curriculum, one for budget, one for administration, and Solide for everything else. He was also on call to the Dean for any problem, whether it had to do with the law school or not. And he was on call for twenty four hours, as Bill could get a call from the Dean at 4 o'clock in the morning. Bill was a graduate of Essex Law but also had an accounting degree. During his years at Essex, he was student president, represented the student body at American Bar Association meetings, and had an aptitude for getting along with people. On graduation, he stayed on to help the registrar's office with some business problems until he got a job in some law office. Nothing came up that was better than what he was doing for Essex, and Essex found him ever more useful, and so the Assistant to the Dean was created. Technically, his title was Assistant to the Dean, while the other Deans were Assistant Deans, but the distinction proved to be without a difference.

Bill was of average height, average intelligence, and average looks. There was a sharpness to his appearance. His nose had an edge to it, and his eyes looked like they could dart around corners. He was never in one place, and he never stood still. It was as if he was expecting a call from the Dean at any moment. He once confided to Tom, that it was his ambition to one day say to the Dean, "If you need me, don't call." And it was with Tom that he was most comfortable and most confiding. And Tom had great respect for Solide. He never used his authority to bully anyone, and he did carry out his assignments, which included hiring and firing, with dignity. When Tom came to him in need of funds, or any matter, he listened carefully and, if he said he would talk to the Dean about it, Tom had confidence it would happen. When Tom approached him on setting up a computer lab for the law students, Bill was not skeptical but told him the administration would be. "I'll bring it up, Tom, but you are asking for a good hunk of money. If it is approved, and I'll push for it because I have confidence in you, but I warn you if the money goes down the drain, your life is in jeopardy." It took six months, but the money came through, the lab was built, the students responded most favorably, and Bill remarked to Tom, "You made a lot of skeptics unhappy."

One of the skeptics was Dooley and not just because the lab succeeded. Since Tom came aboard, he was looking for the chink in his armor. This was not that Tom was a special target. As second in command, he thought it obligatory to have something on everybody. He was like a policeman who joins the force so he can legally beat people up.

But Tom became a special target for two reasons. One: the projects that he asked for were successful despite being downgraded by Dooley, and two: his relationship with Mary McCarthy. This latter came to a head, when it was announced at a faculty meeting that the Dean was having a get-together at his home in New Hampshire on the weekend. Tom approached the Dean and informed him he would not be able to attend. Said that Mary McCarthy had urged him to come up on a serious matter. Dooley was within hearing distance and he broke in.

"If this has to do with your history of the law school, forget it. I'm not authorizing the expense."

Both the Dean and Tom looked askance at Dooley. Tom spoke first with anger in his voice. "I'm having a conversation with Dean Oberal, Dean Dooley. But to allay your suspicion, this is a purely social, and maybe a business engagement that will take place on my time and my money."

The Dean added, "Dooley get a hold of yourself."

"That senile woman is spreading false rumors about me, Dean. I won't have it."

" John, if they are false, you have nothing to worry about. My God, she hasn't been around here for twenty years. What's eating you."

Dooley's eyes narrowed. "That crazy woman is trouble. Not only for me. The school. And you better instruct your librarian there to remember that."

The relationship between Dooley and Dean Oberal was cordial but not close. When Oberal took over the Deanship, Dooley was the acting Dean, and the Associate Dean under the prior administration. Oberal thought it tactful to keep Dooley in an administrative position, but the other Associate Deans were new.

"Anything to what Dooley is saying," the Dean asked Tom. as Dooley humphed away.

"Nothing that I know of, Dean. I do know that Dooley was very helpful to Mary when she bought a camp up in Mount Desert Island."

"It's none of my business, Tom. You've been up there a couple of times, what gives."

"She's a great lady. Plus I have some great stories about the law school and Seth Adams from her. She may have only been the Dean's secretary, but she played a role similar to what your four associate deans play now. On the personal side, she had invited me and Janet up to her camp. It is the most glorious piece of land in America. Acadia National Park is just the beginning. She does want to talk to me about something personal – if I had to guess, she is well in her eighties and wants advise about a will. If that is the case, I will tell her there are a lot of people at the law school better equipped to give her advise than I am."

The Dean patted Tom on the back. "Enjoy yourself."

It was only Tuesday, and Tom still had a faculty meeting to attend. But he did arrange a flight to the Bar Harbor Airport for Saturday morning, and a car rental for the weekend.

CHAPTER 23

THE FACULTY MEETING

The faculty library was Tom Jones' place for R&R. It was a spacious room lined with second sets of books of most use to law professors: An encyclopedia, the Massachusetts reports, a regional reporter, the *Lawyers Edition of the United States Supreme Court,* and sets and treatises recommended by the faculty; and along the wall, a battery of computers and printers. But for Tom Jones the four enclosed cubicles were where he headed first. Here he could seclude himself in a cubicle and read, write, check sources on the computer, daydream and not worry about the outside world. Even his staff was notified that only an emergency could extricate him from a cubicle.

Not only did Tom use this time for writing up his history of the law school, but also to prepare for his class on Law and Literature and to work on an article on the uses that courts made of references to works of literature. He had searched the web by putting in "Shakespeare" and then the name of one of his plays, and watch the result. Then another play, and so on. That part had been finished and he was now working on Charles Dickens. A search of "Oliver Twist" turned up a judge attributing "the law is an ass" to Finley Peter Dunne. The judge must have had a lousy clerk, Tom mused.

A knock on the door. Tom's forehead creased. He had suggested a list of informal rules for the faculty. One of them was that if you come into the faculty library to talk, have a cup of coffee (replenished every morning, afternoon, and evening), or even read and talk, Fine. But if you are using a cubicle, you are not to be disturbed.

But rules were not made for Associate Dean Dooley. "I know you are in there Tom."

Tom printed out the material on Lexis and reluctantly went to the door. "Yes, Dean."

""Don't Dean me, Tom. I need to harass someone. We have a faculty meeting in an hour, and I want to brainstorm with you. You know the agenda?"

"Yes, Dean."

Dooley stiffened up at this, but then smiled. "I need some input on how we can emerge from being a fourth tier law school. I mean, why should we care? We have no trouble with enrollment. Cripes, we turn away twenty percent of the applicants. We got something that 95 percent of the law schools do not have. Location. Location. Location. But the real Dean – I'm only an associate, Tom: if you insist on calling me Dean, call me Associate Dean – wants us in the third tier. I need suggestions and you librarians know everything."

"Well, we have a building fund that is coming along fine. It will probably provide us with the most technically proficient law school in the country. My suggestion is that we need a few scholars on the faculty. We should improve the quality of people invited to speak here."

"That's long term, Tom. How about what can we do immediately."

"Maybe we should do what some schools are doing. Every year, Yale Institute of Law, run by a librarian, that has a study that lists what schools have faculty members that are cited most. I am convinced that some schools urge their faculties to write long articles, cite faculty members, and otherwise make sure that they rate in the top twenty citation score. For instance, the Michigan Citation Law Forum this month has an article by John Kindley of Brandeis Law that is over one hundred pages long, has over 300 citations, including, I'll bet, some fifty relating to his own productions ..."

"I missed that – what was it about..."

"I think it was a hoax – it had something to do with cannibalism – the law of cannibalism. Dudley vs somebody. But that article will go far to put Brandeis Law School in the top twenty."

Dooley scribbled some notes. "Keep going."

"Well, a lot of law schools are adding law reviews. Thayer of Ohio has three hundred students and six law reviews. A regular law review, an environmental law review, an intellectual property law review – I forget the other three but it means the top 65 percent of students that graduate can include in their resumes that they were on law review.

"That is good, Tom. But where do they get the articles to include in them. When I was in law school, every school had one law review and I can't recall anything ever worth reading in them, except the note I had to write as a law review member. All I remember is that it had something to do with the obligation to save a drowning person if there was a life saver nearby and after you threw the life saver at him, you realized it was the guy who stole your wife, and you withdrew it from his grasp at the last moment. It took me weeks to write the damn thing and I thought I had explored a new avenue of law and you know what – I never got a client with facts even resembling that situation."

"Never write an article Dean, unless you have a follow-up article to cite yourself. But you are absolutely correct if you are telling me that law reviews serve very little purpose in the legal world. I don't think Justice Holmes ever cited anything unless it was fifty years old – that leaves hope for your note – and as far as I am concerned the last person worth citing was Justice Brandeis and his partner when they wrote that famous article on privacy. The point is that it makes smart law students happy and probably has some effect on a school's reputation."

"What about the cost – do you know what it costs us to put out our law review? By the time those idiots send the corrected article back to the professor who wrote it and then he rewrites the article, its like renvoi. Last year we had an issue ready for distribution and the author of one article – Dishcohern – threatened to sue unless we withdrew the issue so that he could update it. We threw out the entire issue – he never updated it – the bastard published it in an ivy league law review. And last year, we received a letter from his agent – the guy has an agent – that he would be happy to be one of our guest lecturers at some outlandish figure."

"Dean, You asked me for suggestions."

"I know – I have that down. What else."

"A graduate program in intellectual property."

"That's it. Tom, I knew I could rely on you. I'll have the Dean call on me first. I make my report and I sit back and take a nap. I may need you to back me up on some of this – see you there. By the way, how is the history coming. I think I will give you a plug and say that your history will do much to bring this school into national repute. Ta ta."

Dooley left the faculty library humming a hymn.

Tom went back into his cubicle but Dooley had taken all the air out of his enthusiasm. He would get a cup of coffee, take a seat on the sofa in the faculty library and relax for a few minutes. Maybe a faculty member would come in and provide some entertainment.

The faculty door from the fourth floor elevator landing opened edgily. Tom saw a forehead and one eye wide open, and then the door flew open. It was Janice Kahn. In she rushed sobbing violently. "I was hoping you would be here, Tom." She sobbed loudly, dabbed her tears with a handkerchief and continued. "Just you, I wanted to talk to you alone."

"What gives, Janet?"

"It's Larry."

"Larry who?" and then Tom realized it must be Larry Flinn, the head cataloguer. Tom had gone to library school with Larry. He finished first in his class at Simmons, far ahead of Tom. He was very bright but not very accommodating. He was someone you had to push to get results. He did not like authority and that was why he was limited in his opportunities. Being a cataloguer was about as far as he was going to get in life and he accepted it. Tom had hired him a year ago when he had moved back to Boston from his job at the University of Chicago law library. His wife had cancer and he decided she could be better treated at the Boston hospitals. Also, his wife had family in one of the Boston suburbs which made life easier for Larry and his family. He had written to Tom about a job, and Tom was happy to oblige him by offering one of his cataloguers a promotion to reference librarian in charge of online searching and faculty assistance. The move was not successful as far as his wife was concerned. She passed away soon after they arrived, and, while Tom would occasionally have a cup of coffee with Larry and inquire how he and his two sons were getting along, that was the extent of their friendship.

"Larry Flinn. Your cataloguer. I knew it was a bad move when you hired him and moved Teresa into the reference department. You shouldn't have.."

"Wait a minute. Whoa! This is the first I have heard of all this. You are head of acquisitions. Reference would have been a demotion for you."

Janice broke down and sobbed so violently that when a faculty member opened the door, took one step into the library, immediately backed out and closed the door. "He's left me." She put her head on Tom's shoulder and Tom patted her on the top of the head. She continued, "We had been going together for six months." She then spat out angrily. "He's been laying me for six months. I told him it's time we got more serious and he's been avoiding me ever since."

"How long has he been avoiding you?" was the best with which Tom could follow through.

"After our argument, I told him he had better think about us and I was going to visit my parents in the Adirondacks for two weeks. I come back and not only do I not hear from him, but I show up at the Law Librarians of New England conference on ethics in librarianship and there he is with some woman at the luncheon. I passed his table and he didn't even say hello. The bastard!"

"Janice, number one, I don't have any rules on this, but you know it's never a good idea to date someone on the staff. You and Larry should have realized this."

Janice shrieked, "But we were sleeping together." Her sobs grew fainter and fainter, her heavy breathing was now relaxed. Her head was comfortably perched on Tom's shoulder, her ample bosoms were vibrating against his arm, and her left hand was on Tom's left knee and edging toward his fly.

Tom watched this progression from a person deserted to a coquettish tease with interest and then impatience.

"Janice, I'm a married man." Janice arose quickly, straightened out her skirt and shot a look at Tom. "Yuh, and that don't stop a lot of your faculty from what I know." And she shot out of the room.

Tom looked at his watch. Ten minutes to the faculty meeting and he had not yet looked at the agenda except for his discussion with the Dean. But looking at it was not to be, for out of the corner of his eye he could see the faculty library door that led out to the library slowly open. That door only opened with a key which meant that a librarian was coming into the library probably to bring in material or to take care of the loose leaf services. Tom's demeanor sank when he realized it was Larry.

"Is she gone?" were his first words. He didn't wait for Tom to speak. "I figured she was coming to see you and I confess I was listening at the door. Tom, the woman befriended me after my wife passed away. She insisted on going on picnics with my kids when we first went out. Next thing I knew she was in charge. I had no idea what she was up to."

"You slept with her, Larry."

"Do you know how I slept with her? We go out one night – I think a movie – come back to the house for a cup of coffee. She disappears. I'm drinking coffee all alone. Where is she? I look for her – maybe she fainted or something. She's in bed. She says to me, 'Larry, come to bed – you don't have to take off all your clothes.'"

"So what did you do?"

"I left on my socks. After that, she took over. She made me buy a new sweater because the one I had on – that I liked very much – had a moth hole on it. But the final straw was when I took her to the Law Librarian's Ball. She decided my Volkswagen wasn't appropriate so we went in her Integra. We drive to the Copley Plaza with the radio playing a Sinatra tune and she was telling me about her divorce from her husband and what a bitch he was, etc. I park the car, get out and close my door, start walking to the other side to open the door for her and then wait for the parking attendant at the hotel to take the car. But she had already gotten out of the car and closed her door, which, much to my surprise, meant I had locked the car with the motor running and the radio on. I say surprise because she realized it before I did, and before I had even got to her side of the car, I heard her shouting, "You fucking asshole – you locked the car.""

"And that was the end of your relationship.":

"Pretty much. What hurt most was the way she emphasized the 'g.' We went to the dinner. The attendant came in later with the keys to the car. Cost me twenty bucks for him to get in there with a hanger or something. But that is the last time we dated."

"She says you had a commitment."

"No commitment. You know what the problem is? I'm a widower. Women prefer widowers. A divorced man, in a woman's eyes, has proven himself a bad risk. A widower could have killed his wife and he's acceptable. Well, I'm not ready for that."

"Larry, how are we going to repair this situation?"

"I have a solution. St. Francis is looking for a cataloguer – now. They can take me tomorrow if I can get your recommendation."

"Come to my office around ten am tomorrow and we'll try and work something out. I am late for a faculty meeting."

They both stood up. Larry shook Tom's right hand with both his hands, and left quietly.

As the door opened, Tom called out, "By the way, Larry, Janice told me she saw you at a library meeting with a female companion. Is their a connection?"

"That," replied Larry with emphasis on 'that,' "was my accomplice."

The faculty meeting lasted two hours. It had to be adjourned at four pm - enough faculty members had classes to discourage its continuance. Dooley, as usual, made his presentation right out of Tom's playbook, but gave him no credit. There was an extensive discussion on the importance of a writing faculty. A motion was passed, and Tom was charged with its keeping: to post quarterly the academic achievements of the faculty. It was suggested that the development office was not capable of doing public relations work, and that a public relations office be set up for the law school. Another committee was formed to look into setting up a graduate program in intellectual property so that the school could be on the cutting edge of the boom in electronics and its ramifications. Another motion proposed a relationship with the Antartica Law School. It was suggested that the school act quickly as United States law schools were gobbling up nations so fast Essex would be left out in the cold. A motion was proposed that all children of faculty be admitted tuition free as this would encourage senior faculty that the school is interested in hiring to consider Essex. The discussion that followed asked who would be included in free tuition. Would it include children from all marriages or only those sperm related. Another question was whether emeriti faculty would fall into this category. At this point the Dean whispered to the Associate Dean and Dooley arose and asked whether this motion was germinal to the discussion on the table. A vote was taken and it was decided that it was not. A suggestion that we use the internet and teleconferencing to accept courses taught at other law schools was proposed by Professor Dawkins, who was presently involved in teaching a conferencing course at the William Mitchell Law School. A raucous debate followed and the sponsor accused the most vociferous attacker of the proposal of being against it as he was an internet dummy. At this point, the Dean judiciously proposed the meeting be adjourned which was voted thirty eight to four.

As the faculty members filed out of the room, some partaking of the coffee, fruit, celery and other cold vegetables, as well as bottles of water, the grumbling could be heard all along the corridor.

"Did you notice there were four people who voted not to adjourn the meeting. I'll bet if we voted on the Dean's health, there would be 20 for, 20 against, with ten abstentions."

"Was anything accomplished at that meeting.?"

"Eversharp is the dumbest shit on this faculty."

"The tuition proposal was the only one that made sense and we vote it down. Crazy."

Tom quietly proceeded to his office when Professor Toole sidled up to him. "You were very quiet at that meeting, Tom. Cat got your tongue?"

"I do all my negotiating before the meeting and let others speak for me, Professor Toole."

"Well, I know you have two children. That tuition thing must have been yours, huh?"

"If you were observant you would have noted that I voted to squelch that proposal. I happen to think it is a good one but it belongs as a separate item on the agenda."

"I happen to think we are a fourth tier law school. We should be happy that we are where we are. But if I were to make a proposal, it would be we should evaluate all our faculty. If we did we would find that at least a third of them should not be teaching at any law school. Let me put it to you this way – Gardner is a disgrace as a teacher. I sit in his class once a year and I can tell you that he cannot teach contracts."

"Professor Toole, I have sat in your class. You are a great teacher – I think one of the best in the country. I even think you think that and you are right. I even suspect that you know what a good teacher is and that you may be right about Gardner. But on the other hand, I think you are one of the most arrogant and divisive persons on this faculty. I have heard you called 'The Imp of the Perverse.' I have only known you for a short time, I admit, and I do not recall you saying anything good about this faculty from the Dean on down. You have even said to my face that librarians should not be on the faculty. But let me leave you with one thought – Gardner has tenure, I have tenure, you have tenure. On that we are all equal. And one more thing, As a librarian I consider it my duty to listen to all faculty. Nothing I have just said should leave you with the feeling that I do not welcome any conversation that you wish to have with me."

Toole looked at Tom's visage, happy to see that he had got a rise out of him. "I take offense that you suggest that I have nothing good to say about anyone. I happen to think you are a good librarian." And Toole jauntily walked to the elevator and pressed the two button with his walking stick.

CHAPTER 24

MARY'S CONSCIENCE

Tom flew to the Bar Harbor Airport located just off the causeway that led to Mount Desert Island, the home of part of Acadia National Park. He rented a car and drove to Bar Harbor to Mary's retirement residence. The Bar Harbor Residence for Seniors was located on an elevation overlooking Frenchman's Bay. By auto, it was just a few minutes from the center of Bar Harbor. The first level was populated by seniors able to care for themselves. If you were incontinent or worse, you were put on the second floor. The third floor was for people who needed constant assistance. The next step was out of the building into a hospice facility or the cemetery. There was a nurse on duty at all time,

Tom was buzzed into the building, identified himself, and spotted Mary in the veranda talking to someone. He walked over and was greeted heartily by Mary who introduced him to Zeke Harper. "Zeke and I go way back, don't we Zeke." "We sure do," said Zeke in that Down East accent, "and I'm not letting her get out of my sight again. I was madly in love with this lady." Mary laughed, "Get out of here Zeke, all you wanted was my body." "That too." "You didn't have a chance." "I ain't given up." They both laughed and Zeke got out of his chair, "Mary told me you was coming, young man, and I will leave you two alone." He slowly lifted his body from the armchair, and arranged himself in a walker, and trudged off.

"Never paid much attention to Zeke. He was a wormer. But I find out that he took over his father's business – grocery store in Southwest Harbor, and did well enough to be able to retire in this human warehouse."

"Don't like it here."

"As a matter of fact, I do. To me, every day is a bonus. I'm eighty eight years old. I thought I was done for when I broke my hip but they pinned it together and I have graduated from a walker to a cane. Pills keep my blood pressure under control. I take pills so my bones won't fall apart. An aspirin every day, and something else I can't remember. Oh, sodium chloride."

"You look great. I don't want to change your mood, Mary, but when Dooley found out that I was coming to see you, he raised hell with the Dean."

"He did. Did he tell you he came up to see me last week?"

"No."

"Wants me to sign some papers. I told him no more signing papers. Tom, I have to trust you. When Bender was librarian I could trust him because he was scared as hell of me. I have faith in librarians that I would never have in any professor. If ever there was a bunch of deceitful, greedy, avaricious –"

"Whoa, Mary, Whoa. You can't tear down the legal elite."

"Yeh, if you gave me time, I would add lawyers, too. I know you are a lawyer but you are a librarian, and you are going to help me."

"Mary, if all you ever did, was introduce me to the glories of Mount Desert Island, I would be in your debt forever. I know you wouldn't ask me to do anything not on the up and up, so I am at your service."

"I am going to boil it down to this. Anytime Dooley has asked me to do anything, it had to do with money. I know I got myself into this. I think I told you that when Seth brought me to Boston, I was not a happy camper. I was rotting away in Southwest Harbor. Slinging hash and being an easy mark. I did well in Boston. Sort of became a lady. But deep inside of me I wanted to get back to Mount Desert. But I wanted to come back as my own person. Seth gave me the education, the position, and I figured when I retired I could spend summers there as I did during my vacations. Then Dooley came along."

"You told him of your longing …"

"I probably was always bragging about the island. Dooley is no dope. He knew that I knew he was siphoning off money. Do you know he has this fancy digs on the Cape – big house – on an exclusive golf course. Has he invited you to play there?"

"No."

"I didn't think so. So when I suggested that I'd love to have a camp up there, he said 'find one and I'll help you.' You know, Tom, when Jesus got on that mountain top and the devil offered him anything in his view, he turned it down. I'm not Jesus. I found that piece of land I wanted. By kayak. Twelve acres with 300 feet of shorefront for eleven thousand dollars. I had the eleven thousand, but now I needed a camp. The funny thing was that Dooley thought a camp was a tent. In Maine, a camp can mean anything from a simple log cabin with an outhouse to even more than what I wanted. I arranged with a local builder – you guessed it, one of the stool sitters at the diner I worked at – to build me a two bedroom, two bathroom camp with a deck, facing the cove, that ran the full size of the house. My dining room and living room faced the cove and was glass-paneled to face the cove. He insisted I put in a cellar, but I turned down insulating the place. Seventeen thousand dollars. Dooley said 'One hundred dollars a month will take care of it.' I knew better. I knew Essex was putting up the rest and my conscience went dead on me."

"Mary, why don't you estimate what you should have put up. Make a gift to Essex and your conscience is clear – well, not clear, but I don't see the value of making a public confession. I think that was what Dooley was concerned with. It would put a blemish on the school if you confessed that tuition money went into your camp."

"It's not that easy Tom. You obviously do not know Dooley Do you know how much the value of this property went up?"

"Quite a bit."

"And Dooley would come to me periodically and have me take out home equity loans. Then I would be involved in land purchases, home building, and God knows what. We built and own the two camps on either side of mine. Both of them are terrible. They belong on Commonwealth Avenue. I didn't know either of them were going up until I awoke one morning to the sound of trees coming down and a foundation being put in. Dooley rents them. You can't believe what the rent is."

"So what you are telling me is that Dooley has made you a lot of money. What is in it for him?"

"My word for one thing. But let me give you an idea of what is going on. I have a caretaker. He takes care of my place, and the two camps we have built on it that we rent. He collects the rent. The money goes to an account that I have in Portland. Dooley is my agent and I am sure that he is putting the money to – bad – use. By the way, we even own the land that this senior residence is on. I have no idea what else."

Tom took out his handkerchief, and wiped his forehead and then sat down heavily in an armchair. You didn't have to be a real estate appraiser, or a tax assessor, to know that Mary McCarthy was probably worth a fortune. Dooley had parlayed a few thousand dollars into probably millions. He probably had another deal going that Mary put a stop to.

"Mary, what do you want me to do."

"Tom, I'm not a religious person. My folks were Catholic, and I do remember something about having communion but I am not a churchgoer. But this whole business is nagging at me. I want to put a stop to it. I want the Dooley burden off my shoulders. I have a few years left in me and I want them to be peaceful. I even feel a push toward God. I can't explain it but you have to help me right wrongs and do right."

"Mary, I am flying blind on this. But let's start with the bank in Portland. Would you call the bank and tell the manager you have hired me to check into your financial worth. I'll need you to give me the power of attorney."

"Of course. I will also give you a key to our safety deposit box at the bank, and authorize you to check it. I never have, and Dooley realizes that I am in no position to do so now. Tom, I am hiring you to look into my financial situation, and if Dooley doesn't like it, he can lump it. Oh, one more thing. This is just an aside. When I walked into my camp for the first time, Dooley came with me. We're talking thirty years ago. LaGrange, the builder, and the guy I hired to be the caretaker, was also there. I went over things with them – I think I signed a couple of papers – and the two of them left. Dooley had driven up in his Jaguar, and was dressed to the hilt. He swaggered as if he had just made the coup of his life. I thought it was hand shaking time for him, but that bastard grabbed me, edged me to the bedroom, and French kissed me. He thought he deserved a reward for all he had done. He got one, a left hook to the eye."

"He is a beaut. Did he apologize?"

. He told me he didn't know what came over him. I told him it came over him not me. And that was the end of it. I sometimes get the feeling that he wants people to think I was one of his many conquests."

"He was a lover boy also?"

"Tom, that guy always came on strong. We had a reference librarian before you came aboard. Very sexy. She was suspicious about Dooley's reputation. She made a play for him, and he takes the bait. She lived on Joy Street, and invites him up for a drink after work. She gets into something cozy, and that Lothario turned limp and ashen, and excused himself. It's surprising how stories like that get around."

"Sometimes the other way, Mary."

Mary looked at him suspiciously. "From what I hear, Tom, and I hear things, you are the real thing." Mary laughed, and reached over and gave Tom a big hug and a kiss on the cheek. Tom found himself blushing and could only stammer, "Mary, we shouldn't mix business with pleasure."

Mary made her call to the Portland National Bank, gave Tom a letter asking the bank to show him every courtesy. Tom then leisurely drove home, stopping first at Ogunquit to walk the Marginal Way to work up an appetite and then satisfying it at Barnacle Bill's restaurant with a pound and a half lobster, corn on the cob, coleslaw, blueberry pie and coffee.

CHAPTER 25

THE FEDERAL JUDGE

Tom Jones' office was on the fourth floor of a six story building. It was six stories for two reasons. One was that the Beacon Hill Residential Committee had an iron hand on buildings. A church had been torn down for the law school structure and the tip of its steeple was the maximum height of the new structure. It was known as the point of law.

It took the Essex lawyers two years to win approval of the height as the Committee fought before the Land Court that the steeple tip should not count which would have limited the law school to four floors and that would have been the death knell of a law school at that site. The head of the Land Court was an Essex law graduate; the lead lawyer for the committee was a Havad professor. Essex won. The Havad people had fought every effort of Essex to exist including an attempt to curtail its accreditation by the American Bar Association. Tom thought about all this as he planned his next interview.

He dialed the Development Office. "Tom Jones – yuh – the new librarian. Yes, Deborah we met at the reception for new faculty. I need a list of the biggest contributors to Essex .. No, I'll come down and get it."

The Development Office was on the first floor as were the Registrar, Admissions, the Clinics, and an auditorium that could seat five hundred or be cut up like a pineapple into slices and chunks for conference rooms. This floor was where the business of the school was conducted.

Tom arrived at A278, mentioned his business, and the clerk pointed to a short, brown haired girl with a constant , puckish smile. She excused herself from an elderly gentleman who was no taller than she.

"Professor Jones, you are so lucky. I have someone working up the list you want, but I received a visit from one of our most illustrious alumni and an ardent supporter and benefactor..."

"And," I added before she could finish, "an eminent judge and Shakesperean scholar. Judge Kaplinsky, I can't think of anyone I would prefer talking to about the history of the law school that the Dean has asked me to write."

"Wonderful! Wonderful! I'm sure you will do an excellent job." The Judge looked at his watch. "Hmm, it's eleven thirty. Mr. eh"

"Tom Jones, judge. Please call me Tom."

"Tom, it's eleven thirty. Will you do me the honor of accompanying me to lunch. I am off to Durgin Park for some scrod and we can talk." Tom was grateful that the judge didn't' tell him one of those awful scrod jokes that Bostonians like to visit upon newcomers.

"Delighted."

Judge Kaplinsky was in his 70s or 80s. It was hard to tell. He had a lively walk. His cane rattled the pavement more like a weapon than an aid. He had a full head of hair with tufts of brown holding out against a panoply of gray. They walked down Temple Place and the Judge acted as a tour guide. "We're crossing School Street – down there was the Old Court House – Justice Holmes was baptized or whatever they do to young ones in the Christian religion over here, that monstrosity is the City Hall ..." and so on until they came to Faneuil Hall. "That statue's Sam Adams .." He looked up at Tom.

"Great man. But we should have a statue for John Hancock. Is there one?"

"By God, I don't think so. You know why? Very short man. Society rarely acknowledges short people.."

"Short sighted," I said.

"Exactly right. My name came up before the Governor's Council I don't know how many times. Never appointed. I've never complained. Every one of those guys on the Supreme Judicial Court, except the women, were taller than me. And I can tell, you, not smarter."

"Judge- everyone knows you should have been on the Massachusetts Supreme Judicial Court. I guess you have to know the governor."

At this time they were at the end of a line that led to a staircase that brought them to the Durgin Park restaurant. "Follow me," said the Judge.

He brusquely elbowed his way up the stairs, looked up at the young man with the menus and was immediately led to another staircase, which they ascended and where they were ushered to a table. Tom had followed loyally behind.

Both had broiled scrod. Tom had baked beans. The Judge had cole slaw. They then shared a biscuit covered with strawberries and overwhelmed with whipped cream. And all through this the Judge talked. "You know, Tom, is it – yes, I can't stand Indian pudding. All the Yankees love it. You know the Indians don't like us pale faces making fun of them. Nevertheless they should be held responsible for that stuff being called a dessert.

"You have to watch what Indians give you."

"You are wrong on that. Indian giving is a wonderful concept. Remind me to explain the concept. But, back to Essex and your history. I hope you'll write up our role in educating the down trodden in our community. We were taking blacks, Jews – do you know I was valedictorian of my class – Boston Latin – top student – and Havad turned me down. My father was a prominent rabbi – Tom Jones – obviously you're not Jewish."

"I'm not sure Judge. My mother was Jewish. I lived in a Jewish neighborhood. Belonged to the Y.M.H.A. I was president of my club once – The Redwings. Our counselor always called me Jonesky."

The Judge laughed. "Jonesky – that is funny – but I've heard funnier. I had an uncle whose name was John Kelly. How did he get John Kelly? The immigration people asked his father what his name was as he came off the boat. 'Yankele', he said. To an Irish immigration officer, Yankele or young boy, was John Kelly..." He waved his hand. "I'm getting off the story. Back to Essex..

"But first my father. He was a prominent rabbi in Boston – In Boston – In America. His temple was right on Commonwealth Avenue. People – Christians even, came to hear him on Friday night. He was an inspiring orator. Beautiful voice. If he spoke of God being in our presence, you would want to touch the hem of His garment. Read his book, 'Shalom for the Soul,' for the best book on faith – any faith – ever written. No sooner written than Bishop Stein, a convert, by the way, wrote 'Jesus for the Soul' and some *meshuganah* – you know what a *meshuganah* is – of course – wrote "Atheism for the Soul.' This father of mine, when I was turned down at a very prestigious law school, whose name I will not reveal to protect the guilty, went to see the President of this august institution.

That *mamzer* told my father that he had so much respect for him and his preaching that he would be glad to knock off a Jew that was accepted and accept his son – but he couldn't do anything about the quota. He actually tried to explain to my father – but never mind.."

"And so you came to Essex?"

"My father didn't like it. I could have gone to Commonwealth but after Havad, as far as I was concerned everyone else comes in second. Besides I lived on Beacon Hill and I could walk to school. I think I got all A's."

"I want you to know Judge that I've read every decision you have written. You did not make judge in Massachusetts but you grace the Federal District Court. You even published an article in the *Havad Law Review.*"

"Yes, on the iniquity of the quota system. I argued that no institution should get federal aid if it could be proved they discriminated. I sent a copy to the President of the institution that turned me down and the *paskudnik* congratulated me on it."

"Let's talk a little more about legal education at Essex. Better than Havad?"

"I was no. 1 at Essex. Would I have been that at Havad. I don't know. Essex adopted the black letter rule that was once the way they taught at Havad. Dean Adams actually – can you believe this – wrote a black letter rule book for every course. They were his Commonwealth law school course notes. I remember Tom Schott – who taught at Commonwealth – complaining in court that I had decided against him on the basis of his own book on Trusts. He told me he was in the process of revising his book and that the statement that I was relying on was completely at odds with his revision. I told him that he may change his mind again when he reads my opinion.

"The point is that legal education is a farce. More than ever, to paraphrase Holmes, it narrows the mind rather than broadens it. I breezed through three years – made law review – was President of my class – the first graduate to work for a State Street firm and the first Jew hired by a State Street firm. The year I made partner was the year I was appointed by Roosevelt to the Federal bench. Do you know why? Efraim Saltonstall, the business manager of the firm, didn't want a Kaplinsky on the letter head. It was alright with me. Oy, my tooth is kicking up again."

Another chance to break in. "'Uneasy lies the head that wears the crown.'"

The Judge laughed. "I thought I was the Shakespeare scholar. I like you

Tom and I'm sure you will do an excellent job on the history. But play up our role in admitting minorities – Blacks, Jews, women."

Tom suggested that it may not have been a civil rights thing with Essex but Essex did it and you have to give Seth credit for it. Kaplinsky added, "If it wasn't for unintended consequences, we might not yet have a theory of gravity. Essex would take anyone who could come up with tuition. Havad took years to accept women. Havad gets the brains and top professors and you have to ask yourself: Is the world any better for it? All it produces is noisy Americans."

"Well, isn't that better than quiet Americans?"

"I wish Graham Greene had time for our noisy Americans."

"Name me a few."

"I'll name you one. And this is off the record. A *lantsman* – Chief Judge of one of our circuits. Havad all the way. A friend of mine graduated in the same class. He was the biggest nerd he had ever met. The most obnoxious student to graduate from Havad Law School, an honor not easily achieved. He not only was sure that he knew more law than anyone in his class, but the class conceded in that opinion. Very smart, yes. Never really earned a living though. From law school to clerking for a judge. From there he became a law professor. Taught at Yale and a year at Oxford. Outstanding authority on economics and the law. Republicans love his theory – it used to be called *laissez faire*. They rushed him to the bench – not a trial court but an appeals court."

"Judge Ginzburg? We used his economics textbook as supplemental reading. Very persuasive guy."

"Maybe. But this guy didn't stop at economics. He is into sex, aging, law and literature, space, politics. Ginzberg has his own five foot shelf of his books, articles, book reviews. And I'll guarantee you, not one of them will outlast him. I read his last one on how to be a judge, and all it was was a regurgitation of all his other books that he was aware that no one had read. Here is a man who idolizes Holmes and Cardozo in print – men whose words you remember like a popular song – someone put out a book of legal quotations – an oxymoron if I've ever heard one – and had several entries by Ginzburg. Ginzburg quotations that includes stuff by Holmes and Cardozo!"

"You really don't like the guy. Is it because he cites Shakespeare more than you do?"

"Tom, you are a very dangerous man. You looked like someone I could handle – now I think I'm the one over a barrel. Of course, I don't hate the guy. We've met. We've exchanged compliments – we've even cited each other. But I think judges should be circumspect in their writing. People like Ginzburg make it sound like judging is an avocation. Ginzburg wants to be in and out of the fray. That's not the way it should work. If he wants to be a public intellectual he should give up judging and show that he can make a living as an intellectual.

"Do you realize that Holmes and Cardozo never wrote a book. Holmes's *Common Law* grew out of a series of lectures. Editors put stuff together that these men had written. I don't think you should quote a legal writer unless he has been dead for fifty years."

"Who was the greatest?"

"Holmes. He had a great life. His father was a famous author. He knew all the greats in the United States and England. Climbed mountains. Liked the ladies. Was a soldier. Wounded three times in the Civil War. His father came after him after his last wound and brought him home. I think Dad was worried about the young lady caring for his wound. He wrote poetry and the greatest legal prose ever produced in the legal world."

"Yuh, but he kind of believed in war. Used terms like 'fighting faiths' and such."

"I'm not sure. In my readings about Holmes, he regretted the Civil War. Thought it was brought about by the overzealous abolitionists and the plantation owner complex. Most northerners were not abolitionists and most Southerners did not own plantations. These small minorities were able to foment more death and destruction over a dying slavery economy by playing to the innocent majority. We needed types of men like our founding fathers instead of fanatics. You see it again and again in our country. People have no idea what political philosophy can carry the day and honor our republic."

"Who was the worst"

"The judge who put the Rosenbergs to their death. I am not defending the Rosenbergs. But the trial was a farce. The defense team ignorant of the implications of their action. The English gave Klaus Fuchs fourteen years and he was the one who was capable of giving away the atom bomb. That Judge wanted to be rewarded with a Supreme Court appointment. I have it on good information that Frankfurter made sure that it did not happen.

He looked at this case as he looked at the Sacco-Vanzetti case. Tom, you know what happens to people who have a lean and hungry look."

"Judge, no one will ever leave Durgin Park with that look."

By this time, they had left the restaurant. The judge insisted on paying the bill and they were now at the entrance to the Federal Court Building.

"Tom, I hope this is the first of many meetings. I occasionally use your excellent library and maybe we can meet for lunch again."

"Thank you, Judge. It has been memorable. And I will remember that Essex stands for being first in the hearts of minorities."

Tom returned to his office and was checking his calendar to catch up on any problems or obligations that remained for the rest of the day.

"A visitor to see you, Mr. Jones."

When Tom gave up his spacious office for a computer lab for the law students, he literally emptied out a broom closet for his office. There was room for a small desk and two chairs. No pictures or diplomas on the wall. No curtains as there were no windows. That was it. To Tom, running a law school library did not require heavy lifting or intellectual leanings and particularly a spacious office. It required a lot of delegation and interruption. At any time, a faculty member, a student, an alumnus or alumna, a salesman would drop in and announce his or her purpose. There was also lunch to be considered, and faculty members looking for company felt free to see if Tom was available for that purpose. There was no room for chit chat or browsing and that pleased Tom. And then there was that piece of paper that Tom always carried around with him when making the circuit of the library. People seemed to respect Tom's privacy when he was on the move with a yellow legal pad or invoice looking form and let him proceed on his way to wherever he was going.

So, it was somewhat of a surprise when one of Elizabeth Hughes' workers announced someone at the same time as that person barged right in.

And Tom was not particularly pleased when he saw Ernie Browder shuffle into his office and take a seat. Ernie had been the librarian for Commonwealth forever. The usual conversation with Ernie was about the faculty refusing to promote him to full professorship. It was common knowledge among librarians that he would arrive at Commonwealth at 8:00am, proceed to his office with a large lunch and a suspicious looking bottle, leave the office at 5:00pm, and then go home. His only conversation was the grievances he had against the administration, the faculty, and the students. Tom did not want to have lunch with him, but he also did not want to appear rude, so he decided to see how this visit would turn out. Maybe he would get lucky.

Ernie broke the silence. "I'm having my office redone and thought I'd drop in and see if I could get some ideas from you." Tom let an amused look settle on his face.

"Just kidding, Tom. Remember me. I'm the guy who shared my room with you when you showed up in L.A. without a room at last year's convention."

"And you kept me up all night telling me your troubles. Things a little better now?"

Tom had resigned himself to sit down and Ernie pulled his chair closer to Tom's. "Haven't had sex with the wife for five years. Can't get an erection." Tom searched for something to say but was silent. "Not really a problem. I'm 70, Tom. She understands. Fortunately, I have a brownstone in Back Bay. I have a floor, she has a floor, and the kids have a floor."

"Well, I'm glad you've worked out that problem. And you don't look any the worse for it. I presume you are here for a reason, Ernie. What can I do for you?"

"I just dropped in to say hello. I have an appointment with your tax guy, Zaltman."

"Why don't you use one of your Commonwealth guys?"

"They're not trustworthy Tom. A couple of things I said to a tax guy got around the building. I'll take my chances with Zaltman."

"Heh, Ernie. You are a graduate of Havad. I'm sure they will keep things confidential and you'd probably get a professional discount."

"Hah. You know, Tom, I happen to know you are doing a history of the law school. Mentioning Havad reminded me of it. I think you should take this down." And Ernie, picked up a yellow legal pad from Tom's desk and put it on Tom's lap. "You should interview me."

Tom blinked. "Yes, I went to Havad Law. I didn't live in the dormitory. I was a commuter. Brookline. You read *One L* about study groups. Where you divide responsibility and pool your notes and interpretations. Where alliances are forged, friendships sealed, and networks established. I studied alone."

"You couldn't get in a group.?"

"The groups I could get into, I didn't want. The groups I wanted wouldn't have me. Tom, I graduated into the most snobbish, successful group of law students in the history of the law school. These guys are in banking, investment, academia, best selling authors."

"I gather you have the distinction of being the only law librarian? I seem to remember you telling me last year that not one Wall Street firm would even give you an interview."

"That's right. I sat right next to Homer Ferguson, whose father is a senior partner in Ferguson, Lipton, and Cawalder. The guy would look at my briefs in class. He came into class so drunk one day, I carried his books out of class for him."

"Ernie. You don't have to look up to anyone. You have a great job. Your bibliographic work is recognized internationally. You'll probably be president of the American Association of Law Libraries some day."

"Tom. I'm a Havad graduate. I should get some respect. I called up Ferguson last year and invited him to lunch. Never got beyond his secretary."

"Forget it Ernie."

"No. It's an obsession with me now, Tom. Every month, I call up a different member of my class and ask him out to lunch."

"It's not worth it Ernie."

"Do you know that Alger Hiss was a student while I was in law school?"

"Turned you down?"

"At least he answered the phone. The guy is a jailbird, and he's too good for me."

Tom, at this point, rose from his seat. "Ernie, I find this all very depressing. I can't take it anymore. You can sit here until your appointment with Zaltman, but, please, no more."

Ernie looked at his watch. "Another ten minutes, Tom. Let me just leave you with this thought. You should put some of this in your interview. Essex kids get out of law school without the trauma that I have had to go through. Private school guys, insufferable smart broads, faculty guys monopolizing the air waves, hallowed halls, ghosts of the past haunting every discussion. What was my mother thinking of? I should have gone here. I might have even made law review."

Tom walked out of his office leaving Ernie mumbling to the bare walls. There was something to what Ernie was saying. It would have to be subtle, but he would work it in. As Tom sauntered toward the elevator, a piece of paper in hand, all he could mutter was, "No sex for five years!"

CHAPTER 26

THE DISCOVERY

Tom arrived at the law school at 8:30am and went to the cafeteria in the basement for his morning coffee. The Dean motioned him over.

"Good morning, Tom. I just got news about the team that is going to inspect us." He showed the list to Tom.

"I think we are in good shape, Dean." Tom looked over the names. "I know the librarian. He has already called me and asked that I put an office and secretary at his disposal. He thinks he is a very important guy."

The Dean frowned. "The nerve!" But Tom smiled. "No problem, Dean. I told him he could have my office, and that I have no secretary."

"You don't have a secretary, Tom?"

"Dean, when I need someone to write a letter, or do something for me, I just call Elizabeth and ask for one of her people. I find a secretary a bother. I can't stand seeing someone doing nothing, and that is the nature of the job ninety percent of the time."

"How you coming with Dooley? I wish you two would get along. If I may, I would like to offer some constructive criticism. I know Mary McCarthy was an institution at this school, and it was a good idea to interview her, but I would keep a distance from her."

Tom's forehead crinkled at this. He deliberated for about thirty second. "You know Dean, constructive criticism is sometimes worse than the other kind." And Tom headed up to his office.

Elizabeth Hughes ran the library. She kept all the records. She paid the bills. She hired the law students that worked part time in the library.

And she ran the cataloging department. That was what she did before Tom came, and Tom was perfectly willing to let her continue. Tom hired the reference librarians, and he also took over buying the books. That was the one thing he took away from Elizabeth, and she was wise enough to realize that he was better at it than she was. Tom did not consider himself a delegator, but that was in effect what he was doing. And by doing so, Tom had pretty much worked himself into a plush position with a middle income salary that brought him contentment and, if not prestige, a bit of envy to some who watched him in action. What he had to do may have taken one hour a day. And part of that hour, was to walk through the library unannounced. Let the staff know that he was there. By lunch time, Tom had checked through two issues of *Publisher's Weekly*, the latest Oxford University Press catalog, walked through the library, and asked one of his reference librarians to page proof an article he had written for *the Library Journal* on "Mr. Dooley on Law Librarians."

Tom then walked into Elizabeth's office. "Elizabeth, I have some business in Portland. I can catch a train at North Station in half an hour. I should be able to take care of things in half an hour and catch the train back by 3:30."

"Mr. Jones." She stopped. "Tom. Don't rush. We'll take care of things."

If Mary so much as looked distressed at his request, Tom would not have gone. He had learned that Elizabeth expected respect, and he wanted her to know that he relied on her. Having passed the test, he was off to Portland.

The train ride to Portland was a pleasure. Tom had purchased a sandwich at North Station, had the *New York Times* to read, and within four hours was at the bank.

Fortunately Jeb Figgis was in his office and he amiably and anxiously agreed to talk to Tom.

"Miss McCarthy wants me to check her safety deposit box which, she tells me, she leases jointly with Professor Dooley

"Yes, Mr. Jones. And I have pulled out her files and accounts. I will give you all the information that it is legal to give you." With this Figgis turned full face for the first time to Tom Jones. Tom took one look, and let out a squeaky noise.

"Is anything the matter, Mr. Jones?"

Tom hesitated. "Eh, no. I just felt a little pain in my shoulder. Arthritis."

Figgis had no idea that Tom thought that he was looking at an atavar. This face was the striking image of a painting that hung on the wall of Dean Oberon's office. The face of the founder of the law school, Seth Adams. Unmistakable large ears, eyebrows that spanned the depression at the beginning of the nose. The thick upper lip that obscured the space below the nose. This was the face that launched a thousand law students.

It immediately struck Tom that this Mr. Figgis could be Mary's son. That face could only come from the portrait on the Dean's wall.

Tom kept his composure. Made notes. Checked the box and found some securities, and most interesting, a will that left all her property to Dean Dooley. Did Mary know that? There was also a list of properties, deeds, insurance documents, and other material that Tom would not have time to check over at this time. A quick observation made Tom realize that he was dealing with a woman who had assets that were into six figures.

When Tom finished, he thanked Mr. Figgis. The bank was closing at this time and the two strode out together. "Heading back up to Mount Desert, Mr. Jones?" "No, I am heading back to Massachusetts. I have a class tomorrow, and have to get ready for it."

"Can I ask you a question, Mr. Jones?"

"Of course."

"You are a college professor?"

"Well, I have that status, but I am also the law librarian."

"Have you worked for Miss McCarthy long?"

"I wouldn't say I work for her. She is getting on in years and has asked me to make sure her accounts are in good order. Maybe make some recommendations."

"Please don't take this amiss, Mr. Jones. But the bank has to report all deposits over ten thousand dollars."

"Yes, I noticed that. Property rentals have gone sky high in recent years and her caretaker collects them, turns them into Miss McCarthy, and when she gets around to it, she mails them into you. She is a bit tardy but after all she is in her eighties. One of the first things that was obvious to me. We will correct it."

"They have gone sky high. I manage to take a week of my vacation up there. I used to stay in Southwest Harbor. I now stay in Ellsworth, and me and the family go into the Acadia National Park every day from there to do our kayaking, swimming and what not. And she does have prime locations." There was envy and suspicion in Figgis's voice as he said this.

"I'll tell her that," answered Tom thinking the man may have been looking for a good rental deal from his client.

"Well, in case you are not aware, and I assume you are new in this business, this state and the Federal government do quite a lot of investigating people who make large deposits."

Tom laughed. "Miss McCarthy is a pretty old gal. I don't think she has much to worry about."

They stood face to face. Figgis nodded, turned and went his way.

All Tom could think of as he trained home was the striking resemblance between Figgis's face and that painting on the wall of Dean Oberal's office. As he entered his house, there was Janet, her arms folded, sitting at the kitchen table and looking at him with disgust.

"Aren't you ever home, Mr. Jones?"

"You are getting formal, Mrs. Jones."

"I decided to take a day of sick leave. Grampa and my sister have agreed to take care of the kids, and we can go to my class reunion."

"Your class reunion. I'm honored," and then with a bit of sarcasm, "I am sure I am your first choice."

Janet scowled and off they went to The Club. Locals called the Concord Country Club, The Club, as if it was the only golf course in the country. It was a private course, and Tom, a very occasional golfer, had never played there, been there, or even, to his knowledge, knew any of its members. And Tom did not relish the idea of going to a class reunion with his wife as a prime way to spend an evening. And Janet did not disappoint him, She spent the evening introducing him to what seemed like the football team. They kissed, they hugged, and Tom did his best to hide his chagrin at the bar.

As he sat on a stool, he turned when addressed by his neighbor. "You're Janet's husband?"

"Good guess."

"My name is Alfred Higgins. Janet was the editor of the school paper. I was the business manager. Your wife was the best student in the school."

Higgins was about five ten. One hundred fifty pounds. Bespectacled. Prematurely bald. And he was the first person at the function to take an interest in him.

"I'll bet she was voted most popular."

"No. That was Ellen. She's over there wearing that strapless gown that could come off any minute."

"And where is her husband."

"He's sitting on my other side."

"Maybe we should be introduced."

"No, I suspect in about twenty minutes he will work up a rage and grab his wife and carry her into the car. The guy has a nasty temper. I just told him that you were Janet's husband and it made him feel better."

"I gather you are a peace maker."

"No. But I have always wanted to meet you. You married the girl I am in love with."

Tom was about to say something, but Alfred interrupted. "I didn't say I wanted to marry her. Janet has a great mind. Believe it or not, we could talk into the night about things. She wrote great editorials for the paper. Do you know that one of her essays that appeared in the Concord Free Press was reprinted in the *Congressional Record*. And I'm not surprised that she works for *Item*. Quite a gal."

"And you talked into the night."

"Don't get me wrong. That was it – talk."

"Is your wife here."

"No. I am single. I am a traveling salesman. I sell Oshkosh clothing for little tots. And everything you have heard about traveling salesmen is rubbish. I live two streets down from you. The house I live in is even older than your house. Built in the 1840s. My mother is still alive and we have ten rooms for two people."

"Alfred, maybe sometime we can get together and have a cup of coffee at Brigham's."

"I'd like that, Tom." Alfred got off the stool just as Janet came along. She was walking and hugging a big, bald, burly guy who was the only person there not in a suit. He was wearing overalls and looked like he came from work. Janet pushed him ahead of her. "Hi Alfred. You met my husband. And this is Tom Hubbard, Concord's greatest football player." Tom wasn't talking. "Tom, not you, Tom Hubbard, Tom, this man was the fullback on the greatest team in Concord's history. Undefeated all three years. Say something, Tom."

"Hi, Janet, I got to go, my wife is over there and she will get pissed ..."

Janet's face was flushed. Alfred got between Tom Hubbard and Janet. "Janet, you haven't said a word to me all evening. Don't you remember me?"

Janet looked pleasingly at Alfred. "Oh, Alfred," and she hugged him, "you and I were the real lovers."

Alfred wiggled out of her embrace. Tom Hubbard was ambling over to his wife. The situation was diffused. "We were, Janet, we were, and I want you to know that I took the liberty of meeting your husband. You both have my congratulations." And Alfred strode off.

Janet looked at Tom. Tom looked at Janet. And as if by signal, they both said, "Let's go home."

CHAPTER 27

BIRTHRIGHT

"Mary, this is Tom Jones. Do you have a minute?"

"Of course, Tom. I've been waiting to hear from you about the bank. What did you find."

"I don't want to talk over the phone about that. You have given me an important assignment, and to carry it out, it means I have to look at all aspects of it."

"That's what we agreed on, Tom. I want you to clear the air."

"Well, I have run into a snag – no hold on – if I am out of bounds with what I am going to tell you, let me know, but I have to clear this matter up."

"Shoot."

"You said you had a baby. I have checked the birth records of Mount Desert Island for the date you gave me and for a period before and after and there is no record of Mary McCarthy having a baby."

There was a pause.

"Tom, I think I should know if I had a baby."

"No record."

Another pause.

"Is there a record of Dr. Adams delivering a baby?"

"Yes. On the date you gave me he delivered a baby to a Mrs. Figgis."

"That's my baby."

"OK. I thought it strange that the birth certificate was stamped two weeks after the baby was born. I also looked into Mrs. Figgis. She was fifty-two years old when she gave birth."

"Dr. Adams was probably a good doctor, but I would not put anything past him. I think I told you that the baby was a spitting image of Seth. He had no intention of having his Yankee son marry an Irish girl, whose mother, his cleaning woman, he was probably having his way with. Where do you think Seth got his ideas from."

"So he found this woman who wanted a baby and just avoided adoption."

"More than that, Tom. When I had the baby, I was living on Ripple Road in a shack with an outhouse. My father had a pick up truck, and when he was sober, and sometimes when he wasn't, would use it to get food in Southwest Harbor. He would also drive Mom to do her housecleaning. I think I told you she would take me along. He lived on Long Pond. Seth and I used to go skinny dipping there. The doctor had a great camp right on the water. Sailboat. I'll tell you about Seth and me on that sailboat. "

"Where does Figgis come in."

"Probably one of his patients. Mr. and Mrs. Figgis lived outside of Bangor. They had a vegetable stand. No children. My guess is that Adams wanted that baby as far away as possible. This couple must have wanted a child. Adams convinced my Mom that Ripple Road was not a good place to bring up a child, and that he had a nice couple who would take care of him. He took me there and I stayed with them two or three weeks. Then one day, he came to the house and took me back to the shack on Ripple Road. Just like that. I never saw that kid again."

"Oh, my God. I can't believe things like that go on in this country. Mary …"

"Yes."

"Can you take a shock."

"Anything you can hand out."

"Your son is the bank manager handling your account."

No response.

"I did a little checking on him. Nice family. Three children. Right age. Has an accounting degree. And get this, He has his suspicions about you. What is a retired secretary doing accumulating all that money."

"Oh, my God. My kid is going to be my downfall. Tom, I had a feeling about this whole business."

"Mary, I know you well enough not to panic. I have some suggestions and I want to know what you think of them."

"God bless you Tom. I feel better knowing you are on my side. Shoot."

"Call Dooley and tell him you will sign anything he wants."

"What does he want? Let him have everything and get me out of this."

"Mary your fingerprints are on the whole works. Here is my take on the guy. He had no idea that by giving you a camp would do nothing more than put you in the same camp as him, if you will forgive the metaphor."

"The what?"

"Never mind. Suddenly, the guy finds himself churning property. The more he buys, the more equity. The more equity the more he buys."

"Tom, I'm not clear on this. If he uses the equity, doesn't that mean he owes a lot of money. Doesn't he have to pay off these loans to buy more."

"Mary, that is what is called leveraging. Dooley is a pretty smart guy. He can cash in tomorrow and the two of you will end up with a million bucks each. I think this country is in the infancy of a real estate bubble."

"Great. Then we can lose the whole thing and I will feel better."

"Mary, I have a plan – it may only be an intuition but I think we can get out of this without anyone getting hurt and your conscience cleared."

"Please God, I hope so. Tom, you are a Godsend. Do you know I went to church last Sunday."

"Did you go to confession."

"It turned out to be a Protestant Church. The sign said St. something so I thought it was Catholic. Turned out to be Episcopalian."

Tom laughed. "When this is over, Mary, I'll go to church with you. In the meantime, I want your permission to offer your son a week at one of your camps. He loves Mount Desert, and I'd like to get on the good side of him."

"Well, Dooley has asked me to let some of his friends use my camp at 72 Mill Marsh Road in Marshfield for two weeks. I'll tell him he can only have it for one week. Maybe you'll drive me up there and I can get a look at my son." Mary laughed.

"And also your grandchildren."

"And daughter in law."

"Mary, I'm going to sign off now. I feel better about this already but we still have a lot of work to do."

"Tom, you are a doll. For the first time in my life I don't feel like an underdog. If you know what I mean."

Tom dropped the receiver and wiped his brow. He shook his head and said to himself, "If I know what I am doing, nobody will be hurt. In some ways it feels like Magellan all over again."

Tom thought about his one foray into finance. Throughout his library career he made it a habit always to arrive at his place of work early. Go to the cafeteria, get the *New York Times* and a cup of coffee, and relax until it was time to go to work. There would always be a faculty member or two and sometimes a Dean. Tom would sit alone minding his business. Occasionally, the Dean might look his way, and if the spirit moved him would call, "Tom, come on over." Tom made it a point of avoiding making appointments with Deans. You would have some project in mind, but before you could get to it the Dean would have some onerous task for you. In the cafeteria, you sat across as an equal and you would have a chance to sow the seed of an idea in his head and often get results. Tom did not mind if the idea took hold and the Dean forgot it came from him.

On this occasion the Dean was occupied with the business manager for the university, but while Tom was turning the pages of the newspaper, Adjunct Professor Isadore Zaltman plopped his coffee opposite Tom, and asked, "Who are you? You're reading the *Times* so you are not a student. If you were reading the *Herald*, I wouldn't speak to you if you were the President of the University. *The Globe* – I would sit and let you speak first."

"Tom Jones – the law librarian."

"Tom, I've used your library three times in my life. Each time I found what I wanted. I haven't had the same luck with my alma mater's library."

Tom knew that when someone mentioned their college without specifying its name, the person was obviously from Havad. Tom did not ask the name of the college which got a respectful nod from "my name is Zaltman, adjunct professor. Teach taxation every Tuesday morning at nine a.m."

Isadore Zaltman was a respected tax lawyer in Boston. Like many practitioners, he liked the prestige of being connected with a law school. There was a cachet being introduced not just as a lawyer but as a professor. And the average client did not know the difference between the degrees of professorship.

"Did I interrupt your reading?"

"No, professor, when I was young, I read the funnies. No funnies in the *Times*. Now, I look at the headlines, then turn to the Arts section, and you caught me checking the business pages."

"I get the *Times,* but I have to admit *The Wall Street Journal* and *Barron's* take up more of my time. Holmes once said taxes are the price we pay for civilization, and I say civilization is at risk. It's good for tax lawyers, but it is so full of loopholes, exemptions, earmarks by lobbyists, that it no longer has a valid philosophy."

"I can understand why you practice it, but why do you teach it?"

'Memory. It is good for the memory. At my age, memorizing things keeps the mind young. My class sounds like we are telling jokes by the numbers, or a quarterback giving signals. All I have to say is Chapter 11, and I can eat up an hour with student recitation." Tom laughed. "Can I ask you a tax question?"

"Shoot."

"There is an article here that says if you put $2000.00 in a mutual fund, there is a tax break of some kind. Why?"

"Tom, you are on to something. That is true. The government is trying to get the American public to save money. If we spend, spend, spend, and don't put money into savings accounts of some kind, the nation will go bankrupt. It happens to be the only sensible provision in the tax code."

"So, you are telling me to invest 2000 dollars. Can I lose it?"

"Of course you can lose it, but risk is good for your health. If the fund goes up, it's good for your adrenalin. If it goes down, same thing."

Tom asked, "Where do you put your money?

Zaltman answered, "I never tell people where I put my money, but I don't think you can go wrong with Magellan."

"Magellan? I don't know Magellan from Vasco de Gama. What is Magellan?"

"It is a fund run by a guy named Lynch, you are looking at an ad for Fidelity that runs the fund right now."

And Tom looked and started putting 2000 dollars in the fund each year and taking the tax advantage. And he suggested it to Janet, and she did the same.

Tom now had a decent nest egg for his retirement, and that coupled with his retirement account and Social Security should provide him with a cushion for his old age. It did not resemble what Dooley had done for Mary McCarthy, but Tom felt very smug about his decision to invest in Magellan, and his desire to help Mary out of her not so bad predicament.

CHAPTER 28

LIBRARY CHAPTER

Fifty Dixwell Street was a one hundred fifty year old structure. It had three floors, the third with walls slanted to accommodate a Mansard roof. The house still had a Franklin stove that heated, if inadequately, the first floor. The former coal burning stove in the cellar had been converted to oil, and worked on the principle of forced heat to take care of the second floor, and keep the third floor occupants from freezing to death.

The third floor was Tom's refuge. Except in the extremes of weather, he found it ideal for writing, thinking, reading, and meditating. The three rooms it contained each had a different purpose. One was for his library, one was for his writing, and the third contained a couch, which he used for meditating, and when he and Janet were on the outs. It was also a refuge when Grandpa Wright went on a talking rampage. He had a habit of only hesitating in the middle of a sentence, so that getting in a word edge-wise, always appeared impertinent. An ardent despiser of F.D.R., he not only spoke endlessly of the attributes of Alf Landon, Thomas Dewey, and Wendell Willkie but wrote them letters as to how they should run their campaigns. He once refused to drive his wife to vote unless she swore she would support the Republican candidate. Age had withered his activism but not his penchant for incessant philosophizing about the Republican way of life. Only when Tom's marriage was wavering did Tom decide that he could leave grandpa midsentence and head to the third floor.

And Tom was meditating. Writing two histories of the law school posed some problems. On the one hand, he was not going to do a cut-and-paste job. It would be an accurate history of Essex that rose from an idea in Seth Adams' head to a law school that filled a need in the community. The Jekyll side would commemorate his fight against the established order of the ivy league law schools, but it would not indulge in outlandish claims. It would be tempered, factual, and prophetic. On the other hand, his Hyde analysis would not only show the warts, pimples, cancers of Essex but also of law schools in general. One would end up in the mail to thousands of alumni, faculty members, donors, other law schools, high school advisors to students contemplating law school; the other would rest unseen in his study, and in Tom's Gray's vision, like a flower in a hidden bower, born to blush unseen. and waste its fragrance on the desert air.

So Tom meditated on his project. What factors go into a history of a law school. The caliber of its faculty past and present. Did the graduates tend to go into corporate law or public service? How many actually practiced law? How many graduates were Judges? Senators? Governors? Were any employed as clerks to the United States Supreme Court?

And then there was the issue of books. Libraries loved to claim how many books they had. He remembered Professor Powell of Havad Law, when asked whether Havad was the largest law library in the world replied, "I am sure it must be because it is the only library where three hundred thousand books can be lost at the same time." Tom knew of one law library that bought multiple sets of the National Reporter System to bulk up its count. And Tom, himself, when told by the Dean that he would like to say the library has 200,000 volumes, immediately spent $50,000 on microfiche that qualified for that count despite only occupying two file cabinets.

Tom had already been on three inspection trips to law schools that the American Bar Association and the Association of American Law Schools sponsored to check on the caliber of law schools. These trips were like the trips of royalty during medieval times. First the Dean of the inspected school made sure the inspection committee was properly wined and dined at the best hostelries in the city. He knew of one professor who was often on an inspection teams and would not consider an inspection unless it included tickets to sporting events. There was also constant bickering as to what constituted a satisfactory inspection.

Internecine warfare would break out on the faculty of the inspected school. What should be the minimum LSAT score for admittance. Faculty size and salary. Physical plant. Esoteric courses. More clinics. Dooley would go into a tantrum when these standards were discussed. "By God, all this has to do with upping the cost of a legal education. All the ivies are trying to do is make us go bankrupt. They have the money because of their endowment. They do it because they are subservient to their rich law students and alumni."

A particular rivalry existed among teachers who taught introductory law courses. Probably more articles have been written, and more syllabi drawn, in teaching this course than any other law course. At Cahn, one professor threw philosophy and jurisprudence at his first year students, wrote an article about The New Law Student, and then abandoned the course to others. In short order the school went back to having the students write a brief and compete in oral arguments. In the meantime, other schools would follow suit The end results were always the same. The smart kids came out on top, the average kids were in the middle, and those that bore the stigma of "passers" passed. The only difference to legal education was that Havad made sure that other schools felt the same pain, cost, and inefficiency that they did or their tuition would be out of proportion to non ivy league schools.

The most notorious and outspoken objector to these standards was the Dean of Essex. He ignored their fanciful courses. He railed against the case system, and against any authority telling him what the ratio of faculty to student should be. He conceded that Havad had great teachers. He agreed they wrote the essential treatises. But when it came to teaching, where were they? Their assistants, or neophyte faculty members, did most of the teaching. That was not the way it would be at Essex. He was particularly wrathful about book counts. He scoffed at schools that boasted the ratio of books to students. Essex, he claimed, was a block away from the State Law Library, it was a block away from the Boston Athenaeum, it was a block away from the Social Law Library. What idiot would downgrade Essex because it did not duplicate collections within its grasp. "Why gild the lily," he would roar at meetings discussing standards.

And then there was the requirement that professors should not have full time jobs, in effect, should not have a practice. This was insane to the Dean. His faculty could practice all they wanted as long as it did not interfere with their teaching He kept to himself the belief that a good many law professors were teaching because they couldn't make a living practicing.

It was sort of the opposite of the old adage that those who can't, teach. As for the requirement that law students not hold full time jobs, he gave that lip service. Tom had read all about this battle between the Dean and the higher authorities. And while his sympathies, in this regard, were with the Dean, he knew that the Dean had lost the battle.

Anathema was the word he used for exotic courses such as Law and Literature, Seminar on the First Amendment, States' Rights vs Federalism. To Seth Adams, law was contracts, torts, civil procedure, equity, constitutional law, agency, and a few other topics that he had turned into black letter hornbooks that his students had to buy. "Elective courses," he would shout, "what a euphemism." Intellectual subjects were something that you get in college or on your own. The great announcements on the rights of man did not come from law schools but from Henry David Thoreau and Thomas Paine and Nat Hentoff and Anthony Lewis and Stanley Fish. The teaching of jurisprudence was an impediment to passing the bar and an unneeded luxury for the lower and even middle class students who came to Essex. Adams remembered one of his law teachers expounding that a student would be better prepared for any legal problem in law if he spent his three years just studying contract law. The concept of consideration as an element of contract could take a whole semester.

Seth Adams not only lost the battle but he was ousted. The school that he had invented, nurtured, and had achieved some recognition in the community dropped him ceremoniously. By law, Essex was now required to have a Board of Trustees and all the accoutrements of other colleges. The law school faculty was able to exert pressure on the Board to force the Dean to seek acceptance by the American Bar Association. There was now a development office bringing chaos into order in the billing procedures of the law school. Not only did Adams find himself ousted as Dean but an accounting of his procedures was undertaken and he was asked to reimburse the school for over one million dollars. Seth Adams, disgraced and disgruntled, successfully fought the suit and retired to the Cape where he became a successful cranberry harvester. A sad note occurred, when in his nineties, Adams was sued in court in a paternity case by one of his employees. When Tom informed Mary of this, her terse comment was, "If it wasn't for me that poor guy would have spent his life in jail."

During the forties, and after World War II had ceased, the law school realized there was money to be made from the GI Bill, which opened up education to all GIs. This influx of college students would become fodder for the law school. The school petitioned for college status, it was granted, and GIs flocked in. GIs applied in record numbers all over the United States that would profoundly effect the direction of the country. Every excuse for a college sprang into existence, and every excuse for putting up college buildings and educational extravagance came with it. GI's tuition was paid for, their books were paid for and they pocketed $75.00 a month if they were single, more if they were married. The colleges made money, the students were double dipping between their classes and business opportunities. Tom was astounded at how many GIs received their bachelor degrees at Essex, flunked out of law school after their first year, and had jobs at the post office, banking institutions, and investment houses.

Every year when the first year law class filed into the auditorium to be congratulated on its achievement of being accepted at Essex Law School, Tom would wince. The Dean would roll out the statistics. "You, first year students," he would announce, "are the select. This year we received 7000 applications and we are proud to say that of that number, you, all 470 of you, are that select group and we promise to provide you with an education that will turn you into the ablest lawyers in this Commonwealth." Then the head of Placement would talk, then the President of the student class, and so on. But it was Associate Dean Dooley who would outdo them all by repeating a mantra probably used in many law schools. "I want you to look to your right," he would say usually pointing to the left when he should be pointing to the right, "and I want you to look to your left. You will not see one of those faces at graduation time. I hope I am wrong, but we have a rigorous program here and our professors are like drill sergeants in the Marines. You will be subjected to the best training in law that you can get but you must be prepared for the rigors of a legal obstacle course. I wish you well." And Dooley may have believed what he was saying as he was aware that the man that delivered mail to the law school, used to be one of his students.

Of course, Tom knew that the big lie was that law was an obstacle course. He remembered one of his teachers telling him that the only requirement for getting through law school was a cast iron bottom. Tom taught an introductory course at Cahn. Students were initially totally bewildered by such terms as "*certiorari*," "precedent," "*stare decisis*," "*decree nisi*," .and it was hard for them to adjust to Socratic teaching methods.

By the end of the first year, except for "passers," it was just more of the same. Tom was required to provide students with an issue and then pair off the class to argue that issue. They had to write briefs and then argue the case before him as if he were a judge. One student came to Tom and took exception to his side of the issue. He could not in good conscience argue that side. Tom dismissed him with the caveat that if he did not argue it he would flunk the course. When the student appeared before him, he looked at him sternly and remarked, "Counsel, I believe you came before me in chambers and argued that you could not in good conscience represent your client in this appeal." The student broadened his shoulders, looked righteously at Tom and said, "No, your, honor, as I am about to argue, I have the law and cases on my side." On another occasion, a student passed out as he was arguing his case. Someone brought him some water and he was revived and, as he was about to continue, opposing counsel suggested that he had used up his time. Tom once concluded his course with the observation, "When you first came into class I had the idea that you thought I knew everything, now that the semester is over, you now think you know everything." The round of applause he received, made it worth the semester's effort.

When Tom came to Essex and the Dean asked him what courses he would like to teach, Tom indicated that he would have enough to do running the library. The last thing he wanted to do was teach an introductory course. But teaching does get into your blood, and Tom, once he felt secure in his job, ventured to ask the Dean to teach a course in Law and Literature. In Seth Adams' time, he would probably have been fired for asking, but Essex had joined the fraternity and now had a curriculum that looked like most other schools. Tom gave assignments and lectures on Dickens, Trollope, Whitman, Rattigan, Benet and others. Shakespeare's *Measure for Measure* was acted out in class, fiction about the law, poetry about the law, and even assignments as to how judges used literature in their opinions. One member of the faculty asked to audit the course, and submitted a novel he had written as his writing assignment. Tom gave it a C and lost a colleague. But the exchanges with students were far more interesting than in his introductory law course. One student came to Tom and wanted to write about Essex and had a few questions to ask. Tom invited him to the cafeteria for a cup of coffee where they could discuss his paper.

"I'd like to know how Essex got its name? For one thing it is not in Essex County."

"I've looked into that myself, John. There are various stories. One is that because we are in Suffolk County, to call the school Suffolk we would be confused with a hundred other entities called Suffolk. You may have noticed that there is a construction company called "Suffolk Construction." There are a dozen buildings under construction by that company and they put up a big sign with only the word "Suffolk" on it. Too confusing. Another theory is that the founder of this school was a Yankee. He wanted a name that resounded English history. Essex is a venerable name in English lore, and there is no trademark law that would deny its use in Suffolk County."

But John had a coy look on his face. "Did it have anything to do with sex being a part of the name?"

Tom deliberated. Stories about the Dean, the Associate Dean, and stories Tom was not aware of proliferated at the school. The influx of female students certainly contributed to the proliferation and the Associate Dean was not called "The Silver Hedgehog" because he was in the fur business. "Where did you go to college, John."

"Duke."

"Duke, my friend, was founded by a gentleman who made his fortune in tobacco. That man probably is responsible for more deaths than occurred in the Civil War. Take Rockefeller University. Mr. Rockefeller bankrupted companies, despoiled our land, and his encouragement to use oil may yet cause enough global warming to destroy human life. Jefferson founded the University of Virginia and you and I know that slaves probably hid their daughters when he made the rounds of his plantation. Mr. Brown was in the slavery and molasses business. And Leland Stanford was in railroads and he was probably a robber baron. John Havad …"

"Enough," shouted John, "Do I have your permission to pick out another topic?"

CHAPTER 29

MARSHFIELD

As Tom looked deeper into the land acquisitions of Mary McCarthy, he could only shake his head at the acumen of Associate Dean Dooley. That little piece of land at 72 Mill Marsh Road had spawned an empire. Dooley squeezed the equity out of it to purchase most of the cove. Backed by the deep well of tuition money pouring into Essex, he had no fear of failure. It was a gamble on a giant scale that was still paying off. Tom could even trace the down payment on Dooley's house on the Cape to the original investment, and that house was now assessed at close to a million dollars.

But Tom knew a few things that Dooley did not know. Dooley knew nothing about Maine. His obvious interest in getting the camp for Mary was to keep her quiet. She was smart enough to know that she was an accessory and the consequences of her talking could incriminate her as well as Dooley. And, after all, what harm was done? It is not as if Dooley was stealing money. Seth Adams paid his faculty the lowest wages in the country. Seth, himself, originated the idea of using the money, and not just for lunch. It was very easy for Dooley to justify his actions, and he even felt that he had done a good turn by getting Mary that little plot of land so that she could return home when she retired (and be where she could do no harm).

Dooley had no idea that Mount Desert Island was the main home of the Acadia National Park. He had no idea the Rockefellers lived there, had a great deal to do with creating the carriage roads that made it a national treasure, that it was a playground for the rich, and, with the advent of the automobile and a concourse to the island, becoming a playground for anyone that loved hiking, bicycling, swimming, mountain climbing, all sports that were foreign to the South Boston boy Dooley.

And he did not know what Tom discovered as he went over deeds and land purchases at the registry. Mary's cove was in Marshfield, the least developed part of the island. Marshfield had no stores, no Main Street; it was all birch trees and pine trees, and water. Water, water, everywhere. It was fifteen minutes by car to Somesville, where one country store with a gas station served the community. There was the post office where most people came to pick up their mail, say hello to their friends, or eye the new renters. Marshfield was as close as you could get to the feel of what this country once looked like.

But how long would it last? Was Marshfield to go the way of Bar Harbor? Bar Harbor was tourist country. It wasn't the Hamptons or Provincetown, but during July and particularly August the streets could overflow with tourists. The two main streets, Cottage and Main, were lined with stores selling T shirts, local products, and, of course, lobster dinners. The parking lot at the pier was usually crowded with cars bearing license plates that could be from all fifty states. Liners would anchor in the harbor for a day and discharge their cargo of sightseers. The newspapers would report what current celebrity had bought a cottage (not a mere camp) on the island, and had a yacht anchored at Northeast Harbor. Bar Harbor did not look gaudy, but there were local people in Marshfield who had never been to Bar Harbor.

But Tom had made a few discoveries. For one, an investment tycoon named Svenson had been buying up property in Marshfield, particularly in the area that led to Bosc Landing. If he were buying shore front property, Tom would not have paid any attention to the purchase. But he was buying property that led up to shorefront property. And, as Tom had noticed, as he drove the seven tenth of a mile path that led to Mary's camp, he had been clearing the area. Where once had been fallen trees, and thick growth, was now a pleasing view of well-placed healthy trees (the others had been cut down and chopped into mulch). A silken moss was growing in areas, and rock masses now showed up that were pleasing to the eye. Tom remembered visiting the Rockefeller Gardens that rivaled Versailles in its beauty, and how the winding path to its entrance resembled something out of a fable – a Brigadoon - with its stately trees and rug of moss.

Marshfield had an organization that met in a little house on a side road. It held pot-luck meetings during the summer, and Tom, who was now checking Mary's mail, noticed that she had an invitation. Tom suggested that they go to the meeting, but Mary felt she was now an outsider living in a retirement home just outside of Bar Harbor. She was only an absentee landlady, but she didn't mind if Tom went. It turned out to be a wonderful meeting. Tom went to the market in Southwest Harbor and bought cold cuts as his pot-luck contribution, but was put to shame by the lasagna, lobster stew, crab rolls and other home concocted foods brought to the meeting. There were people there who had spent their lives in Marshfield. There was also a matronly lady, who Tom was sure was a Rockefeller or something similar. He learned a bit of the history of the area, and that Mill Marsh Road once contained a mill. Mr. Svenson was also there.

And there were people there, Maine people, who didn't care if Mr. Svenson was the second coming. He was grilled. Svenson lived on a road just off Bosc Landing. The road led to a point where his large but not grandiose cottage faced Bosc Island. It had a pier and you could see from the sail boats and other craft at the pier, that the Svensons took advantage of their wealth and love of the sea. His answer to those questioning him was direct and sounded sincere. He loved Marshfield and he farmed the forest land so that the trees could breathe. He also made money selling the trees that he cut down. He was a tax paying resident of the island, he and his family were more than just summer residents, and one more thing. He employed a number of local people to work on his property, and working the land made it possible for him to employ them year round. It was a very convincing talk, particularly the last part, as four young locals in the group sported "Svenson & Co, The Trust Company You Trust" red shirts with white lettering.

And then there was Bosc Island. This island could be seen from Mary's camp. It could also be seen from the pier at Bosc Landing which was about a mile from where Mary's path led to the road and off to the right. The island was owned by the descendants of J. P. Pebblepal, the railroad tycoon of robber baron days. The family was now into banking but kept a low profile. Tom had once dined with Mary at a gourmet restaurant in

Seal Harbor, a sanctuary for the vieux riche that had only six tables. While Tom was dining, a gentleman came in with four other people. The maitre d', also the owner, rushed to put a table together for the group. David Pebblepal walked by their table, and introduced himself, shook Tom's hand, A conversation began and continued until the group was ready to be seated, and then Mr. Pebblepal excused himself and joined his company.

Bosc Island was basically inhabited by one person. Miss Pebblepal, an elderly woman who was spending her senior years breeding cattle. Whether it was for a better kind of beef, or for religious purposes, no one really knew and no one was going to find out because she passed away shortly after Tom became familiar with Mount Desert. Except for the breeding area, Bosc Island was the forest primeval. From Mary's camp it was a perfect green, and when the sunset became a deep red, it created a picture that Van Gogh would have given his other ear for.

Mary would make her camp available to Tom when he came up to see her. Ordinarily Mary would rent her camps for fees which Tom thought outrageous, but she knew Tom had developed a special love for the area so she kept 72 Mill Marsh Road open for his visits and had the caretaker keep it supplied with wood for the fireplace, well water running, and all the basic necessities of life. Even in the hottest days of the summer, Tom found he had to make a fire in the morning or he would have to bury himself in blankets, turn on the electric heaters, and even the stove. It gave him the feeling of a pioneer without the risks. Tom loved walking down the path to the road, and then to Bosc Landing, but he carried a heavy stick despite assurances that his life was not in danger from bear, deer, moose, fox, hare and other forest animals. He was once frightened when he accidentally hit a bush with his stick and a pheasant almost flew into his face. He would walk out on the pier and gaze out at the lobster boats and other craft in the water. A very busy industry was kayakers. Tourists and kayak carriers would drive to the pier. The leader would give the tourists instructions on paddling and off they would go. Tom noticed that they would paddle the length of Bosc Island, right by Mary's camp, and to another cove where they would be picked up and driven to the home base. What an experience to tell your neighbors. Tom's children were testimony to its value. He also noticed that the "Beau Island" motor boat limited its trips from the pier to Bosc Island. The skipper was a friendly person and told him the family doesn't use the island as much since Miss Pebblepal passed away, but that the family kept him busy with one thing or another. All Tom could think of was the thought that in his day and age there were people who owned islands big enough to establish a town.

A person cannot be thrust into other people's lives that make their own pedestrian and drab, and not have dreams. Mr. Svenson, Mr. Pebblepal, Associate Dean Dooley, Mary McCarthy. They were just people. Nothing really special about them. And here they were making real castles, if not in Spain, then in a far more hospitable place called Mt. Desert Island. It struck Tom that if you went north to Calais, you would not be impressed. If you went south to Portland, all you found was a pleasant, but pedestrian, city. But Mt. Desert was magic. People who came here had to leave their mark. On Northeast Harbor a simple walk up a stairway with a landing that gave you a view of the Harbor, and you would find a plaque to Gordon H. Felt. The Rockefellers are given credit for the magnificent carriage roads that are a paradise to walkers and bikers. Jordan Pond, with its gorgeous view of the twin mountains and its restaurant that featured popovers and strawberry jam had pictures of its founders. On and on it went. And what was going to be Tom Jones' contribution to this island's legend. Tom punned to himself: "That remains to be scene."

CHAPTER 30

DIVORCE

It was Sunday morning, and Tom was awakened by a tingling in the sole of his foot. There was Janet, in her nightgown, smiling at him.

"Wake up lazy bones. That bike ride you went on yesterday must have worn you out."

Tom stretched, rubbed his eyes to make sure that it was Janet. "As a matter of fact it did. I must be getting old."

Janet snickered. "I saw you off with our neighbor, the gay divorcee, yesterday. With those big boobs, it's a wonder she don't roll over going down hill. Riding your bikes into the sunset?" She smiled suggestively.

"We belong to a bicycle club, Janet. We bike to the Sleepy Hollow Cemetery. About twenty of us. Then we were transported to the Cape and we rode the bike route to Provincetown. I can get you in the club."

"No thank you. Got home very late, I imagine she invited you in for coffee," Janet suggested. "On the other hand, she may be a little too old for you."

Tom shrugged. "Ben Franklin recommended older women, you know. No, she didn't invite me in for coffee, but we all had a lovely time. No scandal."

"Nothing like that catalog girl you got tangled up with?"

Tom was indignant. "Nothing happened there either."

"Well, I am going to find out." Janet peeled off her nightgown and snuggled up to Tom. Tom acted helpless as she removed his bottom pajama, and after an inspection tour that satisfied her, straddled Tom until they were both satisfied. She then rolled over on the bed. Looked around and then sniffed, "I wish you smoked."

"Janet, no salmon smokes better than you do." Neither laughed. Tom put his pajama bottom on, went down to Janet's room, and brought her a pack of cigarettes. They both lighted up.

"So how are things with you and that women you are seeing in Mt. Desert."

"Janet, you can't believe what is going on there. I am on Mary McCarthy's payroll. She really needs someone and I intend to help her."

"She was a secretary, wasn't she? And you are her knight in shining armor. I think you are up to your old trick of saving a girl in peril," and Janet added mischievously, "Like me."

"There is that, Janet. There is that. But I think there is something else, and I'd like to make you a part of it. Interested?"

Janet lit another cigarette, and listened.

"Mary is worth over a million dollars. She is in her eighties and wants to give it all away and for good reason."

"She's put you in her will and you want me to find a hit man."

"Janet, please be serious. Without going into sordid details, Mary made her money in real estate. Mountains of money. Mount Desert is Treasure Island."

"Yes,"

"Well, I'd like to buy some real estate. Property values there are going up every year. I could find some good property. We make a down payment. In a few years, we have equity, and with that we buy more property. In no time, we could be in Mary's camp, literally and figuratively."

"Where do I come in."

"Janet, you work for *Item*. Remember when I asked you to invest in Magellan. We are doing very well with that. But Magellan is small potatoes to what I am suggesting."

"And?"

"Janet, you make more money than I do. And if I must say so, you contribute nothing to the upkeep of this house. I pay the rent, the taxes, take care of the kids, etc."

"Tom, all you had to do was ask."

"Well, I am asking. I found some nice properties in Bass Harbor. Where Mary is is all taken up. I have about ten thousand. If you can come up with twenty, you will be a two-thirds partner and we will both make out like bandits. With a decent down payment of thirty thousand, I have my eye on what could be a bonanza. While I am taking care of Mary's financial problems, I can be taking care of ours. What do you say."

"Tom," and Janet looked very serious, "I have been spending money very foolishly lately. If you must know, I have fallen in love with a great guy. He's an actor. He has a great role in a remake of "A Streetcar Called Desire," you know the guy who thinks he's in love with Stella's nutcase sister."

"Does falling in love have anything to do with spending money?"

"Well,. I have moved to a nice apartment in Greenwich Village. And I'm in with an interesting crowd. Etc., etc., etc."

"And you are here in my bedroom, and he is there. What are you doing here?"

"He wants to marry me."

Tom said nothing.

"I came here to ask you for a divorce."

Tom had been lying down in the bed. But he got up and sat beside Janet. "Janet, you turned me down, but let me be the first to congratulate the two of you. Would you like me to dig up those papers for the Dominican Republic?"

"No hurry, Tom. I just want you to know that you deserved better than me. I know that I am a lousy wife, and not much of a mother. I hate housework. I hate cooking. Tom, if this *Item* job didn't come up, I assure you, I'd be in the loony bin by now." Janet dabbed her eyes with the bed sheet. "I want the best for you, Tom. I want you to find the right kind of gal, and I'm doing this as much for you as for me. As for the real estate deal, right now is a bad time."

"I understand Janet. You know I think you wore me out. If you don't mind I think I'll try and get a couple hours more sleep."

They kissed, and Janet put on her night gown and went downstairs. Tom shook his head. All he could think of was that girl Fantine and how she came to ruin because of her illegitimate child. The cruelty of men who leave women in distress. Did Victor Hugo ever think of the guys who marry the girls that get pregnant?

Tom slept soundly but the summer sun's rays reached into his attic room and woke him. He dressed and found Janet sitting at the breakfast table, and her father at the stove cooking breakfast. Fred had put a batch of fatty bacon in a cast iron frying pan, and when the gas heat had melted that bacon into a soup, he cracked open some eggs and dropped them into the pan. On this morning, Fred had his usual three day beard. Summer and winter, he wore a flannel shirt, and there was a gusset in the old pair of pants that he had on which he had probably made himself to accommodate his increasing girth. The heel off an old pair of shoes had been cut out to perform the duty of slippers.

"I'll make you a batch, son," said Fred as he split the concoction with his daughter. He then poured coffee into cups. The coffee was made by pouring ground coffee into boiling water. Fred cooked as if he was on a camping trip.

"No thanks, Dad. I feel like some cold cereal and milk."

Janet ate quickly. A horn beeped. Janet jumped up. "It's Beverly. See ya." Tom noticed that it was Beverly Brooks and that two men were also in the car.

Fred looked at Tom. "You should take better care of that girl."

"She wants a divorce, Mr. Wright. She told me this morning."

"Is that what I heard thumping on my ceiling this morning."

Tom laughed, then got serious, and decided to change the subject.

"Mr. Wright. What did you pay for this house?"

"This house was built by my Dad around 1850. Do you know I had trouble paying the sixty dollars a month in principal and interest when I fixed it up around 1950?"

"I'll bet you could get – I don't know – twenty times that today," and then Tom had an inspiration, "you could probably get a home equity loan – I don't know – maybe thirty forty thousand."

"What would I do with it."

"Fix the house up, invest it – I don't know."

Fred was now pouring himself another cup of coffee, grinds and all. He looked quizzically at Tom. "Tom, why are you burdening yourself with this house. And what do you know about this home equity stuff. When I retired, God knows when, I was in charge of the estate division of the Merchants National Bank. You're a librarian."

"You are right, gramps. All I am is a librarian that is getting divorced from your daughter." And Tom left the kitchen without his cereal, and his dreams of avarice joined the stench of burning lard, overcooked bacon, stale cigarette smoke, and coffee grinds.

CHAPTER 31

FOR THE LOVE OF MAINE

Tom began spending every weekend possible at Mary's camp. Mary kept her camp open until October. Tom would either drive up, fly to Bar Harbor Airport, or fly to Bangor and rent a car and drive the 20 miles to Ellsworth and the twenty more to the camp in Marshfield. He would take the kids, if they wanted to go, and they would drive up Cadillac Mountain to watch the sunset, climb Beach Mountain, swim at Echo Lake. Sometimes he would arrange for the caretaker to take them to Sands Beach in the Acadia National Park or they would ride to the fire road and swim in Long Pond.

Tom would park himself on the recliner on the deck to the camp and ponder his future. His dreams of avarice were shattered. Janet would divorce him and that would end his last hope. At one point, he thought that his father in law could be the solution. The guy was 84 years old, substantially overweight, smoked at least a pack a day, and was advised by Dr. Piper that if he was working in the garden and suddenly felt short of breath, to lean against a tree and take a nitroglycerin pill. Obviously the old guy had angina. If he passed away the house would pass to Janet and her sister. They would make a deal with the sister, and he and Janet could own the house as tenants in the entirety and then he could work with the equity in the house to buy property. But that dream was shattered with news of the impending divorce which he would not contest.

Tom's children were just as anxious as he was to get to Marshfield. They were now big enough to get on their bikes, plow down the path to the road, ride the seven miles to Somesville, or another five miles to Southwest Harbor, or even make a day of it and head to Bar Harbor. When the Island introduced the Explorer, a free bus that would take you to the major terminals on the island, including your bike, it expanded their horizon to Jordan Pond, Eagle Lake, and inlets and outlets that Tom had no knowledge of. They had met the children from the other camps and they would report to Tom on their schedule for the day. Tom marveled at how well-behaved his children were. They seemed to ignore the friction between their parents, because, in fact, their parents didn't fight or argue. At one point, Janet was angry with him because of something they repeated to her that was derogatory about her. "I don't say anything bad about you, and I expect the same courtesy from you." Tom was numb as she spoke, and that was the end of it. Although Tom didn't know what could be bad about himself, he thought he had learned a good lesson.

The leisure of not having a wife to entertain, and children to play with, provided Tom with much time on the deck of Mary's camp. It made him think about all the things he could be doing in Maine. He took out books at the local libraries. He read about living in the woods in *A Place Called Maine* where people spend the entire year in interior Maine, enduring the bitter cold, living in a winter house in winter, and a summer house in summer. There was even something romantic about going to an outhouse at three o'clock in the morning in a driving snowstorm with maybe a moose in your path. These pioneers would fish the lake, act as guides for hunters and fishers, cut wood for winter, harvest blueberries in summer and write about it as if they had achieved nirvana, or at least were not bothered by neighbors or visitors. Then he would read about sailing. How navigating from Newport to Monhegan Island could be a perilous journey. He daydreamed about the *Caine Mutiny* and saw himself testifying against Captain Queeg at the Court Martial; he knew his dad served aboard the U.S.S. Bangust which was caught in a typhoon in the Pacific which saw three destroyers in his task group sink in the storm; he remembered *Mutiny on the Bounty* and wryly decided that Captain Bligh would address him as "Mr. Jewish." He would read about E.B. White and his fishing experiences. He would learn about lobster boats, and worming, and turn the pages on picture books about the Wyeths and other painters that tried unsuccessfully, in his opinion, to imitate nature. Tom had been to Ogunquit and Booth Bay, and once visited a friend in Calais, but Mount Desert came to mean to him the ultimate experience in beauty and preservation. Beauty preserved in such a way that this island at once mimicked the origins of the planet and man's ingenuity with nature. Only a Mainer like Longfellow could have written "This is the forest primeval." Except for a few streets in Bar Harbor, every road on Mount Desert led to forests, lakes, and miniature mountains. Every experience, in Tom's stay here had to do with the origin of life. Tom had climbed Beech Mountain and witnessed with sheer joy the panorama of looking down on Southwest Harbor from that elevation. But he preferred reading about those that climbed Mt. Cadillac or the Beehive. He decided that his idea of roughing it was making a fire to ward off the chill of the cold Maine mornings despite the fact that the afternoon would bring temperatures in the eighties, or a walk to Bosc Landing, or a ride to Seal Cove, or take the kids to Wonderland or the Sea Wall, or just reading about it.

"Heh, Dad, wake up, we're back." It was Janice breathless from their trip to Jordan Pond. "Dad," threw in Jack, "I brought you back a popover with strawberry jam. Delicious." Tom looked up at his children and then spotted his caretaker, and then he blinked at the two other people on the deck with his children.

"What are you two doing here?" It was Vivian Gefelche and Shem Willkins.

Vivian spoke first. "You kept telling us about the biking up here and Shem and I decided to give it a whirl."

"We biked Eagle Lake to Jordan Pond, and saw your kids."

"Yuh, Dad," added Jack, "we biked to the Village Green in Bar Harbor and took the Explorer to Jordan Pond. You said we could."

"And Vivian recognized the kids and we decided to surprise you and we all took the Explorer to Somesville and bicycled here," added Shem.

Tom blinked his eyes. "I'm ashamed of myself. I just love sitting on this deck and watching the kayaks glide by, or a sailboat sweep into the cove."

Vivian eyed Tom mischievously, "I suppose you do it in your sleep. Look, we just thought we'd drop by and say hello."

"And we also wanted to see what you are up to. This camp is unbelievable. When Jack opened the door – do you know your front door is really your back door – and I saw water, sky, trees, and then you – Tom, you were holding out on us. You wake up to this every morning?"

Tom was now awake. "No, no. You two are going to stay here tonight. I have bunk beds, and the study has a couch that opens up so that the kids can sleep in. We can check the refrigerator and dig up some supper."

"Can't," said Shem. "I'm staying with friends."

"And I'm at the Kimball Terrace. But let's have dinner at the Terrace. You and the kids."

"Great idea, Put your bikes on the back of my Camry and off we go. Let me just wash my face. God, I'm glad to see my biking buddies."

Janice and Jack looked morose at all this and Tom said, "What's up."

"The Pattersons have invited us to a pajama party at their house and all of us to dinner."

"Well, what if I call them and excuse myself and you go with your friends and I will go with mine?"

The two jumped with joy. The call was made. They packed their pajamas and skipped through the woods to the Patterson camp next door.

They loaded the bikes onto Tom's car and Vivian jumped in the front seat as Tom started up the car. Shem was in back and they drove to Kimball Terrace.

"All alone out here, Tom?"

"Well, I think I told you that I am trying to help out an elderly woman that has a problem with the property you found me asleep in. It means going over her accounts for the past forty years or so, driving from here to her bank in Portland, meeting with her at her retirement home, and ..."

"Sleeping in her camp. I'd love to have that problem."

"Vivian, what may not look like a problem to you, to someone else borders on the tragic. This woman needs my help, and I think I can help her."

Vivian put her hand on Tom's wrist, "I'm sure you will, Tom. I know if I had a problem I would entrust it to you in a minute. By the way, is your wife here?"

"No, Vivian. Janet is not a happy camper. She also has a habit of lighting a cigarette and tossing the match away as if she was in a bar. The island has had one fire too many already. She has asked me for a divorce," also escaped from Tom's lips.

Vivian eyes widened noticeably. "Tom, this could be the beginning of a beautiful friendship."

Tom then took charge. He took the scenic route to Northeast Harbor down Sargent Drive which Vivien exclaimed was more beautiful than the

Amalfi Drive in Italy. They dropped Shem off at the Kimball Terrace and proceeded to Abel's where they had their lobster al fresco facing Somes Sound with a full moon overhead.

That night Vivian returned with Tom to the camp and spent the night. Early the next morning Tom drove her to Kimball Terrace where they had breakfast with the bicycle group Vivian had come up with. And Tom drove home to his camp to prepare to go back to Essex the next morning where he had agreed to substitute for a faculty member and conduct a class in Professional Responsibility.

CHAPTER 32

CLASS ACTION

To Tom Jones, Jr.

From the Office of David Furness

The following stenographic notes were taken by Doris Burke, secretary to David Furness. They are for the sole use of Tom Jones, Jr., law librarian, Essex Law School. You have Mr. Furness's permission to edit them but, if they are to be published in any form, the galleys must be shown to Mr. Furness. Please acknowledge. FAX 807 369 2041

TJ: It is a pleasure to meet you, Mr. Furness. I appreciate your giving me this opportunity to interview you.

DF: Sit down, young man. My secretary tells me that I am to be interviewed for your history of Essex Law School. I postponed a golf trip – uh, uh, uh – don't think that you are denying me anything. I take golf trips frequently, play cards in Vegas, and occasionally do a little work. [laughter]

TJ: Is that how class action business works?
DF: For me it does. Tom, I have put in seven day twenty four hour weeks when the occasion warrants it. I have also had slow periods that I use for my pursuits. And often I pursue business during my pursuits. But let's get down to business. I'm happy to do this interview as I have ulterior

motives. Much of my business is referral. I want to be in your history. If I get one case from it, it could set me up for a year. So what do you want to know?

TJ: How do you get to be a class action lawyer.
DF: Number one – I am not a class action lawyer. There are three lawyers here. Steven, my brother, does negligence cases, such as slip and fall and automobile accident cases. Michel Dodd handles disability cases. But we work together as needed. We also work with other lawyers. If a medical liability case comes my way, I refer it to Nate Silverberg. If Nate gets a disability case he refers it to us. We also go to court occasionally as Steven is a very good trial lawyer. You have a case, he'll try it.

TJ: According to my information you did quite well handling fen-phen diet drug cases.
DF: Back to class action. Tom, lawyering is marketing. I spent a couple of years working for Dynamic General. They manufactured things, they serviced big equipment. They also had a legal department to handle suits against them. The job of my department was to decide whether to settle the case, go to arbitration, go to court. We made decisions. If we decide to go to court, we hire local firms to handle the cases. That's how I got to play golf. We'd be sued in Ohio and hire local counsel. They want to be nice to us so that we would continue to use them, so they would invite one or two of us to play golf at Firestone Country Club. I once stayed in the Arnie Palmer room at Firestone. I once shot the same as Arnie. Of course, he just had a hip replacement.

TJ: Sounds like a good job.
DF: Not bad. They had a restructuring in my department and I was eased out of the possibilities of getting golf perks. That was part of the reason I left. The other was that I recognized risk. Companies put out products that they know are going to kill and maim people. They price their products so that they can please their stockholders and pay off those who run into trouble using the product. Tom, I had documents cross my desk that were so incriminating against the company that I think I could have put Dynamic out of business.

TJ: Whistleblowing

DF: Tom, when I work for someone I am loyal. I don't whistleblow. Besides, have you ever seen the movie, *The Insider* with Al Pacino? The story of a lawyer suing the tobacco industry. The whistleblower suffered death threats and his life was ruined. So I went into business for myself with a plan that would accomplish whistleblowing and make a living for myself.

TJ: And that is?

DR: Class action is an expensive business, Tom. Do you remember that class action movie? Travolta starred in it: *A Civil Action*. They had a good case, but lost because they were up against a behemoth. Very expensive and the lawyer went bankrupt trying to win the case. Expert fees, discovery, medical records, you name it. I knew from the start that there had to be a better way.

TJ: And that was.

DF: I arranged to meet lawyers who could afford to fund the cases such that they would opt out of the class action to pursue individual cases. By negotiating this accumulation of cases outside of the class action, we were able to resolve our cases most remuneratively.

And to my surprise, there were lots of little guys like me referring out cases to the same firm who then had strength in numbers to deal with the manufacturer. In my situation, I was more involved with my clients than simply referring them. There is more to this than meets the eye.

I would use marketing to find out who was injured by breast implants, fen-phen diet drugs, etc. I would get the information from these people and if I was sure they had a claim I would funnel it to my parent firm. Other lawyers throughout the country would pursue a class action procedure but that was not my style.

It might take years but stockholders like settlements that don't bankrupt the company. So do I.

TJ: How do you get these cases?

DF: Simple. TV, internet, advertising, word of mouth, referrals. Tom, drug companies are nothing more than the snake oil salesmen you read about in *Huckleberry Finn*. They do with drugs what the butcher does with cows. Find every possible use for it. A drug may be good for asthma, but some advertising maniac may decide it is good for a guy who can't keep his feet still. They cross market. The FDA approves a drug for one thing, they try and palm that drug for something else. An example. Zyprexa is approved for psychotic behavior. They promote it for depression. Oh, they're careful. They try and stay within the law. They caution the public about side effects, etc. Anything to keep the stockholders happy, the bonuses rolling, and the advertising business sprouting. To be fair, sometimes a drug used for killing rats is found to be good for growing hair.

TJ: So you see yourself as the savior of the beset upon average man.
DF: More than that, Tom. I see myself as the Food and Drug Administration. I see myself as a policeman. Tom, there was once a doctor named Sabin. He found a cure for polio. He was asked why he didn't patent it and make millions. The question never entered his mind. We live in a strange age where people want to make money curing diseases. Who ever heard of doctors making thousands of dollars speaking on behalf of pharmaceutical firms?

TJ: Do you think Essex prepared you for this?
DF: I hadn't thought of it. But, yes, it did. You don't go to Essex planning to defend pharmaceutical companies. They won't even let you in the door. We are the bloodhounds, searching out the bad guys.

TJ: Well, Mr. Furness. You know what the tort reformers say. Frivolous law suits, junk science, breast implants.
DF: Tom, I've had clients with breast implant problems that would make you sick to your stomach. No question they are sick. They think it is the silicone. Take fibromyalgia. Client is helpless with pain and inertia. He and many like him say it is caused by a drug they have taken. The pharmaceuticals say there is no such ailment. Try and get a doctor to testify against the biggies. If we have the goods or the stamina, they settle. Soon after, a pharmaceutical company comes out with a cure for fibromyalgia.

Frivolous law suits – the courts do not allow frivolous law suits. Check the rules. If we can trust juries to determine whether a defendant should live or die, shouldn't we trust them to determine the amount of damages corporate America should pay for causing damage to one of its consumers? Look Tom. It is a cat and mouse game. Lawyers like me find a niche.

We exploit it to make a living. The companies round up tort reformers – an oxymoron if I ever heard one – and they work up preemption laws so that when the FDA approves a drug, the patient is denied action in a state court.

One more thing, Tom. Law to me is more than a business. It is more than a profession. It is way of life. We do a lot of military disability work here. It pays the rent but it exposes us to the tragedy of life. I spent an hour with a guy whose life turned into a shambles after he was honorably discharged. He had army related injuries that were patched up and the VA doctor filed a report that means he has no redress for disability. Right now I am working on an appeal for a veteran that a veteran's organization asked me take on a pro bono basis. We are happy to do it. Steve spent last week at Essex judging student moot court cases.

TJ: Well, Mr. Furness. This has been fascinating, and I assure you that you will get a good hearing in my history. By the way, the development office asked me to thank you for your annual gifts to the law school. I hope you will excuse me for noticing, a vial of pills on your desk. Beginning of a class action there?"

DF: Tom, handling these drug cases has given me stomach problems. These things are for acid reflux. And the damn things work.

CHAPTER 33

KNIGHT'S MOVE

Mary McCarthy was getting along well with just a cane.

"I tell you Tom, it is just remarkable. They pinned me together and I thought I would be a cripple for life. I didn't think I would ever get out of a bed, but the rehab people were wonderful. Then I thought I would be stuck with a walker, but here I am with a cane and I am now thinking of when I can get rid of it."

"Mary, you Mainiacs, are made of steel. Do you like being called a Mainiac – it just slipped out."

"Doesn't bother me none, Tom. I look back on my life, and I think I am the original Mainiac."

"You are one of many. My biggest peeve on this island is the local drivers. They can't stand a license plate from another state being in front of them. Lately, I spot a Maine driver, I slow down, pull over, and insist he or she pass me. Sometimes they give me a flash to thank me."

"Are you here to talk about Maine drivers or do we have business to discuss?"

"We have business. A couple of things. One. I know that you have told Dean Dooley that you were through with any business transactions. You won't sign any more papers."

"That's right."

"Tell him you have changed your mind. He can do anything he wants to do. You are sick and tired of arguing about it. You have enough to do taking care of yourself."

Mary looked quizzical.

"When he brings you papers to sign, give him some excuse – tell him anything – I want to see what he is up to. If possible have him mail them to you. I pretty much know from the Portland bank what you two own, but I think he may be up to something that these papers may reveal. Two. I want to invite Jeb Figgis and his family to spend a week at your camp. I hate to do that because I have been spending a lot of time there and I love it."

Mary sat up in her chair. "That's my son, isn't it?"

"Yes, and he is very suspicious of his mother. He knows that you were a mere secretary at a law school. He thinks you are up to something funny. He also loves Mt. Desert Island. Takes his family there every year. I've hinted at it to him, and he usually goes up the first two weeks in August."

"Tom," said Mary, suddenly twitching in her chair," I think I'd like to see him."

"And if he sees you, he will know you are not up to any shenanigans."

"One problem. I just remembered that Joseph Francis Xavier Dooley has just asked a favor of me that conflicts with your timing about my son – what's his name again?"

"Jeb Figgis."

Mary wrote the name down on a pad that she kept on a string around her neck. Then she looked at another note. "Yup, Dooley has asked for the same time – he told me his son would like to come up with his buddies for a week."

"His son, eh. That I don't like Mary. Sean has given his father lots of trouble. I am heading back to Boston and I will try to work the dates out."

"Talking about dates. Here comes my dinner date for this evening. I get one meal a day at this place and who sits at my table – I'll tell you later."

The last remark was caused by the appearance of Zeke Harper, a big lumbering fellow who was laboring as he maneuvered his walker within range.

Mary introduced the two again, and Tom gathered up his notes, and excused himself. "I have lots to do Miss McCarthy, glad to meet you Mr. Harper," and Tom skedaddled to his rented car, and headed back to Boston.

His first task was to get in touch with Sean Dooley to head him off from using the camp. Sean had none of the virtues and all of the defects of his father. He had a poor but passable record at St. Mary's. He was reluctantly accepted at Essex but had no affinity for the law. He had to take the bar exam twice to pass, and was twice unable to hold positions his father had obtained for him. He was sued for divorce by his wife accusing him of abuse and violence. He defended himself so ineptly and was so abusive to the judge that he was suspended from the practice of law. He was required to take an anger management course or go to jail. He did have an aptitude for sports but was kicked off every team for either not going to practices or arguing with his coaches. As his divorce required him to pay support for his two children, and he was faced with jail for lack of payment, he agreed to take a job as assistant coach at Essex, a job made possible by a substantial gift to the athletic program of the school by Sean's father. The reason that job held was that it meshed with Sean's propensity for gambling, and hanging out with a crowd that his father constantly warned him would bring him to no good.

Tom caught up with Sean in the locker room. He had looked for him on the field but one of the players suggested the locker room. There was Sean smoking a cigarette.

"Sean, I'm Tom Jones, the librarian at Essex."

"Hi," was all Sean could muster.

"I understand that you asked your dad if you could use the camp at Mt. Desert Island."

"Yup."

"You asked for two weeks, and it turns out that is impossible."

Sean tossed his cigarette on the floor and stomped on it. Then he thought twice. Picked it up, and deposited it in a waste basket. The team was coming into the locker room and he waived his arms to spread the smell of the smoke.

"What has that got to do with you?"

"Miss McCarthy owns the camp. I do some work for her, and she asked me to let you know that she has rented the camp for the first week in August. You can have the second week."

"My father has told me I could have it those two weeks, and no librarian is going to tell me otherwise."

Tom shrugged. "My job was to give you a message. I have done that. Goodbye."

The next thing Tom knew, Sean had grabbed Tom's shoulder and spun him around. And the next thing Sean knew, he was being spun around by Coach Kelly.

"I do the spinning around here, Buster. Now get out on the field, and round up the equipment and then you can go home."

Sean's mien immediately changed. "Right coach," and then he yelled at the disappearing Tom, "Heh, librarian, I'll talk to my father."

And talk he did. And Dean Dooley made it clear to both Tom and Sean that Mary had the final decision on the camp. That cleared the way for Tom to call Jeb Figgis and confirm that the first week in August was his.

Tom decided that he should speak to Dean Dooley and make sure that no feathers were ruffled. But before he could leave his office, Peter Toole stepped in. A first rule of librarianship is to expect to be interrupted. It could be a student, an alumna, a faculty member, or just about anybody who required your audience. It was as if you had nothing to do with your time but to make it available to the general public. And Tom had no misgivings about making his time available. Students came to him with problems with the plumbing, air conditioning, hours of the library, structural deficiencies of the building, exam scheduling, the building being closed on New Year's Day, traffic noise, and even domestic squabbles. Tom did have a couple of defenses. If he was on the phone for more than three minutes, or someone was in his office for more than three minutes, a worker would come in and say the "Dean wants you on the phone." That would give Tom the opportunity of excusing himself or making his guest feel important that he was keeping the Dean waiting. On one occasion, the Dean was in his office when this message came in, and the two had a hearty laugh over the incident.

"Dean Toole, it is good to see you."

"It's been a while. I've missed you, Tom. I thought you might be on a sabbatical."

"Well, we had a New England Law Librarian's Convention in Portland early this week. I also did an interview for my history of the law school. It was very interesting."

"Spare me, your interviews. I'll read it when it makes the *New York Times* best seller list. I thought you might have been to Dean Dooley's celebration."

"I wasn't invited. What were they celebrating?"

"I think he was being installed, or mounted, or stuffed. I'm not much for celebrating my Catholicism, but he revels in it."

"Is that the right word? Nothing wrong with being a good Catholic, or a good Jew, or a good Christian, is there?"

"Yes, there is. Particularly if you are Boston Irish."

"Are the Boston Irish different from say, New York Irish," asked Tom.

"As a Bostonian you know there is. For a group that was persecuted by the old Yankees, you would think they would know better. But they attended rallies by Gerald L. K. Smith, they were nailed to their radios when Father Coughlin spewed hatred against the Jews. I stopped attending Irish meetings because I couldn't stand their stiff-necked racism. Do you know we had a mayor who when things went right for him would express his joy by saying, 'I killed a Jew today.'

I can't stand people like Dooley who enjoy their religion at other people's expense. They want you to know they go to church every Sunday, that some member of their family has taken one for the church by becoming a priest, that their piousness proves their religion is better than yours."

"And New York Irish are different?"

"New Yorkers are New Yorkers. It's who you are and what you do that counts. A bum is a bum in New York whether he is Jewish, Catholic or Protestant. And if someone became a Sir Knight in New York, it wouldn't become common knowledge like Sir Knight Dooley. That irks me."

"It doesn't bother me, Dean Dooley a knight? Is he a knight of the round table?"

"You've never heard of the Knights of Columbus?"

"Just kidding."

"I don't think you were. You should be impressed. I understand he is a Fourth Degree Knight. I had one of my Catholic students – a convert by the way – tell me that a priest told him that Dooley is planning a big gift to the diocese. That the diocese is planning a trip to Rome with an audience with the Pope to announce it. You'd think he was a Kennedy. I don't like it."

Tom took careful note of this and then, as if in thought, brought his left hand up to cover his chin and lips. "I guess the man wants to be remembered. Can you buy yourself into heaven?"

Toole shrugged his shoulders and cackled. "Mr. Jones, one day we will all be forgotten but every day is a bonus." And Professor Toole turned and went his way.

Tom shook his head as he watched the Professor make his way out of the library.

"Touché," was all he could think of.

But Toole had put Tom on to something. What was Dooley up to? Was his latest coup with sending papers to Mary to sign have anything to do with it? And Tom decided he had to act fast on Mary's behalf.

CHAPTER 34

THE BREAKDOWN

Tom had a monthly meeting with his professional staff. The computer program that Tom had installed in the law school was a great success He had taken over what was the housekeeping supply room for his temporary quarters. Elizabeth Hughes, who had watched the computer program with little empathy, and had stood by while the reference people enthusiastically began computer classes for both student and faculty, now joined reluctantly in its success. But Elizabeth, who was six feet tall and big boned, was not about to meet in a housekeeping room that would accentuate her girth. She insisted on her spatial office. This was fine with Tom.

Tom had added an additional reference librarian to his staff who had a technical background, and Tom had invited two law students, who were employed at the Digital Computer Company, to the meeting. Janet Klein, now Chief Reference Librarian, reported on her plan to cosponsor a course with the Essex Center for Legal Advancement on "The Use of Computers in Law Practice." There was also plans for cooperation among New England law schools for the storage of books, and the creation of a combined catalog of all the law schools. The slate for the next election of officers for the Law Librarians of New England was announced and Tom Jones was to be President Elect. At that point, a secretary knocked on the door, and upon being admitted, walked over to Tom and whispered in his ear.

"Will you excuse me. Elizabeth will you continue with the meeting?" and Tom followed the secretary to the catalog room, where Elizabeth had instructed her staff to monitor the calls. Tom got on the phone, "This is Tom Jones."

"Tom, this is Beverly Brooks, your wife's friend."

Tom hesitated before answering. She certainly was his wife's friend. Beverly was divorced from her psychiatrist husband, who had married his receptionist. The two were inseparable at coffee shops, bars, and particularly at the Riverdale Community Theater where both were mainstays. They were either acting or producing or being stage hands. Tom would come home from work and find a note "at a rehearsal" or work late at the law library and find a note "striking the set." Sometimes the note would be more convivial "join us at Murphy's for Irish coffee – Janet 10pm." Tom would oblige on occasion and Beverly loved to tell how her lawyer wrangled every dime out of her husband for alimony and child support. Tom always felt that message was for him. Since Tom had taken the job in Boston, and Janet was in New York, he assumed the two were up to whatever they were up to. And as Janet had told him she wanted a divorce, he was in no mood to talk to this woman, who he thought, contributed mightily to Janet's behavior.

"I'm listening."

"Your wife is very ill. She is in the hospital."

Tom hesitated again.

"Tom, I know you two are not getting along, but you are her husband, and this is very serious."

"How serious."

"She is in Mount Beth Misery Hospital. Complete nervous breakdown. Went absolutely berserk."

"Miss Brooks. I don't even know where Janet lives. That's number one! Number two: Where is this guy she told me she is marrying? Number three: I have two children to take care of."

"Tom, she's asked for you. Do you want her to commit suicide?"

"Alright, Where is this Mount Beth? How long has she been there? Give me..."

Beverly gave Tom the information. He returned to the meeting to find that it had been concluded. He went to Elizabeth. "Elizabeth, my wife is in the hospital in New York."

Before Tom could add anything to that Elizabeth, who at the time was busy with one of her staff, said, "Don't worry about a thing, Tom.

We'll take care of everything." And while Tom strode off he could hear her say, and intentionally, "I could have told him there'd be trouble living in different cities."

Tom notified his father in law and sister in law of the problem. For once Fred Wright was sympathetic. But all he could say was, "She should have married a psychiatrist." Tom flew to New York and took a cab to Mount Beth Misery, and was directed to Janet's room. He asked at the desk if he could speak to someone about her case first, and, after a few calls, was told to wait in the anteroom of the fourth floor. There he was met by a very tall man who still had on a black hat and a black cape. He wore a white shirt and a red bow tie. He was rail thin and his ears seemed to point north and south, one of which was decorated with what looked like a two carat diamond. He sported a trim goatee that was flaked with gray. Tom did not know whether he had just come in, was going out, or that this was his working wardrobe.

As they faced each other all Tom could think of was Gounod's *Faust* and that a deep bass voice was going to break out and offer him a way out of his predicament. Instead, Tom heard a pleasing, soft, and soothing voice that was both calming and assuring.

The facts that Tom learned was that Janet was picked up by a policeman on Riverdale Avenue and 246st Street in broad daylight. She was naked, and nonchalantly walking down the street with an empty martini glass in her hand. The policeman commandeered a trench coat from a passerby, wrapped her in it, and unable to get any information from her brought her to the police station. There she became very vocal. Berating the police for depriving her of the right to walk the streets in whatever way she deemed fit, she insisted they call her lawyer. The lawyer happened to be Beverly Brooks' divorce lawyer. He got in touch with Beverly Brooks. By this time, the police had enough of Janet who was either belligerent or making passes at one particular policeman, so they transferred her to Misery.

When Beverly arrived at Mount Beth Misery, Janet had become so unmanageable that she was placed in a padded cell to protect herself and the hospital staff. She had been sedated, and by nightfall she was asleep.

"And when did all this happen, Doctor Manberg?"

"Four days ago, Mr. Jones. Ms Brooks has been in attendance every day. I didn't know you existed until this moment. I apologize. But I think it was for the best. She has calmed down remarkably. You will find her quite coherent. But you must remember that we are dealing with a borderline patient. My only problem right now is you."

"Me?"

"I don't want to set her off again, Mr. Jones."

"Doctor, I don't remember the last time she's taken her clothes off for me."

The Doctor looked very sternly at him.

"The woman has asked me for a divorce. I agreed amicably. Janet has done a few things that made me think she could use help, but what you are telling me is way beyond her conduct. I sometimes think she has things under control better than I have."

"I'm relieved by what you tell me. Apparently there was a Mr. Watson that she had some unkind words about as we tried to make sense of her conduct. I also was able to get her medical records. She was on a diet and taking pills that do bring on behavior such as we witnessed in her."

"Well, what do we do now, Doctor."

"Please call me Stephen. As I said, Janet has made a remarkable recovery. She asked to wear the clothes Ms Brooks brought for her. She is being sedated very slightly, and we have her walking about in the main room. She is a model patient, and has done wonders in calming down a young lady that was brought in the other day. It is a secure room, but it gives our patients an opportunity to walk and talk normally."

Dr. Manberg led Tom into the room, and let him find his wife. There was Janet talking with a young girl, holding her hand, and saying, "Mary, you are very pretty, and ..." and then she saw Tom. "Well, my librarian in shining armor." And with insouciance, "What brings you here, darling?"

Tom laughed and noticed that the hand that Janet was holding had a bandaged wrist. Tom hunched his shoulders. "I don't know. They told me it was visiting day."

Tom sat next to Janet. "I suppose they told you all about me? You know, if they just brought me back to my apartment, I would have been OK. My love had deserted me. Can you believe that. I couldn't believe it. I staked the bastard. Got him what he wanted and he is now in Hollywood under contract. I think I would have been all right. But he wanted to thank me. If I wanted thanks ..."

"You would have stayed with me."

They both laughed. "I know I'm stupid. Heh, look at that black guy.

Look at the size of him. A beautiful hunk of man and they have him so sedated, he doesn't even know his name."

"He is big. I'm not sure I want to be around if he isn't sedated."

"Tom, you are so practical. I think if you had one trait – smoking cigars, playing poker with the boys, wearing a regulation Yankee outfit with Yogi Berra on the back – we might have made a go of it."

The imbecility of this remark got to Tom. As if his conduct was the source of their incompatibility.

"Janet, you just struck out. My God, Janet. What are you doing here? You sound perfectly normal to me."

At this point an intern approached the group. Janet still held the young girl's hand. "Folks, we are going to have a meeting in the recreation room. Doctor Manberg would like to have a chat with you." He then looked at Janet. "Miss, you will have to go in the guest room until the meeting is over." He then locked arms with Tom and the girl with the bandaged wrist and started herding them to the recreation room. Tom shook his head and decided to go along until Janet piped up, "Wait a minute, feller, he's the guest, I'm the patient. He looks that way because he is my husband." The intern apologized and Tom said his goodbye to Janet and promised to return the next day.

Tom found that once committed to Misery getting out could be a problem. It turned out that Misery had a quasi court where residents, as they were called, could petition for release. The procedure required the psychiatrist to testify as to the condition of the resident, the resident to testify as to her ability to adjust to society, and for someone to assure the court that the resident would have security, safety, and sustenance in the outside world. A magistrate of some kind presided over the hearing, and after a morning of testimony, he released Janet in Tom's recognizance. This procedure took three trips to New York City.

Beverly Brooks was present on the day of release, and the three took a cab to Janet's apartment in Greenwich Village. The apartment was in Washington Mews, As Janet opened the door, she was met with hugs and kisses by a greeting party from *Item Magazine's* editorial department. People were dancing. Tom recognized Sidney Rosen, an editorial writer for the publication. He was the guy, Tom remembered, that Janet barged in on and suggested he use "regrettably" instead of "regretfully" in the magazine's back page editorial.

At the homecoming, Rosen was wearing an intern's costume, had all kinds of medical apparatus on him, and was listening to Janet's heart the minute she came in the door. There were people dressed as nurses, and a few people acting as they thought Beth Misery inhabitants acted. Janet loved it. Tom silently made his way out of the apartment and headed to Penn Station for a train back to sanity. The thought occurred to him that going crazy must be considered a perfectly normal activity among the literary class in New York City.

But Tom had more important things to contemplate than his wife's rapid recovery. She was back at work as if nothing had happened. She made what seemed like an obligatory trip back to Boston to see her children. She was obviously no longer on amphetamines or whatever it was that she took to try and loose weight, and was now a bit too heavy. Her mood was so good that Tom agreed to take her to HoJos to listen to music and her behavior amused Tom no end. She sat for a few moments with the piano player, greeted some of her old friends, drank just below her threshold, and agreed to call it a night at Tom's suggestion.

Tom even agreed to drive her to New York on Thursday and stayed to take in a few plays. Janet's work week began on Thursday and lasted until the magazine went to bed on Sunday. In the meantime, Tom would drop in at Cahn Law School and have lunch with acquaintances on the library staff. Janet made no effort to resume their marital ways. They were now friends. Janet would not get through with her duties until after midnight. On occasion, she would be working until two or three in the morning. Tom would return to the apartment after the theater and he would always buy a couple of Danish at Balducci's and make himself an instant coffee or hot chocolate before going to bed. On occasion, Janet would get home around the same time, and they would both chat civilly.

"You know, Tom. I didn't thank you for coming to get me at Misery considering – I was in love with another guy. I ruined your plans for buying camps? What was that all about?"

"Janet, I'm grateful you are OK. The camps? Pie in the sky. I do have to get back to my history, and without going into detail I do want to be a librarian in shining armor."

"Oh, that reminds me. How are you doing with that gefilte fish girl. I thought she was a little old for you. But she could ride that bicycle. I can see you two riding into the sunset."

"Very funny, Janet. I think women look at boobs more than men do. Yes, she was a bit older than me, but if I had taken Ben Franklin's advice, going out with older woman might have saved me a few heartaches. She did have possibilities, though."

"Listen, Tom, Age had nothing to do with it. And I detect a little bit of past tense in your relationship with ..."

"Vivian Gefelshe."

"A nice Jewish girl. What happened? I'm curious. Dad told me you spent a lot of time with her. My sister told me you were *shtooping* her. I think that's the right term."

Tom laughed. It's all over. I've dropped out of the bicycle club. We pass each other like ships in the night."

"She wasn't good in bed?" Tom said nothing. "You weren't good in bed?"

"I'll leave that up to you, Janet."

Janet was nonplussed for a moment. "Tom, bedrooms don't make or break a marriage. We didn't make it because I drink and you don't. Because I like jazz and you don't. Because you like kids – you like the institution of marriage and I don't. Don't demonize yourself about it. I'll bet Vivian meets all of your requirements and being Jewish might be just the *schmaltz* to make it palatable."

"*Shtoop, smaltz*, you have become a New Yorker." He deliberated a minute before he decided to answer her comment. " I thought so too until a couple of weeks ago."

"Tell me, maybe I can help."

Tom laughed. "I'll tell you, but only because I have met your opposite."

"Now you have to tell me"

"She drove me absolutely mad in bed."

"How does a woman do that?"

"First we'd have sex. No, first she would put on a record. Bolero or something. Then sex. Then she would edge my hand to her you know what and want a massage."

"So far, so good."

"But it was never ending. All night long. If I stopped she would cry and moan about her fate. Her big boobs. Her failed marriage. Her need for love."

"Maybe you should carry a vibrator with you."

"That's the end of the story."

"Are you telling me that was what killed the romance?"

"I guess so. We now pass like ships in the night. You know what I found out. Being married and being eligible has its advantages. The word gets around that you are separated from your wife. That you are a faculty member. I get an invitation to a party by Fannie Kleindienst, who teaches judicial administration, and runs what amounts to a salon in her home. There I was with judges, members of distinguished law firms, the President of the University, and me. Why was I invited? Fannie's friend, it turns out is a vice president of an investment company. His daughter has just been divorced, and Fannie decided I was a possibility."

"What happened?"

Well, we were the only unattached people there. I felt obliged to offer her a ride home."

"And,"

"It turned out that Judge Lamar, a distinguished judge, the main speaker at the law review dinner that week, an 85 year old lecher was going to ditch his wife and take her home. She turned him down for me."

"And where was I at the time?

"That was when we broke up and I lived in the Cahn dorm, and you had the apartment and were suing me for more support."

"That's right. You're living it up with this dame and I am absolutely miserable with the kids. As I recall, you sent me a letter telling me you had found your real love."

Tom was silent.

"Well, go on."

"She liked ballet. I actually fell asleep watching "Candide." Her parents lived near the Carnegie and had a beautiful apartment. They would go to Spain each year and scour the art world for the next Picasso. He looked me over as if I was his daughter's next disaster. Mother wanted to know where I lived. I decided not to impress her. I told her the Bronx, instead of Riverdale."

Janet folded her hands. "The worst period of my life and you are striking gold. What happened next. You forgot your vibrator."

"No, I'm sure you remember this. I had the kids for a weekend, and I brought them back to you. It was a Sunday afternoon. I was pretty sweaty from biking with the kids. We had just begun to talk civilly to one another and I went into the bathroom to wash my hands and face. When I came out and was prepared to leave, Jack joined us and the three of us went to the car together while we talked about my next visit. Do you remember that?"

"Yes, and you and I were holding Jack's hands and he somehow put our hands together."

"He's such a loving kid. And you suggested we go back in the house and have a cup of tea."

Janet looked doubtful. "Alright, I suggested it."

"And there we sat. In silence."

"And you, Janet, suggested that I would probably marry again. And I kindly suggested that you would find the man of your dreams."

"And then you followed with 'and the result would be four miserable people.'"

"And I followed that with we should do the humanitarian thing and get together and save two people from miserable lives."

"And we both went up to your lair, if I may use the expression, and consummated our new resolve."

CHAPTER 35

TOM MEETS BOSTON BLACKIE

Tom had copies of the documents that Dean Dooley had asked Mary to sign. They listed the property that Mary owned, their assessed value, the certificates of deposit they had accumulated, the amount of rent they had collected over the years. They also owned the land on which Mary was now residing, as well as the sardine factory they had converted into condominiums. It was an impressive portfolio and Dooley was asking for five percent for each of them upon a sale of the property with the rest to be donated to a charity to be determined by the two of them. Based on the assessments, which Tom considered to be far below market value, and actual accumulations, Tom figured that package was worth up to ten million dollars.

When Tom was considering buying property for his own aggrandizement, he went to the real estate people that handled the renting of the property. Jim Grolier was a man that Tom found straightforward, a real Maine person. He was in his seventies. He wore a shirt and tie, and his chinos had an edge that looked like it could cut through Vermont cheddar cheese. He walked very erect and had a slight limp that he made no effort to hide. What made him stand out in Tom's mind is that he not only had his trousers secured by a big buckled belt but he also wore suspenders. He was Maine. You knew instinctively that he was sound, direct, and terse. His accent was as Down East as the rocky coast.

"Mr. Jones," he said to Tom as they sat opposite each other in his office in Southwest Harbor, "land is getting expensive here. I know that you are doing work for Mrs. McCarthy. My God, that woman has resurrected herself… I knew her when she worked in the café. Somehow, she went to Boston and," he threw his hands up in the air, "got an education or something and come back here and did herself wicked. All these Boston and New York people coming up here and buying up the land – but I'm glad a local person is getting some of it."

"I'm not from Maine, Mr. Grolier, but …"

"It's alright, son. I'm a real estate man and I sell real estate. I've got a suggestion for you. Listen carefully. When the Putnams sold what became the camps that Mrs. McCarthy bought, it was three separate purchases." Mr. Grolier then went to a cabinet and pulled a plan of the area. "This sliver was left out because there was no way you could build a camp there. Drainage problem."

"What would I do with it?"

"Buy it and hold it. May be worth something some day. I can get it for you for ten thousand dollars. One third of an acre. It separates the McCarthy land from the log cabin camp at the head of the cove still owned by the family that once owned it all.

Jim Grolier folded the plan and put it away as if waiting for an answer.

"I'll think it over, Mr. Grolier. Give me a couple of days."

"I'll do that son," and the meeting was over.

If Tom could have laid his hands on ten thousand dollars without any trouble, he might have bought the property. But the more he thought about it, the more he thought that destiny had decided he had a more important role to play than just make a few dollars on a real estate transaction. Why was that useless quarter of an acre that Grolier was trying to push on him valuable? Was Grolier testing him? Trying to find out if he was just a Boston wheeler-dealer? Maybe seeing if he had his own interests at heart rather than "Mrs." McCarthy, a bona fide Down Easter?

And Tom had more important things to take care of. He wanted to make sure that that Jeb Figgis was having a good time. He also wanted to make sure that Boston Blackie and his boisterous buddies took care to respect the property when they took it over from Figgis. That was the second reason he was in MDI. It was now Saturday, and he decided to call Figgis and ask him if it was alright to come over.

"Mr. Jones. I thought you said we could have the camp until Sunday.

There is a group of people here that claim they have the place and seem insistent that we leave."

"Put someone on the phone."

"This is Boston Blackie. Who are you?"

"Mr. Blackie. I am the agent for the property. Your rental does not begin until Sunday."

"Not on your life, buster. We are here and intend to stay here."

"Mr. Blackie. I am going to call the police and tell them you are ..."

"Wait a minute. Don't call the police for Christ's sake. Let's solve this like gentlemen. How much do you want – we take over."

"Mr. Blackie. I make the terms not you. I am doing a favor to Dean Dooley in letting you have the place for the week. There is no charge. I know of you Mr. Blackie. I will be right over to take charge of the matter. Should I come with the police?"

"No, no. Come on over, we can settle this thing."

Tom came over in his rental car and there was Jeb Figgis, fidgeting with his hands in his pockets. Out on the cove was his family on their sailboat waiting for their father. There was Boston Blackie sitting at the kitchen table smoking a cigarette. Walking nervously around the apartment were four men, one of whom was Sean Dooley.

Sean spoke up. "Hi Professor Jones, remember me. I'm ..."

"I know who you are." He then turned to Boston Blackie. "Mr. Blackie, I specifically do the renting here. I have in my possession the arrangement that we made with you. You take possession tomorrow. Is that clear?"

Blackie took out a roll of bills. "Mr. Blackie, put that money away," said Tom. "I told you that you cannot take possession of this place until tomorrow."

Sean went to Blackie and whispered in his ear and Blackie shook his head. He then started to plead. "Mr. Jones, we got no place to stay. We made a mistake. Can't we give this guy a few hundred ..."

Tom interrupted. "Mr. Blackie. This is Mount Desert Island in August. I doubt if there is a room on the island. My suggestion is that I will give you my room at the Kimball Terrace. I'll tell you how to get there. And maybe Jeb Figgis will put me up for the night." Jeb nodded in agreement.

"There's five of us. You gonna put us in one room."

"The alternative is driving to Ellsworth. Twenty miles. You'll probably be able to get rooms there."

"C'mon, guys," decided Blackie, "Let's go to the Terrace. But you guys are sleeping in the car." And then he slapped one of the guys in the face, "You idiot, telling us we had the room."

Jeb thanked Tom, and then headed out to the beach to join his family on their last day of sailing the cove.

That night, Tom got to meet the family.

CHAPTER 36

THE DRUG BUST

Tom's next task was to keep his promise to Mary. That evening he had called Mary and suggested she come over in the morning and that Mary, Tom, and the Figgis family go to the Asticou Inn in Northeast Harbor for brunch. Mary, who no longer drove a car, came with her friend, Zeke Harper, and they all participated in a hearty brunch. Mary was very quiet, very tentative, in meeting with Jeb. "By God," she said to herself, " he looks just like Seth." Inwardly, Mary fumed. "The old man didn't want trash toting around his grandson. I could buy and sell the son of a bitch, now."

The Figgis family drove back to Portland that afternoon. Tom was still edgy about the Blackie gang being at the camp and he called the caretaker to ask him to look in on them.

"I already have, Mr. Jones. People in the camp next to them called me to complain that they were acting a little crazy. One of them, probably drunk, almost drowned using the kayak. It tipped over and if he wasn't close to the shore he would have been upended and drowned. They keep the lights on all night and somehow they got a speed boat moored to a buoy. Probably rented from Bar Harbor. I tell you, Mr. Jones, I don't like the looks of it. I told the neighbors they should call the police if they make a ruckus."

"Do you have the telephone number of their camp? I think I'll call them and talk it over with them. I also left my suitcase in Mary's camp."

Tom called the camp and they were overjoyed that he would come over so that they could get a little peace. They were afraid to take out their sailboat with these idiots racing around with their speedboat that was twice the size of a lobster boat. "These men don't belong in Maine, Mr. Jones."

Tom drove Mary and Zeke back to the retirement house and then headed to Marshfield. He noticed a car was following him from the time he entered Somesville and onto the road to Bosc Landing. It was a Jaguar and the top was down, and he could see the silver mane that could only mean the Silver Hedgehog. As Tom made the turn into Mill Marsh Road, he slowed the car down, then brought it to a stop, forcing Dooley to do the same on the one lane path. Tom got out of the car and faced the Associate Dean.

"Dean what are you doing here?"

"I'm worried about my kid. I'm going up to take him home. I should never have agreed to this. I was stupid."

"Just worried about your kid, Dean?"

Dooley snarled at Tom. "One of these days, Tom." Dooley caught himself. "I'm sorry, Tom. I'm worried about everything. I wont go into detail, but Mary and I have some plans." Dooley threw his hands up in the air. "But I am worried about my kid. And, by the way, what are you doing here?"

"Dean Joseph Francis Xavier Dooley. I am worried about those guys setting fire to the entire island. They seem to be drinking, kayaking when drunk, pushing a speed boat to its limit. I just spoke to our caretaker, and I am on my way to the camp next to where your son is. They asked me to come and I decided to see if I can reason with Boston Blackie to behave himself, and if not, call the police."

"Good. Let's try and do this without the police."

"Dooley, two is an army. I suggest you go grab a bite at the Deacon's Nest in Southwest, and I will join you in an hour."

"No way. I am going to get my kid." And you could practically hear Dooley's head spinning with conspiracy. "Look, I'll park the car where the mill foundation is, and we'll go in your car. We are both representing Mary's interest. What say you?"

Tom nodded and Dooley hid his car in a little opening that led to the foundation of what used to be a mill on the path. They then proceeded to the neighbor's camp, the path of which was about one hundred feet from the path leading to Mary's camp where Blackie and his gang were staying.

Tom parked his car in a space next to a Jeep. As he approached the house, he could see a male pushing a curtain aside just enough to see who the visitors were. Then the door opened and a loud voice said, "Please identify yourself."

"Hi, I'm Tom Jones and this is Dean Dooley. I spoke to you on the phone a few minutes ago." Tom and Dooley entered the house. Tom, in an aside to Dooley, said, "I'll do the talking Dean." "Good," said the Dean, "because I am heading to the toilet. Those fried clams and French fries are killing me". Dooley took off. The door closed, and in the next few minutes Tom and Mr. Patterson exchanged pleasantries while their two teen aged children stood at attention.

The pleasantries were interrupted when one of the children shouted, "Dad, someone else." In the doorway was a tall figure, dressed in camouflage, with enough gadgets around his waist and dangling from his shoulders that he looked like he had just emerged from jungle warfare.

The man held up his hands. "Please do not be afraid. I represent the Drug Enforcement Agency and we are on an important mission. You are all to sit down," and as he said this three more similarly dressed men positioned themselves in the room, "and please be quiet."

Tom interjected, "Are we in any peril, officer?"

"No, as long as you do as we tell you. My men will watch you carefully, but you can go about your business. Put some food out. Drinks. Talk. Put on the television. We are only interested in an operation that we believe has nothing to do with you."

Tom started to say something, but the man put his hand up to quiet him. "I have nothing more to say at this time. Please go about your business. Act natural. My superior in this operation, Michael Connolly will be here shortly. He is doing some reconnaissance." The narc then took his seat.

Steven Patterson came over to Tom. "What do you make of this?

"We have no alternative but to do as he says. By the size of these guys with their short haircuts and neat appearance, I would say they are on a drug bust and our friends across the way are the culprits."

"We're paying five thousand a month for this. I would think you would have enough sense not to rent to a bunch of gangsters." Patterson was now getting angry.

Tom shushed him. "It's a long story, Mr. Patterson. I would suggest that this is a bad time to get into a rage and find yourself screwing up a drug bust and maybe getting your head bashed in."

Patterson brooded in a corner while his wife put some cold cuts on the table, a bottle of wine, some potato chips, crackers, cheddar cheese, and some fresh crab meat.

At this point there was slight rustling outside, and pushed into the room, in handcuffs, were Dean Dooley and his son. Behind them were three more similarly dressed men, one of whom seemed to be in command. One of the men had a gun aimed at the handcuffed two and putting two seats parallel ordered them to sit down.

Tom's eyes widened when he saw the commanding officer. It was Michael Connolly, a graduate of Essex, who had just last week appeared on a panel at the law school debating the legalization of marijuana. Connolly recognized Tom as he was the moderator of the program but only their eyes met.

Connolly began to speak. "Agent Craven, I see, has oriented you to the fact that we are on a very important mission. Your cooperation is essential. That means that none of you are to leave the premises." And he looked at the handcuffed two. "These two were apprehended apparently making their way to a Jaguar hidden in the woods. You will all be interrogated but first we must proceed with our mission. I believe Agent Craven has told you to be at ease, stay in this room unless you get permission to do otherwise. I see Mr. Jones here which suggests to me that you are a law abiding group and will not only do as you are told but, if necessary, assist us in any way to bring to justice a criminal group located nearby which is presently engaged in a criminal activity." He then sat down and welcomed the fact that Tom Jones gingerly approached him.

"Can I have a word with you, Mr. Connolly?"

"Professor Jones, first let me say that you are going to be questioned as well as all the people in this room. We are about to clamp down on one of the biggest drug busts in this country. The crime de la crime. And nicer people than you have been caught up in things like this."

"Mr. Connolly, I have been suspected of a lot of things but not as a supplier of drugs. But I would like to talk to you about those two people in handcuffs. One of them is the Associate Dean of Essex Law School. The other is his son Seth. The reason I am here is that the people in this camp complained about the noise and drinking going on over there. I am an agent for Mary McCarthy who owns the camp and was the secretary to Seth Adams, the founder of Essex Law School. Dean Dooley was here because he came to get his son away from that camp."

"Well, my friend, Dean Dooley is in big trouble. He could have screwed up this whole operation. We followed him as he almost broke his neck climbing down from the toilet of this camp, sneaking over to the other camp, and grabbing – you say it was his son? – one of the gang, and before the two of them could make a getaway. Our men subdued them and brought them over here."

"Mr. Connolly. Seth was in debt up to his ears to Boston Blackie. I believe the gang knew his father had a camp and they agreed to forgive the debt for a week at the camp."

"Even if I believe that story, we got him as an accessory. The Dean – I recognize him now – had him for real property – The Silver Hedgehog – pompous old guy – look Tom, on your say so, I'll let the two of them go and put them in the same category as the rest of you. Craven, take the cuffs off – those two," and he pointed to Dooley and son. As the handcuffs were removed, and both tried to rub off the pain of the clamp, Connolly spoke a reprimand, "You are both still under suspicion but I am releasing you on the recognition of Mr. Jones here, do you understand?" They both nodded.

CHAPTER 37

THE DRUG BUST II

I t was an all night affair. The Pattersons were allowed to use the bedrooms, but the rest were ordered to find rest as best as they could in the large dining room-parlor arrangement. The narcs took turns on watch. Connolly, gone most of the night, returned at daybreak. His men had brought in breakfast for all purchased at a shop near the airport. Connolly was in a good mood. As all were ordered to sit around makeshift accommodations and were fed orange juice, coffee, and bites of blueberry pancakes, Connolly announced, "Ladies and gentlemen, and you young people, I have an announcement to make that will please you. I have instructions to release all of you. The Dooleys in Mr. Jones recognizance. Our mission has been successful and I want to thank you for your cooperation, except for Dean Dooley. I will report, as I am required to do, that you were in the building at the time all were asked to remain in the building. I will also report that your son was in the same camp as the drug runners. What happens to be in your favor is that we may never have been clued into this operation if we weren't tailing Mr. Sean Dooley on another matter and his tie in with Mr. Blackie led to a freighter bearing a Liberian flag that was veering off course to drop one of the biggest loads of drugs here in good old Maine."

Connolly then dismissed his men and sat next to Tom to finish his breakfast. Connolly was a big man, broad chested, and walked like the marine he had always wanted to be, but was discouraged by his father, Big Steve Connolly. Steve had been a cop for many years and had achieved sergeant status, and that made him think higher. He decided to go to law school nights. After Essex Law School, he decided that being a defense lawyer might be more to his liking. He knew what made criminals tick, and he knew how to make criminals talk. When Big Steve was accused by a prosecutor that criminals consulted him before they committed crimes, he would give forth with a bellowing laugh and suggest that company's do the same thing when they enlist corporate lawyers. Bank robbers were Big Steve's specialty and he achieved some sort of notoriety in defending the First National Five who were apprehended some miles from the scene of the robbery. The case against them was meticulously detailed. The prosecution was sure it had an airtight case. Big Steve let everything in. He made no objections to the prosecution's case. But Big Steve's ace in the hole was that Federal District Judge McClernon permitted closing arguments large range. And Big Steve's entire defense was in his closing argument. He looked each jury member in the eye and recited each point against his clients. "What a symphony," he would exclaim after each point. As he orated, he would make a motion as if playing a violin. Another point. Everything meshing to perfection. "Bach, Beethoven, Lennie Bernstein could not have written this symphony, my fine members of the jury. Only a prosecutor bent on conviction. And I say to you, it is more phony, than symphony." The jury acquitted and Big Steve's reputation was made. The press ranked him with Lawrence O'Donnell, of whom it was said, "He has never been accused of understatement, timidity, or excessive modesty."

The problem was that Big Steve wanted his son to follow in his footsteps. But Michael Connolly was an observer of the First National Five case. He had been with his father when they went to visit the five in jail as they awaited trial. He had great sympathy for these men - They were black. They had no formal education. They were victims of a society that discriminated against minorities. Their chances of a decent life were slight if they existed at all. But nevertheless they were guilty. Michael followed his father's wishes and attended Essex, as his father, and actually spent a year practicing with his father. But he left the firm without notice and joined the Peace Corps. After two years in Africa, he came home and, probably unconscious of his need to undo the guilt he felt for his father's practice, entered the law to do justice. He picked drugs because he knew his father had his limits on what kind of criminal he would defend, and drugs and prostitution were off limits in his practice.

"Professor Jones, where do you go from here?"

"I'm going back to Boston, Michael. You seem relieved that the operation was a success." And then Tom added, and as he said it, wished he had not, "Unless your dad takes their case."

"My dad doesn't take drugs or prostitution cases, Professor Jones. That's why I am in the drug business."

Please call me Tom, Michael. I feel like I am being pandered when called professor."

"I probably was doing just that. Any chance of our driving back to Boston together? I'd like to talk to you."

Tom went over to the Dooleys and gave Sean the keys to his car. Dean Dooley looked suspiciously at Tom. "Dean, he asked me to drive with him. Believe me, I don't think Sean had anything to do with this and I will also try and keep Essex's name out of this business. He seems like a reasonable guy."

And Tom was true to his purpose. They stopped at Portland for lunch and made it back to Boston before nightfall. Michael and Tom both had a good laugh at the Dean scrambling out of a narrow window in the toilet, his impeccable dress in shambles, and his always carefully contoured hair bathed in sweat and hanging over his forehead. And then being followed by agents down to the shore where they watched him literally drag his son to the car. They were then apprehended by the agents and brought to the house.

"I know a little about Sean, and if I had a son like that, I don't think I would have risked my life for him," said Tom.

"You're not Irish, Tom."

"You mean I'm not Boston Irish."

"Maybe I mean that. I only know that kind. Frankly, I didn't think the old man had that in him. He was willing to risk his life for that kid. If I didn't know you and the Silver Hedgehog, he would be a goner."

Michael and Tom stopped at The Hilltop on Route 1 in the Saugus area for a steak. Then Michael drove Tom home. They agreed to have dinner some night together and Michael drove off. Tom could not shake the thought that Michael had lingering doubts about Tom's possible involvement in the drug business. A true detective. And an episode that will not go unreported in his hidden history.

CHAPTER 38

THE EULOGY

Tom had one sure method of relaxation in the law library. He would make the rounds of the various departments. Stop at cataloging; work his way to reference, then to the computer lab, and then to the staff room for coffee around ten am to chat with the staff. If there were no problems and no long conversations he would descend to the archives, say hello to Billy Connolly, and then proceed to the file cabinet that contained Ed Bender's memos. You could pick at random and be entertained by this collection. At Tom's suggestion, Billy had diligently applied himself to indexing the Bender memoranda.

Tom was asked to be one of the representatives for the school in eulogizing Samuel Cohen who had passed away while Tom was embroiled with the drug bust in Maine. So Tom entered "eulogy" and up came "Norman L. Thomas."

And Tom settled in a chair to read Bender's memo. "There is no one better at giving eulogies than Dean Oberal. No notes. Complete sentences. Absolutely mellifluous. No one can say less with such sincerity and poise than a Dean. And what is even more remarkable is that they can do it without repeating themselves. And timing. Twenty minutes each. I have timed them. It obviously comes from his years of practice and the ennui of collegiality. Norman was a capable teacher and he was worth twenty minutes, but not the pap the dean threw out. And who can forget this final line, 'Norman belongs in that pantheon of great law professors who have brought this law school to its present promontory,' followed by Josh Wittberg's aside, 'None of whose names he can recall.'

Not only will names be forgotten but the rush to take the place of the fallen begins before the burial. Mark Anthony was never on a law faculty.

Tom read on: "He should have mentioned that when you walked into Norman's office, the first thing you saw was his Havad Law diploma. Beneath it was three years of the *Havad Law Reviews* shelved prominently in crimson binding with gold lettering specifying the volume number. Lettered slightly smaller on the bottom were his name and the years he was on the law review. No one that I know could turn a conversation around to Havad like Norman. If he couldn't place a person, he would discreetly ask, "I think you were at the law school when I was there." His articles, and there were many (and I should add they were more than competent), cited ivy authors and ivy law reviews on at least ten to one basis over other authorities. Norman was on many law association and bar association committees as well as an author of books. He never included Essex in his credentials. Of course Norman came to us after forced retirement from Havad at 65 and has had visiting professorships at a number of universities, and also served as staff on Congressional Committees when Republicans were in power. Yes, he had many credentials but it was notable that *Who's Who In America* neglected to mention that Essex was the place of last repose for this gentleman scholar."

Tom had no such intentions of using Bender's sarcasm. But he was right on the mark as far as Dean Oberal was concerned. When Tom first came to Essex, he didn't know a soul. He began writing his own memorandum for the hidden history: "Here I was coming to a new institution. I knew of Essex, but didn't think much of it. Jewish kids didn't go to Essex, and here was a nice albeit half-Jewish librarian coming to an institution sprinkled like jimmies with an Irish faculty, Irish secretaries, and God save me, Irish cleaning people. The students were not all Irish and that was because the school was a haven for the poor. That let in Christians of all sorts, a few unhappy Jews, whose parents insisted they become lawyers or doctors even if they couldn't get into a decent law school, a few blacks, and politicians, who, it is unfair to religion to place them in any other category. I should mention St. Mary's in Holyoke. You could be the dumbest person in the world, if you graduated from St. Mary's, there was a place for you at Essex. One reason for that could be that Father O'Reilly, the President of St. Mary's was an Essex alumnus.

And this is where Samuel Cohen comes in. My first day at Essex, Samuel came over to me and asked me to lunch. He said 'Let's go to Durgin Park.' I acted innocent and said, 'I didn't know there was a Durgin Park.' He said, 'It's not a park, it's a restaurant. Let me tell you about Boston. We have the Boston Common. That's a park. We have the Public Gardens. That's a park. There is also the Arnold Arboretum. A Bostonian term for a park. Then we have Park Street, which isn't a park. Then there is that famous family: The Parkmans. And don't forget The Parker House. So let us go to Durgin Park, which is not a park, that is located in Fanueil Hall, which is part of Quincy Market. In Boston we distinguish ourselves with nomenclature.'

Through Samuel, and by the way, never call him Sam, I met other faculty and was thereby eased into the Essex community. Throughout my stay at Essex, Samuel was my mainstay. The man was brilliant in unimaginable ways. He taught taxation and commercial law, but faculty would come to him with problems in their discipline. If I had a mechanical problem in the library, he would either find a way to fix it or know someone who could. If you had a personal problem, and I wont go into the few I had, Samuel was there to offer solace, not advice. The problem that I had with Samuel was that there were times I would only want him to listen to my problem, and not drop whatever he was doing and attend to me.

What kind of a teacher was Samuel? I don't know. Professor Toole thought – not thought – spoke derisively of his talents. But I have been to many law school events and witnessed lawyers coming up to Samuel and thanking him for his teaching skills.

I sat in on a few of Professor Cohen's classes. By the way, Samuel always referred to going to class, as 'I am going to meet my class.' He would illustrate a point in commercial law by taking a cane and turning it into a snake. He would open his tax class by stating that the tax code was the most begotten piece of legislation ever written and rewritten. It had more loopholes than boy scouts had knots to tie. There was no possible way to make any sense of the code and to teach it was a task no Hercules could ever accomplish. And then he would say, "Now let us begin."

Professor Cohen died on the job. He was 92 and the longest living active professor at Essex. He said, 'If Holmes could stay on the court in his

90s, why not me on this faculty.' His passing away was a phenomenon. He had driven his bike from Newton to the law school, a good three miles, and had reached the area where bikes were secured when he passed away astride the bike. How long he was in that rigid position and how the bicycle held him up and did not topple can only be guessed at. But a security guard thought it peculiar and when he approached the bike, Professor Cohen tipped over in his arms."

Tom finished writing. It was time to head to the synagogue and to sit up front with the family and the other eulogists. He would be short, and he would be diplomatic, but he made it a point to ask Connolly to start a new file and begin it with his eulogy.

CHAPTER 39

TOM vs DOOLEY

The library committee had just concluded. The Dean and Associate Dean were over in a corner and Dooley seemed to be unduly upset. Tom was engaged in conversation with Peter Toole.

"Talk it over with Tom, Joseph. I'm sure you can come to some agreement on this." And Dooley walked over to Tom and Peter.

Tom and Dooley stared at one another.

"If neither of you have anything to say, I will begin the conversation," began Peter Toole. "The alumni dinner is tonight. I am staying at the Havad Club for the weekend, and I wondered if either of you gentlemen would like to join me for a drink and then walk over to the Copley Plaza for the festivities."

"Well, before I answer that question, I want Dean Dooley to know, that I do not favor setting up a separate law library for the law review. I think there should be one for the four reviews that the school has authorized."

"Tom," replied Dooley, "I appreciate your democratic tendencies, but the law review is the big jewel in the tiara of this law school, and ..."

"They don't want to associate with the serfs on the other reviews?"

"You may put any interpretation on it that you like. Peter what is your take on this. I don't recall your weighing in on the matter."

"Simple. Tom, give it to the law review. I guarantee you the library will be overrun by the entire student body. You are both in error, though. The law review has enough privileges already. They don't have to attend classes, they have the biggest budget in the law school, they throw a lavish expense paid dinners, and they get the best jobs. They don't need a library and I want an answer to my invitation."

"I'll be glad to meet you Peter. How about you, Tom? Is your wife coming?"

"No, she is in New York, and yes, Professor Toole I will join you."

Toole was never content to let an opportunity for getting at any joint in the harness. "Tom, your little lady was certainly in her cups at the last alumni dinner."

And Dooley hastened to add with a slight nod to Toole, "And out of her cups too."

Tom stiffened at this and, in a calm voice, added, "As a matter of fact she didn't come home that night."

Dooley laughed. "Well, don't look at me."

"I was told that she was seen leaving the Copley in a Jaguar."

At this, Toole took off abruptly, only adding, "I hope to see you two at the Club later."

Tom and Dooley stared at one another. "Heh, lots of people have Jaguars." And then glared at Tom. "So that's it. Even-steven. You've been at me over this property business for some time. Poisoning my relationship with Mary McCarthy. And you almost got my son hooked up with that gang." Dooley began stomping around the room. He was taking deep breaths, and his face was red and puffed. "You got nothing on me, Tom." Dooley's hands were opening and closing. "I warned the Dean about hiring you. We could have had Hughes for half the price and got twice the value. We'd have made the third tier of law schools without you, Tom. And sucking up to the Student Bar to get their achievement award. And it was a Jewish student president." Tom stood silent waiting for Dooley to finish. "You know your problem, Tom? You're nothing. You're not Jewish, you're not Catholic. If you were either one I could deal with you. I can't deal with half breeds." He began to walk away.

Tom calmly called after him. "Dean Dooley, I would love to be in the confessional booth to hear your confession, and by the way, I will definitely take Professor Toole's offer of a drink.

CHAPTER 40

THE NEW DEAN

If Dean Dooley had one quality, it was to act as if he had no grudge against those he considered to be his worst enemies. His rages would simmer down to a smile. His madness was his method. Like a soldier it was the uniform he was saluting not the dumb idiot wearing the stripes. Dooley was an Associate Dean and he recognized that faculty were his commanding officers. If he had ambitions to succeed Dean Oberal, he was the first to scoff at the idea. He often pontificated that his family was his only obsession. A wife, he claimed to be wonderful, that few on the faculty had met as she never came to law school functions. Nine children, one of whom he proudly claimed took one on the chin to join the church. One an officer in the army. Eleven grandchildren. "Not a beatnick among them," as he proudly proclaimed. After his scuffle with Tom, they greeted each other as if nothing had happened. The only difference was that while Tom did not feel a grudge, he also did not hide his low opinion for the man he dubbed Mr. Pecksniff.

The Deanships were divided like Gaul in three parts. Dooley handled administrative matters. Another dean handled curriculum matters, and the third handled appointments. Then there was the assistant to the dean who oversaw placement, development, alumni functions and was on call twenty-four hours a day. Dean Oberal was a delegator with Machiavellian instincts. You would never know that he had an opinion one way or the other at faculty meetings, unless you were aware that he would have a point man to achieve his wishes. If he did not want a person to get tenure,

244

he would make sure someone on the faculty would make the argument for him. The same went for curriculum matters, budget apportionments, and course assignments. When the Dean decided that a contract professor was making a nuisance of himself by refusing to abide by marking on a bell curve and flunking too large a percentage of his classes, he went to work. First he found a replacement in a talented young man who had written an excellent treatise on the subject. Then he called the mark in. He expressed sorrow that his wife was quite ill at the time. Suggested that at fifty-five he might want to take advantage of the law school's buyout program. It was just his way of showing appreciation for his loyalty to the school. They had talked about the winter place the family went to every year in St. Petersburg, and he could put in a good word for him to the law school down there. That did the job. Law professors know when the game is up. No overt hard feelings. Everybody acts satisfied. There was even a delightful interview in *Cert* on his departure. And the school even threw in a set of golf clubs.

To T. S. Eliot, April is the cruelest month, but in law it is May. That is when decisions are made for the next calendar year. Who is in and who is out. The beauty of a street fight is that it is generally over pretty quickly. A bloody nose, a black eye. Law professors are not so lucky. The psychological traumas pervade the entire body like a slow acting drug. Even tenure does not save you. A contract professor is suddenly told he will only be teaching professional responsibility. Where there is a three year rule, you have an agonizingly long wait to know if you will be on a tenure track. If not, you are sent out into the legal world to fend for yourself. And woe to the newcomer who shows up a tenured professor, or whose skills and popularity diminish his betters, or who considers himself an equal to his colleagues. Hell has no fury like a tenured law professor scorned. And no despondency is greater, after a stellar performance in college and law school, to find that your colleagues hold you in low regard. And this is usually done with panache and the blackball. And every Dean knows his responsibility in staffing his faculty.

The Dean was so good at his job and the President of the University, Augustus Friedrich, so out of his element in the opinion of many, that it was only natural when the latter's contract was up it was a simple matter for the Board of Trustees to decide on Dean Oberal as his successor.

On the matter of the outgoing President, Dean Oberal was not diplomatic. When Friedrich took office, he assumed his authority exceeded that of the Dean of the law school. What a mistake that was! The Dean never appeared at the President's monthly meetings. In fact, President Friedrich wasn't invited to law school's functions, and when he did come he was never asked to speak. Oberal actually rebuked one of the speakers for acknowledging his presence. He never learned that at Essex, the law school tail wags the dog. But the President was dogged in his determination to run a university. And truth to be told, he did not do a bad job. He got accreditation for the business school, increased enrollment, particularly by attracting foreign students, and made many positive structural improvements. But for five years he was known only for his forced smile. Dean Oberal never forgave him for assuming that his Presidency included the law school.

And now Oberal was asked to take over the university. The trustees implored him. The alumni association begged him. The students and faculty had no idea that all of this was taking place. Tom Jones did because as law librarian he had many dealings with the university administration. Because the law library's budget was larger than the university library budget, Tom and the university librarian worked together on many projects. Tom had also undertaken to teach a course for paralegals at the university and that had brought him into contact with their faculty. The resentment of the university faculty to the law faculty was that the law faculty had salaries that many times doubled that of the university faculty. They were not step-children – they were orphans.

And so the Dean accepted the presidency. Now the race for the new law dean was on. It was astounding to Tom how many people came out of the woodwork to be Dean. Suddenly faculty he had not spoken to since arriving at the school wanted to have a cup of coffee with him and dwell on their meager achievements as if they were earth shattering. Even strangers. Tom got calls from professors at other schools making inquiries about the job. A committee was set up to sift through the applicants. To be sure, Oberal had a hand in appointing the committee. And the committee narrowed the list to five names. One member of the Essex law faculty, a Dean of a neighboring law school, a member of the legislature who was an alumnus, a member of the board of trustees who was also an alumnus of the law school, and a well known personal injury lawyer, who, as it happens, was a friend of the now President Oberal.

Professor Toole made his weekly pilgrimage to the library for the sole purpose of seeing if he could antagonize Tom. He always felt he came away second best in his exchanges but this time he thought he had an ace up his sleeve.

"I notice you have been attending the interviews for the new Dean, Tom," said Toole after he patiently waited for Tom to end a telephone call.

"I just had a call from a leading labor lawyer asking me when Justice Holmes said 'that it is not only that justice must be done, but it must be seen to be done.'"

"Sounds like something he'd say."

"Fact is that he didn't say it. I happened to be reading a book by Megarry and it was Lord Hewitt who said it and I am going to look up when he said it and call the man back."

"Are you planning to be demoted to reference librarian? Maybe we should strip you of that professor title you have?"

"Dean Toole, considering your opinion of some of the faculty here, I should consider it a promotion."

They laughed. "But to get back to the interviews," asked Tom, "I'd like to get your undoubtedly honest opinion of the candidates."

"Well," said Toole, "let's eliminate Bradford first. Groton, Havad, and teaching at this lowly school. Maybe the Deanship will get him back in the family's good graces. Coleman: Father a Federal judge, had a good career going at Cahn but his wife couldn't stand New York so took a Deanship in a small town. Then he was divorced and he can't stand being in a small town. The Board of Trustee guy. Ridiculous. He was a student of mine. Smart. Went to work for a big Boston firm. Didn't make partner. Went into business for himself. Three man law firm. Very active in Essex affairs that got him on the Board of Trustees. Wants to get out of the rat race. Sees the Deanship as a raise in pay. No way."

"We're running out of candidates, Professor. How about you? Maybe this time around ..." Tom didn't finish as he could see Toole's lips twitching.

Toole caught himself. "Tom, I do the needling, if you don't mind. Where were we? Oh, yes. Mr. Mitnich. Very successful tort lawyer. Million dollar verdicts. Very thorough. I've done some work for him on a military case. Good friend of Oberal."

"Do you think the Board would go for a Jewish lawyer?"

"I think they should go for Fitzgerald, his being Irish not the least of things in his favor. A good legislator but a Republican. His only avenue, and that is why he is an applicant, is to become a Dean here - he is an alumnus – if he does a good job and uses the school as a bully pulpit I see him as a Governor."

"So that is why you are here – to get me to vote for him."

"Tom, the reason I like you is that you want everyone to think you are naïve. Yes, I want you to vote for him but the Dean has his army out for Mitnich. The faculty will be asked to narrow the list down to two, and the Board will pick Mitnich."

"Why?"

"Because Oberal wants him. How can the Board that begged him to be President turn down his request. Probably owes him a favor. Mitnich is bored with his job. His partner will take over the firm. You will find Mitnich and Oberal celebrating at the Ritz-Carlton with a couple of – let's leave it at that."

"Well, I think I'll vote for Bradford."

"I can see why," threw in Toole as he walked toward the exit. "You both come from families of settlers."

CHAPTER 41

THE NEW PRESIDENT

And sure enough, as Toole predicted, Sol Mitnich became Dean. Oberal came away from the fray knowing he owed favors to many. It was all the alumni association could do to control its outrage at the selection. The association was top heavy with alumni who had protested school integration, still lived in Irish conclaves in South Boston, and revered James Michael Curley, the rogue mayor that the city had blessed with not one but two statues. Framed and signed photographs of Father Coughlin could still be found in many of their homes.

Sol Mitnich was well aware of the mixed feelings at his arrival and took steps to calm it down. He had membership in "12 Park Street" an exclusive club on 12 Park Street that catered to the elite of Boston, and arranged for luncheons, at his own expense, with all members of the faculty. He made it a point to talk individually with faculty and office personnel. This included maintenance, and a luncheon with Tom Jones and his professional staff at Locke-Ober's, a non-exclusive dining establishment that catered to those that could afford its prices, and satisfy the tourists that came to see the painting of a naked lady in the downstairs area once only accessible to men..

And Tom and his staff made the short trek to Locke-Ober Café, located on a *cul de sac* off Winter Street in the heart of Boston. A room on the second floor had been reserved for the group and such specialties as lobster bisque and finan haddie were gobbled up by the group.

Sol Mitnich was of medium height, an oval face that was always flushed either through two much drinking or genetically. Unlike many trial lawyers, his dress was moderate and looked off the rack. He did not wear tasseled shoes. Some said his success was due to his ordinariness. He made no attempt to overpower juries with either his dress, his demeanor, or his voice. He never raised his voice in cross-examination and although he had more million dollar verdicts than any other lawyer in New England, he rarely made headlines. Sol was sixty years of age but looked much older. There was a sag to his shoulders, and a roundness to his belly, and his speech in conversation was slow enough to cause the listener to lose concentration. He was an inspiration to lawyers of similar appearance. But here he was, about to give a short talk to Tom Jones and his staff who were used to Dean Oberal's Demosthenes-like oratory.

"Tom," and he began, "I want to welcome you and your staff to this luncheon and I want all of you to know that I think the law library is the backbone of a law school. I myself worked in the Commonwealth Law School library when I was going to law school. I want you all to be free to come into my office at any time to talk to me. And ..."

At this point, a waiter intruded and asked if there was a Tom Jones in the room.

Tom raised his hand and was told there was an urgent message from a Mary McCarthy on the phone and would he like to answer it. The Dean nodded to indicate that Tom was free to leave. When Tom tried a quick explanation, the Dean said, "I know Mary McCarthy. Go to it, Tom."

"God, I'm glad to get you. What the hell are you doing at Locke-Ober's." Mary suspiciously added, "Did you come into an inheritance? Tom, I'm in big trouble. They want to kick me out of the home here."

Tom took the trouble to explain the nature of the meeting and then asked, "What happened, Mary? Why?"

"Please come right away." There was a frantic note to Mary's plea, and Tom felt he had no alternative but to say, "Mary, I'll catch the first plane out of here."

"Thank God," and Tom could feel the click of the telephone had a note of relief in it.

The next plane out of Logan to Mt. Desert was at 6pm. When Tom arrived at Mount Desert Island, he rented a car and drove to Mary's retirement community on Frenchman's Bay. Tom was let into the building upon identifying himself and located Mary at the sick bay attended by a nurse practitioner.

"She's not feeling well today," was the nurse's verdict. "People have been coming in and out of her apartment, including Mr. Sheffield, the supervisor. She finally had enough, and refused to see anyone until you came along. And we brought her here for observation. Good luck."

Tom walked in and there was Mary on what looked like an operating table. Her legs were dangling, her hair was untidy, and her eyes were bloodshot.

The first thing she said was, "I guess you're going to have to find me another place to live. They've given me notice. They want me out immediately."

"Calm down, Mary. Give it to me slow and easy. "

Mary looked around to make sure she was alone with Tom Jones.

"Do you remember that fellow that came with me one day that we met? Old guy with wobbly knees. We were very friendly. He used to come to the hash house I worked in way back when my prospects were dim. I never took a fancy to him. Wouldn't let him drive me home. He was a wormer. Imagine making a living digging worms out of the tide. Boots up to your hips. Smelly business. It's a wonder he didn't get sucked in and joined them."

"I'm listening."

"Well, what. It's thirty years later and here he is retired – knobby knees and all – and he introduces himself to me. Tells me how much he admired me. No longer a wormer. Took over the family business."

"They don't allow residents to be friends?"

"Not if they spend the night with you."

"Mary."

"The man was in love with me. I was in love with him."

"There's something else here Mary."

"Here's the whole story. He and his wife have an apartment here. Same size as mine. She must weigh 300 pounds. Has diabetes. Is asthmatic. Needs oxygen. The only way she can get around is when an attendant wheels her out to the porch for some air. She is a nice lady but immobile. That is why Zeke is here. He may be eighty years old but he can get around. But he brought her here so she would be comfortable, and sold his home in Surrey."

"So they have a moral code here?"

Mary shook her head to indicate that things were a little more complicated than that. "I'm glad you're not squeamish Tom. Zeke is old. We fell in love. He wanted to have sex with me when I was at the eats place. I wasn't interested. So now I'm interested and the poor guy, much as he tries, can't perform. Like putting a marshmallow in a piggy bank. By the way, I never did oral sex in the old days, but, to make him happy, we both lapped ourselves to sleep."

"And Mrs. Zeke?"

"We thought she was out of it. Immobile. Had to have an oxygen tank wherever she went. Zeke paid for a nurse during the day, and she slept peacefully during the night. If she had a problem, she just had to press for an attendant."

"Mary, I'm getting squeamish."

"The worst is just beginning, Tom. Zeke comes hobbling into my room last night. He's in his pajamas, and sticking out of his fly is a rather substantial erection. "Eureka," he yells. "I don't know whether it's the name of a drug, or he found the thing somewhere. He jumps on the bed and I have no objection, except that since I had pins put in my hip when I broke it, it was a little painful getting into position. He has terrible knees – probably from the suction while he was worming, and he is trying to get into position but has no leverage. It was taking a while, but he was finally achieving satisfaction, when his wife arrives."

"I thought she was immobile."

"So did we. Somehow she got someone to put her in one of those electric scooters and made it to our room, caught us in the act and started screaming bloody murder."

Mary stopped and waited for a comment. Tom just kept staring at her. "What could be next," was all he could think of.

"The poor woman dropped dead, Tom."

"Ooh, my God," exclaimed Tom

"And so did Zeke." Mary shook her head. "It was terrible. There he was on top of me. In the middle of an orgasm. It took two orderlies to pry him lose. And the idiots could not stop laughing. Didn't sleep a week all night. And seven o'clock in the morning in comes the superintendent and I don't know who else and tell me I have to leave immediately."

"Mary," and this was all Tom could think of, "you're what? 85 years old. What are you doing having sex? My God, that's awful."

Mary looked kindly at Tom. "Tom, you may be too young to have sex, but you are never too old. I finally find a man that I am comfortable with in bed – he loves me and I love him – and this has to happen."

"That Eureka is certainly deadly," was all Tom could add.

"I don't think so. I think they both died of natural causes. I wish it killed me too."

"Don't say that Mary. Look, let me talk to some people here and see what I can do. You sit tight – I mean relax – and get a good night's sleep."

Tom located the chief financial officer the next morning.

"I'm sorry, Mr. Jones, there is nothing I can do. We think we can be sued for what went on that night. We cannot have that kind of conduct in this establishment."

Tom went right to the point. "Mr. Cartwright, do you know that the lease you have on this building is owned by the McCarthy Associates?"

"What has that to do with our discussion, Mr. Jones?"

"Number One – Mary McCarthy is McCarthy Associates. When she authorized the lease, she agreed to your request for most favorable terms as you were a non-profit association. I am Ms McCarthy's lawyer, and I am preparing her will as well as other matters for her, and you might want to reconsider your harsh terms. She regrets the incident, and I want to remind you that it was not she who invaded another's apartment. If there is to be any suing, I think she is as likely as any to bring charges."

Mr. Cartwright looked perplexed. He rose from his chair and excused himself. Tom sat calmly and looked out the window. The retirement home was built on a rising that overlooked Frenchman's Bay. There were sailboats in the bay, and a big liner seemed to be steaming into Bar Harbor. The sky was a deep blue and the Mt. Desert Island mountains looked like a pod of whales. Tom was thinking that maybe Mary was healthy enough to accompany him to a nice fish dish at the Coach House that was but minutes away. Sure enough, Mr. Cartwright returned.

"Mr. Jones, I have just spoken to the administrator. You are right. We have acted hastily. But please tell Miss McCarthy that we are trying to run a respectable home here."

"Mr. Cartwright, all I am going to tell her is that you acted hastily. She is rather wrought right now, and I don't want to imperil her health. But thank you and goodbye."

Tom suggested that Mary go to her room and take a nap. He would go to his room at the Asticou Inn in Northeast Harbor and freshen up. He would then pick her up and they would go out to dinner rather than Mary eat in the retirement dining room and have to face all her neighbors. Mary shrugged and agreed.

And Tom and Mary drove to the Coach House and gorged on plates of trout and salmon, with a crab cake appetizer and some blueberry beer just for the heck of it.. They lolled on the deck and looked out on Frenchman Bay in search of pirates

Tom drove Mary back to her retirement abode. Mary was relieved to find that she wasn't locked out and that her room was still hers. She invited Tom in.

"Mary, I'm a little hesitant about going into a room with you."

"That would be encouraging Tom, but I think I have to lay low for a while."

Tom wasn't sure just what that meant, but got down to business. "Mary recent developments suggest to me that we have to come to a conclusion about your dealings with Dean Dooley."

"You tell me what to do, Tom"

"First, let me give you the layout. That little camp that Dooley brought you has spawned a fortune. Dooley used the equity to practically buy up the cove. He also bought some other tracts on the island, including the one you are living in now. The property is in your name, but he is your agent. He determines the rents, pays the real estate taxes, and takes a salary. He thinks he has clean hands."

"I put everything in his hands, Tom. I got what I wanted. But, hey, I now have a son that I'd like to do something for. Any problem with that."

"We are getting a little ahead of my story, Mary, but let's get to that. Your son is the bank manager who has been handling your account. Frankly, I don't trust the guy."

"What do you mean?"

"He is a CPA, Mary. He has great suspicions of what is going on."

"Like what?"

"Like the fact that you are sitting on what could be millions of dollars. Like the fact that Dooley sometimes get carried away with his role as agent. Without much trouble, I, myself, traced his down payment to his house on the Cape to your account."

"Tom, I don't begrudge him his house on the Cape. For God's sake …"

"Hold it, Mary. I know you don't but there are transactions that can be easily accumulated to being over ten thousand dollars that can arise suspicions and reporting by a bank officer. And Jeb Figgis is keeping an eye on me thinking, I believe, that I'm in on something." Tom thought it best not to mention that Jeb could reap a reward for discovering tax irregularities.

"Something illegal?"

"Mary, the whole business is illegal. The money that bought your camp. The equity from it that bought the cove. The purchase of property that – Mary, I'm not trying to make Dooley out as a villain. He did you a good turn. His motive may not have been of the best, but you got what you wanted. Then his real estate instincts took hold. He had money, not his own, to invest. Every gambler's most ardent desire. He succeeded beyond the dreams of avarice. And Mary, he now wants to give it all away. He's not the devil's apprentice exactly."

"What should be done with it?"

"We'll talk about it tomorrow. I have a room at the Asticou Inn, and I would like you to come over tomorrow for lunch."

CHAPTER 42

THE RECKONING

Mary took a cab to the Asticou. Sitting on the porch was Dean Dooley and Tom. Mary's eyes tried to reach her eyebrows as she paid the cabbie, and slowly, and a little painfully, made her way up the stairs. Dooley descended to help her but she whisked him away.

"I don't need any help, Dean. And if I did need any, I'd want a young guy like Tom."

Tom took Mary by the arm, and the three of them slowly made it to the luncheon area out on the deck. The view of Northeast Harbor from the Asticou was of gracious lawns, towering sailboats, yachts, and the hum of sea-going activity. It was a very quiet lunch. Mary had not been told that Dooley would be there. Tom only had stomach for clam chowder. Mary had a crab roll and coffee. Dooley, not a fish eater, had a hamburger and a beer. Tom then suggested they go to his room.

Dooley began the proceedings. "First thing I'd like to settle here Mary is this – you and I have done pretty well in our dealings. What right have you to involve Tom in our dealings."

"Cause I'm leery of you, Joseph. I want to do the right thing and I don't want you to talk me into doing the wrong thing."

"Mary, what have I done wrong?" He spread his arms out wide as to indicate that he had given her everything she ever wanted.

Mary looked at Tom.

Tom answered, as he shook his head. "You stole money, Dean Dooley."

Dooley rose up. His face was livid. At that moment if he could have struck Tom dead, it would have happened. But Dooley's rage, as always, was short lived. He laughed weakly.

"Tom, I presume Mary has told you things that may or may not be true."

"I have corroborating evidence. Ed Bender has left some very incriminating information about some of the practices of you and the founder of the law school."

"That schmuck." Dooley laughed. "He's dead – and long before you got here."

"You'd be surprised at what librarians leave behind."

"All right," said Dooley taking a more pleasing tone, "forget the statute of limitations, forget that what I and the Dean did was common practice. There was Miss McCarthy with a pail between her legs collecting tuition fees, and, yes, I was guilty of doing what the Dean was doing – with his permission. I took the faculty to lunch with the money, cab fares, etc. Let's say, I took fifty thousand dollars. Which is crazy. Do you know how much I have donated to Essex in the past twenty five years?"

"Exactly fifty thousand dollars," said Tom.

Dooley was able to suppress any surprise at this. "Do you know what that bastard paid us for salary. I taught every course in the curriculum. I ran the school. I had day classes and night classes. In that pail was our salary, and Seth knew it."

Tom said nothing.

"And now for the *coup de grace*. Am I going to use that money to build a castle? To buy a yacht? I am going to give it all to charity. Now, Mr. Jones, what do you say to that?"

"You have nothing to give, Mr. Dooley. Not without Ms McCarthy..."

Dooley looked at Mary. "I have an agreement with Mary."

"All I can see is a will ..."

Dooley interrupted, "That is good enough for me."

And Mary blurted, "It's not good enough for me, Joseph. I have a son."

Dooley was unable to suppress astonishment at this. And Tom added, "And he happens to be the bank manager in Portland that handles your account. And if I am not mistaken he may have suspicions of irregularities. It's possible that one miscalculation by us could send the two of you to jail."

Things were clearing up for Dooley. He was now picturing the bank manager and seeing his face blend in with that of Seth Adams. The ears, the eyebrows that had no break on his forehead, the Roman nose, and even the Maine argot. "Mary, why didn't you tell me?"

"I never saw him. Tom recognized him."

"To me he was just a dumb hick. When I decided to get a new Jaguar, I tried to make a nice deal with him for my old one. Practically give him the car. I think he was interested but decided it wouldn't look right. Now that I think of it, it wasn't a good move. But he's your son, Mary." And Dooley looked first at Mary, then at Tom.

"Let's get back to charity. What charity?"

"None of your business, retorted Dooley.

"Maybe not, but Professor Toole tells me you are planning to get some Knights of Columbus recognition, that you are planning a trip to Rome, and ..."

"Toole's a fool. And what if I am planning to give the Church some money?"

"Dean Dooley. That money belongs to Essex. And how can you give stolen money to the Church?"

Dooley laughed. "Tom if you were Jewish I could talk sense to you. If you were Catholic I could talk sense to you. I have always had suspicions of half-breeds. They have no loyalties, and are always anti-Catholic. Mary may be a lapsed Catholic, but we have an agreement and I am sure she will keep it."

"Joseph, I may be a lapsed Catholic. I have made a lot of mistakes in my life. But for once in my life I want to do the right thing. I am a thief. You are a thief. I am 80 something years old. I may want to go to confession before I die and I want to do the right thing. And I want you to do the right thing.

Dooley sat down. Got up. Paced around the deck. And then walked out. Tom waited a minute and then could hear the unmistakable roar of a Jaguar spitting gravel from under its tires.

CHAPTER 43

THE CENTENNIAL

Celebrating a hundred years anniversary may not be an auspicious occasion in Boston, but to the Essex Anniversary Committee it was momentous. They arranged for a tent the size of a football field to accommodate the luminaries and students that were invited. As the administration marched up Bowdoin Street, paraded by the State House, down the steps adjoining the Shaw Memorial on Beacon Street, and the length of the Boston Common where a huge tent was set up facing Charles Street and the Public Garden. Few pedestrians thought it an unusual sight. Faculty marched in their academic regalia where purple and red seemed to be at war with each other. Student guides kept the procession in order, occasionally keeping a participant, who had alcoholically prepared himself for the event, from falling on his or her face, and steadying the person the rest of the way. Processional music blared from the school's band.

Behind the dais were seated one hundred people all of whom would be introduced with a number. Number One Hundred was going to be President Oberal of this great university. The first was a one hundred year old graduate of Essex, who appeared to have been dragged or drugged from his home in Pittsfield. A microphone had to be brought to the gentleman and a sigh of relief could be heard from the arrangers of this event when he took out a piece of paper from his pocket and read, "Essex University has made me what I am, and I wish it well for the next one hundred years." No one knew just what Essex had made him.

Fortunately Caleb Cushing, who would have been the oldest alumnus of the law school, and was anxiously looking forward to the event, passed away just shy of his 100th birthday. Dean Mitnich, aware of Tom's interview with Caleb had stopped to talk to Tom as Presdent Oberal was heading toward the speaker's platform.

"Tom, can you imagine that guy on the platform? I knew of his propensity for farting at an American Trial Lawyer's annual meeting. No one sat within ten feet of him."

Tom joined in, "The band would not have needed the cymbals if he came."

"By the way, whatever happened to that case. Oberal told me about it. Someone should have written it up for the *Boston Bar Journal*.

"The Judge recused himself which is what Cushing wanted. Got a plaintiff judge and the case was settled."

"Sounds like the sour smell of success," and Mitnich headed toward the platform.

Sitting quietly in the front row were Seth Adams' three sons. All Havad Law graduates, they sat uncomfortably as guests of the school. As they stood to be introduced as children of the founder, all Mary could say was, "Thank God he had only boys."

Then followed two Federal District Court Judges, twenty two, Massachusetts judges from the district and superior courts, four judges from Rhode Island, one judge from Maine, Vermont, Connecticut, and New Hampshire. There was also one judge from Colorado and another from New York, but they were announced as having prior engagements. Then followed legislators, lawyers, civil servants, business entrepreneurs and other citizens who the school believed had achieved some measure of success in life.

The event was opened with a prayer by Father Dooley, the son of the Associate Dean. There was a slight disturbance at this point as the exPresident of the United States, Alexander George Twigg, a bit unsteady as he had recently had some hip problems from his annual parachute event, rose to the platform unannounced. Oberal rose to meet him and they exchanged words. Oberal seemed to have the last words and Twigg stepped aside. "It is a great pleasure for me to introduce at this time the former President of the United States, Alexander George Twigg. He has insisted, correctly, I may add, that he doesn't need an introduction, and so I present, admittedly a little out of order – I am a great admirer of President Twigg and had a most impressive …" President Twigg all this time was edging Oberal away and Oberal finally gave in and turned the microphone over to the President of the United States. "Mr. Mmm – a great president of a great university. I'm not going to say very much as I don't want to spoil your day. You know the old saying of General MacArthur that old soldiers never die, they fade away; well, old deans never die, they lose their faculties, old lawyers never die, they lose their appeal. How about exPresidents. Apparently they never die, they just look for opportunities like this to be reminded they once were President." The President laughed, The people behind the dais laughed, and even those in the audience out of the range of the loud speakers laughed. This seemed to invigorate the President and he continued, "Old bankers never die, they just lose their interest." At this point, a tall, young man who had followed the President while all this was going on whispered in his ear. The President nodded. "Ladies and Gentleman, I have a golf cart just outside this tent that is going to take me to a limousine that is going to drive me to the airport where I will board an airplane. I have been asked by the government," and the President made a motion not to be believed, "to represent the United States at an exhibition to be held at St. Andrews, Scotland." And off the President went to the customary applause.

Tom and the library staff were asked to usher at the event. And the seating of the two thousand attendees was handled expeditiously. Lavatories were carted in and placed in convenient locations. There were representatives from all schools including a number of high school valedictorians. The only glitch was an encounter with Dean Dooley.

"You're doing a great job, Tom," said the Dean.

"I try and do a great job whatever my assignment, Dean."

"I'm really sorry about that history you wrote. I hope you don't think I had anything to do with it."

"What! That Gibbons is doing it? I wrote the history and sent it to Mitnich and he decided to get Gibbons to incorporate it in his history of the university. No problem."

"I think he gave you a footnote, or did he?"

"I didn't notice. Shouldn't you be making it up to the podium? I understand you have an announcement to make."

"Tom, believe me, I tried to get you on the podium, but you and your staff were too valuable down here. So help me, no one could have done a better job."

"You are so right, Dean Dooley.

And Dean Dooley, garbed in crimson from his masters degree in law from Havad Law School, ambled proudly to the podium.

Tom was amused that Dooley thought he was putting one over on Tom. Writing the two histories was fun and both will be preserved in the archives. It may take a hundred years for them to be found by another inquisitive librarian but just the thought of it made the colloquy with Dooley worth while.

The afternoon droned on. The elite one hundred were introduced with a few words as to their year of graduation, their accomplishments, and their family life. They stood, were acknowledged, and then sat down.

Then the main event. The Associate Justice of the United States Supreme Court, the Honorable Justin Fryer was introduced. No one could beam like Fryer. He could have been a lighthouse. The self-satisfied look on his face told you that he felt that everyone in the audience was looking at him with envy. A graduate of Groton, Havad, Havad Law, a longtime teacher of administrative law at Havad, he still kept a home in Cambridge, and spent his summers at Martha's Vinyard. He considered himself as one following in the footsteps of Holmes, Brandeis, Frankfurter. His book on the deregulation of the air waves was heralded by a noted daily as the beginning of a a new era in law. Soon the market would regulate itself and a new era of prosperity would spread to the four corners of the world. Another daily had a column, "Man's Ingenuity to Man" that predicted that more needless *chotkes* would be invented to choke homes like clogged chimneys. "Creative destruction would reach its zenith," the article said." and destroy the universe."

The Justice's speech was a marvel of learning. It traced the common law from the Year Books to the right to privacy with frequent quotes from Holmes, Brandeis, Frankfurter, and even Cardozo. For twenty minutes he impressed himself, if no one else, with his learning. And for twenty minutes he never mentioned Essex University.

Then the President noted that in the program a special announcement would be made of significance to everyone connected not only with the university, but with the city of Boston, the State of Massachusetts, the United States of America, and even the entire English speaking world. For months Oberal had made it known that Essex was heading for great things. Every speech he gave, and even in run of the mill announcements there was a hint of things to come. A press agent had been hired to create this wave of excitement and it was very successful. It was successful enough to keep everyone in their seats even during the Justice's speech. The program for the event had a last listing of a "SPECIAL ANNOUNCEMENT."

And then the drum beat began. Then it accelerated. Then it grew louder. Finally a clash of cymbals. The President was thanking the Associate Justice, who quietly made his way out of the tent. He was a bit irate that he did not follow the President in speech making, and did not have the nerve to do what the President had done.

Tom knew what was coming. He had convinced Dooley that Jeb Figgis was on the edge of reporting to the I.R.S certain irregularities in the McCarthy Corporation dealings. There were several transactions that if combined would show large amounts of money being transferred. Tom convinced Jeb that his job was to take over the accounting and the business profile and to uncover any irregularities. Jeb had not been swayed by his spending a week in Mary's Mt. Desert camp, although he did appreciate it. But his duty as bank manager to report any improprieties overrode any personal advantages he might get from a client. In fact, he felt that the invitation was an attempt to keep him quiet. And he would not have kept quiet if Tom did not promise to cooperate with him.

Jeb convinced Tom he was not going to report any irregularities because he might be rewarded for his efforts, although he would not turn it down if the IRS thought he deserved a percentage of the illegal transactions. No one who, every working day and probably on weekends, wore a belt and suspenders to hold his pants up could be considered anything but upright.

That is what he thought until Tom lowered the bombshell on him. Tom waited until Jeb had everything in writing. Every transaction that had a shady look. Checkbooks, rent payments, stock transactions – a stack that was an inch thick lay on his desk when Tom took from under his arm, a rolled up piece of cardboard. He unfolded it. There was a painting of Seth Adams. Then he opened his brief case. There was a birth certificate. And then a one page explanation of the relationship between Jeb and Mary McCarthy.

Jeb closed the door to his office. Tom spoke. "I want to make one thing clear to you Jeb. When Mary invited you to the camp, it was not to get you to cover anything up. She wanted to see her son. Number two:

when Mary asked me to help her get out of the clutches of Dooley, I had no idea who you were."

Tom remembered this scene vividly as he waited for the announcement. President Oberal rose and beckoned Associate Dean Dooley to accompany him. "My friends, I have an announcement to make that promises to make our next hundred years even more successful than the last hundred. One hundred years ago, Essex Law School was founded by our exalted leader, Seth Adams, to educate lawyers. His quarry was not the homes of the rich and favored, but the huddled masses yearning for the opportunity to make good in this free society. Seth Adams gave meaning to democracy. He reached out for the poor, the minorities, the lower middle class and gave them the opportunity of a lifetime. Not just reached out, my friends, he extended a helpful hand. You have heard today, and read in our publications, that we pioneered in providing free tuition, loans without guarantees, and other benefits. We proved to the world despite opposition from the elite law schools," and Oberal turned to look at Justice Fryer but found only an empty seat, "and bar associations. You may remember they tried to eliminate evening law schools, they said you can't make carthorses into trotters. Seth Adams proved them wrong. Essex Law School now attracts law students from all over the country. We are now a third tier law school. We have arrangements with European and Asian law schools to spread our learning. Our publications are renowned for scholarship and attract scholars from around the world.

"The one thing we lacked that the so-called elite law schools had plenty of was endowment. My friends, I am here to announce that through the good works of our Associate Dean Joseph Francis Xavier Dooley, we have solved that problem. Through an anonymous benefactor, brought to us by Dean Dooley I announce today that we have received a gift of twenty million dollars with a promise of more to come through an arrangement with a real estate investment trust set up in a pristine location in Maine. Maine, you know, used to be part of Massachusetts." The President stopped for a moment. He sported a wisp of a smile. "We are finally making a profit out of that sale." The audience laughed. Then cheered.

"This endowment will have immediate repercussions," he began again. "First, we will immediately set in motion to build a new law school that will be the most technologically advanced in the history of architecture. Second, that two new programs will be immediately instituted. A graduate program in intellectual property will begin next semester and propel this law school, nay, this university, into the upper echelons of intellectual achievement.

But, my friends, we cannot subsist on bread alone. Dean Dooley and I are putting our heads together and will soon announce a new ecumenical program in Jewish and Catholic legal thought. This great city of Boston has a legacy of great accomplishments by these two religions and they will unite in thought and prayer for the good of the Commonwealth and beyond."

There was more applause. It was the signal for Tom to start up the music for the clearing of the tent. By arrangement, the people of the podium were ushered out. Then row by row the audience began to leave in an orderly procession. Tom could see that Dooley had a quizzical look on his face as he marched out. "I have a feeling that Oberal put one over on him, It sounds like a half-Jewish and half-Catholic program," Tom mused. Tom had asked Mary and Jeb to stay put in their seats after the event was over, and he walked over to them.

"We have a golf cart just for our use," he said to them as they went out a side entrance. "We have been invited to the most prestigious party of all – the President's party at the Ritz. Champagne, caviar – the crème de la crème of Boston will be there – at least they have been invited."

"Do you think they will come, Tom. I understand they invited the President."

"I'm sure he had a subsequent engagement, Mary. But the dignitaries will come as they know the school has spared no expense and that there is a chance that their picture will appear in the newspapers – even the *New York Times*. The law school has done some advertising in national papers and that usually insures some coverage of the event."

Mary looked at Tom quizzically. "You seem so matter of fact, Tom. Without you none of this would have happened. You have brought me and my son together. He is bringing his family up here and has a job with the Pebblepal organization. Dooley gets a chair named after him. It should have gone to you. Without you Essex would have got nothing. I wished I had insisted that you got a chair also."

It was true. Dooley had all but tied up Pebblepal, the owner of Bosc Island, and Svenson, who owned vast acreage in Marshfield except for the five hundred feet of shore line on the cove that McCarthy Enterprises owned. Marshfield was on its way to becoming a development and lose its pristine charm. What was once the quiet side of Mount Desert Island would now be the book end to Bar Harbor.

The sad part was that when the Rockefellers and the ultra riche discovered Mount Desert and built their cottages it was too far from New York City and Boston to consider turning it into a Disneyland. Trains and Model Ts were too far from the sites of power, except for the few, to use as a vacationland. But slowly Bar Harbor grew into a thriving vacation spot, and planes and fast cars made weekends possible. And what was once for the few seeped down to the *nouveau riche*, then the *riche*, and then even the *bourgeoisie*. Now the plan was for a golf course on Bosc Island, cottages on the perimeter, and on the Bosc shoreline. There would be sailing, kayaking, and trips to the carriage roads. There would be a seaplane base. Hiking, cross country skiing, climbing the mountains, graded by skill and endurance. It would be planned not for the many but for the few. In a time of uncertainty, it would be good for the chosen to have a place of refuge when no city was safe from destruction, There was even talk in some of the boardrooms that even if the United States failed, they could become part of Canada. And Dooley was able to extract what he thought was extortion, but what the buyers considered a bargain. His only failure was to misjudge Mary, not only to ward off his dishonorable intentions but to renege on her promise to give him carte blanche. And Tom became the catalyst to thwart Dooley's ambitions to become a hero of the church. Being adaptable, Dooley became a hero to Essex, much to the chagrin of his alma mater, St. Francis, and the local Cardinal, with whom he had confided his plans for the church.

"Mary, it is all a dream. For you, for me, for Jeb. My real happiness is for you, Mary. You have had it pretty tough. You have had to live with some pretty tough memories. You can now live in peace with yourself. I really think the chair should have been named after you."

"God forbid. I've had all I want of chairs."

The three of them were soon at the Ritz ballroom. Mary and Jeb found it uncomfortable being with all the big shots and took their leave of Tom to head back to their camp in Maine. Mary was to live with her son and family on a camp they had purchased in Long Pond where there was fishing, sailing, hiking, and mountain climbing to satisfy their taste.

Tom found a seat at the perimeter of the ballroom and watched the proceedings. There was Dooley in his tuxedo with his arm around his priest son. He was surrounded by faculty and alumni. Congratulations were in order.

Tom left the Ritz and walked through the Public Gardens, then to the Boston Common where they were still dismantling the tent and stowing the stacked chairs into a van. Remarkably there was little littering and what there was was being picked up and put into large paper bags. Tom proceeded to the law building which was closed. He identified himself to the guard and was let in to the building. He proceeded to the archives and opened the door to it with his master key. Unobtrusively, in one corner was the file cabinet that contained the Bender memoranda. From the bottom drawer, secured by another key, he removed an interlibrary folder that contained some one hundred pages. He then sat at a carrel adjacent to the file cabinet and started writing in long hand. He wrote for one hour. He placed this handwritten material after the last page in the folder. He then opened the top drawer of the cabinet that was marked "A to K." Before the "J" tab he inserted the interlibrary folder that was marked "The Hidden History of Essex Law School by Tom Jones, Jr."

Tom then went to his office where surprisingly, Elizabeth Hughes was sitting at an OCLC computer. "Elizabeth, what are you doing here? You promised me you would go to the President's party." "I was there as promised, but left after five minutes. The reason I'm not a head librarian is that I can't stand making small talk. And you have a letter on your desk that has me worried." Tom looked down on his desk where a stack of mail had been opened. On top was a letter from Norman Dawson, acting dean of Cahn Law School: "Tom, As you may have heard, we lost our librarian yesterday – literally – a deadly aneurism. I am urging you to apply for the job you would have gotten if I had been dean when Isaac retired. Please call me."

Tom looked up. "Elizabeth, you'd make a good law librarian. Don't undersell yourself. I doubt if I am interested in going back to New York, but the procedure in these matters is that you go to the Dean. Show him the letter and he will tell me whether I should apply for the job. He may want you."

Elizabeth said nothing and walked out of the office. "I have to get home and take care of my cats."

Also on the desk was a scribbled note of a call from Leslie Forsyth,

"Tom, I need to talk to you. Come to my office on Monday around three pm. Very important."

Tom then called home. The phone kept ringing. "Hello." "Hello, yourself. Where were you, up in the attic?"

It was Janet's sister. "I was reading a story to Janice and expected one of your two guests to answer the phone."

"Guests?"

"Your wife is sitting in the parlor talking casually to Miss Gefelsche."

"You're kidding."

"I'm pretty sure they intend to stay here until you arrive home. Toss a coin."

Tom tapped his foot for a couple of minutes. He closed his office door, shook his head, and said to himself, "I'm going home knowing 'the great shroud of the sea will roll on as it rolled five thousand years ago.'"

DEDICATION

I dedicate this work of fiction to my three children, Lida Bander McGirr, David Bander, and Steven Bander, to my son-in-law Rich McGirr, to my grandchildren Daniel and Jeffrey, and to my soul mate, Tema Nason, who has offered me encouragement, advice, editing, and love for the past eighteen years.

ACKNOWLEDGEMENTS

While writing this novel, I notified my peers that for fifty dollars I would put them in the book; for one hundred fifty dollars I would exclude them. No takers! So I had to rely on Chaucer, Henry Fielding, Charles Dickens, William Makepeace Thackeray, Gustave Flaubert, Mark Twain and a few other literary luminaries for my characters. It was a good choice! I drew on many of the anecdotes in my book on legal anecdotes to round out some of my fictional characters. I also consulted articles and histories of Suffolk Law School, New York University Law School, and Harvard Law School, three institutions that made use of my library skills dating back to the 1950s. I also consulted material of other law schools and accumulated much experience attending or chairing meetings of the AALS, ABA, AALL, NELL (consult the index for full name), and many other legal associations.

I also want to pay special thanks to Victor A. Birch who kindly went over my manuscript.

This novel is an attempt to represent that part of the iceberg that is not the tip. Human nature being what it is, my readers may see traits in some of my characters inhabiting a human form. In my life, I have known many Tom Jones' and Mr. Pecksniffs' but they were only shadows of the fictional characters in my novel.

INDEX

(Note: References are to chapters)

Cohen, Samuel, 4, 5, 7, 9, 11, 15, 17, 21, 38

Cohen, Sheila, 11

Coleman, 40

Collier on Bankruptcy, 15

Collins, Thomas, 20

Columbia Law School, 1, 13, 15, 20

Commencement speech
    Lavinia, 15

Commonwealth Club, 6

Commonwealth Law School, 1, 5, 7, 15, 22, 25

Computer lab, 15, 22, 34

Concord (MA),, 2, 14, 18, 21

Concord Academy, 14

Concord Country Club, 26

Congressional Record, 26

Connolly, Archie
    Trustee at Essex, 15, 16

Connolly, Billy
    Archivist at Essex, 9, 15, 16, 17, 38

Connolly, Michael
    DEA, 36, 37

Connolly, Steve, 37

Contracts, 5

Copley Plaza, 39

Copyright Association of America, 19

Copyright,19

Corbin on Contracts, 5

Cottages, 1

Coughlin, Father, 15, 33, 41

Cousell, Howard, 15

Craven, Agent, 36

Curley Building, 1

Curley, James M. 4, 41

Curtis, Tony, 15

Cushing, Caleb,, 3, 43
    Interviewed by Tom, 3

Cusinart, 12

-D-

Darrow, Clarence, 3, 15, 17, 21

Daugherty, Dan
    First faculty, 7

Dawkins, Professor, 23

Dawson, Norman
    Professor at Cahn, 13, 20, 43

Dean, law school
    See Mitnich, Oberal
    Assistant to the Dean
        See Solide
    Associate Dean
        See Dooley, F

Demonstrative evidence, 21

Deutsch, Gerhard O., 6, 13
    Cahn professor, 6
    Elaborate parties, 6
    Moot court judge, 6

Dewey, Tom, 28

Dickens, Charles, 7, 15, 23, 28

Dino's
    Restaurant in Boston, 7, 9

Directory of Law Schools,13

Discrimination, 4, 19
    Law firms, 4

Diversity, 4, 9, 13

Divorce, 16, 21, 30

Dixwell St., 16, 28

Djonovich, Dusan, 14

Dodd, Michael, 32

Dodge, Vicki, 12

Doe, C.J., 18

Dominican Republic, 21, 30

Donavan Honorarium Committee, 8

Donavan, Frank
    Son of Patrick, 4

Donavan, Patrick J.

McCoy, Abner, law clerk to Strong, 8
McGovern, Charlie, 21
McGuire, Fred A., 4
McReynolds, James C.. 6
McSorley's, 14
Memoranda
    See Bender
Merchants National Bank, 2, 30
Mersky, Roy, 14
Methew Bender, 11
Michigan Citation Law Forum, 23
Michigan Law School, 20
Mike"s (North End), 9
Military law, 15
Mill Marsh Road, 9, 27, 29, 36
Minorities, 25
Mitnich, Dean, 40, 41, 43
    Current dean after Oberal, 40,
        41, 43
    Profile, 41
Mohegan Island, 31
Monte's, 18
Moot Court, 4, 5, 6, 13, 17, 28
Mott's BarBQ, 1, 7
Mount Beth Misery Hospital, 34
Mr. Dooley (F.P. Dunne), 7, 21
Mt. Desert Island (MDI) (ME), 1,
    7, 9, 11, 29, 33, 41
Mutiny on the Bounty, 31
Myerson, Ray, 17

-N-
National Reporter System, 15
Nazi Germany, 19
Needleman, Dean Norman
    Cahn Law School, 11, 13, 18
    Laughs at own jokes, 11
Neon sign, 7
New England Law School, 1

Newfoundland, 1
New Hampshire, 1, 4, 5
New Ritz, 14, 21
New York City Abraham Cahn Law
    Centre
    [See Cahn Law School]
No fault insurance, 14
North End, 9
Norman conquest, 13
Northeast Harbor (MDI), 7, 10, 29

-O-
O'Brien, John Duke,
    acting dean in Tom Arnold
        episode, 4
O'Sullivan, Judge, 3
Oberal, Dean
Dean of Essex Law School, 1, 3, 4,
    12, 13, 14, 15, 22, 38, 40, 43
    Description, 14
    Machiavellian, 40
    President of Essex University,
        40, 43
Ogunquit, 1, 24, 31
Old Granary Burying Ground, 7
Otis, James, 9

-P-
Paine, Thomas, 28
Paralegal, 12
Park Street Church, 7
Parker House, 8, 9
Path of the Law, 9
Patterson, Steven
    Renter of camp, 31, 36, 37
Pebblepal, David, 29
Pebblepal, John P., 9, 10, 29, 43
Pebblepal, Ms, 29
Pecksniff, Mr., 40

Williston on Contracts, 5, 15
Wittberg, Josh
    Law Professor at Essex, 3, 7,
        12, 38
Woe Unto You, Law Professors, 17
Women, 7, 8, 13
    As faculty, 4, 13
    As lawyers, 12
    Havad and, 25
    Ladies' Day, 7
    Paralegal, 12
    Seduced by professors, 17
    Seduction of law professors, 20
    Transsexual, 7
Wonderland, 31
Workmen's Circle, 5
World War II, 5, 6, 8, 15, 28
Worsthaus, 18
Wouk, Herman, 31
Wright, Fred, 14, 18, 21, 30, 31, 34
    Family home in Concord,
        MA, 2

Father of Janet Jones, 2, 14, 16
    Republican, 2, 28
Wright, Rebecca, 16,
Wursthaus, 18
Wyeths, 31
Wyzanski, Judge, 15

-Y-
Y.M.H.A., 25
Yale Institute of Law, 23
Yale Law School, 4, 5, 11, 12, 13,
    17, 25
Youngerman, Henry, 13

-Z-
Zaltman, Isadore
    Tax instructor, 25, 27
Zenger, John Peter, 15
Zyprexa, 32

EDWARD J. BANDER

SELECT BIBLIOGRAPHY

Edward J. Bander is Law Librarian Emeritus from Suffolk University. He enlisted in the United States Navy in 1942, served on the U.S.S. Bangust, DE 739, and was honorably discharged in 1946. He is a graduate of Boston University CLA '49, Law '51, Simmons College, Library School '55. He was the editor of volumes 56 and 57 of the Law Library Journal (1963-1964). Recipient of the Dean Frederick A. McDermott award, Suffolk University Bar Association, 1980. On April 20, 2007 he received a lifetime achievement award from the Law Librarians of New England. He was a past president of both the Law Library Association of Greater New York and the Law Librarians of New England. He has served in a library capacity at the United States Court of Appeals in Boston, Harvard Law School, New York University School of Law and Suffolk University Law School.

Mr. Bander was born in Roxbury, and is a graduate of Roxbury Memorial High School. Mr. Bander was married to Frances Waite (deceased 1988), and has three children, two of whom are lawyers, and all three reside in Concord, MA. Mr. Bander lived in Brookline for nineteen years, summers in Mt. Desert Island, Maine, and presently resides in Concord, MA.

Books – select list

Bardell v. Pickwick: The Most Famous Fictional Trial in the English Language. Edited and Abstracted by Edward J. Bander from Charles Dickens' Pickwick Papers. Transnational, 2004.

Breath of an Unfee'd Lawyer: Shakespeare on Lawyers and the Law. Ed by Edward J. Bander. Catbird Press, 1996.

Dean's List of Recommended Reading for Prelaw and Law Students. Selected by the Deans and Faculties of American Law Schools. Compiled and edited with annotations by Julius J. Marke and Edward J. Bander. Oceana, 1983.

Justice Holmes Ex Cathedra. Compiled and arranged by Edward J. Bander. Michie, 1966. Reprinted by Hein, 1991 [with additional bibliographical material]

Legal Anecdotes, Wit, and Rejoinder. Edward J. Bander. Vandeplas Publishing, 2007.

Mr. Dooley and Mr. Dunne: The Literary Life of a Chicago Catholic. Edward J. Bander. Michie, 1981.

Mr. Dooley on the Choice of Law. Compiled and Arranged by Edward J. Bander. Michie, 1963.

Turmoil on the Campus. Edited by Edward J. Bander. H.W. Wilson, 1970.

Articles – select list

The Dooley Process of Law. Case and Comment, Sept.-Oct. 1957, p. 20

The Dred Scott Case and Judicial Statesmanship, 6 Villanova Law Review 514 (1961)

How to Protect Yourself from Legal Experts, 1 Obiter Dictum (Franklin Pierce Law Center) Fall 1975, p. 24

Is it True What They Say About Law Reviews, 67 American Bar Association Journal 509 (1981)

The Justice of Louis Dembitz Brandeis. Selected Excerpts by Edward J. Bander. Commentary, Nov. 1956, p. 453

Legal Humor Dissected. 75 Law Library Journal 289 (1982)

Library Exhibits – Panel Discussion, 58 Law Library Journal 3 (1965)

Mr. Dooley and the Chicago Bar. 54 Illinois Bar Journal 318 (1965)

Mr. Dooley and the Law. 36 New York State Bar Journal, Aug. 1964, p. 336

Mr. Dooley on Law Librarians. Library Journal, Feb, 1, 1964, p. 575

The Novel Approach to Juvenile Delinquency. Edward J. and Frances W. Bander. The Counselor (Ohio Probation and Parole Ass'n), March 1954, p. 23. Also in 1 National Probation and Parole Association Journal 25 (July 1955).

Problems of Area Jurisdiction in Juvenile Courts. 45 The Journal of Criminal Law, Criminology and Police Science 668 (March-April 1955). Reprinted in Glueck, Unraveling Juvenile Delinquency (1957)

Reforming the Massachusetts Official Document Quagmire. Edward J. Bander, Robert Favini and Martin Healy. The Advocate (Suffolk University Law School Journal) Fall, 1989, p. 3.

Some Legal Fiction: Woe Unto You, Novelists! 45 American Bar Association Journal 925 (Sept. 1959)

Under 5'6": They Get the Short End, Commentator (New York University Law School) Oct. 13, 1970, p. 10. Reprinted in New York University Alumni News, Dec. 1970, p. 3

Wading Through the Congressional Morass, 7 New York University School of Law Review of Law and Social Change 345 (1978)